ROGER MEADOWS

D1525017

DEVIL'S LANE

This is a work of fiction. The characters, incidents, and dialogue are products of the author's imagination and are not to be construed as real. The geography of the subject area has also been modified. Any resemblance to actual events or persons, living or dead, is coincidental.

Cover design by xenopixel.com
www.xenopixel.com

ISBN: 1532840314
ISBN 13: 9781532840319

For Ida Pauline Mayers Strong and
Washington Irving Meadows
In Memoriam

CHAPTER 1

Spring, 1880: Anna was frightened. Papa was angry and his face was red. He was shouting in German, and she knew they must be bad words because Mama wouldn't tell her what they meant when he used them. This time it was the horse, Bonner. Papa was trying to get him to back between the shafts of the buckboard and Bonner didn't want to go.

"Eva, get out here!" he yelled.

Mama came out of the cabin, wiping her hands on her apron. She had a worried look on her face.

"Get back dere and get aholt of the trace chains, and hook him up when I get him in dere." He talked to Mama in the same angry voice he used with Bonner.

Mama also looked frightened, perhaps more of Jürgen Friedrich, than of the horse. She timidly crept forward and gathered the chains trailing behind Bonner that were to be hooked into the singletree.

Papa yanked backward on the reins. Bonner's nostrils flared and his eyes were wild. He whinnied and bucked, kicking backward with both hind feet. To Anna's horror, Mama was thrown against the buckboard wheel and fell to the ground with a loud wail.

Anna ran to her and knelt beside her, taking her hand. "Mama, Mama, are you all right?"

Eva's face was twisted in pain and she was moving and moaning. "No, sweetheart," she whispered. "I hurt real bad."

Anna's brother Evan came running from the tall trees at the edge of the clearing, coming back from squirrel hunting. He flung two carcasses to the ground, laid down his rifle, and came to her side.

Papa tied Bonner to a tree and came running. Eva was moaning in pain. "Anna, get the door open," he commanded.

Papa and Evan carried Mama into the cabin and laid her on her bed in the shedded back room where Mama and Papa slept. The bed was a rope bed with a corn-shuck mattress.

"Evan, go get that *gottverdammt* horse and bring him to the buckboard. You're going after Ma Bright. We'll get that sonofabitch hitched. Anna, get Mama some water and put a wet towel on her face."

Anna rushed to get water and a cloth, and Papa and Evan ran outside. She bathed her mother's face with the cool water she'd carried in earlier from the spring. Mama was still moving and holding her stomach where the horse had kicked her.

Anna ran into the main room and got a twig from the shelf behind the cook stove. She lit it in the firebox, lit a candle, and carried it into the dark bedroom, shielding the flame with her hand. She stuck it into the brass sconce mounted over the bed. Mama's eyes were squeezed shut and tears were leaking out and running down her cheeks onto the striped ticking.

She heard the horse neighing and Papa's shouting from outside, but soon there was the sound of the buckboard clattering away. In a few minutes, he came hurrying into the room, his face red and covered with sweat.

"How is she?"

"Not good, Papa."

Jürgen shrugged his shoulders and held his callused hand out to his sides. "But what can we do?"

"I don't know. Maybe we can pray?"

Jürgen snorted. "If *Gott* could help, why in the first place does he let it happen?"

Anna thought to herself that it wasn't God that fought with the horse or told Mama to get behind him, but she knew not to voice her thoughts. She'd gotten in trouble before by talking when she shouldn't. She'd also felt the sting of a keen switch when she displayed the rebellious nature Papa claimed was a product of her flaming red hair.

Jürgen left the room and paced the rough plank floor of the main cabin. What else could go wrong? It had been a dry spring and the corn didn't look good. Deer had jumped the rail fence and gotten in the garden. He'd have to replant half of it, then guard it with a shotgun. Where were Evan and the old lady? Should be here by now. He owed a payment on the meager farmstead, due this fall. Now Eva has to get herself kicked by a horse! Anna was starting to show signs of growing up; starting to get some woman shape. Only fourteen years old, and stubborn as a *verdammt* mule. He went outside, straining for sounds of the buckboard. What if Eva doesn't make it? Then what?

Finally he heard it, the jingle of harness and the sound of the iron wheel rims on gravel. The buckboard came into the clearing, Bonner lathered with sweat around his breast collar and under the straps of harness.

Evan brought him to a halt in a cloud of following dust, hauling back on the reins with a shouted "Whoa!" He leaped out and ran around to help old lady Bright to the ground, practically picking her up like a child. Evan was fifteen years old, and already a man from hard work with his father.

Ma Bright grabbed a satchel out from under the springboard seat and looked at Jürgen, "Where is she? Don't just gawk, take me to her."

Anna heard them come into the cabin and rose from where she had been kneeling on a rug by her mother's bed as Ma Bright came into the room. Ma Bright turned and poked Jürgen in the chest.

"You stay outside until I tell you."

Anna was amazed at the way the tiny lady commanded with such authority. Ma Bright is not as big as I am, she thought. People said she was part Cherokee Indian and knew their healing ways. She delivered babies and came when called to minister to the sick. She now lived alone in a tiny cabin set back in a cove, and subsisted on a garden plot and what people would give her for her services. She had long black hair with streaks of white, the contrast like the back of a skunk, and she wore it in a long tail down her back. Despite the heat, she wore a knitted gray shawl draped about her shoulders.

"How is she?" she asked Anna, her black eyes glittering in the dim light.

"She seems to be sleeping. I can't get her to talk. She moves around and moans a lot."

"Let's get her clothes off her." Ma Bright proceeded to unbutton the front of the homespun dress. Anna was embarrassed, but couldn't look away. Mama would never let anyone see her, not even Anna.

Mama was wearing no undergarments, and her bare white skin contrasted with the great blue bruises where the hooves had struck, just below her breasts which were sagging to each side. Anna wondered briefly if that's how she would look someday.

"Get a cup of hot water," Ma commanded, then she took from her bag a jar of ointment and began to gently wipe it into the bruises, mumbling strange incantations. Eva winced in pain, but remained otherwise unresponsive.

Anna returned with a cup of water from the kettle always on the stove. Ma Bright crumbled a mixture of herbs and leaves into it with her gnarled hands. She stirred it and said, "Let's see if we can get her to drink."

Anna gently lifted her mother's head and Ma Bright brought the cup to her lips. "Come now, dear. Drink a little bit." She managed to get in a few drops, but Eva coughed and screamed in pain.

"Ease her back down, child. It ain't workin.' Need some painkiller in her, but she can't take it. Maybe the poultice I put over the salve will draw out the poison. Didn't feel no broken ribs, but she's hurt bad inside." She proceeded to button Eva's dress and lift the blanket back over her.

"Tell your pa I'm comin' out to talk. Then come back and sit with your ma."

When Anna came back and knelt by her mother's bedside again, Ma Bright smoothed Anna's unruly hair. "Don't give up, child. Say your prayers." She took her satchel and walked out of the room.

Outside, she found Jürgen pacing in the gravel drive and Evan still holding the horse. Both looked at her with concern and came toward her.

"Mister Friedrich, I always speak the truth as I know it. You too, young man, you're old enough to hear it straight. I'm afeered she ain't gonna make it."

Jürgen stared at her, stone-faced. Evan, in the body of a man but still a boy, looked as though he wanted to cry.

"The problem," Ma Bright continued, "is she's tore up inside. I put on some salve and a poultice, and tried to give some medicine, but she wouldn't take much. Keep her easy as best you can. The girl is holdin' on to her, so's she won't be feelin' alone."

Jürgen continued to stare. "Evan, go catch a hen and dig a couple of hills of new potatoes. Thank you for coming, Missus Bright. Wish we had more to give. Evan will take you home." With that he turned and trudged toward the cabin door.

CHAPTER 2

Benjamin Archer baited his hook with a soft-shell crawfish and lifted the cane pole to swing the bait out over the crystal waters of Bull Creek. It sank directly into the bowl-shaped nest of a smallmouth bass he'd watched that morning fanning the gravel bottom into shape. The water was so clear that it had looked like the fish was floating in air, casting a shadow on the nest.

The bass attacked the intruder and Benjamin added it to his stringer. It was a beauty, a little over a foot long and with the five others he had, would make a nice supper for his family; his dad and his brothers and sister.

He loved Bull Creek and spent every free moment exploring it and all it provided. Although the season was a little dry, cold springs and smaller creeks kept it alive all the way down its watercourse; flowing out of the Missouri hills from all the way up in Christian County and down through Taney County. Earlier in the spring he had grabbed suckers and redhorse as they made their spawning runs. In the winter he trapped along its banks. Pa had taught him all the ways of wildlife and he figured he could just about live off the creek, even at his age.

He walked up the path along Hanson Creek, a stream flowing into Bull Creek, shaded by the overhanging sycamores, oaks, and elms. As he headed up the path toward their log house, his little brother Oren came running barefoot to meet him.

"Ben, whatcha got?"

"I got supper. Has Pa come home yet?"

"No. Josie says she don't know when to start cookin'."

"Where's Jimmy?"

Oren trotted sideways beside his big brother. "Josie tole him to go dig some taters 'n carrots, an' he said 'you ain't the boss of me,' an' she said if he didn't, he wouldn't eat." Oren smiled at Benjamin, the sun-light shining on his white-blond hair.

"Did he go?"

"Shore did."

"If you'll go get me a pan and a knife, you can help me clean these fish. Put the knife in the pan and don't run with it."

Oren ran to the house and Benjamin smiled to himself. Oren was a blessing to the family, but he had come at a dear price. Their mother died giving birth to him four years ago, and the family had struggled to overcome their grief. Their father, Thomas, had become more silent, rarely laughing aloud, but caring for his children with more gentleness than Ben remembered from before.

Jimmy Archer stabbed the spading fork into the ground beside a hill of potatoes and pried upward, uprooting the still-green plant. He dusted the dirt off the hen-egg size potatoes and added them to his basket. It was actually fun to see what the earth had provided, but Josie wasn't his ma and she had no right to boss him around. She did it all the time. He wished he had a real ma like before. He had faint memories of her taking him on her lap, hugging him and kissing his cheek. Try as he might, he couldn't make out her face. It was all misty. Some people had pictures, but there wasn't one of Ma. There was a little one of Pa in his Civil War uniform that they kept on the mantel, but they didn't need that. They could just look at him anytime they wanted to.

Thomas Archer led his sorrel mare up to the hitching rail in front of Zinn's blacksmith shop in Sycamore. A giant namesake tree shaded the shop and the dirt street in front as the sun began to descend over the ridge on the other side of Bull Creek.

"Hi, Mister Archer," said George Zinn. "What can we do for you?"

"Beauty's got a loose shoe on the right rear, George. Do you think your dad can tighten it up for me? Or I'm sure you can. I keep forgettin' you're not a kid anymore."

George broke into a broad smile, "It's all right. I'll get a clinchin' iron and hammer and take a look at it. Go on in and see Pa." George looked as Tom imagined Homer looked when he was a young man; broad and muscular, short of stature, thick thatch of black hair.

Archer entered the dim light of the shop, lit by the glowing coals in the forge as they brightened with each stoke of the bellows. Homer Zinn had his back to the wide doorway as he pumped the bellows with a pole suspended from a joist.

"Hi, Smitty. How's business?" Archer called.

Zinn turned, "Tom! How the heck are you?" He stepped forward and removed a heavy glove to shake hands. "'Scuse me, got a hot one here."

"Go ahead. Don't let me interrupt."

Zinn turned back to the forge, picked up tongs, and pulled an iron strap out of the coals. It was white-hot in the center and had holes already punched in each end. He turned to his anvil, picked up a heavy hammer, and started bending the strap into a U shape around the horn of the anvil with ringing blows.

"Whatcha need?"

"Had a loose shoe, but George is taking care of it."

Zinn kept the hammer bouncing as he did the final shaping, the sinews in his forearm standing out with each stroke.

"Double-tree clevis?"

"Yep." Zinn held up the clevis, squinted, then plunged it into a bucket of water where it sizzled in a rise of steam.

Both men walked outside. George had his back to the mare with her hind leg resting over his knee, her hoof between his knees. He grasped below her fetlock, lifted her hoof to the ground, and turned around. He held up the shoe. "I peeled it off and I'm gonna trim her hoof and re-set it. It ain't wore out, but it'll set better."

"Good. I'm goin' over to the store a few minutes."

Tom walked into the Sycamore general store and post office to the jingle of a sleigh bell hanging on the frame. The log store had pigeon holes with glass doors on the left of the entrance behind which the mail was sorted. Glass cases sat atop counters along both sides of the building to house smaller merchandise, with shelves behind them to hold dry goods, shoes, and so forth. Toward the back, there were barrels containing pickles and other supplies. A potbelly stove formed the center of a gathering of rockers at the back.

The proprietor rose as he entered. "Hi, Tom. Come on in."

"Hi, Henry. Where's Mary?"

"She's at the house. She don't stay over here much after the mail sort. Says it's m'pipe."

Tears formed in Tom's eyes and there was a catch in his throat as he replied. "Hard to figure, ain't it?" Henry smoked a calabash pipe stuffed with crumbled twist chewing tobacco.

"Yep. She's kinda cranky sometimes. What can I do for you?"

"Don't need a lot. Saw the "A" mailbox was empty. Four sticks of penny candy. Coupla' pounds of salt. Need shavin' stuff for Ben. He started out usin' mine. Also, let me look at what you got in dress material. Josie keeps growing and she needs to make her something."

Tom took his purchases back to the blacksmith shop, paid Zinn, and shook hands with both men. He led Beauty the short distance to the Jensen mill, set on the bank of Sycamore Creek, upstream from where it emptied into Bull Creek. The Sycamore coursed down the steep and narrow hollow, spring fed and dependably strong. It passed between rock outcroppings, making a natural millrace for the undershot wheel. Olaf Jensen had built the most imposing building in the area, except maybe for Colonel Madison's spread. The first story was all natural stone, a firm foundation for the mill wheel machinery and resistant to high water. The second and third stories were sawn lumber, hauled up from down by Forsyth, after it came up the White River by steamboat.

Tom hitched Beauty to a rail and secured his purchases in the saddlebags.

Hiram Zinn, Homer's younger son, came out to meet him, a bag of flour over his dusty shoulder. "Here's your flour, Mister Archer."

"Thanks, Hy. Is Oley around?"

"He's up by the stones. Go on up."

Tom found him at the grinding station, beside the rumbling millstone slowly rotating over the grist.

Oley smiled through his dusty brown beard. "Good afternoon, Thomas."

"How's it going, Oley?"

"Could be better." He raised his voice about the noise. "We got some bad news. Eva Friedrich's been kicked by a horse and she prob'ly won't make it. You know her, don't you?"

"They live up the other side of Snow Ridge? I think so."

"Yeah. Tell the truth, theirs is a hard place to raise a family. Not much bottom land. But lots of timber."

"She has kids, I think. Boy and a girl?"

"Yep. If she goes, I don't know what happens. We may have to get together and help."

"Let us know. We'll see you at services on Sunday." Jensen preached at the services held in the Sycamore schoolhouse.

The sun was hiding behind the treetops in the west and dusk softened the landscape as Tom Archer rode into the open in sight of his farmstead. I should have made it home a little sooner, he thought. My kids have a burden to bear. They've had to step up and do things they shouldn't have to do. Josie's really just a child, but she's taken the role of mother to Oren and Jimmy, although Jimmy doesn't think so. He smiled to himself. Now it sounds like the Friedrich family's going to be in the same situation.

As he approached the house, he saw Oren run out on the porch. He looked to the left of the house, up the slope where the single grave rested beneath the canopy of a large maple. Elizabeth, maybe I never should have convinced you to move here. We could have got by in Tennessee. It just sounded like a better deal here. Was, until...

Can't undo what's already done. Wish I could.

Life is hard to bear sometimes.

CHAPTER 3

Colonel Perry Madison rode his black Tennessee Walker stallion through a stand of hardwood trees on his farm to the large bottom field where his hired hands were hoeing corn. His two regular hands were cultivating between the rows, driving mules pulling double shovels. He'd hired temporary help to chop out the weeds in between the stalks. Col. Madison preferred English style saddles as they looked more elegant than the western style used by the locals. He didn't consider himself one of them. It was better to remain separate and above.

As he rode out of the woods, he came upon three of them standing in a circle, leaning on their hoes, talking.

"What are you-all doing, standing around suckling your hoe handles?"

The men sprang into action to start back down the rows followed by Madison's loud exhortation. "I'm not paying you to stand around!"

Madison spurred his horse and rode around the outside of the barbed-wire fence enclosing the fertile bottom field. Wire fencing was an innovation the locals had never seen before and increased the mystery surrounding Colonel Madison. They don't know what to think of me, he thought. All they know is I'm way out of their league, but they haven't seen anything yet. One of these days I'll own the whole county. Imagine these yokels are still using split rail fences. And most of them still live in log houses.

After he completed his circuit he rode back up the lane leading to his mansion on the point of the ridge between two converging hollows. Back east it might not be called a mansion, but here it sure as hell was. It was a stately two and a half story, painted white, with a broad veranda circling three sides. No house outside of Ozark or Forsyth used any kind of paint, as far as he knew. He looked with satisfaction at the cluster of outbuildings; a separate cookhouse, smokehouse, springhouse, stables, and stately red barn. Even the outhouses were painted white. All but the barn had clapboard siding, and the main house had three chimneys, one at each end and one in the middle. Smoke was rising from the cookhouse chimney, so the noon meal was being prepared.

He rode up to the stable and tossed the reins to his groom. "Walk Devil to cool him off and give him a rub-down."

"Yes, suh, Colonel Mad'son," the old black man said. Madison had brought him along when he'd moved to the area. Didn't know what to expect from the country people who had plow horses and mules.

Madison walked around to the front entrance of the house, his boots clumping on the front steps and porch he entered the beveled glass front door.

"Agnes, I'm back," he shouted.

His wife appeared at the other end of the main hall. "I'm seeing to dinner," she replied. She was dressed in a long black skirt which swished as she walked. Her blouse was white with ruffled collar and puffed sleeves, tight at the wrists. Her dark hair was piled high, with tendrils over each ear. She was tall, the same height as her husband.

"Come on back to the dining room. Etta just about has it ready."

Neither made an attempt to touch or smile. Any warmth between them was not in evidence for some time now, though they maintained a civil relationship in public and in the presence of their two daughters.

As he entered the room, his eldest daughter, Gertrude, said, "Oh, hi, Daddy!" and rushed to embrace him.

"How's my girl?" he replied, kissing her on the cheek and putting his arm around her.

Margaret, now sixteen, remained standing behind her chair watching her older sister's display of affection.

Madison looked across the table at her. "And you?"

"Fine. Hi, Father."

"Well, let's be seated." He called out, "Etta, bring me some coffee."

The carved mahogany table was set up for twelve, but could be extended to twice that size. Gertrude sat to her father's right at one end and Margaret to her mother's at the other. Madison insisted on maintaining what he deemed proper formality in his household.

Etta, the black maid clad in servant's livery, came in and placed a cup of coffee at Madison's right hand, then bustled back into the kitchen.

Madison took a sip and called out. "Etta! This don't taste fresh."

She hurried back, clasping her hands in front of her. She dipped her head and said, "Sorry, suh. I made it for the missus, not an hour ago. I'll make some fresh."

Madison looked down the table at his wife. "I think she's losin' it. Might be time to think about a change."

"Oh, Perry, she'll be all right. She's been with us for a long time. I'll talk to her."

Gertrude patted her father's hand.

After the silent meal, Madison retired to his study with the intention of having a cigar and reading a Springfield paper he had delivered weekly. Agnes followed him down the hall.

"May I speak with you, Perry?"

He hesitated. "If we must."

When he was seated behind his imposing desk and she had taken a side chair, he leaned back and said, "All right, what is it?"

"I'm worried about the girls. They have no social life out here in the hills so how are they to develop the skills and contacts to make a proper marriage?"

"Our son seems to be doing all right with social graces and marriage."

"It's different for a man. And don't forget, Reggie didn't come to this God-forsaken wilderness."

"Still harping about that, are you?"

"I know you needed to leave Washington after the war, before a new administration came in, but can't we go back now?"

"Are you insane? After all I've sunk into this place? And there are still prying eyes back there. Take 'em to Springfield for a week. Show 'em around. Hell, take a train to St. Louis."

"But that's only temporary."

"Well, that'll have to do. We'll send 'em back east come fall. Anything else?"

"I think we might need some help for Etta. She might be slowing down a little, but she knows how things ought to be. Maybe a girl to help her."

"Whatever works, as long as it don't cost anything."

Margaret Madison climbed the stairs to her room situated on the west side of the house, facing down the broad valley where Hanson Creek flowed toward Bull Creek in the distance. Her room was smaller than her sister's, but she liked it better. She went to the window seat and sat down on the brocade cushion, taking up a framed needlepoint wall hanging she was working on. She looked down the valley, with its green hills and cultivated patches of bottom land. Is this all there is to my life? she thought. She rose, put the needlepoint aside, went to her wardrobes and opened the door of one of them. Just look at my dresses. Who will ever see them? Maybe in the fall when I go back east to school. I wish I could meet some of the people my age who live around here. I'd go crazy if it weren't for Princess. Maybe I can sneak away on some longer rides.

At the north end of the second floor, Gertrude stood in front of her full length mirror. She twirled her long skirt and looked at her image over her shoulder. Daddy's so handsome, she thought. He loves me best. Margaret doesn't show him the respect he deserves. Who cares if we are isolated here? We have everything we could desire. Mother gripes at him too much, too. One of these days he may get too much of it. If she wants to go back to Washington, she can go anytime.

CHAPTER 4

Anna sat in the darkness, holding her mother's limp hand. She'd brought a stool in from the main room and was determined to stay by her side all night if need be. Earlier, her father had looked in and asked what they would be having for supper, viewing his wife without comment.

"Can't Evan find something? There's some ham left over from dinner. I fried up extra."

Jürgen grunted and left.

Anna felt herself falling and snapped awake. She could not tell how much time had passed, but her body ached. The candle had gone out, so she groped into the kitchen and found another, lighting it with a dry splinter she lit from the stove. Her brother was asleep in his loft bed and her father was sleeping in hers behind the curtain that defined her space. She shielded the candle with her hand and carried it back to her mother's bedside. When she put it in the wall sconce and bent to touch her mother's hand, it felt cold. With a sense of panic, she felt for a pulse in the slim wrist. There was none.

"Mama, oh Mama, wake up," she sobbed. Frantically she placed her hand over Eva's heart, still feeling no beat and no rise and fall of breathing. "Please, Lord. Don't take her away," she whispered, but she knew it was too late.

"*Papa!*" she shouted. "Come help!"

She heard stirring and he soon drew the curtain aside. He rubbed his eyes, "What is it?"

"She's gone, Papa."

"Oh? Let me see." He bent over and felt her wrist. He nodded, "Yes, you are right."

"Is that all you have to say? 'Yes you are right?' How about all the years she was your wife and my mother? What will we do now?"

"You mind your tongue! You don't talk to me that way!"

Evan came into the room. He embraced his sister. "I'm so sorry, Anna. I should have sat with you. And now she's gone. What happens now, Papa?"

"I don't know. When daylight comes we call in the neighbor women to prepare her." He lifted the quilt and started to bring it over Eva's face.

"Wait!" Anna cried. She bent and kissed her mother's forehead, then backed away.

When dawn came, Evan was sent in the buckboard to the nearest neighbors, the Harveys on the bordering farm, the Johnsons farther up the hollow, and to Ma Bright, who accompanied him back to the cabin. By then, word had begun to travel down the hollow and over ridges and valleys in the Bull Creek watershed by a process no one could explain. A death touched them all in various ways, mostly sadness; but for some a break in the routine of an otherwise unexciting life.

By midmorning people of the hills began to gather in the clearing around the Friedrich cabin. The women, led by Ma Bright, set to the task of preparing Eva's body for burial. Contrary to the custom of many families with deeper roots, Jürgen opted to bury his wife in the community graveyard in Sycamore rather than start a family burial plot on his land.

Several of the men had brought picks and shovels and headed down the hollow to dig the grave and notify Oley Jensen, the miller, so he could prepare to speak a funeral on the following day.

Anna watched in sadness as the women gently carried Eva's body into the main room and laid it out on the plank table, keeping the quilt draped over her. Edna Johnson went to Anna and put an arm around her shoulders. "Child, let me take ya outside for a little while. When we're all finished, I promise I'll bring ya back inside, so's you can see her resting in peace."

Anna allowed herself to be led out on the porch, where she sat on an upturned nail keg, staring to the west as the morning sun began to light the bald hilltops in that direction. What will happen to me now, she thought. Mama was always kind to me and Evan, even when Papa was not. He doesn't mean to be hard, I guess, but he never smiles or says any good things. Maybe it was the war he never talks about.

Inside, the womenfolk undressed the body and carefully washed it and dressed it in clean clothing. Ma Bright gently massaged the face to relax the expression to that of a sleeping person. When all was finished, it looked like Eva had lain down to sleep. She nodded at Edna, who opened the door and told Anna she could come in.

When Anna saw her mother, she sobbed, and whispered. "Why did it have to happen, Lord?"

Thomas Archer and Benjamin were in the springhouse, skimming cream from yesterday's milk and putting it in the churn. As they came out of the small stone building, they saw James and Oren running up the lane from the creek, Oren struggling behind his older brother.

When James drew nearer, he called breathlessly, "Pa! They's men goin' to dig a grave!"

Oren caught up to his brother and pushed him. "I wanted to tell!"

Archer said, "Slow down. Who is it? What happened?"

"They said it was Miss Eva."

"I was afraid of that. Mister Jensen told me yesterday she'd been kicked by a horse. Guess I'd better ride down and help. Ben, you harness one of the mules and start plowin' out the corn rows. Jimmy, you take the churn down to the house and help Josie churn it."

"Aw, Pa, that's what women do."

"Men do too, if there's no Ma to help. You'll get your chance today or tomorrow when we start hoein' weeds out of the rows. Josie'll probably be doin' that too."

"I'll help," said Oren.

Archer tousled his hair. "Good. Tell your sister I'll be back soon's I can. We'll go down to the service in the morning, pay our respects. You kids check out your shoes tonight, see if they'll hold together 'til we get your new ones for winter."

In the Madison kitchen, Margaret lingered at the breakfast table while Etta cleaned up and washed dishes. She would have helped, but that was forbidden by her father. It was the one opportunity she had to hear about the community she lived in, news from the coves and hollows where "real people" lived, as she termed them in her own mind.

"They's gonna be a buryin' tomorrow down Sycamore," Etta said, as she worked. "Lady name Eva got killed by a horse over 'crost Snow Ridge."

"Oh, that's terrible. How did it happen?"

"Don't know. Say she helpin' hitch him up."

"What time? I think I'll go."

Etta stopped and gave her a look, "Early mornin' after chores. You know what yo daddy say."

"He won't know. He's leaving today for Ozark, to stay overnight. I'll just go for a ride."

Etta wiped her hands on her apron. "Just don't get caught. It'ud kill me, he send you away."

"I'll be careful, Etta. You know Mother and Gertie don't pay attention to me."

Tom Archer rode into the settlement of Sycamore and tied Beauty to a hitching rail in front of the schoolhouse. He headed up the slope to where a group of men were gathered, sitting in the grass and smoking. As he drew closer he could hear the sound of a pick striking rocks. Homer Zinn climbed out of the grave which was now about two feet deep. Two men climbed in with shovels and began to shovel the loosened soil and rocks. Only two could shovel or one could pick at any time, but they all took turns as a way of showing support for the family.

Homer walked over to Tom, wiping sweat with a bandanna handkerchief. "Startin' to cloud up, Tom."

"We could use some rain, Smitty, but I hope it holds off until this is over with."

"Yeah, it's a sad case. Well, I'd best be goin' to the shop and finishin' the pine box."

Rafe Johnson and Charlie Tate climbed out of the grave, and Homer's son George climbed in with a pick in his strong hands and began to dig.

Tom sought out Jürgen Friedrich at the edge of the gathering, standing and talking to Oley Jensen. Oley was saying, "Well, if that's what you want. We'll just say a few words at the grave side, and sing a couple of hymns. You know, folks like to say a proper goodbye."

Friedrich replied, "I guess it will have to do. We can't change anything now."

"I'm sorry for your loss, Jürgen," Tom said, holding out his hand. He pronounced it with a J, as all in the community did.

"Thank you. I don't know now what we do."

"I know the feeling, of course. Short term, you just get by. Long term, it never really goes away, as some folks think it might."

Tom went back to the grave site and stepped in to take a turn with a shovel. The morning wore on, the grave deepened, and talk continued about crops, the prospect of rain, and worry about occasional problems in the community with no law close by.

They reached solid limestone just short of six feet deep, neatened the pile of dirt, and covered it with burlap for the service the next morning. The men dispersed to go back to their work. Tom rode home to join his sons, working in the corn.

CHAPTER 5

Margaret Madison awoke with the morning light and dressed hurriedly in her riding clothes, boots, jodhpurs, shirt, and jacket. Father forbade going out in public except as a lady, dressed in long skirt, riding side-saddle. This was eighteen-eighty, for heaven's sake! He did allow riding in hunting clothes with him on the farm, but he wasn't here, was he? She gathered her long brown hair into a braid and got her helmet from a shelf. Silently she slipped down the stairs and went down the carpeted hall to the kitchen.

Etta shook her head from side to side and clucked her tongue. "I hope you know what you're doin', child."

"Don't you worry, and remember, all you know is I went for a ride. Mother and Gertrude will sleep in. Maybe you could take them breakfast in bed?"

"I can do that, soon's I hear 'em stirrin'."

"You don't mind a little fib, do you? I'll get a two-hour head start, but I'd just left when they woke up."

"I got it." She shook her finger at Margaret. "Now you be careful, child."

Margaret rode Princess down the valley of Hanson Creek, occasionally crossing at fords where the creek switched sides of the valley. After a mile or so, she caught up with a family riding in a wagon, man and woman on the spring seat, and four children in the wagon bed. The man touched the brim of his hat as she passed by.

"Mornin', Miss."

"Good morning, sir, and you, too, m'am. How far to Sycamore?"

The woman nodded and the man replied. "'Bout two-three mile, I reckon. Goin' to the buryin'?"

"Yes, sir. I'll see you there."

The closer she got to the settlement, the more people she spoke to as they came out of the hollows along the creek. All were friendly, but stared at her with some curiosity. The women and girls were all dressed in print dresses and bonnets, and the men in overalls and work shirts, with felt hats, despite the warm season. It had become cloudy and Margaret was glad old Ike had bundled an oilskin slicker on the back of her saddle.

The gravel street in front of a row of buildings was packed with wagons along one side and families were climbing out and moving toward the hillside where the grave stood open. Margaret found a place to tie Princess at a rail in front of Guthrie's store and followed the crowd up the slope. She saw four men slide a wooden box out of a wagon parked near the grave and carry it to two lengths of log beside the grave.

A husky man stood near the grave, dressed in a black frock coat over white shirt and overalls. He was hatless, with a bald head and bushy brown beard. He held a Bible in his hand and surveyed the gathering crowd, now forming a circle around him. She presumed that the man standing beside him was the widowed husband. He was severe-looking, with dark hair and beard. A young man about her own age was beside him, and a younger girl with a mass of red hair.

Not a word was spoken. It was so quiet that Margaret could hear the freshening wind in the trees along Bull Creek. She stayed in the outer fringe of the circle as she knew her hunter green jacket would stand out. Finally, all the stragglers seemed in place and the man with the Bible began to speak.

"Dear friends, we gather to bury our sister, Eva Friedrich, God rest her soul. He has chosen to call her home in the prime of her life. It is not for us to question or to understand, but accept as His will..."

Margaret looked around the faces of the crowd as the part-time minister spoke on. She was fascinated by her first look at the real people of the community. Sadness and sympathy were evident in them, along with the vestiges of work in the sun on the men and older boys; white foreheads and ruddy tan below the eyes where hat brims failed to protect. They'd all taken their hats off when the minister began. And on the women, she could sense a tired resignation to the reality of life in the hill country.

" ...and now let us sing a hymn all of you know. Brother Zinn, will you lead us in 'Amazing Grace?'"

Margaret was surprised when all eyes turned toward a man standing right in front of her. He was broad and muscular, with a shock of salt and pepper hair. Beside him was a black haired young man obviously his son.

Brother Zinn hummed a note for pitch and began in a clear tenor:

Amazing grace, how sweet the sound
That saved a wretch like me.
I once was lost, but now I'm found....

Margaret loved to sing and joined in with her strong soprano. The younger man turned to look at her and drifted back beside her, singing and looking at her with a twinkle in his gray eyes. Margaret stared back at him and a feeling of emotion washed over her at the sound of the young man and the congregation around them singing the beautiful words. She felt a chill down her spine.

When the song was over, the minister began again, but the man came closer and whispered, *"My name's George Zinn. You must be one of the Madison girls."*

"I guess you could tell. I'm Margaret."

He nodded, *"Pleased to meetcha. We can talk later."*

Margaret forced herself to listen again to the service. "...so now we know that she rests with you, Lord, and we return the vessel she lived in back to the earth from which it came, dust to dust. We commend our sister Eva to your care. Please watch over her family in their grief and look on her with favor and give her peace. Amen."

A ragged chorus of "Amens" echoed him.

He closed the Bible and nodded to the four men who had carried the pine box to the grave. They threaded plow lines under the coffin and picked it up, awkwardly moving around until they suspended it over the grave. They slowly let the ropes slide through their hands until it reached the bottom, then two released the ropes and the other two drew them out of the grave. The minister shook hands with the husband, then someone handed him a shovel. The burlap was removed from the mound of soil, and he took a shovel full and cast it into the grave. The rocks and clumps made a loud thumping sound. All of the other men and older boys lined up and one at a time cast a shovelful of dirt into the grave.

George Zinn held up his hand, "Please, Miss Margaret. Wait for me. I'll be right back."

Intrigued, Margaret complied. She watched as he joined the line and came back to her. Some of the men stayed by the grave to finish filling it in. The red-haired girl stood there with her face in her hands. Margaret could see she was sobbing and felt sorry for her. The father came back and grasped her roughly by the arm and led her away.

George came back. "Thanks for waiting. I wanted to ask why you came. Did you know her?"

"You want to know the truth?"

"Of course."

"I was curious, I guess. Father never wants us to mingle. Thinks we're something special. But he's away on business."

He smiled, showing square white teeth, "Maybe you are…something special."

"No. You know what I mean." She looked at the dark clouds scudding before the wind. It was growing darker. "I'd better get going."

A few drops of rain fell. There was flash of lightning and crash of thunder. He took her hand, "Come quick. Let's head for the shop."

She ran down the slope with him to the blacksmith shop as light rain began. As they stopped in the shelter, he said, "You'd better wait. You have to go up Hanson Creek. It could get bad."

'I can't wait. I'm in trouble if I don't get back. No matter what, I have to lie about it."

He smiled at her again. "My goodness. Someone like you lying? Let me catch the Archers." He dashed out into the rain to a wagon getting underway. The man in the spring seat pulled back on the reins and listened to George Zinn. He looked in Margaret's direction and nodded.

George came back, "Let's get your horse. They'll help you get back."

Margaret put on the oilskin slicker when she reached Princess and ran with George to the Archers' wagon, leading the horse. The family were all exposed to the rain, but waited patiently.

"Mister Archer, this here is Margaret Madison. Can you see she gets back up the creek?"

"Sure can. Miss Madison, I'm Tom and this is Ben beside me. In the back there's Josie, Jimmy, and Oren." Ben, the girl, and small boy smiled. The other boy looked unhappy.

James was thinking I wish they'd call me by my name. Jimmy sounds like a little kid like Oren.

"Hello, all of you," Margaret said. "Sorry to hold you up. Thanks for helping me." She waved, "And thanks, George. I hope to see you again."

Margaret climbed into the wagon and held the reins to Princess. They drove the mile or so to where Hanson Creek came into Bull Creek. As they rode along, Oren looked at Margaret with big eyes, his blond hair plastered by the rain. He said, "How come you're wearin' pants like a man?"

Margaret smiled. "They're for riding a horse. Back east, some women ride horses when there is a fox hunt, and on a hunt, sometimes the horse has to jump a fence. You'd fall off if you're a woman riding side-saddle."

"Can your horse jump a fence?"

"If I ask her to."

Oren looked at her in awe.

As they neared the crossing to Archer's farm. Tom looked back over his shoulder. "Miss Madison, you can wait on this side of the creek with your horse. We'll cross over, then Ben will bring the wagon back and take you up across the last ford before your place. The creek's startin' to come up a little already."

Margaret climbed out and waited as the family forded the creek. Soon, Benjamin drove back across with the team and wagon. He ratcheted the brake lever in place and wrapped the reins around the handle. "Miss, I think it would be best if I fashion a halter for your mare and lead her with a rope."

"Sounds good to me. And you can call me Margaret. You're Ben, right."

Ben smiled and nodded. He secured Princess to the rear of the wagon and unsaddled her. He turned the saddle upside down under the wagon seat and put the saddle blanket over it. He then assisted Margaret up into the spring seat. She was dry inside her slicker, but Ben was becoming soaked by the rain, except for the protection of his hat. He slapped the reins on the horses' backs and they surged forward. Steam rose from them and the harness fittings jingled. The wagon rims ground against the gravel lane.

Margret looked at her companion and smiled to herself. A second handsome young man in the space of an hour, but quite different in appearance. Ben looked younger than George Zinn and Margaret guessed he was about her age. Ben was tall and lean with blond hair while George was stocky and dark.

"What does your family do for money?"

Ben grinned, "We don't see much money, but we do pretty well on what we raise. We farm, raise a garden, keep cows and chickens. That kind of thing."

"Well, you must buy some stuff. I think father buys about everything."

"Oh, sure. We buy shoes for winter, coffee, cloth for shirts. Buy some sugar, but mostly use long sweetenin'."

"Long sweetenin'?"

"Sorghum. Forgot you're not from around here. Where *are* you from?"

"Moved here from Washington. Father was in the Department of the Army."

"Why? I mean why move here?"

"I don't know, but I'm glad."

Ben just looked at her. They'd come to the first ford. "Hang on, here we go!" Then to the horses, "Gittup, Barney! Go, Blacky!" The team of Percherons surged into the swift, belly-deep current and drove up the bank on the far side.

"We have two cows, I think, but I don't know anything about them. Do they just keep on giving milk?"

"Well, yeah, most of the year, but they have to freshen once a year."

"Pardon my questions, because I don't know anything, but what does that mean?"

"Well, they eventually dry up until they have another calf, then they start it all up again." Ben thought about the good-looking young woman beside him and regretted the direction of the conversation. Please don't ask how that takes place, he thought. He could feel blood rising in his fair cheeks. Thankfully, she changed the subject.

"What does your friend George do?"

"He and his pa are blacksmiths. They can make just about anything out of iron. His dad made the buryin' box and he'll probably make the grave stone if they want one. They both shoe horses."

"My father had a farrier come from Forsyth to shoe our horses."

"Waste of time and money. They don't come any better than the Zinns."

"I'll remember for next time."

They rode in silence for a time until they approached the next bend in the creek and the next ford. Margaret turned to Ben, "Aren't you getting wet?"

"Like a bullfrog in a pond. Hang on; here we go again."

On the other side of the creek, Ben reined in the horses and jumped down to give a steadying hand to Margaret as she climbed down. She smiled up at him, "Thank you so much for seeing me over the fords."

"I enjoyed it. I hope we'll be seeing you again down in Sycamore."

"Me, too. I may be in trouble, but it was worth it."

"Trouble?"

"I'm supposed to sit around and embroider, drink tea, act like a lady."

"You are a lady. How about you got caught by the rain? There's a bluff that overhangs about halfway between here and your place. You waited and waited but the rain didn't stop, so you came on."

Margaret smiled again, "I like the way you think; and thanks again."

Ben had finished saddling her horse, so she mounted and rode away with a wave of her hand.

Margaret turned her horse over to Ike who was waiting at the stables. He was wagging his head, "Boss man, he be back, Miz Margaret. He not be happy. I tole 'em you went ridin', be back soon.

"Thanks, Ike. I'll take care of it."

She went in the back door, through the kitchen. Etta was preparing to serve the noon meal. She had a worried frown and spoke quietly. "Glad you come back. They's comin' up the hall."

Margaret's father stormed into the kitchen from the dining room, followed by her mother and sister. "Where in tarnation have you been," he shouted.

"Hi, Father. You're back early."

"Answer my question." His face was red.

"I'm sorry to be late, Father. I went for a ride, but it started to rain so I took shelter under the bluff. Finally I decided it wasn't stopping so I rode on home. Ike had put a slicker on my saddle, so it worked out."

Madison's face was grim and he stared at her. "Well, go up and change. We'll start without you."

Her mother looked relieved. Gertrude smirked at her and lifted her chin as Margaret breezed past her.

Alone in her room, Margaret replayed the burial service in her mind and the feelings that rose within her at the singing. Thinking of the hymn and the sadness of the daughter caused a lump in her throat. The drama of the scene was beyond anything she had experienced. Father had taken the family to concerts in Washington and even to a couple of musical plays in New York, but they evoked no real emotion. They were false. Today she experienced reality.

CHAPTER 6

Ferdinand Harvey sat at the plank table in dingy underwear. His sons, Bob and Clint, similarly attired, their hair and beards in tangles, lounged on the benches along both sides. Buford was too young to achieve a beard, but he had hopes.

Ferd banged his tin cup on the plank table. "Stelle, bring me some more coffee."

Estelle turned from the wood stove where she was frying a skillet of potatoes. She handed the wooden spoon to her daughter Rose, grabbed the coffeepot and walked across the room, her bare feet slapping against floor. Though it was early, she had a tired expression. She was thin, her dress hanging off her bony shoulders. Her black hair was twisted into a pile on top of her head, but strings of it hung over her face and her ears.

Her grown sons Bob and Clint held up their cups. Buford, the baby of the family at thirteen, didn't like coffee.

Rose was tall like her mother, but had chestnut hair pulled back in a braid. She brought the platter of fried rabbit and bowl of fried potatoes to the table and sat without speaking.

"When ya gettin' married, Rose?" said Bob.

She glared at him, "Look who's talkin'. You're four years older than I am. Guess you can't find a girl dumb enough to have you."

Bob jumped at her and she flinched. He roared with laughter. "Look at you! Gotcha, din't I?"

Rose ignored him.

"I'm gettin' tired of eatin' rabbits and squirrels," said Ferd. "'Bout time we had us some fresh beef." He paused to pick lead shot out of his mouth. "Wish you'd learn to shoot 'em with a twenty-two, Clint."

"Would if they'd hold still," said Clint.

"As I was sayin'," Ferd continued, "when I was you boys' age and I was ridin' with Alf Bolin, we ate all the beef we wanted. Fact is, did as we pleased. Them was the days."

"You're lucky you didn't get what Alf got; killed with a fire poker." said Estelle.

"Watch your mouth, woman. He just wasn't as smart as I was. I knew when to get out. Say, Bob, you and Clint come out to the barn when we're done. Want to talk about somethin'."

"How about me?" said Buford.

"You stay here."

When darkness fell over the hills that evening, Ferd and his two older sons gathered behind the log barn as they had planned that morning.

"Moon's gonna be up in a little bit. Not full; big enough. We'll just take a pole axe and some rope and a gunny sack. Tie up the dogs. I've got my Colt Navy, just in case, but we don't need anything else."

The three of them walked silently, single file through the corn-field behind the barn. They crossed the rail fence into the neighboring Friedrich farm and climbed the ridge through the woods.

"What'll Friedrich do now, Pa?" Bob said softly.

"Who knows? He ain't doin' too well. Wish I had this piece of land. Lots of timber."

"Maybe he'll leave." Bob said.

"Wait and see. Now be quiet."

They topped the ridge and dropped down the other side, above Hanson Creek, following a game trail just inside the woods that bordered the bald peak of the ridge. It was rough going in the near-darkness as the fringe of the woods was a scrubby growth of blackjack and post oak.

After another hour's walk, they emerged into the open, looking down on the broad bottom land at the confluence of the two creeks that joined to make up Hanson Creek. At the nose of the ridge between the creeks, the impressive white house of Colonel Madison sat, with its barn and outbuildings.

"Whooee," said Ferd. "That man's got money. Don't suppose he'll miss a yearlin' calf. The herd was his'n I seen when I was squirrel huntin' the other day. I don't see 'em on this side of the field, so they may be bedded down on the other side of the ridge."

They walked back up over the hilltop and started down the other side. Ferd stopped and pointed. "See 'em down there, along the edge of the woods? We'll go on down and slip up on 'em through the woods."

When they reached the edge of the woods, Ferd whispered, "See that damn new-fangled bob-war fence? Be careful when you climb over. Hold next to a fencepost and step on the middle war. Don't snag your nuts."

After they had cleared the fence and crept into position, Ferd stopped and whispered, "Gimme the rope. See that calf a layin' between them two cows? I'll try that 'un. Y'all wait here until I get him. Then run out and help."

All went as Ferd planned. He slipped softly and slowly along the fence, a noose prepared in his hand. The resting cattle raised their heads and looked at him, but did not rise to their feet. When he was in striking distance, Ferd charged forward and slipped the loop around the yearling's neck and braced himself. The calf leaped against the rope, yanking Ferd off his feet. His sons ran and joined him so they were able to bring the calf to a halt. The rest of the cattle all leaped to their feet and stampeded across the field in the darkness.

Several hours later, Ferd and his sons trudged wearily back through the cornfield to the barn, the partially-dressed carcass of the calf strung from a pole they took turns carrying between them. They took it into the back of the barn and hung it up. The sky was brightening in the east as they finished skinning and quartering the beef, and hanging it in the springhouse. They washed up in the little stream that trickled out of the spring toward the small creek below the farm.

Ferd looked at his sons as they headed for the house. "Good job. We'll be havin' liver for breakfast!"

CHAPTER 7

Anna Friedrich got up before dawn and kindled a fire in the iron cook stove. The house and her mind were filled with gloom. With Mama gone, what would life be like? Her father always seemed angry about something, and was now grimly silent, not speaking to her and not even looking at her. Anna knew how to cook and keep house, so she did all the things her mother used to do, but with no acknowledgement from her father or her brother, Evan. The day before, after the rain from the burying day had ceased, she had seen them talking together out by the barn, but they said only a few single words inside the house around her. Then it was only to make some demand for food, or coffee, or to wash their clothes.

She set a kettle of water on the stovetop to heat for cornmeal mush and added a little fresh coffee to the grounds that half-filled the coffee pot. As she waited for them to boil, she went to the springhouse and retrieved a shank of ham. It was the last of the cured meat from the winter's butchering. She dreaded talking to her pa about getting some meat from somewhere.

Hank Green, Colonel Madison's overseer, knocked on the front door of the Madison house. After a long pause, he heard footsteps approaching inside and Etta, the housekeeper, opened the door.

"Etta, tell the boss I need to see him."

Etta padded away and in a few moments, Madison stepped out on the porch. "Yes, what is it?" he demanded.

"Boss, I hate to tell ya this, but we lost a yearlin' last night."

"Lost how?"

"Somebody butchered it. Left the head and innards."

"Who the hell did such a thing? They leave any tracks?"

"They was some boot tracks from the rain yesstiddy, but you know how rocky it is in some places. I've got a coup'la the boys lookin' but didn't seem to be no horses."

"Here's what you do. Ride in to Forsyth and get the sheriff out here. I won't stand for this! And we're going to start standing watch with Winchesters. We'll kill any sonofabitch that touches my cattle."

"Yessir, Boss." Hank started to walk away.

"Oh, and Green? Have that storekeeper down in Sycamore...what's his name?"

"Henry Guthrie."

"Yeah. Have him post a notice on that board of his that I want to hire a housekeeper. Have it say, 'pay good wages' and 'contact me or leave a note'."

Hank rode into Sycamore and up to the Guthrie store's hitching rail. On the way, he wondered if Etta was to be replaced. He also thought that his mission to Forsyth would not be successful. There was too much other thieving going on for this one to get much attention. Oh, well, it all paid the same. As he looped the reins around the rail, one of the idlers on the broad front porch called out.

"Hey, Hank. How are things up at the castle?"

"Tolerable, I reckon. Did lose a yearlin' calf last night. Somebody killed it and hauled off the carcass."

One of the others looked around the group. "All right, which one of you fellers did it? I'm hungry for a steak."

There was general laughter.

"Boss don't think it's funny. He sent me to fetch the sheriff," Hank said.

Charlie Tate paused in his whittling and said, "I guess you do what the boss says, but there's a lot of that goin' on. Why, Buford had a couple of hams stole the other night out of his smokehouse."

"How was they, Charlie?" another said, to more laughter.

Rafe Johnson spoke out, "Really, it ain't no joke. Maybe he'll come since it's the colonel. If he does, Hank, let us know. Maybe we could have a meetin' here and talk about all of it. We got a dispute goin' over a line fence over in Hickory Hollow that's causin' a stir. So far it's just fist fights, but it could be worse. Might be settin' up a devil's lane."

The others around the porch nodded agreement.

Rafe's second son, Mark, was with him and tugged at his sleeve. "What's a devil's lane, Pa?" he said quietly.

"It's where two guys can't agree on fixin' fence, so they get mad and both build one with a strip of land between. That there's a devil's lane, and it shows everybody what stubborn is."

Hank stepped up on the porch and clumped across to the door. "I'll let ya know. I've got to post a note on the board. Boss wants to hire a housekeeper."

As he opened the door, the bell jangled. Henry Guthrie was at the back of the store, and another man was standing at the bulletin board. "Hi, Henry," Hank called out. "Want to post a notice."

"Go right ahead," Henry called back through a wreath of blue pipe smoke.

The other man turned. "*Güt* morning, Hank."

"Hi, Jürgen. Sorry for your loss." He extended his hand.

"We get by," Jürgen said, shaking his hand. "What are you posting?"

"Notice to hire a housekeeper. How about you?"

"A sale of all our stuff. We're moving out."

"Really? Where to?"

"Going west. Our farm is not so *güt* for us."

The next morning after she had served breakfast, Anna cleaned the dishes and put them away. Papa still sat at the table, drinking coffee. He'd sent Evan out to hitch one of horses to the buckboard without telling him why.

Finally he spoke. "Anna, if you are finished, get yourself cleaned up and put on your best dress. Use something of Mama's if you need to. And put shoes on."

"Why, Papa?"

"Because I said!"

"Yes, Papa. But I have no shoes. It's not winter yet."

"Just do as I say."

Anna got a pan of water, warmed from the teakettle on the stovetop. She took it behind her curtain and did her best to wash herself. She had only one other dress. The print pattern was faded, but it was clean. Mama was buried in her best dress, so that wasn't an option. She started with her face and work her way downward, at the last folding a clean cotton cloth and pinning it in her drawers, since she was enduring the "monthly curse" her mama had told her about. She hid the dirty clothing under her bed to wash later. She gathered her hair into a long braid down her back.

"Hurry up!" her papa shouted.

"Soon, Papa," she said. What am I doing? she thought. Where is he taking me? I'm afraid. She went into the bedroom and looked under the bed for shoes, but there were none, so she went back into the main room where Papa was.

He merely rose, staring at her and said. "Let's go."

Papa said almost nothing on the two-hour ride down the hollow, down Bull Creek, and up Hanson Creek. Once she had the courage to ask again where they were going, but all he said was, "You'll see."

They forded the creek in two or three places and eventually rounded a bend in the wagon road and up ahead Anna saw the biggest house she had ever seen. And it was *white*! Her anxiety increased. Surely we can't be going there.

Friedrich drove around the circular gravel drive and reined to a halt at the base of a wide set of steps leading up to the broad porch. He wrapped the reins around the brake lever and climbed down. "You wait right here," he said.

Anna sat trembling in the spring seat and gazed up at the house towering over her. She caught a glimpse of a face at a window high above, but it quickly disappeared.

Friedrich climbed the steps, squared his shoulders, and knocked firmly on the oak door. After a short time, a black woman with a white apron opened it

"I'm here to see Mister Madison," he announced, without waiting for her to speak.

"Sir, do he expect you?"

"He does not, but I have something for him."

The maid closed the door and left. In a short time she returned. "The Colonel, he say he need your name and business."

"Tell him 'Friedrich' and it's about his notice down at Sycamore."

The door closed again, but in a few minutes it was opened by a distinguished man with a full head of silver hair combed straight back. He stepped out onto the porch to face Jürgen Friedrich. He looked at his visitor up and down. "What is it you want with me?"

"I brought my daughter for the housekeeper you seek."

"Your daughter? What's she been doing? What makes you think she can do the job?"

"Her mama teaches her everything. She is a hard worker."

"How old is she?"

"Sixteen," he lied.

"Too young."

"She works hard, and you don't have to pay."

"No pay?"

"I go west and she can't go. You give hundred dollars, I leave her here. No pay."

Madison stared at him, thinking. Then he spoke. "Get her up here."

"Anna! Come!"

Madison watched her climb down from the buckboard and walk up the steps to the porch. She carried herself well, but she looked young. He could see a woman's figure starting to develop, however. *Maybe there are some possibilities here. I would essentially own her.*

Anna stood before the man with the silver hair, trying not to tremble, eyes downcast.

"Take off your bonnet and look at me," Madison said.

Anna complied, looking directly at him. Madison noted the luxuriant red hair and the steady gaze of the gray-green eyes. *Young,* he thought, *but some day beautiful if she can be domesticated. Clothing is pitiful and no shoes.*

He twirled his finger in the air. "Turn all the way around."

What am I, a cow to be sold? thought Anna, but she complied, looking straight back at him.

"Anna, you go back to the buckboard," said Friedrich.

"Papa, what is happening?"

"Never you mind. Do as I say."

Madison cupped his chin in his hand and pinched his lower lip. Maybe Agnes is right. We can keep Etta for a while if this filly can be trained to help her. Be interesting to see how she develops. "Tell you what, Friedrich, if we do this, I have to feed her and get her in decent clothes. And she probably knows nothing about how a house like this operates. Make it fifty and you have a deal."

Friedrich extended his hand. "Deal," he said.

CHAPTER 8

The Archer family sat at the plank table eating a breakfast of fried mush and scrambled eggs prepared by Josie. Tom Archer spoke between bites. "Well, now that the rain's gone, we got to get back to work. I think you got about half the corn scratched out, didn't you Ben?"

"Yeah, Pa. Just need to hoe it and do both to the other half."

"Well I'll use the double-shovel and mule on the rest of it, and you kids can start hoein'."

Josie spoke up, "Pa, I need to wash clothes."

"All right. You do that, then. Jimmy can build a fire and help carry water. Oren, you can help your sister in whatever she needs."

"Why can't Ben do that and let me hoe corn?" said Jimmy.

"Ben will get more done. When Josie tells you you're done, you can do all the hoein' you want."

"That ain't fair!"

"Life ain't fair, Son. You'll do all right." Tom rose and patted his son on the shoulder.

Ben started down the first row of corn, methodically scraping his hoe through the roots of the weeds that intruded between the stalks of shoulder high corn. Before the rain, he had plowed out the weeds between the rows up here with a mule and double-shovel. His pa had taken over that task down in the middle of the field. He actually liked this kind of work. You got to make a good clean row of corn behind you and you got to daydream about most anything. His mind was on yesterday. He'd never been around what might be called a "fancy" girl before. He couldn't believe how nice she was. He expected someone from a rich family like that would have her nose in the air. It wasn't that way at all. She actually seemed to be interested in what he had to say.

It ain't going anywhere, though. She may be older than I am and I'll probably never see her again. Still, it was worth gettin' soaked in the rain to take her home. And she admitted she wasn't supposed to be goin' to our buryin'. Glad she did. Oh well. Nuthin' will come of it.

He stopped his line of thinking and picked up an arrowhead. He wiped it off with his thumb and turned it over in his hand. That was another good thing about hoeing corn after a rain. It washed 'em off on the topside. He had a cigar box full and always looked for them in the bottom fields. Actually, it was a spear point. The real arrowheads were much smaller and he had a few of those also. He talked to the old man school teacher in Sycamore, who had explained it to him. His interest was kindled years ago when somebody told him what his last name "Archer" meant.

Josie carried the wash tubs out into the yard. She let Oren carry one side of each one so he'd feel important. Jimmy didn't look happy, but he did what Pa told him. He already had a fire going under the big cast iron pot which sat on square stones from the creek. He was also carrying buckets of water from the small stream that flowed out of the spring. She felt sorry for him, being the second son and unable to do things his big brother did.

After she got the washtubs set up on their stones, she started carrying water also, for the rinsing. As she met Jimmy at the creek, she spoke to him, "I'm sorry, Jimmy, that you have to do things you don't like to do, but I thank you for your help."

Jimmy kept his head down as he filled a bucket. "I reckon you have to do stuff too."

When he set the bucket down, she put her arms around him. "We have to work together. I'm just twelve, you know. We both need a ma to take care of us. But we'll all get through it." Jimmy nodded.

After several trips, they had the kettle and a rinse tubs full. While they waited for the kettle to come to a boil, Josie went inside and rinsed the beans that had been soaking overnight, then set them to cook in a cast iron pot with onion and bacon fryings. She gathered a basket of clothes and Oren followed behind her carrying the washboard. She carved shavings of lye soap into the heating water. Edna Johnson had helped her make the soap last winter.

The sun was climbing in the east, beating down on Ben as he worked. He was making good headway, leaving clean rows of corn behind him. Also, he'd found two more flint points. As he worked he thought about the future. Wonder what I'll do when I get older? No more schoolin'. I'm too old for that. Guess I'll try to get a piece of land like Pa has and someday get married. That last thought caused some inner confusion. How do you find somebody like that? When he was going to school winter before last, he kinda had his eye on Rose Harvey, but she lived over Snow Ridge and he never saw her anymore. Her family didn't come to church services.

His thoughts were interrupted by Jimmy approaching in the next row, hoeing in the opposite direction. "How's it goin', Jimmy?"

"Good. Better since I got out here."

Clean clothes were hanging on the line, flapping in the light breeze that had sprung up, when the men of the family came in from the field at mid-day. Oren ran to meet them and took his father's hand. Josie could see him chattering at their father and she smiled. Someday, she thought, I'll be grown up and maybe have kids of my own.

She stirred cornmeal, a little flour, bacon grease, and baking soda in hot water and set it to cook in a skillet to make a johnny cake to go with the beans.

The field crew all washed in a pan at the end of the porch and came inside, the boys immediately sitting at the table. Tom approached his daughter standing at the stove. He noted the sweat on her face and her roughened red hands. It troubled him to expect so much of her. He put his arm around her shoulder, "I'm sorry you have to work so hard, Sweetheart."

She smiled up at him, "It's all right, Pa. We do what we haf'ta to do."

As they ate their noon meal, they discussed the afternoon.

Tom said, "While I was followin' that mule, Rafe Johnson came by and said there's a meetin' down in Sycamore this evenin' at five o'clock with the county sheriff. I'd best be goin'." He looked at the mantel clock. "I might be finished in time, but if not, Josie, will you send Oren to get me in plenty of time? If I have to leave, Ben, you can take over the mule."

"Sure, Pa," said Josie. "I'll be ironing and puttin' the beds back together."

Tom Archer rode into Sycamore in time to join the men gathering in the schoolhouse. Sheriff Horton rode in shortly after, coming from his meeting with Colonel Madison. Like any good politician, he shook hands with Tom and many others as he made his way to the front of the room. His spurs jingled as he walked across the small stage and stood behind the teacher's desk. He was wearing those jeans called Levi's, cotton shirt, and large western hat. He hitched up his gun belt, lined with loops holding brass cartridges. It also suspended a long-barreled Colt .45 Peacemaker in a holster down his right thigh. He really looks like a sheriff, thought Tom, from his ample belly to the star on his chest to the drooping white mustache.

Horton cleared his throat and began, "You fellers wanted to get together and talk about all the stuff goin' on over here on Bull and Swan Creeks. I just been up talkin' to the Colonel. He had somebody come in and butcher a calf, and I hafta say he ain't totally happy with what I had to say. Let's hear from you-all and I'll come back to his problem."

Hands were raised and the sheriff called on the men one by one. Most of the problems were similar: stolen pigs, stolen chickens, stolen beef. One man reported a stolen horse. Rafe Johnson mentioned the fence dispute in Hickory Hollow.

The sheriff listened to each complaint, clumping back and forth on the stage. "All right. You might not like to hear what I have to say, just like the Colonel didn't, but it's the truth. This is a big county and there ain't many of us. If somebody steals sumpin' small and eats it, there ain't a whole lot to be done unless somebody saw them do it and can testify. Now a stolen wagon or a horse, assumin' he ain't gonna eat it"—laughter

44

from the room—"we at least have a chance. I'll take down anything you got on the horse, and I'll see about this dispute thing. In fact, I'll do that this evenin' if I can find a place to bed down here tonight. For the rest, I suggest you have some get-togethers and figure out ways to keep watch on each other. If anybody sees who's doin' it, we'll take action."

Oley Jensen, the miller, held up his hand. "Sheriff, you can bunk at my place tonight, if you're a mind to."

"Thankee," said the sheriff. "Now let me talk to the feller lost a horse, and you, Rafe, about the dispute."

The meeting broke up and the men milled about the room talking in groups. After Oley Jensen spoke to the sheriff, he came over to Tom Archer.

"Tom, can we step outside. Got something you might be interested in."

"Sure, Oley."

When they were out of earshot, Oley began, "I was at the bank in Forsyth today and the manager approached me. Now I don't want to be accused of dancing on a grave, but it might be something you'd want to look into. He heard about the Friedrichs and he holds the paper on their property. He might not should have told me, but he's way, way behind on the mortgage. He figures Friedrich may just skip out."

"Skip out without sayin' anything? And why me?"

"It happens. That oldest boy of yours may want a place of his own someday and you may be one of the few who could swing the deal."

Tom rubbed his chin, thinking. "Hadn't thought about it, but I might be interested. Depends on what they want for it. I thank you for letting me know."

They shook hands and parted ways.

CHAPTER 9

Anna was up at dawn in the somber atmosphere of her home. She built a fire in the cook stove to begin preparing breakfast. Papa was still not talking. Anna maintained her composure, too stubborn some would say, to outwardly display her grief. Within herself, she longed for someone to share her feelings. Mama was gone but no one seemed to care.

Papa and Evan came in and sat at their usual places and she brought them coffee. Instead of waiting silently for her to serve them breakfast, however, this morning her father spoke. "Anna, come and sit," he commanded.

She slid the skillet off the burner and sat across from him.

"I'm telling you what is to happen," said Jürgen. "Your brother and me, we leaving to go west."

Anna started to rise. "What about me?"

"You stay here."

"Stay here? How can I do that?" she cried through her tears.

"No use to cry. It is all settled. You know where we went the other day, they will take you in until we get settled. Then I come back for you."

"Why can't I go too?"

"Sleeping out along the trail is no place for a girl."

Anna wiped her eyes. "I can do it!"

"No, you do as I say. You will work for those people for your keep, just as you do in any family. You get your food and a place to sleep."

Anna whipped off her apron, threw it on the floor, and ran behind her curtain, falling onto her narrow bed. She buried her face in her pillow and released her emotions at last.

In moments, Papa pulled the curtain aside. "Get in here and finish cooking the breakfast," he shouted.

She sat up, wiped her eyes with her hands and stared at him. "If you and Evan can cook on the trail, you can cook your own breakfast!" she shouted, her chin thrust forward.

Jürgen slapped her face and shouted back, "You do as I say!" He grabbed her roughly by the arm and yanked her to her feet and dragged her toward the cooking area. Evan, still seated at the table, watched with concern.

Anna gave in to his superior strength and the threat of more violence, but said to herself that Papa, from this day forth, was as dead to her as Mama. Now Evan was her only living family and he was powerless to help her.

Later, she cleaned up the remnants of breakfast, eating nothing herself, and retreated to her curtained space. Jürgen followed behind her. "Get your stuff together and we will go."

"What stuff? There is almost nothing."

"Anything of yours or Mama's."

Anna spent the next half-hour gathering her meager belongings, putting clothing, knitting needles, and yarn in a pillowcase. She got her mother's Bible with names of ancestors written in it, a hand mirror and brush, a rag doll her mother had made, and a cigar box with childhood treasures: pretty stones, a marble, some arrowheads, and a tiny locket. Last, she carefully folded the quilt her mother had made, and sat on her bed to wait. Her face still felt hot where she had been slapped.

In moments, Jürgen jerked the curtain back. "Are you ready? We go now."

Anna rose and picked up the folded quilt with the other items stacked on it and followed her papa outside. Evan was holding Bonner by the bridle, a sad look on his face. He came to meet her and took the things from her as they approached the buckboard. He placed them in first, then turned to face her. He enveloped her in a fierce hug and whispered in her ear, "I'm so sorry Anna. So sorry. I will see you again someday."

Anna felt numb, but said, "I'm sorry, too, Evan. I know there is nothing you can do about him. Goodbye."

She climbed in beside her papa and they drove away.

"God be with you, Anna!" Evan shouted as they drove out of the clearing.

They repeated the long drive down the hollow, along the banks of Bull Creek and back up the valley of Hanson Creek to the great house on the hill. Neither spoke. Anna was lost in a turmoil of thought. Her life was going to change, and she had no idea what to expect. She was determined to display no emotion in front of this man beside her, who was no longer her papa. No more anger or crying. That was going to be only on the inside from now on.

Friedrich drove the buckboard around the same circular drive to the front steps. He'd sent Evan here the day before with the message that he'd be bringing his daughter the next morning. He climbed to the front door and knocked.

Madison's announcement to his family that he had hired a girl to help the housekeeper had met strong reactions. His wife, Agnes, and daughter, Gertrude, were both shocked that he would bring someone from the local population to work in their home. Margaret was secretly amused and delighted, but said nothing. She heard Mother and Gertie throw back to Father all of his prior statements about how inferior the local people are.

"How do we know she won't steal everything she can get her hands on?" demanded Mother. "Will she be unclean? Will she be lazy?"

Father's response was to slap his hand on the table with a force that rattled the china, "It's done! Make it work!"

Etta watched the family debate and took some pleasure in the chance that she'd have some help and might get to keep her place in the household. She hoped the girl worked out and could lighten her burden just a bit, especially climbing stairs and lifting some of the heavier loads.

Now she opened the door to the man who had brought the girl before. At his request, she found the Colonel in his study and found the Mistress in her bedroom sitting area. The daughters had noted the arrival and descended the staircase, so all were waiting in the wide entrance hall as Jürgen Friedrich escorted his daughter across the veranda and inside.

Anna was aware of her worn clothes, her bare feet, and her meager possessions as all eyes of the assemblage were on her. I'm a person created by God, just as they are, she said to herself. She quelled the inner tremors, held herself erect and walked gracefully into the room. Before anyone else had a chance to speak, she said, "Good morning. I am Anna Friedrich."

Friedrich's mouth was open, but he closed it again. Madison replied, "Good morning, Anna. Etta will take you out back." Then he motioned Friedrich to follow him back out the front door.

Friedrich said, "Anna…" but she turned her back and began to follow Etta down the hall..

Madison gave Friedrich the agreed price and sent him on his way. He came quickly back into the house and said, "Wait a minute, Etta. Margaret, come here."

Margaret had been surprised when she saw Anna enter the hall, immediately recognizing who she was. This is even better, she thought. Now she approached, "Yes, Father?"

"See if you have some old clothes that will fit her, nothing fancy, and help Etta get her cleaned up. Draw her a bath out in the kitchen house. Make sure she isn't carrying anything."

"*Father!*" she whispered.

"Well, just do it. We'll have to decide what to do with her; where to put her."

Margaret hurried to catch up with Etta and Anna. She smiled and said, "I'm Margaret Madison. I'll help you get settled in."

"Thank you. I'll do my best to earn my keep."

"I'm sure you will. To get started on the right foot, go with Etta and she'll draw you a bath. I'll get some of my things that might fit and I'll be right out."

Margaret's mother and sister had said not a word, watching without expression. She knew that some conversations with her father were soon to take place, but she hurried past them and up the staircase. This is going to be like having a real sister, she thought, although I will have to hide the fact when the others are around. She hastened into her room, threw open her wardrobes, and began to take out dresses, skirts, and blouses and lay them on the bed. She opened drawers and took out undergarments and stockings, and looked through her collection of shoes. After choosing the plainest and smallest, she gathered an arm-load, picked up bath salts and French soap, and dashed downstairs. As she passed her father's closed study door, she heard animated conversation coming from inside.

She hurried out the back door and into the cookhouse. Etta and Anna were standing by the great iron stove with a large copper boiler heating water over two burners. The firebox was roaring with seasoned split oak, occasionally popping sparks. An oval bathtub was set up in the side room, so Margaret took the clothing in there and hung it on hooks on the wall.

"Well, Anna, I have lots of clothes I've outgrown, so we may be able to find you something. Also shoes and stuff. After your bath, we'll see what fits or if we have to make some changes."

"Thank you Miss Margaret."

"You're welcome. You can leave off the "Miss" when the others aren't around. They're stuffy."

For the first time since before her mother died, Anna smiled.

The tub was tin-plated and had high sides. After Anna helped Etta carry the hot water and added cool water to temper it, Margaret shook scented powder into it and smiled at her. "Don't be bashful. We'll close the door. Call me when you're finished. You can wrap yourself in a towel and I'll come in and help sort out some clothes for you."

"Thank you Miss...er...thank you Margaret."

"After this, you will be serving others, so enjoy it while you can."

Anna sat in the tub of scented water and used the wonderful soft soap to wash her hair and the rest of herself. She had never experienced anything like it and knew that she had never been so clean. She looked around the small room which was lined with shelves. They contained kitchen utensils and pots and pans, also food supplies: bags of flour and cornmeal, jars of vegetables, and all manner of bounty.

When she felt she must give up the luxury of the bath, she reached for one of the large fluffy towels on the chair by the tub and stood, drying her hair and wrapping the towel around her. She stepped out on the braided rug, and said, "I'm finished."

There was a tap at the door and both Etta and Margaret came in. Etta set down a bucket and spoke first, "I'm startin' the dinner. When you get dressed we start showin' you the ropes. We can carry out the water later."

When Anna came into the kitchen a half-hour later, Etta turned from the stove. "My, my! Look at you, child. We better put a' apron on you or they think some fancy lady come for dinner!"

Anna blushed and Margaret laughed. "I've warned her that my family are all pretty stiff, Etta. She knows she's here to help you, so you can start her training any time. I'll see you later."

"I will. I need help and I bet she know how to work."

"I'll do my best."

"You have any problem workin' for a colored woman?"

"No, no, no. I'm just a kid and you know what you're doin'."

"Jist had to ask, get that out'a tha way. Now. I gotta roast in the oven and green beans and new potatoes on the stove. We go in the main house and I show you how the table is set."

Anna followed her into the house and through the warming kitchen where a low fire was kept in the range. They went into the dining room and she marveled at the gleaming mahogany table and white tablecloth. Etta began, "Now I done it already, but I show you. The Mister and Miz Gertrude sit at that end. Missus and Miz Margaret sit up here. Make more sense they all sit together, but ain't for me to say. This be a simple meal, so simple setup. The knife, he go on the right with sharp side to the plate, and miz spoon, she keep him company. Mister fork by hisself on this side, but the napkin go right by him. See the open side of the fold go toward the plate, so's they can whip it off and right on they lap. For a fancy dinner, there be lots more stuff and sometimes they want to sit and make you put the napkin on 'em. Missus tell us, if that be so."

Anna nodded, "Why don't they sit together?"

"We don't know that stuff. I s'pose it looks fancier. But it means we have to stay here and carry stuff back and forth. When you're in here, you don't say nuthin. 'Cep for Miz Margaret, they ack like they can't see you." She pitched her voice in a higher register and leaned back. "I look like a ghost to you?" Then she flashed her white teeth in a giggle.

Anna couldn't help but join her. "How do you know all this stuff?"

"My mama a house slave. She learn it all and she teach me like I gonna teach you. Then I was a house slave in Virginia and my brother Ike kept the horses. When Mister Lincoln freed the slaves, we walked for many nights, hidin' in the days, and made it acrost the river into Washington. We called it 'crossin' the Jordan' and we hooked up with the Madisons. They pay us a tiny bit so's it ain't slavery, so's we say we free."

Anna listened with interest and began to feel like this might not be so bad, after her sadness and dark thoughts of the morning.

CHAPTER 10

A different discussion was taking place in Colonel Madison's study. As soon as Margaret left to find clothing for the girl, Agnes fired the opening salvo. "Perry, I can't believe what you were thinking! Why, that girl is straight out of the backwoods! No shoes! Did you see her clothing?"

"Now, Agnes, she'll clean up, and we can put better clothes on her. Don't forget it was your idea. I wanted to get rid of Etta, and you're the one that whined about how long we'd had her. Remember? You said, 'get a girl to help her.' What do you think that was that walked in the door? And where, for God's sake do you think you'd find a cultured English maid out here? Huh?"

Gertrude sat back, amused at the interplay between her parents. The same points were made and rebutted endlessly back and forth. This was going to be fun.

"Where will we put her?" demanded Agnes. "She can't sleep with the colored."

"We'll think of something," said Madison.

Gertrude sat up straighter. "I've got it. You know the little attic room in front, the one with the window? There's some stuff in there now, but it has a stairs to it, and we could have an 'upstairs maid' like in a book I'm reading."

They both turned to look at her, both in thought.

"She'd be handy in case Margaret or I needed anything at night, some of the work is upstairs anyway, and she wouldn't really be living in the same quarters."

Just as Margaret entered the room, Madison said, "You may be right."

"About what?" Margaret said.

"Gertie suggests we put the girl—"

"Name's Anna,"

"—put *Anna* in that little attic room above yours."

"I think that's a great idea, Father. Can we get one of the men to come up and clear it out and set up a bed?"

"I'll talk to Hank after we eat." He pulled a gold pocket watch out of his vest pocket and flipped it open. "Let's go in."

When the Madisons were all seated in their customary seats, Etta entered from the warming kitchen with a large roast of beef on a platter. Following closely behind, Anna carried a gravy boat and waited as she had been instructed until Etta presented the roast to be carved. Then she hurried back in to the warming stove and brought in the large bowl of potatoes and green beans, then a basket of rolls, and did the same, arraying the dishes around the Colonel.

Agnes Madison stared at Anna as she entered and followed her with her gaze each time Anna traversed the room. Margaret had to suppress her amusement at her mother's surprised look.

Etta nodded at the roast beef and Anna carried it to the other end of the table. They spent the rest of the meal shuttling the dishes back and forth as the family called for them, invisible as ghosts, Anna thought to herself with amusement as she glided back and forth.

Margaret noted that Anna's hair had dried and she'd braided it in one long braid down her back. It was deep red and shining, with curls framing her face. She will be a beauty someday, she thought. Wonder what Mother thinks now? She noted how her mother followed Anna's every move except when she was watching Father watching Anna. Gertrude was watching both parents with a calculating expression. I wonder what's going on in the head of my dear sister, thought Margaret.

After coffee and blackberry cobbler were served—serve from the right, remove from the left—the family left the table and Etta and Anna cleared, and washed, and cleaned. Etta took Anna on a tour of the house and began an explanation of household duties, telling her they would do everything together for a while and sort it out later.

Hank sent in a couple of men to work under Margaret's direction to clear out the garret room and install a single bed and chest of drawers. She found an unused wardrobe in the attic and they carried it in also. She found Etta and Anna and showed them her handiwork, so the two set to work making up the bed and bringing Anna's meager belongings. They used Anna's quilt as a counterpane. Margaret carried in more unwanted clothing and they sorted through it to find spare outfits for Anna to be reworked to fit. She produced a bolt of black fabric and explained that they would be making a simple dress to put her in uniform if they ever entertained fancy people sometime.

After a long and tiring day, her youthful energy depleted by excitement and adrenalin, Anna knelt by her bed and searched for a way to begin. "Dear Lord, I hope Mama's there with you and I hope she doesn't hurt anymore. Thank you for bringing me to a safe place and bless Miss Margaret and Miz Etta for being nice to me. Amen."

Jürgen Friedrich spent the next two weeks selling all unwanted possessions for whatever cash they would bring, then in the darkness of an early morning he left the log house in the clearing with Evan sitting beside him on the wagon spring seat. The wagon was pulled by two mules, and two saddle horses and a spare mule were tied behind. They forded Bull Creek and drove the gravel wagon road west to intercept the Springfield-Harrison mail road. The sun was showing itself in the east as they turned north toward Springfield.

CHAPTER 11

The heat of summer began to wane over the Missouri hills and the citizens of the Bull Creek and Swan Creek watersheds followed an established routine to prepare for the coming of winter. The Archer family had all worked together to gather and can vegetables, pick gooseberries and blackberries for jelly, and dig the mature potatoes for storage in a root cellar. Cabbages were shredded and put in vats of vinegar to make sauerkraut. Black walnuts were hulled, dried, ready to be cracked on the hearth on cold winter evenings by the fire.

They were owners of a cane mill and evaporating pan to make sorghum. Once Tom had it set up, he let the word out that others were welcome to come and use it. By tacit agreement it was first come, first served, after the Archer family, so neighbors coordinated with each other to keep the process moving. It took on a carnival atmosphere as neighbors helped neighbors harvest and process the sorghum cane. The tall cane had to be cut at just the right time while the sap was still in the stalks. Leaves were stripped and the long canes hauled to the barn lot where Tom had set up the mill. Others brought in wagonloads when their turn came. Those from longer distances stayed overnight, camping out. They kept the mill and evaporator pan going night and day until all were finished. It was a time for women to gather and visit, and children to play together before the start of school.

The mill was powered by a long pole extending on top to hitch to a mule. As the mule walked in a circle, stalks of cane were fed into the mill to be crushed, the sweet sap draining out into buckets. Tom let Oren walk behind the mule with a stick to keep him moving. It helped motivate the mule, but also kept Oren away from the boiling syrup and made him feel an important part of the process. All of the children liked to have short sections of cane cut and peeled to chew on for a sweet treat, or they would stand in line for some of the sweet foam skimmed from the surface of the boiling sap.

By October's first frost, corn was in the shocks to cure and pumpkins harvested. Hay was stacked outside near the barn behind rail fencing. The Archer barn was built with two log cribs connected by a platform of logs. Hay also filled one crib and the log loft, while one crib was used for horse stalls. A shed was built all along one side were the cows were milked and equipment was stored.

The start of school in Sycamore and other one-room schools was timed to allow harvest to be completed, so it varied with the weather. In preparation, Tom Archer gathered his family one evening for a foot-measuring. Each child in turn stepped on a sheet of paper while Tom traced the foot's outline. The journey to Forsyth and back was a bit long for a team and wagon to make in one day, so he planned to ride alone the next day.

"Well," Tom said. "I'm gonna leave before daylight tomorrow morning, so's I can get back in one day. What do we need besides shoes to start school?"

"I could use a few yards of calico to make another dress," said Josie. "Ought to have two to switch off. And Jimmy needs a shirt or two. Maybe some store-bought socks if we can. I'll darn everything we have that'll hold together."

"I'm all right," said Ben. "I won't be goin' to school anymore."

"Yeah, I reckon not," said Tom. "You'll all have to do the chores tomorrow without me. May be late when I get back."

"We will, Pa," they all said in unison.

"Ben and I need to talk out on the porch. The rest of you go ahead to bed."

They looked puzzled, but obeyed.

When Tom and Ben were seated in rockers on the front porch, Ben looked at his pa with a serious expression. "What is it, Pa?"

"I have other business in Forsyth, Ben. You know about the Friedrichs lightin' out after the missus died. Well, they left the bank being owed most of the money on the place. They'd bought the place from the original homesteaders, but couldn't make the payments. So the bank is finally doing what they call a foreclosure. It means the bank can sell it to get whatever they can to help pay off what's owed. I've been thinkin' if I could get it cheap enough it might be something for you in the future. You ain't quite ready yet, maybe, but if we could manage it, we'd have it ready when you are."

Ben looked at him with eyes wide. "That's something, Pa. I hadn't even thought about such a thing."

"Well it's called plannin' ahead. The place doesn't have a lot of bottom land, but lots of good timber. I'll just have to see what the deal is."

They rocked in silence for few minutes. The night was clear and cool. Suddenly they heard geese honking and both jumped off the porch and looked up into the night sky. High above them in the moonlight were several long Vs of geese flying south.

"Sure sign of the winter to come," said Tom.

Anna Friedrich stood in the cold crisp moonlight, staring at the harvest moon as it climbed out of the treetops on the hill to the east. She had just made her evening trip to the outhouse before going up to her cozy garret bedroom. As she always did, she looked up at the night sky and wondered if heaven was up there as some said. Was Mama able to look down and keep a watch over her daughter?

The weeks had flown by since that morning when Papa had delivered her here. She still resented the feeling of abandonment and told herself she never wanted to see him again. However, in some ways, things weren't so bad. Etta was almost like a mother to her, treating her kindly and helping her learn her duties. She was used to hard work, so it was easy to do everything expected of her. There were good and bad parts. Margaret had treated her almost like she thought a sister might, although she had no basis of comparison. The older daughter, Gertrude, was different. Gertrude seemed to think up things for Anna to do beyond what the rest of the family required.

Her chamber pot was a good example. Etta had told her about this pail with curving sides and a lid that each of the family kept in their bedrooms in a little box they called a "commode" so they wouldn't have to go outside at night, particularly when cold weather came. It was now Anna's duty to tend to this chore each morning and make sure they were ready in the evening. The rest of the family never seemed to use theirs, at least through the summer. After Anna came, she never saw Gertrude go to the outhouse again. Instead, she'd call Anna at all times of the day and night to empty her "chamber," as she called it.

It was a mixed blessing, therefore, when Margaret had told Anna one morning a month ago that she and her sister were going back East for "finishing school," whatever that was.

"I'll miss seeing you each morning, Anna," she had said.

Anna remembered pausing in her bed-making duty, "Me, too, Margaret. You've been really nice to me. When will you come back?"

"After the winter. As soon as I can. Father and Mother insist I need to become more of a 'lady'."

"To me you're already a lady, 'cause there's kindness in your heart."

"Thank you Anna." Margaret had hugged her. "I think you're a lady, too." Then she changed the subject. "I have more books for you to read. Take that stack on the desk to your room and read 'em while I'm gone. There's an arithmetic book there also, one I had in school. I don't know how much you got to go to school, but maybe you can figure it out."

"I didn't get to go much, but Mama helped me some. I'll try to work through it. Thank you ever so much for treating me so nice."

Anna's thoughts were interrupted by the whisper of wings and a dark shadow passing overhead. Must be the hootie owl I've been hearing at night. Maybe he's huntin' for his dinner. Reluctantly, she turned from the moonlit landscape and made her way silently into the house through the back door. As she crept down the hall toward the staircase, she remembered her encounter there with Missus Madison. It was the day after the Madisons had returned from taking the daughters to the train in Springfield. She recalled being summoned into the sitting area of Missus Madison's bedroom.

"Anna, come in please. I want to talk to you."

Anna stood before her with concern showing on her face. She had never seen Margaret's mother smile and she wasn't smiling then. She had seemed to watch every move Anna made and it made her nervous.

"Anna, when my husband first brought you here, I was against having you helping in the house."

"Yes, Ma'm."

"I want to tell you I was wrong about you. You have done everything asked of you and more, and you have done your work with good spirit."

Anna couldn't believe what she was hearing, spoken by this lady with the stern face. "Thank you, Ma'm. I try to earn my keep."

"You've gone beyond that. I think that you can make something of yourself if you keep your good attitude. I've decided to start paying you a little, despite whatever my husband might think. From now on, I'm giving you a dollar every month and here's the first one." She had handed Anna a silver dollar, almost smiling, but not quite.

Anna had been stunned at the time, but had managed to stammer, "T-thank you, Ma'm. Thank you. I never had any money before." She'd even bent her knees in a semi-curtsey, like Etta had taught her, as she accepted the large coin.

Now as she climbed the staircases to her room she felt good inside, almost a feeling of belonging. She could look forward to rising with the sun each morning with confidence that she could do her work and feel rewarded for it.

After she donned her long nightgown, she checked the cigar box under her bed and hefted the heavy silver coin, more money than she had ever before held in her hand. She knelt on the braided rug and said her prayers before sliding under the quilt her mother made for her.

Tom Archer rode into the clearing of his homestead under the light of the full moon. There was a lamp burning in the window, but he made his way to the barn, unloading the sacks holding his purchases. He unsaddled Beauty, rubbed her down with a gunny sack, and put her in a stall in the barn with a generous wad of clover hay.

His children were all sleeping when he silently entered the house. His trip to Forsyth was successful. The Friedrich place was coming up for auction in a week and the banker had given him encouragement that he wouldn't publicize it a great deal. He'd told Tom that it would make him happy if Tom could just take over the payments and own the place.

CHAPTER 12

The next day after Tom Archer returned from Forsyth he gathered the eight steers he had been fattening and drove them to a local auction barn in Ozark. He allowed Jimmy to accompany him, conscious of Jimmy's need to feel more important to the family. Ben was left in charge at home. They were gone overnight with their small cattle drive and Tom came home with a substantial fund of cash to apply to the land auction coming up.

A few days later he came home from another trip to Forsyth with a bill of sale in his hand for the Friedrich farm. When he came into the log house, where his family was eating supper, he waved the paper in the air and shouted, "We got it!" Only Ben knew what his mission had been, so the rest looked puzzled.

"I just bought another farm," he said. "Time will come as the family grows up that we'll need another place. I got it cheap, thanks to the way it was handled. There was only a couple of land speculators bidding against me and they just wanted to make a steal. We'll have to make payments before we get the deed, but we should be able to do it."

"Good goin', Pa," said Ben. "When do we get to see it?"

"How 'bout tomorrow? We'll pack a dinner and all go in the wagon."

He seated himself at the table and Josie jumped up to get him coffee and a plate of beans and cornbread. "School's startin' in a few days, so we'll take a day off and go have a look."

The following day dawned clear and bright blue, cool enough to wear a jacket or sweater. Tom hitched the team of black Percherons to the wagon and Josie packed a basket with bread and ham and apples. It was a rare thing, the whole family taking a day off from the relentless chores of life on the farm. Still, they'd be back for evening milking and most of the critical harvest work was under control.

Fall foliage was in full color, with only the tops of trees beginning to shed their leaves. By mid-morning a light breeze had sprung up, causing more of them to release and come swirling down. They made their way up the wagon road on the east side of Bull Creek, eventually passing around the tip of Snow Ridge and up the hollow on the other side. Tom enjoyed the laughing and singing of his three younger children as they rode along. He found the wagon trail up the side of the ridge and followed it to the clearing where the Friedrich house and homestead stood.

The log house and surroundings presented a forlorn appearance of neglect. It had been over four months since that fateful day that Eva Friedrich died. The rest of the family had cleared out shortly after. Weeds and sprouts had flourished in the absence of human habitation and the only window facing the front had been broken out. The front door stood open.

"Gonna take some work," Tom said, as his family climbed down from the wagon.

Oren ran to the front steps and stood beside a poke weed that towered over his head. It was laden with clusters of purple berries. "Look, Pa," he shouted.

"That's one big weed, ain't it, Oren?" replied Tom. Then to Ben, "Well, what do you think?"

"I can do it, Pa, if you can spare me. I'd look forward to cleanin' this place up and puttin' it back to work. Let's see what's inside."

The cabin was still in good condition for the most part, but there was evidence of animal intrusion and some trash had been left behind. At least the cast iron stove hadn't been stolen yet.

"I can help clean this up," said Josie. "We have a couple of days before school starts."

They next went to the barn and surroundings. The garden was overgrown with weeds and there was no hay in the barn or corn in the granary. The cornfield still had withered stalks. It could be checked later. If there had been any firewood, it was gone now. Rail fencing needed some repair.

"Well, we got it for the land. Kinda expected this is how it would look," Tom said, as his family gathered around. "I've been thinkin'. Why don't we go back home and gather up what we need and come back tomorrow? We can all put in a good day here, and maybe Ben can stay over and keep at it. How does that sound?"

"Good by me," Ben said, excitement in his voice.

"All right, then. We'll let you have the old wagon and a couple of mules. We can load it up with spare tools. Later on, you can have one of the milk cows. Looks like a full time job, cutting winter's wood and puttin' things right."

They gathered on the front porch and ate from the basket of food Josie had prepared. They were observed from the surrounding woods as they climbed back into the wagon for the journey home.

Opening day of schools in the county arrived on a Monday in early October. Most of the children who were able to go donned new stiff shoes and whatever garments they could sort out to look their best as they nervously converged on the one-room schools. Only two of the Archer family were going this year. Ben was too old and Oren too young, so Josie and Jimmy set out to walk the nearly two miles to Sycamore unless they could catch a ride on the way. They figured on two main possibilities. The Johnsons lived far enough up Bull Creek and they had four children going so they usually hauled them down in a wagon. Their Matthew, like Ben, was deemed too old, but that left Mark, Luke, Mary, and John, while the little girl, Rebecca, stayed home.

If they didn't hook up with the Johnsons and crossed the swinging bridge over Hanson Creek there was a chance they'd catch a ride with the Bowmans as they hauled their load of jewels to school. Mrs. Bowman's name was Jewel, so she named her children Opal, Pearl, Ruby, Garnet, and Sapphire. Little Sapphire was too young for school yet. Garnet was the only boy so far and there was some speculation in the community what they'd name another boy if they had one, or even another girl, since most of the citizens didn't have much knowledge of such things as jewelry.

The opening day of school was chaotic and not much was accomplished as the schoolmaster had to sort the students into classes, not by age but by how much schooling they'd had. It was not uncommon for children moving in from some places to have lived too far from a school to attend, so some of the classes were a wide range of ages. The schoolmaster, Abraham Phillips, did his best not to embarrass older students who had to start at a lower level, allowing them to sit with others nearer their age until time for them to perform. He was unique in Taney County, being a retired college professor, over-qualified for rural elementary teaching. He viewed it as a missionary calling in his retirement to the Ozark hill country. He had moved from back East somewhere to help start up Drury College in Springfield, then found his retirement cabin on Bull Creek across a swinging bridge from Sycamore.

County funds for schools were scarce. The county tried to have enough to pay the meager salaries of teachers, but the rest was mostly left to the communities. Buildings were built by volunteer labor and materials, and families with children contributed what they could, often supplementing the schoolmaster's income by giving him or her produce. It was also a tradition to have fund-raising in the form of pie suppers and turkey shoots to help pay for books and other needs.

After days of hard work, Ben Archer was making headway with the task of cleaning up the Friedrich place. He was happier than he had ever been, working hard but feeling pride in the results. Josie had helped that first day to clean out all the packrat nests and filth from the cabin and Ben had since re-strung the rope bed frame with new rope. He'd put a brush blade on the scythe and cut all the weeds around the house and barn lot, including the garden plot. The mules and his chestnut gelding, Charger, were installed in a two-acre pasture behind the barn.

On this morning, he was digging potatoes from the hills that had been hidden by the weeds. He already had a bushel and expected two or three more. His new friend, Bone, gamboled about, getting in the way, nose to the ground trailing rodent scents and insects. On his last visit, Pa had brought him the little redbone hound pup to keep him company. It was from a litter Homer Zinn had just weaned.

Ben was startled by the sudden appearance of three men on horseback. They rode up to the rail fence that encircled the garden. They were all bearded and rough-looking. "What the hell do you think you're doin'?" The older one asked.

"Diggin' potatoes," Ben said, staring back.

"Well, yeah," the man said. "Who do they belong to?"

"Us."

"Us! What the hell kind of answer is that?"

"Us means my pa, Tom Archer, bought this place"

"How'd he do that?"

"At auction in Forsyth."

"How come I didn't know about it?"

"Don't guess I can answer that, Mister Harvey. That's who you guys are, ain't it?"

"Watch how you talk, kid. We'll be back." With that, he nodded his head at the two young men, who had been sitting, staring, and they whirled their horses and rode away, the horse's hooves throwing clods of dirt into the air.

Well, Pa is coming up today with a load of hay. I'll ask him what I should do or if it means anything.

CHAPTER 13

Tom Archer arrived about noon with a load of hay on the wagon. He'd put the racks back on to widen the load and forked the hay out of one of the stacks behind his barn. Behind the wagon trailed Goldie, a Guernsey cow, wearing a halter and rope, not looking happy with this outing.

"Hey, Pa. Thanks for the hay," Ben said, calling from the porch.

"Hey, Son. I think this might be enough for the winter for your mules and horse. And Goldie will want her share."

As they unloaded the hay, pitching it into the barn loft, Ben told of his morning visitors.

"What do you think, Pa? They didn't look too happy."

"Well, I expect we ought to go talk to them. They're your neighbors now, so better get it over with."

"They looked kinda tough."

"Can't do much about that. Need to talk, anyway."

Ben shut Bone up in the smokehouse and they walked through the woods toward the Harvey place, climbing over the rail fence into the Harvey cornfield.

"That fence don't look too good," said Tom. "Needs fixin' up if it's to hold cattle when he plants his corn in the spring. We'll see what he says about it."

They walked across the stubble field through the shocks of corn and approached the log house from the side. Two dogs came out from under the porch and began to bay at them. As they drew closer, Ferdinand Harvey came out on the porch with a shotgun and squinted at them, shielding his eyes against the bright October sun with his left hand.

"What do you want?"

"It's Tom Archer and Ben, Ferd. Don't think you'll need the shotgun. Just want to have a neighborly talk."

"Well, all right then, I reckon," Ferd said, then yelled at the dogs, "Bell, Spot, shut up! Get back here!"

Ben and Tom climbed over the rail fence and went around to the front of the house. The surroundings had a run-down appearance that reminded Tom of the abandoned Freidrich place when they first saw it. Dried weeds bordered the cabin and a wagon with a broken wheel sat to one side, dried weeds obscuring the undercarriage. The two hounds retreated at Ferd's command and crawled under the porch.

Without a word, Ferd leaned the shotgun against the wall and sat in the only rocking chair. Tom and Ben sat on a bench across from him. Ferd sat staring at them.

"Ben says you and the boys dropped by, so I thought we'd return the visit. Didn't want there to be any misunderstanding how I came to own the place."

Ferd said nothing.

"I heard in Sycamore that Friedrich left the bank holding the bag, so I checked it out."

Ferd finally spoke. "Well, me and my brother Clyde over on Swan Creek was aimin' to see if we could get it. He's got two boys comin' up and I've got three. Seems ya bought it out from under us."

"Well, I'm sorry if it seems that way. I had no idea who else wanted it."

"Even talked to my brother-in-law, Charlie Tate, about it. 'Course he ain't got any boys."

"Did you check it out with the bank in Forsyth?"

"We was goin' to, but hadn't got to it, what with gettin' the corn laid by and such."

"Like I said, I'm sorry, Ferd. I truly am. Wish you'd had a chance to bid. I hope it don't cause hard feelings. We'll do all we can to be good neighbors and I promise if I hear of any land coming free, I'll personally make sure you know about it."

Ferd picked up a tin can and spit a stream of tobacco juice into it. "Well, reckon I can like it or lump it. We'll see where it goes."

"While we're here, I noticed the line fence between us is going to need some work before spring. What kind of deal did you have with Friedrich?"

"We done it all together a few years ago, me and my boys and him and his'n."

"Well for keepin' it up, my deal with neighbors at the other place is, we step off halfway and each take a half. Would that work for you?"

Ferd picked up the can and spat again, "I reckon."

"Which half do you want?"

Ferd rocked in his chair and stared at Tom, thinking. "Maybe we'll take the part from the lane down yonder up past the corn field, wherever half is."

Tom rose and held out is hand. "It's a deal."

Ferd looked at the proffered hand and finally grasped it. "Deal."

"Well, Ben, we'd best be gettin' back. Thank you for your time, Ferd. We'll be seein' you."

Tom and Ben stepped off the porch and started around the house, almost running into a young woman. Rose Harvey was carrying a basket of eggs.

"Oh!" she said, startled.

"Hi, Rose," said Ben. "Haven't seen you since we were kids in school."

Rose looked down, then smiled back at Ben. "I don't get out much."

"Well, you ought to come to Sunday meetin'."

"My pa doesn't hold with that."

Tom watched the interplay with amusement. Then Ben said, "Well, we'd best be goin'. Good to see you, Rose."

After they had climbed the fence and gotten some distance away, Ben said, "Pa, how come men like her brothers are so ugly-lookin' and she's not too bad? I mean, they have these bushy beards and they look like they don't ever wash."

Tom laughed. "That's just the way it is. Maybe if she had a beard, she'd be ugly, too."

"I don't even want to think about it."

Back at the Friedrich place, as they had come to call it, Ben carried a couple of bushels of potatoes to the wagon. The team was hitched and ready to go. "This doesn't look like much of a trade, but there's more than I can eat. Soon's I get them all out, I'll see what I can get out of the corn-field. It's full of deer tracks and I've heard turkeys out there. Probably coons, too."

"I'd better get going. You need to let that pup out of jail. Next time I come up, I'll bring you the Winchester. Maybe you can get a deer or two. That twenty-two of yours is not enough."

"I appreciate it. I've got to get started on wood for this winter, too. Pa, can I say something? I just really like what I'm doing, what you're letting me do."

Tom walked over and gave him a hug, a rare thing. "I'm proud of you, Son."

He climbed into the wagon, slapped the reins, and was gone.

Rose Harvey found her father still sitting on the porch in the rocker. He'd pulled out a large clasp knife and was whittling long shavings off a stick.

"What were they doing here, Pa?"

"They got the Friedrich place." Ferd's mouth was set in a firm line and he increased the pace of his whittling.

"They moving in?"

"Don't think so. Just the boy looks to be workin' the place, most likely. But you'd best not be worryin' about it, 'cause it don't concern you."

Rose looked at her father, then turned and went in the house. Nothing is any of my business, she thought. One of these days I'll figure out how to get away from here.

CHAPTER 14

Abraham Phillips, better known as "Abe" or "Professor" walked across Bull Creek on the swinging bridge in the crisp cool morning. He was headed for his duties as schoolmaster at Sycamore school and it promised to be a long day. Might be able to get a little schooling done in the morning hours, but the afternoon would be used to get ready for the pie supper that evening. It was the social high point of the fall season, but Abe knew nothing about it when he moved to the hills the prior year. Since he would be in charge, it had been explained to him by Oley Jensen, owner of the mill, who was always drafted to be the auctioneer.

"Here's how she goes," Oley had said. "The women and older girls are all supposed to bake a pie and decorate it to look purty. Then the men all bid without knowing who baked the pie, then if they get it, they eat the pie with the lady who baked it. Now you can imagine some cheatin' goes on. You can bet there ain't a man who don't have orders from his wife and have pounded into his head which one is hers. And if some young lady and young man have taken a shine to each other, you know there's signals passed.

"Always have a cake walk, too. Some bring cakes and they draw a big circle on the floor with chalk, with numbers on the squares. A secret number is drawn, and folks buy chances for maybe four bits. They all get in the circle and start walkin' to music. When the music stops, the one on the secret number gets the cake. Naturally, all the money from the cakes and pies goes to your school."

Abe chuckled to himself as he descended the ladder on the Sycamore side and headed toward the schoolhouse. He had taught college sociology and psychology classes, and was delighted to watch the process the preceding year and looked forward to it this year. There would be mischief-making that increased the funds for the school.

Now, as seven o'clock approached, the schoolhouse was bustling with citizens. Dusk was approaching, so numerous coal oil lanterns were lit, hanging from the ceiling on wires. The school desks on runners were stacked outside and chairs brought in by the families. The school had a supply of folding tables set up around the inside. School children had cut out fall leaves and stuck them to the walls and twisted ribbons of crepe paper looped from the corners to the center of the room. Planks on sawhorses were set up on the stage and were now filled with decorated pies and cakes. Some were quite elaborate with satin fabric and ribbons, others simply adorned with colored crepe paper Henry Guthrie always stocked this time of year.

Oley took the stage, asked for heads to bow, and said a short prayer. Then he picked up the first pie and started the evening, "Get your money ready. Let me hear a dollar. One dollar, one dollar,"

"Six bits."

"Six bits, six bits, got six bits, let me hear a dollar. C'mon men. Got a dollar, let's have dollar and a half…"

And so Abe watched the bidding continue, and pies sold, until mischief began. Almost all knew where pressure was highest. When Israel Bowman suddenly started bidding, his wife Jewel watched like a hawk. Some of the young hired hands started bidding against him, running the price up to five times the normal going price. Finally they let him win so he could stay out of trouble at home, but lighter in his pocket.

Tension in the room rose again when Oley picked up the most elaborately decorated pie. It was encased in black and white striped satin, drawn up and tied with a red ribbon. It was no secret that it was brought by Azalea Ward, herself packaged in a fancy store-bought dress, wearing jewelry and makeup, and her dark curls swept up atop her head. She had appeared in the community some two years previously and no one seemed to know where she came from. Everyone did know she lived alone in a cabin set back in a wooded cove and had no visible means of support.

All of the married men in the schoolhouse pretended that no auction was taking place and Oley was not holding a pie aloft. Instead, they looked at the floor until it was over. The young single men, however, set up a spirited bidding, the winner paying a record amount.

Abe knew another pressure point was coming when he saw a strange, wizened little old man often seen roaming the roads in the community, begin bidding. He knew the girls in his school had confessed dread that he would win their offering. Opal Bowman turned out to be the unlucky one, but she managed to keep her composure when time came to eat pie.

Ben Archer had come early and kept watch, so was able to wind up with Rose Harvey and a blackberry pie.

"Well, Rose, this looks mighty good."

"I hope it is." She smiled shyly. "Ma helped me."

"Guess your pa told you about the Friedrich place."

"Yep, and he weren't too happy."

"I could tell, but I'll do my best not to cause trouble."

Rose suddenly looked up over Ben's shoulder, her eyes wide.

A harsh voice intruded, "Rose, what the hell you doin' with the likes of him?"

"Clint, you get out'a here. You got no business messin' with us."

Ben turned. There was a strong smell of liquor and tobacco on the bearded young man. He said calmly, "You heard her. Go away and leave us alone." He started to rise and Clint shoved him into the table. Before he could recover, four nearby men jumped up and dragged Clint outside. The room was silent, everyone staring, then they went back to eating their pie.

"I'm sorry," Rose said. "He's been drinkin' shine, I think."

"I'm sorry, too. I hope it doesn't cause trouble at home."

Tom Archer, one of the men who had ushered Clint outside, came by and patted his son on the shoulder. "You did fine," he said. Tom had bought his daughter's pie, rescuing her from fears of a partner not to her liking. Jimmy and Oren had joined them from outside when the pie-eating started.

George Zinn had talked with Ben earlier after scanning the crowd. "Don't suppose the Madison girls come to a thing like this, huh, Ben?"

"Doubt it. Besides, I heard somewhere they go back east for the winter."

George looked disappointed. He later wound up with Mary Guthrie, then generously invited Henry to join them.

Anna heard all about the pie supper the next morning from Etta, who got all the community news from her brother, who heard it from the hired hands. She wondered what it would be like to be part of the community, to go to such a gathering. She was too young when she got to go to school a few years, and later her pa never let the family attend anything social in the community. She could only look forward to the coming of spring, when Margaret would return.

CHAPTER 15

A late February snow blanketed the Ozark Mountains. It had started as a mist of freezing rain in the preceding afternoon, but changed to snow at night as colder upper air moved in from the northwest. Now, in the early morning hours, skies were overcast and very few creatures were stirring except for a few blue jays crying *"thief, thief"* and a crow cawing from a distant treetop.

Charlie Tate trudged slowly along the west bank of Bull Creek, running his trap line. His breath blew clouds of vapor in the cold air. He carried one mink and two muskrats taken during the night, so it was a good morning. It would go a long way toward taking care of his wife and two daughters with some much-needed cash money.

As he approached his next mink-set in the edge of the water, just on the other side of a rock outcropping, he jumped to a snow-covered boulder, forgetting about the freezing rain that preceded the nighttime snow. His foot flew out in space and his flailing arms flung his rifle and the carcasses into the air. The first part of his body to make contact was the crown of his head against the boulder. His body launched into a deep pool of cold, crystal water and he floated motionless, unconscious.

Rebecca Tate stood looking out the window of the log house, across the snowy field, at the white-blanketed forest. Wasn't like Charlie to be late for breakfast. He was out before daylight and always looked forward to coming in and warming beside the fireplace with hot coffee, then having breakfast. Jenny and Essie were both up and dressed, waiting for Daddy to come in so they could eat. Then hoping he'd take them outside to play in the snow.

Estelle, the younger of the two, tugged at her mother's skirt. "When's Daddy comin'? I'm hungry."

"I don't know, Essie. He may be slowed down by the snow. Tell you what. I'll go ahead and feed you and Jenny, and maybe by then he'll be here." Besides, it might take her mind off her own worries.

After the girls were fed, nearly an hour had passed and Charlie still had not come in. Time to really be concerned.

"Jenny, can you be really careful and take care of your sister for a little while? I'm going to ride over to Uncle Ferd's and get help."

"Yes, Mama. I'm big now and we won't get in trouble."

Ferdinand Harvey knew something was up when his sister rode in, clumped up the steps, and knocked on the door. When he opened it, she was stamping the snow from her feet.

"Come in, Sis. What's up?"

"Charlie didn't come in yet from running his traps. I'm really worried."

"Well, it might just be the snow. Me 'n the boys will saddle up and take a look. His trap line started about Spring Creek, I think he said. You go on back home and we'll find him."

Rebecca again stood at the window, staring at the divide in the dark tree trunks on the other side of the field where Charlie would appear. The rest of the landscape was white, with dark green of the cedars showing beneath their caps of snow. She'd put the horse away, hoping to find Charlie home; hoping she'd been foolish to go to her brother's place for help.

The girls were there to greet her the moment she entered the house. They weren't aware of the tension in her mind and asked if they could go play in the snow.

"No, girls. Sorry, but you have to stay inside until Daddy's home."

They protested, but she made them some hot chocolate and set them to writing on their slates. Jenny was learning to write her name, but Essie was content to make scribbles.

Rebecca continued to stand vigil, growing numb as hours passed. At last she saw movement in the woods in the distance. She was horrified when she saw two mounted riders and a man leading a horse. She flung open the door without thinking of her coat, turning to shout at her older daughter, *"Jenny! Watch your sister and don't come outside!"*

She bounded out the door, down the steps, and started running down the lane, now buried in snow, to meet her brother and nephews, fearful of what she would find.

Jennifer and Estelle stood in the doorway, watching their mother running across the white expanse toward the men and horses.

"What's Mama doin'?" said Estelle.

"I don't know, but that looks like Uncle Ferd. Maybe Daddy's with him."

They both stood in the cold of the open door and watched Mama go to the man on foot. It looked like there was something on his horse. Mama bent over, then she fell down in the snow.

Rebecca Harvey Tate did not sleep that night. After she finally got the girls to settle down in the loft, she couldn't bring herself to go to the empty bed she had shared with her husband. She knew also that the turmoil in her mind would not allow her to sleep. She bundled herself in a quilt and sat in a rocker in front of the fireplace all night, occasionally stirring to maintain the fire. Even now, as the gray, cold light of winter began to filter in the window, she did not feel sleepy. Only numb.

Ferd and his sons had laid Charlie's body on some planks across sawhorses in the smokehouse. Ferd pointed out clumsily that "he'd keep" since it was cold, as though he was talking about a deer kill or butchered beef. Rebecca had fetched a quilt to cover the body, trying to avoid the lifeless, staring eyes. After she tried to explain to the girls what had happened and what it meant, they wanted to see him, but she put them off until he could be properly laid out.

Despite the cold and snow, a procession of neighbors began to appear late in the afternoon, bringing food and condolences. Among them, they made plans to return the next day to take care of what needed doing for the burial. Rebecca was dreading what that would entail. For most of the long hours of the night, however, her mind replayed the past and alternated with fears for the future.

She thought about being a late arrival in her family after two older brothers and a series of miscarriages that left her mother a weakened shell after her own birth. Her mother died when she was nine and her brothers disappeared not long after, hiding from conscription during the war. She was relieved in her late teens to meet Charlie Tate at a church meeting in Chadwick. He seemed a decent sort and she agreed to marry him.

In the darkness of a long night, she struggled with her thoughts. Was it selfish and uncaring to worry more about her future than she mourned Charlie's death? Charlie was a good man, by all measures she knew. He made a living for them and he never beat her. Neither of them knew anything about romance; life was too demanding to daydream or think of anything but the necessities of life. With his passing, what would become of her and the girls? She couldn't farm the place by herself and she had no family except for her two brothers. Ferd and Clyde were both living in the past, dwelling on their exploits with lawless men during the war, preying on the weak. Now they were barely able to make a living for themselves...

Winter light was growing stronger, so she forced herself to rise and start a fire in the iron cook stove. She adjusted her clothing and combed the tangles from her dark brown hair. People would be arriving after morning chores and she had to be strong also for her girls. Maybe some kind man would offer to milk the two cows and feed hay to the horses. She had a lot of thinking to do.

The first to arrive was a young man who looked familiar, but she was unsure of his name. He was driving a team of mules and had a load of wood. When she opened the door to his knock, he said, "Good morning, Ma'm. Well, I'm sorry, that may not have been right to say. What I really mean is, I'm terrible sorry for your loss."

"It's all right, and I thank you."

"My name's Benjamin Archer and I'll stack this wood on the porch, if it's all right. It's all I could bring. All I do is cut wood, and I'll bring more if you need it."

"That's very kind. Thank you. Come in and have a cup of coffee. The girls are eating breakfast." He was a handsome young man, tall and lean, with blond hair and clear blue eyes.

"Don't know if you know, Ma'm, but my pa bought the Friedrich place next to your brother, so I stay there."

"I did hear that, and please call me Rebecca."

"Yes, Ma'm," he said, then grinned, bashfully.

Second to arrive was his father Tom. Must be a family thing, she thought. He arrived on horseback and came to the door carrying something in a feed sack.

"Rebecca, I'm sorry for your loss," he said, when she opened the door.

"Thank you, Tom. Come in and warm yourself. Ben just got here and is having a cup of coffee."

"I brought you a ham from the smokehouse. I figured other folks might be bringin' stuff they cooked."

"We'll put it to good use. We're getting a mite low."

After the two Archer men were seated at the table with coffee, Estelle came around and tugged at her mother's apron. "Mama, is Daddy still dead?"

Rebecca bent over and picked her up, finally losing her composure, "Oh, honey, I'm sorry." she said, tears streaming down her face and dripping from her chin. "Daddy is gone to heaven and he won't be coming back."

Ben, speaking quietly, rose from the table. "Thank you, Missus Tate. I'll stack that wood now."

Tom rose also, patted Rebecca on the shoulder and said, "Don't suppose your cows have been milked. I'll take care of things out at the barn."

Rebecca nodded without speaking, still holding Essie close, with her arm around Jennifer.

The rest of the day was marked by a ritual too often repeated in the hills. Neighbors came from some distance to express sympathy and assist in making ready for burial. George Zinn arrived with a pine box his father had made. Someone brought Ma Bright to assist with the laying-out. Since the deceased was a man, some of the men performed the initial tasks of cleansing and dressing, but leaving the women to wash the face, comb the hair, and pose the body in the quilt-lined box.

Ferd and his family all came in mid-morning, after the Archers had left. Aunt Estelle Harvey told Rebecca that her daughter Rose came prepared to stay and help take care of Jenny and little Estelle as long as she was needed. Ferd suggested they bury Charlie's remains at their place, sort of start a family plot. Rebecca agreed, leaving unspoken the questions about the future of her own place, that it could soon be lost to the family.

CHAPTER 16

April had arrived and the hills and fields were turning green. Coves were white with dogwood and pink with redbud trees. Most of the residents took little time to notice the beauty around them, but were thankful for the warmth and a chance to begin the cycle of planting their crops after the unpredictable March weather. After the spring warming, another little cool spell came for a few days when the blackberries were in bloom and the residents all felt assured that this "blackberry winter" was the last of danger to crops.

Tom Archer walked a furrow as the moldboard plow turned the earth, releasing the fresh earthy scent. He had been plowing for two weeks now, first his own fields and now the fields Charlie Tate would have been plowing if not for his untimely death. The plow occasionally scalped off rock and had to be wrestled back into the furrow. It was nearing noon, and Rafe Johnson had come earlier, following behind with another team and a spike harrow with a drag behind it that Rafe stood on.

Tom was grateful for Rafe's presence. It would be unseemly for a single man, a widower like himself, to be spending too much time with a recent widow, one as attractive as Rebecca Tate. Tom kept telling himself that his willingness to help at the Tate place had nothing to do with the lady of the house. It was too soon to have any thoughts along that line, and here was Rafe, working just as hard as he was, proving the point. Benjamin had kept her in firewood to finish out the winter, and others, he knew, were doing what they could to keep the family afloat. Rebecca had admitted one time that she had seen little of her brothers, but said they had a lot to do on their own farms.

As Tom was having these thoughts, he looked up and saw Rebecca approaching from the house, carrying a basket. He hauled back on the reins and hollered "whoa." The team of Tate's grays stopped and tossed their heads, ringing the buckles and bits on their bridles. They swished their tails and flopped their ears against the gathering of flies that pursued them.

"Hi, Tom," she called as she came closer. "Thought you and Rafe could use a bite to eat."

She was wearing a bonnet and long print dress with an apron cinched around her slender waist. Her long brown hair flowed in curls down her back below the bonnet.

"That's right nice of you, Rebecca. I was thinkin' on plowing 'til it was finished."

She looked up at him and smiled, "It's the least I could do. I don't know what we'd do without you…and, uh, others."

Tom waved at Rafe, on the other side of the field. "Why don't we go sit on that log over by the fence?"

Rafe kept his team going until he reached their side of the field. "Well," he said, "What've we got here?" Rafe was tall and thin with a fringe beard and a nose that was flattened and pushed to one side. He perched on the log on the other side of Rebecca, gave a sigh of relief and said, "That's right nice of you, Miz Rebecca."

"Least I could do." She took ham sandwiches and pint jars of buttermilk out of the basket and handed them to the men.

"I think we can finish in about an hour, don'tcha think?" said Tom.

"Yep, I'd say so." Rafe looked up at the sky. "If this weather holds, we could get the corn in the ground tomorrow."

"Tell you what, let's see if we can bring Ben and your Matthew and we can get it done in one day."

Lunch over, they stood to get back to work. Tom and Rebecca faced each other without speaking for a long second before turning away. Rafe observed with a slight smile.

Anna Friedrich and Etta were preparing breakfast in the cook house. Anna was excited to hear from Etta that the Madison girls were coming home for the summer. "They's goin' right after breakfast in the new surrey the colonel bought and stayin' overnight in Springfield to meet the train."

"Wow! That's good news," said Anna.

Etta grinned. "Well I reckon it's half good."

"You always say 'we have to take the bitter with the sweet.'"

"That's right, child. And we know which is which, don't we?"

They laughed together as they worked.

Anna had gotten two letters from Margaret during the long winter, one at Christmas and one in March for her birthday. Both were filled with good wishes for Anna and expressions of wanting to return to Taney County. She opined that Washington society was not to her liking, but had said that her sister seemed happier there. She described parties their older brother had for their benefit, all scenes unfamiliar to Anna.

For her part, Anna settled into her role in the household and continued to study her arithmetic and reading. She had laboriously written one letter back to Margaret, entrusting it to Mrs. Madison to post for her.

Her collection of silver dollars was growing steadily with the passing months. She also noted changes in her body. Her waist was becoming slimmer and her hips wider. He breasts were growing and she attempted to confine them by wrapping a cloth around her upper body. Maybe Margaret could tell her what to do, because she had caught Colonel Madison staring at her at times, which made her uncomfortable.

Sheriff Horton made several trips into Bull and Swan Creek communities during the winter. Some were as a result of complaints and some, along with a deputy or two, to show interest in his voting constituents. There were two more incidents of calves stolen and butchered, but no luck in finding the culprits. One farmer on Swan Creek caught a miscreant in his chicken house and marched him all the way to Forsyth at the point of a shotgun, a rope around his neck.

Israel Bowman told Tom Archer about an incident, but swore him to secrecy. Israel had discovered a hole on the back side of his corncrib, thinking some animal was getting into it. He hid after dark one night and saw a man sneak up with a sack. Israel challenged him with a shotgun and heard a sad story. The man, who he would not name, had run out of food for his family and didn't know what else to do. Israel said, "I got plenty corn, he'p yourself. Just don't tell anyone, 'specially Jewel."

When the Madisons arrived after the long drive from Springfield, Anna followed Etta out to meet the surrey. Ike hobbled out to hold the team in place while the Madison family dismounted. Two of the hired hands came to carry in Margaret's and Gertrude's trunks, while Etta and Anna carried in the smaller valises. Neither Colonel Madison nor his wife spoke, favoring the assembly only with a nod. Margaret, however, rushed to give Anna a hug and greeting, "Hi, Anna. It's good to see you," drawing a frown from her father.

"I'm glad you're back," whispered Anna and she scurried up the steps and opened the front door.

Gertrude was wearing a stunning long dress of narrow black and white vertical stripes, with a black ruffle that began at the waist in back and curved around the hips to about the level of her knees. The dress had a long train in back held out by a bustle. The train was also trimmed with a black ruffle that trailed along the ground. A black hat and gloves completed the ensemble. Anna had never seen anything so grand.

Margaret wore a simpler long dress of light gray with a white lace bodice and circles of white lace around the skirt. She wore no hat or gloves and her brown hair was pulled back in a bun. She really looks nice, thought Anna.

Gertrude immediately called for a bath, so Anna and Etta began endless trips up the stairs with buckets of hot water that Etta had been heating all afternoon in the cookhouse and on the warming stove. An hour later they began the cycle again for Margaret.

After Margaret was dressed for dinner, her father summoned her into his office.

"Sit down, Margaret. I need to speak to you about your decorum."

"My decorum?"

"Yes. You should know that as a lady, you're not to be too familiar with the help. They could get the wrong idea."

"Are you talking about Anna? What on earth do you mean, 'wrong idea'?"

"Don't use that tone of voice with me, young lady. Yes, Anna."

"As you wish, Father." At least when you're around, she added to herself.

After the evening meal was served and everything washed and put away, Etta went to help Gertrude unpack and hang her clothing. She knew Anna wanted to spend time doing the same thing with Margaret.

When Anna came into her room, Margaret shut the door and took her hand. "Father spoke to me about you," she said softly. "He had this crazy idea that I shouldn't be friendly with you, so we'll give him what he wants when he's around. When he can't see us, you're my sister." She smiled at Anna.

"I don't want to be trouble for you. You're so nice to me."

"You're not trouble. My life got better when you came. It was too stuffy before. Now, let's unpack and we can talk while we work. First off, you really look good. You're growing into a beautiful girl."

"Oh, don't say that. I'm not beautiful."

"Yes. You just don't know it. You're developing a nice shape."

"It makes me uncomfortable. I've started to jiggle when I walk...up top, I mean." She looked down, embarrassed. "I wrapped cloth around myself and it helped."

Margaret giggled softly. "It happens. I'll show you what the fashion world does." She dug into the trunk and pulled out a contraption with shoulder straps and a body portion that would reach below the waist. It had buttons in front and was laced up the back. "See, you put this on if you wear a fancy dress. This curved sort of shelf in front is for them to sit on and you get help to cinch up the back so your waist is thin. It has these whalebone stays going up and down."

"Sort of like saddling a horse?"

Margaret giggled again. "Pretty much. It's torture. Gertie likes it, though."

"She had a beautiful dress on today. Was she wearing a thing like that under it?"

"Oh, yes. And a bustle, too."

"A bustle?"

"You notice how her dress stuck out behind? That's it."

"You mean fancy women want their butt to look big?"

Margaret snorted in laughter and tears streamed down her face. "Oh, Anna," she gasped.

Anna looked concerned, then joined her in laughter until they were both consumed by it, trying to be quiet at the same time.

When Margaret was able to breathe again, she explained. "The fashion look is to squeeze your waist as tight as you can stand and make it look even smaller with the bustle and the ruffles around the hips...even if it presents a big behind." She lost composure again and gasped for breath. "Anna, you're really something."

CHAPTER 17

On an April Monday noon, a stranger rode into Sycamore on a rented horse. He looked about him and reined in at the hitching rail in front of Guthrie's store. Conversation halted among the men sitting on the porch as they studied the newcomer. The man was tall and thin, and wore a derby hat and a long-tailed coat over a dingy white shirt. He was clean-shaven except for a thick black mustache.

As he mounted the steps, he stared at Ferdinand Harvey, who was closest. "Sir, might you give me directions to the Madison residence?" he inquired.

"I might if I could think of a reason why I ought," said Ferd, to chuckles from the others.

"Perhaps I can come up with one or two," the stranger said, drawing back the tail of his coat on the right to reveal a heavy revolver. "And this," he said, showing a star pinned to his left breast. "U.S. Marshal. Now, can we proceed, sir?"

"I reckon we can," said Ferd. "Ya turn around and go back yonder the way you come from and in about a mile, jest before ya cross a creek, ya take the wagon road that follers up the creek. In three-four mile, you'll see a big-ass white house perched on the point of the ridge. That-there is it. Whatcha want with the colonel?"

The marshal ignored the question. "Thank you, sir. I'll be on my way."

"What do ya suppose that's about?" said Israel Bowman.

"Could be the colonel's got his tail in a crack," said Ferd.

"Couldn't happen to a nicer feller," said Billy Roberts, to general laughter.

"We'll have to wait and see. Maybe we'll hear something from the hands," said Ferd. "Well, I reckon I'd best see if my corn's ground, and get on up the road."

Anna was helping Etta clean and wax the dining room floor, when there was a knock at the front door. "You can get it," said Etta.

When Anna opened the door, a tall man in dark clothing stood there. "Can you fetch your father, young lady?"

"I'm the help," said Anna. "Please wait here and I'll see if the colonel's in his office," she continued, as she had been instructed.

When Colonel Madison followed her back to the front door and she opened it, the stranger said, "Colonel, I'm Elbert Strong, U.S. Marshal. I need to have a word with you." He thumbed the lapel of his coat aside to reveal his badge.

Colonel Madison looked surprised, then turned to Anna. "Don't just stand there gaping. Go on back to the kitchen."

As she scurried away, she heard him invite the stranger in.

When Madison was seated behind his large oak desk and his visitor in a straight chair, the marshal brought a paper out of his breast pocket and handed it across the desk. The folded paper bore a wax seal.

"That is a subpoena to appear before a select committee of Congress," Strong said. "For the past few years, the Inspector General and Congress have been attempting to clear up any and all questions remaining from activities during the War. President Hayes was determined that no questions would linger after his term ended, but he didn't make it. Garfield is going to keep everything going as before."

"What does this have to do with me?" Madison demanded.

"Not for me to say, Sir," said Strong. "I understand you were in the Quartermaster Corp, related to procurement. They originally thought to send me to invite you to come, which you could have declined, then thought better of it and sent that subpoena, considering the distance and travel time."

"So I have no choice?"

"That's about it, Sir. I'm to accompany you to Washington as expeditiously as possible. We are to leave on the train out of Springfield tomorrow noon."

"Timing is awkward. We'd have to leave immediately and take rooms tonight in Springfield."

"That's correct, Sir."

Madison rose and went out into the hall, his mind racing. They have nothing on me. Nothing was written down. I'll soon take care of this. He shouted, "Etta, Anna, come here!" When they came down the hall, he said, "Anna, go find Hank, wherever he is and get him in here. Etta, get Mrs. Madison, and lay out my large suitcase in my bedroom." He clapped his hands, "Quickly!"

He turned to his visitor, "If you'd be so kind, Marshal, you may wait on the verandah."

Within an hour, Colonel Madison was being driven away in the surrey. He had explained to his wife that the President needed him to help sort things out in Washington. He gave Hank Green instructions about running the farm while he was away, and left his wife and two daughters standing on the front porch staring after him.

CHAPTER 18

Benjamin Archer was working harder than he ever had in his life, but couldn't be happier. All winter, he had worked the woods and had produced several hundred fence rails and a good supply of railroad ties, in addition to a shed full of fireplace wood for next winter. Hacking ties had resulted in a huge pile of joggles, the chips that resulted, which were perfect fuel for the cook stove. He'd hauled a couple of loads of wood to Mrs. Tate to help her out. He also ran a trap line and had sold several pelts down at Sycamore to start a nest egg of cash money for things he couldn't grow on the place.

He loved the freedom of being on his own, but was sometimes a little lonely, especially at night. Many nights he sat by the fireplace shelling corn off the stunted ears he'd gleaned from the crop left in the field. Still, it yielded a good supply of grain and plenty of cobs for the outhouse.

He did have his dog, Bone, to keep him company when he was out and about. Bone was more than half grown and starting to take an interest in trailing and hunting. He followed Ben everywhere. Even when Ben was following the team of mules around and around, doing spring plowing, Bone trailed at his side all day. Now he was through with spring planting and decided to spend the next two days hauling ties to Chadwick, known as "Log Town,' where the railroad spur ended.

He loaded the wagon the night before and set out shortly after daylight on this April morning for the twelve mile drive. His mules were big and strong, so he was able to haul twenty-one ties in one load. After driving there and waiting in line, he was able to sell eighteen ties at a nickel apiece, for ninety cents. Pa told him the inspectors would always reject three, but not to worry, just mix them back in the next load. Ben got a kick out of the fact that the next day they rejected three again, but not the same ones.

After two days of hauling, a dollar and eighty cents richer, he was seeing to the fence that separated his place from the Harveys. He'd previously stepped off his half, the rougher portion that snaked its way through the woods to his corner, marked with a crib of rocks. Since his cow and mules were on his side and their corn on the other, it needed to be in good shape. He drove his wagon and team of mules through the scattered trees and along the fence line, unloading new twelve-foot rails anywhere it looked like the old ones needed replacement. He could see across the field to the Harvey place. A curl of smoke rose from the chimney. Maybe Rose was fixing breakfast for her ugly brothers. He thought of her with a scraggly beard and laughed to himself. The way she really was, she was right comely. Not much chance of seeing her up close, not with the ugly brothers around.

The Harvey hounds detected movement and set up a chorus of baying, looking in his direction. Bone returned the insult and Ben could see the Harvey men spill out on the porch, looking in his direction. He continued running his fence line and looked again toward the Harvey place to see two men walking across the field toward him, one carrying a long gun.

As they approached, sure enough he saw it was the ugly brothers.

"Well, if it ain't the boy farmer," said Clint. "What d'you think about that, Bob?"

"Looks like he's buildin' fence," his brother replied.

"Hi, guys. You're right. This fence is in pretty poor shape, and I'm fixin' my half."

"Your half?" said Clint, shifting the double-barreled shotgun to the crook of his right arm.

"Yes. My pa and yours agreed we'd each do half and he wanted the other half. I stepped it off and marked it with a little pile of rocks. You can check it out. Pa says good fences make good neighbors."

"What if we don't want to be good?" said Clint, elbowing his brother and laughing.

"Well, I reckon we all make our choices," said Ben. "I'd better get back at it. Got to keep the livestock in."

"You go right ahead, boy. And tell your pa we don't like him sniffin' around Aunt Becky."

"All he's done is help her keep the farm afloat, which you'd think her family would be doin'"

"You don't know nothin'!"

"I know she's old enough to make her own decisions. Now I got work to do." Ben climbed into the wagon and slapped the reins on the mules' backs and drove away, leaving the brothers glaring at him.

In the colonel's absence, the three Madison women all sat at one end of the table for breakfast the morning after his departure. Anna heard bits of conversation as she ghosted into the room with platters of bacon, eggs, grits, and toasted bread, and bowls of canned peaches.

"What's this all about, Mother?" said Gertrude.

"I don't know, dear. Your father said the President needed him, so of course he had to go."

"I think the subpoena said he had to go," said Margaret. "Isn't it a little strange they sent a U.S. Marshal?"

"What are you implying, Margaret?" said her mother.

"Nothing. It concerns me a little bit, is all. What could the President be needing from him when he has a cabinet and all those congressmen to help?"

"Father is a very important man in Washington," said Gertrude. "There are many reasons the President might wish to consult him."

"I'm sure we'll find out soon, when your father returns," Agnes responded. "Just don't worry about anything. We'll just keep doing what we normally do. The hired hands have their instructions, so everything will be fine."

"Well, that being the case," said Margaret, "I think I'll go for a drive in the buckboard and take Anna with me to scout out blackberry patches while they're in bloom. Later, we can have her and Etta pick some for us when they bear."

"That'll be fine, dear. Just don't go too far."

"It may take most of the morning, but I'll try to have her back in time to help with the noon meal."

"That's fine, dear."

Anna heard enough of the conversation to realize she was going to get to go away from the house for the first time since she'd come here. She was excited.

They were soon flying down the gravel road along Hanson Creek at a fast trot. Anna was thrilled to be free of all duties for a time, especially since there were no prying eyes watching her and Margaret.

"You can look at the hillside across the creek if you wish, Anna. There are tons of blackberry vines in the woods over there. You can see the white blooms. That's not what we're after, of course."

"It isn't?"

"No, but I had to say something. We're going down to Sycamore. Couple of things I want to check on."

"Like what?"

"Well, I've never spoken to you about your mother's burial service. I didn't want to bring up a sad subject. Anna, I'm really sorry you lost her. It must have been terrible."

"It was. I felt lost. But you were there? I didn't know."

"Of course you wouldn't, but I saw you there. I was thinking only of myself until I saw you and realized what a painful thing it could be. I went because I wanted to see what the real world is like; interact with real people for a change."

"And was it what you expected? I don't remember it much. "

"I can understand. For me, it was moving to see so many people come together, sharing in your sorrow."

They came to the first ford, where Ben had parted with Margaret on that rainy morning. Now, as they drove through, the creek was sparkling clear as it rushed over the gravel bed.

Margaret continued. "On that morning, everyone took care of me, unlike what my father would have led me to believe. I had also lied that day about where I was going. The blacksmith's son, George Zinn, helped me to shelter when the rain began and arranged with a family to help me get back up the creek through the fords when the creek came up. That family, the Archers, treated me with kindness. The oldest son, Ben, saw me safely across that last ford we just crossed."

"That's how most of us are," Anna said, "but we have good and bad, just like anybody, I'd guess. But what is it you want to check on?"

Margaret turned to her and smiled. "Since you asked, there were two handsome young men helping out a damsel in distress. I'd like to see them again. I don't know about Ben, but George works right in Sycamore, so I should be able to find him. The other thing is, school should still be in session. I want to talk to the schoolmaster if he'll see me. I've thought a lot about what I should do with myself. I can't see spending my life as a society lady, even if I could. No life of tea parties and getting dressed up for balls; no dressing up in a corset, laced up like saddling a horse, with a bustle to make my butt look big."

They both burst into laughter. When Anna recovered, she said, "You want to be a teacher? You'd be good at it."

"I think I would. Not a word to my parents, though. They would think it 'beneath me'." She imitated her mother's voice with the last two words.

In due course, they drove down the gravel street of Sycamore and stopped in front of the blacksmith shop. A short distance away, the usual idlers on the porch of Guthrie's stared in their direction, and there were a couple of whistles. Margaret and Anna ignored them.

George came out of the dim recesses of the shop to greet them. "Well, if it ain't Miss Margaret. What a pleasure!" He was dressed in a leather apron and his sleeves were rolled up to his elbows. He carried a four-pound hammer in one hand.

Margaret smiled down at him. "Just came by to thank you again for shelter during that rain."

"Glad to have helped. Will you step down? Sit a spell on the bench in the shade?"

Margaret glanced at Anna. "We'd like that, but we'd better not take the time. George, this is Anna Friedrich. She's staying with us."

"Pleased to meet you, Miss. So sorry about your mother."

"Thank you, sir," Anna replied. "You are kind to say so."

"Sure you don't have time?" George smiled a broad smile. His black hair curled around his ears, and his face was beaded with sweat.

"Not this time. You see, we're not supposed to be here."

George grinned, "Like last time, huh?"

"You remembered."

"I remember everything about you," George said. Then he looked at Anna. "Do you realize this woman may lead you astray, Miss Anna?"

"In my eyes, she can do no wrong." Anna replied, smiling back at him.

Margaret said, "I hope we meet again, soon, George. But now we need to make a stop at the school."

With that, she picked up the reins and urged the horse forward, making a turn in the street and going back a short distance to stop in front of the schoolhouse, setting the hand brake and wrapping the reins around the lever. They both stepped down and walked across the street, up the steps, and quietly opened the schoolhouse door, entering a short hall with coat hooks along both walls. Anna remembered her early years here with regret that she wasn't allowed to continue with her schooling.

As they entered quietly at the back of the room, they noted all of the students, from small to large, were bent over desks, working. At the disturbance, however, the schoolmaster, Abraham Phillips, looked up from his desk on the stage at the front of the room.

He rose and started toward them down the aisle. "Keep working, children. I have visitors, but I'm sure they don't want to interrupt your work."

He smiled as he approached them. "To what do I owe this pleasure?" he said softly. "I'm Abraham Phillips."

Margaret extended her hand. "I'm Margaret Madison, Professor, and this is Anna Friedrich. Pardon me for the interruption, but do you have just a few minutes?"

"Of course. What may I do for you?"

"I believe I would like to teach. My parents send me back East for schooling each winter and I believe I would qualify for a certificate. The only problem is my father. He thinks ladies are only for ornamentation, so I may have to defy him." She smiled.

Phillips smiled back. "There is quite a demand for good teachers. As you may know, I taught at the college level, and am teaching here mainly as a personal duty in retirement. Perhaps we can think it over, but one plan might be for you to apply for certification and we could see about replacing me. I don't plan on much longer, probably not more than next school year. Or, if it all worked out, maybe only half the year. All speculation, but something to think about."

"Oh, indeed it is!" Margaret said. "Thank you so much. We'd better not take more of your time."

"You're quite welcome," he replied, smiling. "And how about you, young lady?" He turned to Anna.

"I was able to come to school here for only three years before my parents would no longer bring me, but Margaret is helping me now to learn."

"Well, good for both of you. And thank you for coming by."

The sun was straight overhead as they pulled into the lot in front of the stables. Ike had heard them coming and met them there. "You-all go right on, Miz Margaret. I'll cool him down."

"Thanks, Ike. We appreciate it."

Both rushed into the house, Margaret to change for the noon meal, and Anna to help serve it. Clandestine mission accomplished.

CHAPTER 19

R ebecca Tate was up before dawn to milk her two cows and turn them out into the pasture. She put the milk to cool in the springhouse and skimmed the cream from yesterday's milk. She put it in the churn and carried it into the house to churn while the girls had their breakfast. As she walked toward the house, she noted her corn crop, planted by men from the community. It was nearing the end of June, and it was looking healthy. Looked like it would be "knee-high by the Fourth of July," as the old saying goes. As positive as that might be, in her mind her situation reminded her of the old hour glass she inherited from her grandparents.

She liked to play with it when she was a little girl, watching the sand run out, then turning it over to repeat the process. Would the community continue to gather; to help her through each turn of the seasons, or would time run out? Could she continue to accept their good will and charity?

Her daughters were waiting for her when she came into the house, standing in their long nightgowns, rubbing the sleep from their eyes.

"How are my beautiful girls this morning?"

"I'm hungry," said Jennifer.

"Me too," said Estelle, who ran to her mother to hug her legs.

"We'll do something about that," said Rebecca. "Jenny, help Essie change clothes and I'll get some pancakes going."

The girls ran to do her bidding and they were soon happily eating their pancakes and drinking fresh milk.

Rebecca sat watching them, pumping the dasher up and down in the churn. And what about my girls? she thought. The sad fact is there is no work for a woman in the hills except that of a wife, and now I'm not one. Something will have to change. It might be possible to sell this farm and move to one of the towns. I've heard of women who open a shop of some kind or work in restaurants or hotels. There is re-marriage if the right man can be found. How long is a long enough wait to consider that? I know Charlie would want me to do the right thing by the girls and for myself. In the past, I've known people in the community to be forgiving about widows and widowers, knowing the decisions we have to face.

Ben Archer milked Goldie that same morning, and found himself talking to her, as he did to his dog. "Well, Goldie, we're going on a trip today. You're going to spend a little time with your sisters and the father of your future baby." He chuckled to himself. People would think I'm nuts, talking to a cow.

He spent a couple of hours weeding his garden after breakfast. He'd raised the fence a couple of rails to help keep the deer out. He'd had no trouble with them since Bone was also on patrol at night.

It took some coaxing to get the halter on Goldie. Maybe she remembered her journey up here. If only she could know what was in store for herself, thought Ben, and he laughed to himself. He soon had Charger saddled, and with Bone trotting along and Goldie shaking her head and complaining, they were off.

Oren ran down the lane to greet the procession as Ben approached his family home. It had been a month or two, and he could see a change in Oren. I do miss my family, he thought.

"Why'd you bring the cow back?" asked Oren, breathless from running.

"She said she was lonesome for her sisters."

"She did not. Cows can't talk."

"Why, sure they do. Maybe you don't know their language."

Oren grinned up at his brother. "You're just funnin' me ain't you?"

Ben dismounted and wrapped the reins around the rail in front of the house. He picked Oren up and hugged him. "I might be. Hey, you're gettin' bigger."

Oren wriggled to get down. "I'm not a little kid anymore. Hey, we was eatin' inside. Come in before it's all gone."

After the family meal, when all were happy to be together again, Tom said, "Thanks, Josie. That was real good. Now I hate to break this up, but we'd better get your cow in the pasture, Ben."

Jimmy and Oren started to follow, but Tom said, "Sorry, boys, but I'd like for you to stay here for now. I've got to talk some things over with Ben, then we'll come back in a little while."

Ben and his father led the cow and horse out to the barn. Ben unsaddled Charger and put him in an open stall with a scoop of oats. They led the reluctant Goldie and turned her into the pasture. The other cows and the bull were at the other end of the field, but the bull saw them, raised his nose in the air, and came trotting toward them.

"Looks like he's happy to have another subject," said Tom.

"Yep. What was it you wanted to talk about, Pa?" said Ben.

"Let's go sit in the shade and I'll tell you."

They went to the backyard of the house, where there was a bench under a maple tree. "You're pretty much grown up now, Ben, so I feel like I can talk to you man to man," he began. "It's been over four years since your mother passed. We won't forget her. But it ain't fair to Josie for her to keep workin' so hard to be the mother. It's time for me to think of marryin' again, making the family more complete for her sake and for the boys."

"Got anybody in mind?" said Ben, knowing what the answer would surely be.

"Well it may be too soon to talk about it, but the fix Rebecca Tate is in is what got me thinkin'. She's a real nice lady and she might see the sense in it. Only thing is, I'd have to bring up the subject with her and I don't know how without seemin' to take advantage, if you see what I mean."

"I guess so, Pa, but I don't think she'd take offense. I will say her brothers might. They don't seem too keen on us right now."

"That so?"

'Yeah, you saw how Clint was at the pie supper. And the other day the two ugly brothers came by when I was fixin' fence." He proceeded to tell his father about the incident.

"Sniffin' around, huh? Well, I hope that wasn't how she saw it, or others in the community saw it."

"I think you have to consider where it came from, Pa. I wouldn't worry about it. Say, what if I was to find some excuse to check on her and say something like, 'my Pa really admires how you're keepin' on after your loss,' or some such and just see how she acts. Without overdoing it, I could mention how our family misses having a mother for the younger children."

"That might be a might bold, but if you can handle it gentle-like, I'd appreciate just a hint of what might could be."

On a sparkling late June morning, Anna set forth for blackberry picking. Morning chores were done, so she put on a bonnet and left the house with two split-oak baskets, one over each arm. Margaret told her she'd like to go along, but her mother forbade her doing anything that looked like labor. Anna, for her part was happy to be alone, breathing the clean spring air, and enjoying a chance to walk in the woods. She made her way down toward the creek and searched along it for a crossing.

Daisies were in bloom along the lane and wild roses grew in clusters on the opposite bank of the creek. She finally found a spot with large stones close enough together for her to hop from one to the next to reach the other side. From there she moved into the shade of the scattered trees, up the slope toward large patches of blackberry vines, the tall canes loaded with ripe fruit. They grew in the more rugged terrain, among scattered boulders.

Butterflies of all description flitted about, lighting near her as she worked, to seek sustenance from the fruit. She worked quickly, happy to be away from the household chores, thinking of the pies she and Etta would bake and the preserves they would make. Moving from one patch to another, she was proud of how soon she filled one basket. She took the heavy basket and set it in the shade of a large boulder and began to fill the other. She hummed to herself as she worked, and realized it was the hymn that was sung at her mother's burying. It gave her a measure of peace.

She was startled out of her reverie by a voice from behind her.

"My, ain't you a purty little thing!"

CHAPTER 20

Anna almost dropped the basket as she whirled around to confront a man, grinning and staring at her. He was dressed in shabby work clothes and battered felt hat. He dangled a shotgun in his right hand.

"Who are you?" she managed to say.

"Ain't who I am, but we could get better acquainted. I been watchin' you for quite a spell."

"Go away and don't bother me. I have work to do."

"Oh, you could stop and have a little fun."

The look in his eyes chilled her. She dropped the basket and ran, scratching her arms on the briars as she crashed through a small opening in the vines. He dropped the shotgun and came after her, shouting, "You want to play games, huh!"

Anna ran for her life around gooseberry bushes and undergrowth, gaining some distance between herself and her pursuer. When she was out of his sight, she went downhill and doubled back, skirting some large boulders, slipping in between two of them, making herself small and quieting her breathing. She heard him thrashing around in the brush a short distance away.

"Where are ya, girl? I ain't aiming to hur'cha. But ya know I'll find ya. I got plenty a' time."

She knew he was right. All he had to do was stand and wait. He had to know that she must be hiding and couldn't be far away. The only thing she could think of to do was put more distance between herself and her pursuer. She was afraid of what he might do if he caught her.

Keeping low, she crept out of her hiding place, gently easing each foot down on the accumulation of dried leaves on the forest floor. She moved around the larger boulder and kept it between herself and where she thought he was. As she drew farther away, she gradually increased her speed until she was practically running, bent over at the waist. She made the mistake of turning her head to see if he was following and stepped on a small rock that rolled with her foot. She went sprawling on the ground.

It was enough to give away her position. Anna leaped to her feet and sprinted downhill toward the creek but her larger, faster pursuer was too much for her. He caught up and grabbed the skirt of her dress, pulling her down and falling on top of her, driving her face into the leaves and dirt.

He grabbed her wrists from behind and rose to his feet, dragging her upright. "Now, little lady, you shouldn't a' run from me. You're gonna pay for causin' trouble."

He turned her around, letting go of one hand long enough for her to swing her fist and hit him in the mouth.

He laughed at her. "You are a feisty one! This is gonna be fun."

Anna answered with a kick to his groin, but the momentum caused her to lose her balance and she fell on her back, with him on top of her again. He smelled of sweat and tobacco, and grinned through his beard. Anna felt behind her on the ground and found a fist-size rock and swung it at his face, hitting him on the cheekbone below his left eye.

"All right, that does it!" he said and pinned both her wrists in his large left hand. He swung hard with his right fist, catching her on the side of her face. Her head hit the ground, and everything went black.

When Anna awoke, he was gone. She was lying on her back on the leaves and stony ground. Her thoughts were confused as she recalled the struggle. When she sat up, she found her clothes were in disarray. Her pantaloons were draped over a bush and she was in pain. When she looked down, she was bleeding and blood had soaked into her petticoat. She had little direct knowledge about such things, but she knew what he had done to her. She put her face in her hands and cried in shame and anger. Now I'm ruined, she thought. The bleeding has stopped, but how will I ever explain how I let this happen?

Gradually, her sobs subsided and her anger and determination took over. She managed to stand, recover her underwear, and limp down to the creek. Cold water washes out blood. She found an eddy of clear water concealed among willows in the edge of the creek, removed her shoes, dress, and petticoat, and washed herself. Next she washed the petticoat until all traces of blood were gone. She draped it over a branch of the willow to dry. There was also some blood on the hem of her dress and she washed and wrung it out as best she could. She put on the dress and pantaloons and thought about her situation. Her bonnet was still tied around her neck, but on her back. She took it off and combed the leaves and debris out of her hair with her fingers and put it back on.

She assumed her attacker was gone. Her head throbbed from the blow and she experienced some double vision. Maybe it would be best to rest and give it some time before going back to the house. She would have to think of some explanation for the bruise.

Anna made her way slowly back up the slope to where it all began. The basket she dropped was still where she left it, but had spilled. To focus her mind on the present, she carefully picked up the fallen berries and began to pick more. By the time she had it filled and recovered the other basket, she had reached a decision. She would find Etta in the cookhouse and tell her she had slipped on a stone crossing the creek and hit her head. She'd had to go back and pick more to replace those spilled. Her petticoat had gotten wet. That should work.

He hurried through the woods and brush, branches slapping his face, climbing the ridge. It was her own damn fault, he thought. It wouldn't a' happened if she'd been friendlier. Why'd she hit me with a rock? She didn't need to hit me with a rock. I wasn't gonna do nothin'. She was all soft and purty. Somebody's gonna ask what happened to my face. I'll tell 'em that I tripped on a root and fell.

When Etta heard her story, she said, "Oh, you poor sweet chile! Let me look at that bruise on your face. My, my, Etta's gonna fix a poultice to draw the pain out. But look at you! Troubles like that and you still picked all them berries!"

Etta left to make the poultice. Anna experienced some pain when she went to the outhouse while Etta was gone. There seemed to be no more bleeding. She hoped no permanent damage had been done to her.

When Anna returned to the cookhouse, Margaret was there with Etta. "I heard what happened, Anna, and I'm so sorry. Does your head hurt?"

"Some, but I'm better now."

"Well, you're going to take off the rest of the day. Etta's fixed you a poultice. Just go up to your room and lie down for a while. I hope you'll feel better soon." She gave Anna a gentle hug and sent her to the house to rest.

As the weeks went by, Anna was able to leave the trauma of that day behind her. It was less frequently in her thoughts with the passage of time, but occasionally appeared in her dreams, causing her to awake, trembling.

She had been determined to not let it destroy her, so only two days after, she asked Margaret if her mother would let her go on an expedition, as long as Margaret just observed. Margaret, no stranger to subterfuge, secured approval so both girls enjoyed the outing together returning with four baskets of blackberries they had both picked. Without telling Margaret, Anna had concealed a kitchen knife under a cloth in the bottom of one of her own baskets.

Now under the direction of Etta, Anna was helping can and preserve vegetables from the garden. There was an abundance of tomatoes, sweet corn, and green beans, put up for the winter. They made large crockery batches of pickles, and similar vats of sauerkraut.

One evening, Anna was taking a bath in the room off the cooking area and a thought occurred to her. It was past time for her monthly curse. She thought immediately of that horrible day. Did he damage something in my insides? I know it hurt and I bled. Mama said the monthly had something to do with what women's bodies did to prepare for having babies, but I don't understand that part. Does my lack of the curse mean that I might not now be able to have babies if I ever get married? Marriage is probably not going to happen to me anyway. What chance at a normal life will I ever have? Probably I'll grow old like Etta, working for some family until I die. Well, I guess I'll take whatever comes.

CHAPTER 21

Ben thought of a proper excuse to visit Rebecca Tate after the talk with his father. He'd spent the night with his family and ridden Charger straight to the Tate place, arriving in late morning. His arrival was announced by whinnies from the Tate workhorses, answered by Charger. Bone added a deep bark. Rebecca and the girls came out on the front porch.

"Good mornin' Miz Tate," called Ben.

"Hey, Ben. And remember I asked you to call me by my given name. Come in."

"Thanks. I just stopped by to check on the corn. Looks like it needs the centers scratched out and maybe a little hoein'."

Jenny and Essie ran down the steps and Bone went to meet them. "What's his name, Ben?"

"I call him 'Bone,' 'cause he's a redbone hound."

"Can we pet him?"

"Sure."

Ben dismounted and tied up his horse. "Maybe we can sit on the porch a spell?"

"Yes," said Rebecca. "I'll get you a cup of coffee."

While the girls and the dog romped in the yard, Ben first discussed plans to get a few men to help and get the corn taken care of. "I've done my own and Pa has done his."

"I've done some hoeing, but haven't got very far."

"We'll see that it gets done. Won't take long."

"You know I appreciate all you folks do. Makes me feel kinda' helpless."

"Naw, not at all. You have a lot to worry about." It was the opening Ben was looking for, so he launched into his rehearsed speech about his father's admiration, trying to sound like it wasn't rehearsed.

Rebecca responded the way he hoped. "Your father would be the one to understand, raising a family like he has after he lost your mother. It can be a lonely and worrisome thing for anybody. I admire how all of you have turned out. He's a very special man."

Ben was emboldened to come up with a plan on the spot. "Say, are you-all plannin' to go to Sycamore for the Fourth of July picnic?"

"Hadn't planned to, although the girls would like it. It's just a little too much for me."

"How about this? What if I came by and hitched up your wagon and drove you down there. I know Pa's going, and we could go as two families?"

Rebecca looked uncertain. She twisted her apron in her hands. After a moment's hesitation, she looked at Ben and smiled. "We'd like that. Thank you."

Instead of going to his own place, Ben rode back down to his father's and gave him the plan. After he delivered the news, they made plans to work in Rebecca's cornfield. They'd skip a day to get the word out and plan on meeting at her place, with help from Rafe Johnson if he didn't have anything else. He'd bring his Biblical sons, Matthew, Mark, and Luke with their hoes. Jimmy and Ben would be there, of course.

Ben's master plan worked perfectly. He told himself it came off without a hitch, except for hitching the horses. Well, there was one other unexpected change which pleased him. Rebecca was waiting with the girls dressed in matching dresses, with ribbons in their hair. And beside them was Rose Harvey.

"My niece was visiting me, helping with the canning, so I invited her to come along. I hope that's all right. She said you know each other."

"We do. Sure it is. Hi, Rose. Just hope it don't get your brothers all stirred up again."

"Hey, Ben. They don't know about it. Pa says the Fourth is a Yankee holiday and he don't want any part of it."

Rebecca had prepared a hamper of bread and fresh vegetables and had baked two pies. For this occasion, folks in and about Sycamore contributed to the roasting of a whole pig for the main course.

Ben hitched up her team to their wagon. He'd brought the Winchester in a saddle scabbard, because it was usual to have a shooting contest during the celebration. Part of his plan was to get both families in his pa's wagon and he'd ride Charger alongside. Now it looked like a better plan to drive one wagon with Rose beside him and Rebecca riding with Pa, dividing the kids however they wished. He unsaddled Prince and put him in a stall in the barn, bringing the rifle with him in the wagon. Rebecca sat beside him on the spring seat, and Rose sat on folded quilts behind them with the two little girls.

When they arrived at the Archer farm, Ben's family was waiting, all ready to go. He was surprised to see his father appear bashful when he approached Rebecca. Still he managed to greet her, "Glad to see you, Rebecca. I hope you are well."

"I surely am, Tom. Thank you."

Oren, bashful like his father, hung back with his hands in the pockets of his overalls, scratching at the grass with his bare toe. After all, there were two little *girls* present. When Jenny and Essie climbed down and started petting Bone, however, Oren soon joined them and all was well.

Ben took charge while the two parents smiled at each other and tried to think of what they should say. He managed to get Rose in the Tate wagon with him, and Josie and Jimmy joined them. The three younger children rode with their parents. Although Rose was a little older, Josie and Jimmy knew her from school.

When they were underway, driving down the lane dappled in shade, Ben nodded at the wagon ahead and said quietly to Rose. "What do you think about them two, Rose?"

"I think it's just fine. Don't know what my family's gonna say, though."

"Why do they seem to hate us?"

"It's just how they are. I think they're jealous of your pa anyways, and then him buyin' the place next to us really got under their hides."

"Clint acted pretty ugly when we were at the pie supper."

"Well, he was drunk, but he's kinda that way most of the time. I get tired of it. Wish there was some way to get out of there."

"Really?"

Josie, sitting behind them on the quilts, spoke up. "Yeah, Ben. You know there ain't much future for girls except to keep right on doin' what we're doin'. Right, Rose?"

"You're right, Josie. I don't know any woman that did anything except maybe get married and raise a family and take care of the menfolk."

"Same thing with men," Ben said. "Well, they do some different things besides farmin'. There's Mister Zinn and Mister Jensen and that schoolmaster."

"Proves my point," Rose said. "I guess I've heard of nurses and woman school teachers, but how do you get to do that?"

They forded Hanson Creek and followed the Archer wagon down the east bank of Bull Creek, continuing to speculate about what life might be like beyond the ring of the surrounding Ozark Mountains.

Tom and Rebecca rode in quiet conversation about everyday subjects, discussing the weather—it would be hot today for the picnic—and the cornfields and vegetable gardens. They avoided the most important subject: are we doing the right thing for our families, being together today? What will the people of the community think? They faced the latter subject as they drove into Sycamore and searched for a place to park the two wagons. All those arriving and those already there turned to stare in their direction. Best just to act normal; gather the families and join those already in the shade of the trees between the schoolhouse and Bull Creek. The air was filled with the smell of roasting meat and newly cut grass where the men had scythed it down that morning.

Ben stayed behind and unhitched the teams, one at a time, leading them back up the road to tie them in the shade of the scattered trees. He also tied Bone to the Tate wagon, so he could lie in the grass in its shade.

When he returned, he went in search of George Zinn. He found him over by the creek bank, nailing up a wood panel to use as a target for the shooting match to come. On the other side of the creek was a high, wooded bank to act as a backstop. Bull Creek was flowing full and clear, making music over the stones.

George looked around. "Hey, Ben! How are you? Long time."

"I been workin' hard. No time just to fool around like some people."

George flashed a big smile. "Yeah, it's really nice, sittin' around in the shade. Say, did I see you arrive with the Harvey girl?"

Ben grinned. "It's a little complicated. Since I live up past her, I told Miz Tate, I'd drive her down. Well, when I got to her place, Rose was there, so what could I do?"

"Just hope her brothers don't come after you."

"Me too. So what's goin' on with you?"

"Got a surprise visitor a while back. You remember the Madison girl, Margaret?"

"Yeah."

"She showed up one day. Had the Friedrich girl with her, you know, who lost her ma?"

"I thought they skipped out."

"Her pa and brother did. I heard rumors her pa put her to work for the Madisons, and there she was with Margaret. By the way, she's grown up some. She's young, but she's gonna be a looker."

"I'll be. Surprised you'd notice her, with Margaret in the picture."

"It took some effort. But she has that pile of red hair, really makes her show up."

"Don't suppose they're comin' today?"

"Doubt it. Seems like she has to slip away to mix with us common folks. Tell me about your pa and Miz Tate." George turned to nail a can lid, painted black, in the middle of the panel.

"Not much to tell. Pa's been alone for several years. She's not been a widow long, but she don't have much of a chance on her own. We've been puttin' in her crops and helpin' out, but you can tell she feels bad about it."

"Yeah, it's tough on a woman on her own…'cept for Azalea Ward, I reckon." George grinned again.

"Not funny, George."

"You're right. Sorry. You shootin'?" He nodded at the scabbard Ben was carrying.

"Naw, this is in case I have to fight off a mad squirrel. Of course, I'm shootin'."

Tom Archer and Rebecca Tate found a spot in the shade of a towering elm and spread their quilts on the grass. Rose and Josie carried the baskets of food. As soon as the younger children saw where home base would be, they ran off to chase after the other children. Jimmy, as usual, felt alone, not a child and not a grownup. He drifted over toward the blacksmith shop, where the men were gathered around the roasting pig. Mark and Luke Johnson were there, so he was able to talk with them.

Tom helped Rebecca to a seat on the quilt. "Rebecca, if you don't mind, I'll go over and see if they need any help. I won't be long."

"Take your time. I'll walk around after bit and visit."

The men were ringed around the roasting pit, except for the downwind side where the light breeze wafted the smoke toward the blacksmith shop where it curled up over the roof and dissipated. The pig, a hundred-pound shoat, was flattened in a frame sitting on four iron posts. Homer Zinn had made the setup. The pig had been roasting slowly since dawn, turned over from time to time.

The men, among them Homer Zinn, Rafe Johnson, Israel Bowman, Oley Jensen, and Billy Roberts were passing a pint jar of clear liquid around the circle, looking over their shoulders at the women before taking a sip. They all nodded and spoke in greeting to Tom.

"Be careful not to get that close to the fire," Tom said.

"Yeah, wouldn't want to blow the place up," said Billy, to chuckles around.

Tom moved over beside Oley, and spoke to him. "Can we talk a moment?"

"Sure. Let's go check out the target." As they walked away, he said, "What's on your mind?"

"Well, you may have noticed Rebecca Tate and her girls came along with my family. I don't want to rush things or reflect poorly on her, since it's not too long since…"

Oley stroked his brown beard and turned to face him, "Tom, you're both honorable people, and we can't know what the future holds. You can't worry about wagging tongues. If you both do what you think's right, you'll be just fine."

116

"Thanks, Oley. I've been alone a long time, and it ain't good for my children. I don't know if she'll have me, but I'd like to start keepin' company with her."

Oley slapped him on the shoulder. "You'll be fine. Now let's go think about eatin' some pig."

When the roast pig was declared done, four men donned gloves and carried the frame to a plank table that had been scrubbed clean. Homer unlatched it and removed the top frame. All the families gathered around with their plates ready. Oley Jensen raised both hands in the air and said, "Let us bow our heads in thanks." He spoke a short prayer of thanksgiving for the food and the privilege of freedom, a nod to the significance of the day.

At the chorus of "amens," the kids first, ushered by their mothers, lined up with plates held high. Oley and Homer went to work carving. After the children were settled back on their pallets, the women and elders were served, then the men.

The next hour was spent feasting on roast pork and the fresh vegetables and pies brought by the families. There was much laughter and moving about, kids chasing each other and men and women of the community renewing acquaintances, since several had traveled some distance and many did not come to Sunday services.

Henry Guthrie, owner of the Sycamore general store, waited until the meal was well over, then he brought out a dozen packages of firecrackers and distributed them to the older boys. They were admonished to stay in a space away from the families, between the shade trees and the creek bank. Soon the air was filled with smoke and noise.

The last event before cleanup was for the men; shooting competition. Each competitor was limited to three shots at two bits each, if he wanted to pay for that many. He could take them all at once, or string them out to see what the odds were for risking a second and third quarter. In the end, the winner got the whole pot. Henry Guthrie agreed to be the spotter. He would stand to the left, behind a big sycamore, then step over and write the shooter's name by his bullet hole, showing where it was with a black disk on a stick.

Rafe Johnson went first, to jeers and catcalls. Billy Roberts hollered, "Look out, Henry. That tree ain't big enough!"

Rafe ignored them and loaded a cartridge as long as a finger in his Trapdoor Springfield .45-70. He spit a stream of tobacco juice off to the side, took aim, and fired. The seventy grains of black powder produced a loud boom and a great cloud of smoke. Henry walked over and spotted the shot low and right, about six inches from the can lid. Rafe shook his head. "That-un ain't gonna win."

More comments, "That one might kill him if he's fat enough," "You gave it a scare," and "Let's see you do better."

More took their turns, some getting closer. First to nick the edge of the lid was Grandpa Ned Bowman, who lived with his son Israel and his family. He showed up with a Kentucky flint-lock squirrel rifle. After the ritual of muzzle-loading powder, patch, and ball, and priming the pan, the old man took steady aim and disappeared in a cloud of smoke as the pan flashed. Henry held the spot over the lower left edge of the lid. This time the men cheered and clapped Grandpa Ned on the back.

More turns were taken with a variety of weapons: .44 rim-fire Henrys, Winchesters, and Springfields. The wood panel was riddled with holes and the prize money grew. They shook their heads in disappointment, as Grandpa Ned's shot still held. Ben sidled up to his father. "Pa, are you going to shoot?"

"I don't think I will, Son. You're better than I am. Go on ahead."

Ben stepped forward. He'd been by the fire pit and taken a burning green stick to blacken the sights of the Winchester .44-40.

"'Bout time, young Archer," "Pot's there for the taking," "Ned, does he scare you?"

Ben's first shot was an inch outside to the left. He paid another quarter and tried again. This one barely missed on the right.

The onlookers were now watching quietly, with only mumbled comments: "That kid can shoot," "He's got one more try," "Third time charms."

Ben felt calm after two near misses. He took several deep breaths and lifted the Winchester again. Deep breath, let it half out and hold it, get the sight picture, squeeze the trigger and be surprised when it goes off.

The can lid fell from the target. Cheers erupted. Henry Guthrie walked over to the target and picked the can lid off the ground. This time he walked back to the crowd at the firing line and displayed the lid. Ben's shot had driven the center nail back through the panel. Men gathered around and clapped him on the back.

Henry said, "Shall I nail her back up?"

Oley Jensen looked around the group, "Anyone else want to shoot?"

He was met with shaking heads.

"Looks like nobody does. Ben, I declare you the winner. Here's the purse."

The group broke up and Tom went to shake his son's hand. "Proud of you, Son."

"Thanks, Pa. You taught me real good. This'll go a long way to makin' the fall payment on the farm."

"We'll worry about that later. But you go ahead and keep the Winchester with you."

"Thanks, Pa. Just think how many loads of ties this is. Lot easier way to make money!"

The clouds of smoke and the distinctive smell of burning powder took Tom back to the noise and carnage of the battlefield, memories he was usually able to force into the depths of his mind.

After the picnic was over and wagons were loaded and on their way home, Tom finally mustered the courage to say what was on his mind. The young children were worn out and dozing on blankets in the back. He took Rebecca's hand. "Rebecca, I don't want to say anything out of line, but I have to speak my mind."

She looked at him, eyes wide.

"I've known you and Charlie for a long time, and admired you both. Charlie was a friend of mine. Now, I don't want to be hasty, but when you feel ready, I'd like to call on you."

She smiled. "I understand. I admire you, too. You've done a good job of taking care of your family after your dear wife passed. Today was a good beginning. I'd welcome spending more time with you."

Tom squeezed her hand. "We'll take our time. I promise I'll never disappoint you."

CHAPTER 22

The heat of August had arrived in the night with towering thunderstorms moving over the hills with crashing thunder and brilliant lightning. Anna had lain awake in her garret room, listening to the hammering rain. In the early morning hours the storms passed over and she was able to sleep.

Now she was in the cookhouse frying bacon while Etta cracked eggs for breakfast and prepared cornmeal mush. For the first time in her memory, the bacon had a strange odor. "Etta, does this smell right to you?"

"Why yes, dear child. Ain't nuthin' smells good as bacon."

"It seems different."

"Nope. Jest like always."

"I don't like it." She wiped her brow with the tail of her apron. "Etta, I don't feel good."

"That storm wake you up?"

"Yes, but I went back to sleep…oh, Etta, I'm gonna be sick." Anna moaned and dropped her fork. She went running out the back door, letting it slam behind her. She barely made it to the soggy grass behind the cookhouse and fell to her knees, retching and vomiting.

Etta took the pan off the stove and followed Anna outside, bringing a cool wet dishtowel. "Let me help you up."

"Oh, I don't think I can," Anna said. "I'm so sick…"

"Come on, Honey. We'll get you inside. You're gettin' all wet."

She helped Anna to her feet. "Let me wash your face. Feel better now?"

Anna's skin was white beneath the scattering of freckles over her nose. "Oh…oh. I don't know. I feel so weak."

"Come on inside. We'll put you on that little bunk back in the storeroom until you feel better."

"I need to help with breakfast," she whispered.

"No you don't. I can do it and if anybody gets nosy, I'll just tell 'em you was feelin' poorly."

Anna was too weak to object and welcomed the chance to close her eyes to the light. Soon she was sleeping.

Colonel Madison had returned from Washington the day before and hired a driver to bring him home before the storms came. His daughters were already sleeping. He had given no notice to his family and his wife was surprised at his return. Now they were gathered for breakfast in their usual arrangement, separated to each end of the table.

Noting Etta scurrying back and forth to serve them, he asked, not looking at Etta. "Where's the girl?"

Margaret spoke up. "Etta, is Anna all right?"

"She's feelin' poorly. May be a touch of summer flu. I thought it best she not come in, handlin' food."

"Probably wise. I'll check on her after breakfast."

Colonel Madison snorted. "Hmf. I expect people to stay in shape to do their duty."

"Speaking of duty, Father, did you finish your duty in Washington?" Margaret asked.

"No. Summer recess. Things move at a snail's pace in Washington. I have to go back in September."

"Are you in any trouble?" asked Agnes, staring at her husband.

"Of course not! Why would you ask such a question?"

Agnes did not reply. She turned her attention to her breakfast.

Anna awakened after sleeping for an hour. Etta peeked in to check on her and saw her stirring.

"How ya doin'? Feelin' better?"

"Oh, I think so." Anna sat up and rubbed her eyes.

"Miss Margaret is waitin' to see you."

"Tell her I'll be out in a minute. I need to rinse out my mouth and drink some water." Anna rose and straightened her hair and clothing. The wet spots on her skirt and apron had dried, but were stained with grass and soil. Finally she walked into the main room of the cookhouse. Margaret was sitting at the small table on one wall. She arose when Anna entered the room.

"Are you feeling better?"

"I think so. I feel weak, but not sick now."

"Good. Etta said you might have a touch of flu. Let me feel your forehead....You don't feel hot, so maybe it was just something you ate."

"Maybe so. I'll change my skirt and get to work."

"Are you sure?" Etta said.

"I think so. Today's the day to change sheets and gather laundry for tomorrow. I'll start on that and see how it goes."

"Tell ya what. I'll make a slice of toast. If you can eat that and feel all right, you can go, but stop if you feel bad, ya hear?"

"I will."

Anna took two bushel baskets in, leaving one in the lower hall, and taking the other up the stairs. She went up the steep stairs to her room, changed her bedding, and changed out of her skirt and apron. She poured water into her wash basin, washed her face, and let down her hair. She brushed it out and braided it again, coiling the braid into a bun at the back of her head. "What is the matter with me?" she said aloud to her reflection in the mirror.

She started with Gertrude's room, making the bed with fresh linens and plumping the pillows. She was glad Gertrude was not there. Next came Margaret's room, the bedding and towels added to the basket. Still feeling well, if a little weak, she went downstairs and into the Colonel's sleeping room and changed towels in the adjoining bathroom. As she turned to reenter the bedroom, Madison was blocking the doorway, leaning against the frame. Anna gasped and jumped back.

Colonel Madison smiled, "Don't be afraid. Sorry I startled you."

Anna stared at him, eyes wide.

"Wanted to tell you I'm back, and I've been noticing the changes in you. You're becoming a very pretty girl."

Anna cringed inwardly, remembering a similar statement out in the woods. She looked down at the basket in her hands and spoke softly, "Thank you, Sir."

She looked up and he was still smiling at her. He slowly turned aside for her to pass. As she did do, he ran his hand up her arm and over her shoulder, caressing her back as she passed.

Benjamin Archer scraped the bottom of his cornmeal bin the night before, so he decided to ride down to the mill in Sycamore in the cool of morning. He tied a sack of shelled corn behind the cantle of Charger's saddle, whistled to Bone, and headed down the ridge toward Bull Creek. It was clear and the air was clean after the rain, with scattered white puffy clouds floating in the blue. He decided to go straight there and maybe drop by Pa's on the way back.

Hiram Zinn, George's younger brother, waited on him when he carried the sack of corn in. Hiram hoisted the sack up and hung it on the steelyard, moving the larger balancing weight along the notches until it balanced. "You wanta' wait to grind it, or take some already ground?"

"I'll take some of yours, Hy. Might be better than mine anyway."

"Who knows? Yours looked good. Had to turn some away the other day, had some blue smut on it." Hiram measured out the percentage. "Say, you wanta hear somethin' funny?"

"Sure."

"Had a kid come in, I won't give his name, had the corn in one end of the sack and a big rock in the other end to balance it over the saddle. One of the fellows pointed out he could just divide the corn." Hiram laughed.

"That is funny."

"Poor kid's ears turned red. I felt sorry for him."

Ben went next to the store and wrapped his reins around the rail out front. As he climbed the steps, he was greeted by Grandpa Ned Bowman, sitting on the whittler's bench, "There's that young feller took away my prize."

"Sorry, Mister Bowman. It was a lucky shot."

"Weren't no luck to it. The other two was good, too. And I'm just joshin' you. You won fair and square."

"Thank you, sir." Ben shook his hand as he walked by. Israel, sitting by his father, and others on the porch, watched the exchange.

Ben went inside and purchased salt and coffee, then added six sticks of candy for his visit by the home place.

When he came back out carrying the packages, his eyes were filled with tears from the smoky interior of the store. He was confronted by Bob and Clint Harvey who were climbing the steps to the porch. Clint was in the lead. He walked up to Ben and bumped his chest against him. "Look what we got here! Thought I told you to stay away from my sister."

"It was her choice to come to the picnic with her aunt, if that's what you're talkin' about."

"An' it was your choice not to bring her," Clint said. Clint grabbed Ben's shirt and shoved him to the porch railing and over it before Ben could react.

Bob made no move to restrain his brother, but several men leaped up and dragged Clint to a bench and sat him down.

"What the hell you doin'?" shouted Israel Bowman, who had both his hands on Clint's shoulders holding him down.

Billy Roberts went down the steps and helped Ben to his feet. "You all right, Ben?"

Ben dusted himself off and said, loudly enough for all to hear. "I reckon so. Only a coward attacks a body without warning."

He went back up on the porch and into the store, as if nothing had happened, ignoring Clint who sat red-faced, restrained on the bench. The coffee and salt were spilled on the ground, so he went inside and replaced them. When he came back out, he said, "Good day to all you gentlemen." He mounted his horse and rode away.

The men released Clint, and Grandpa Ned, who had observed the incident, said, "Young feller, you jest made a complete ass out of yourself. Yonder goes one who acted like a man."

CHAPTER 23

Throughout the month of August, Anna had repeated episodes of nausea. Some days she was fine; on others it would arrive without much warning at different times of the day. She began to worry that something bad was wrong with her. It wasn't uncommon for people to sicken and die at all ages, from children to older people. She kept a bucket by her bed just in case it happened in the night. Etta covered for her, making excuses for her absences, coming up with various tasks to keep her occupied out of sight of the family.

Anna noticed Etta studying her during these times with a worried expression. She was even kinder than usual, producing a cool, wet cloth or helping Anna to lie down. One day, however, when the family were all in other parts of the house, and no chores to be done, Etta took her hand and said, "Anna, girl, let's go into the storeroom and have us a talk."

Puzzled, Anna followed. They sat side-by-side on the bunk.

Etta put her arm around Anna's shoulders and spoke softly to her. "When you gone tell me what really happen that day you pickin' blackberries?"

"What do you mean?"

"I think sumpin' happen besides fallin' in the creek."

"Why do you say that?"

"Tell me. You have the woman's curse lately?"

Anna was concerned. How does Etta know? She looked down at her hands, twisting them in her apron. "No, Etta. Is something wrong with me?"

Etta sighed. "We could say that. Was they a man happen to you?"

Anna burst into tears. She said through her sobs, "I ran from him. I fought him. I hit him with a rock..."

Etta took Anna in her arms and rocked back and forth, "Oh, sweet Jesus, child. Not you fault. You don't know why you be sick, do you?"

"No. Am I gonna die?"

Etta took a deep breath. "Not hardly. I think you be with child."

Anna sat bolt upright, gray-green eyes staring. *"What did you say?"*

"I say, I think you gonna have a baby."

Anna's face was wet with tears, her expression bewildered. *"Etta, I can't do that! Why would you say that?"*

Etta took Anna's hands in hers. "Here's how it is. Man, he do somethin', you no more have the curse, you have what they call 'mornin' sickness. It all add up."

Anna put her face in her hands. *"What's going to happen to me, Etta?"* she cried.

Etta patted her knee. "Don't rightly know, girl. We'll have to think on it. Be a while 'fore it shows."

"Etta, I'm just a kid! I can't do that!"

Etta put her hand to Anna's face, wiping the tears, "Honey, I been seein' you grow up, and now for shore, you ain't a kid no longer."

Anna looked at her, her face set in pain.

"They's some can make it go away, but I don't know who."

Anna still stared at her, trying to absorb what she was saying. "You mean take it out of me?"

"That's what I mean."

"Would it be alive?"

Etta shrugged. "Let's not think about that right now. We got time to ponder. Now, let's go about our business, let it soak in. Then we talk some more." She rose and took Anna's hands, lifting her to her feet and hugging her. "One way or 'nother, it'll work out. Women been doin' this for thousands of years."

Anna washed her face and tried to regain her composure. She trembled inside and realized she would never be the same as before. She had no reason to doubt Etta's wisdom, though what she said was hard to comprehend. She replayed the events of that fateful June morning in her mind, seeing each scene with clarity, reliving her fear and her anger.

Etta had put her to work peeling potatoes and she was thankful to have a familiar task to occupy her hands. Anytime she was standing, walking about the kitchen, she kept reaching to touch her stomach. It felt as it always had, flat and smooth. She made it look like she was straightening her apron when she caught herself. *Is Etta right? Is there really something growing inside me? I wonder what it looks like now, after only a couple of months. Does it look like a little person?*

Anna continued with the routine of kitchen tasks. Etta had a beef roast in the oven and would make brown gravy to go with the boiled potatoes and carrots. Anna put a spoonful of bacon fryings in a dutch oven and added water to steam a halved head of cabbage. *When will my belly get bigger?* Anna clapped the lid on the dutch oven and ran across to the main house and began setting the table. As she did so, she tried to think of when she was a small child and there was a woman with a baby who visited her mother. It wasn't a tiny baby so it couldn't have been new-born. Her family never visited others as she grew older, so she had no recollection of seeing a woman about to have a child. Papa had cows that calved, but they didn't look much different before and after.

As she was finishing her task, Margaret came into the dining room, but Anna did not notice her until Margaret spoke. "Anna, you look so serious. Are you all right?"

Anna recovered and tried to smile. "Yes, I'm fine. I was just thinking."

"I know you've been sick some. Are you over it now?"

"I think so."

"So why the serious frown?"

"Sometimes I start wondering what will happen to me."

Margaret came to her and hugged her. "Don't worry. I'll always be here for you."

"Thank you, Margaret. I know you will try to be, but sometimes things happen we can't control." *Oh, Margaret, if you only knew.*

"My, my. You sound so serious. Try to look on the bright side."

Anna smiled weakly. "I will. Now I have to run over and start bringing supper over here."

The meal was served as it usually was, Anna and Etta gliding back and forth from warming kitchen to dining room and back. Anna felt the

Colonel's eyes following her, but he seemed now to make no effort to hide his interest. Or was it curiosity? Can people look at me now and know something is different, or is it my imagination? Anna had been careful ever since his return to avoid being alone with him, but it hadn't been easy. She was preparing to serve dessert, a peach pie Etta had made, when Colonel Madison's announcement brought her mind to the present.

"Well," Madison began. "I will be leaving in the morning to return to Washington. All of you know what is expected of you. Girls, we have your train tickets booked the following week to head back east to school. And Agnes, I've given Hank his instructions about finishing the harvest, and so forth. You should have nothing to worry about."

"That's the problem," said Agnes. "Nothing to worry about, nothing to do, nowhere to go."

Madison frowned at her from the other end of the table, "Your words are inappropriate at table. We'll discuss this later."

The rest of the meal resumed in silence, tension in the air.

Anna was awake most of the night in her garret room. When she said her nightly prayers, she asked God to tell her why this had happened to her and what she was supposed to do now. She expected no answer, assuming people have to figure out for themselves how to get out of trouble that comes to them.

When morning came, she willed herself out of bed, washed herself, and went down to her usual routine of starting the cook fires and setting up to cook breakfast. Before Etta arrived, Colonel Madison came into the cookhouse and walked up behind her as she stood at the stove. He moved against her and put his arm around her waist. Anna jumped.

"It's all right," he said softly. "I won't hurt you. Just wanted to tell you I'm going away."

Anna tried to move to the side. "Yes, Sir. I heard last night."

At that moment, the back door opened and Etta came in. "Good morning, Suh," she said brightly.

Madison quickly stepped back. "I'll have coffee as soon as it's ready!" he barked.

As soon as he left, Etta went into her high register, "What's that old goat think he's a doin'?"

Anna gave her a weary look. "I don't know, but I'm glad he's gone."

Colonel Madison had made his early departure, being driven in the surrey to the Springfield train station. The Madison ladies were gathered for breakfast at Agnes's end of the table, as was their custom.

As Anna brought coffee and tea service in to the table, Gertrude spoke, ignoring her. "Mother, I heard sounds of disagreement coming from Father's office."

"It's not polite to eavesdrop, my dear."

"I didn't hear what was said."

"Well, I'll enlighten you both. I told your father I'm not going to be imprisoned here, and if he wishes to have someone here to supervise, then hire someone. I'm going to New York to visit my sister."

"Mother! What did he say?"

"He said lots of things, but I'm not changing my mind."

Margaret watched the conversation, eating her scrambled eggs. She said calmly. "I have the perfect solution."

They both looked at her.

"I'm not going back east to school this term. I've had quite enough now to make some decisions of my own. I'll look after this place."

"Whatever do you mean?" said Gertrude. "Did you discuss this with Daddy?"

"No, I did not," said Margaret. "What good would it have done? Easier to ask for forgiveness later." She turned to her mother. "Looks like we are both in rebellion."

Anna listened with interest, making several trips in and out of the dining room. She persuaded Etta to stay in the warming kitchen and let her do all the serving.

Agnes looked stunned. "Margaret, do you realize what might happen?"

"Can't be sure. What he doesn't know won't cause trouble. The longer you both keep it a secret, the better off we'll all be."

"What will you do?" her mother asked.

"Like I said, look after the place. In addition, I plan to understudy the schoolmaster and apply for a teaching license."

"Become a *common teacher?*" Agnes snorted.

"There's nothing common about teaching. It's a noble thing to do. Much more noble than tea and crumpets, boring balls, and crocheting doilies."

CHAPTER 24

After two days of packing, Agnes Madison and her daughter Gertrude left for Springfield, planning to spend the night in a hotel before beginning the long train journey the following day. During those two days, Margaret endured continuous criticism for her decision and warning about her bleak future if she defied her father. At times, Agnes was able to summon tears from her normally dry eyes, displaying emotions Margaret felt were insincere, considering her mother's own decision to defy her husband. Margaret endured, and was relieved to bid them farewell on the early September morning.

After they left, she sent Etta to summon Hank Green, having him report to her father's office. Hank entered, removing his hat with some deference, nodding his head and greeting her. "Good morning, Miz Margaret. What can I do for you?"

"Have a seat, Hank. Just wanted to fill you in on a change or two. Missus Madison has left to visit her sister in New York. She left me in charge of the farm. I don't expect to change any of the tasks my father left for you, but if you have any problems, let me know. We'll talk every few days and you can bring me up to date on progress. And I'll be handling any financial transactions and keeping the books."

"Fine, Miz Margaret. I know what needs to be done. That'll work for me."

Margaret rose and reached to take his hand. "Thanks, Hank. I know I can count on you."

Hank bobbed his head again, shook hands and left, clapping his hat on as he left the room.

Margaret got up from the desk and went out the back door to the cookhouse to find Etta and Anna. They were both working away, cleaning up from breakfast, getting ready to start on the noon meal.

"I hope I can slow you two down for a few minutes," Margaret said, with a smile.

They both turned to her.

"Can we sit at the table a moment?" Margaret said. She walked over to it, and pulled out a chair. Anna and Etta joined her, taking the other two chairs, wondering what was to come.

"Not to worry," she began. "You know the rest of my family is gone for a while. I want to change a few things, so I'll get right to it. There's just the three of us. The hired hands come and go, taking care of themselves, going home at night. Hank and his wife have their own cabin. So that leaves the three of us, and your brother, of course." She looked at Etta. "No change there. So we three are going to have out meals together right here at this table…and nothing fancy."

"Are you sure, Miss Margaret?" Etta said. "I've never done such a thing."

"It's time you did. We can do it their way when they come back, but let's do what makes sense while we can. This is no plantation. We'll close up most of the house—their bedrooms and that big dining room; cover the furniture and so forth. What do you think?"

"Amazin' is what it is," said Etta, shaking her head.

"What will we be doing?" said Anna.

"There will still be plenty," said Margaret. "I'll keep Father's office open." She smiled. "I get more respect if I sit behind that big desk of his."

"Let me say, I shorely do 'preciate it, Miss Margaret," said Etta. "We'll do anything you ask, just you say the word."

Margaret patted her gnarled hand. "I know you will. Time you get to slow down for a little breather. Now, here's another thing I have planned. Anna and I sneaked down to Sycamore awhile back, Etta, and talked to the schoolmaster. I'm going to see if I can work two or three days a week for him as a teacher's aide, see if I can learn the ropes."

"That will be fine!" Anna said.

"Maybe you can go with me once in a while," Margaret said.

"I don't know." Anna looked at Etta, then down at her hands, folded on her lap. "Uh…Margaret…there's something you must know about me," she said in a small voice.

Margaret looked at her, waiting for her to explain. "You can tell me. What is it?"

Anna looked up, her face set in pain. "Etta says I'm going to have a baby."

"What? How can that be?"

"When I was picking blackberries, I was attacked by a man. I lied about falling in the creek." She burst into tears, and sobbed, *"I'm sorry. I didn't mean to."*

Margaret jumped up and knelt by Anna's chair, clasping her hands. "Oh, Anna! It's not your fault. We'll figure it out somehow." She rose and pulled Anna to her feet, embracing her. Over Anna's shoulder, she saw Etta rise and look at her, wagging her head sadly from side to side.

After Anna's shaking began to cease, and after more words of comfort, Margaret said, "Let's sit back down and talk about this. First, do you know who he was?"

"No, I don't. I don't know many people, because we didn't go anywhere much, but I'd know him if I saw him. But what good would that do?"

"I won't try to mislead you," said Margaret. "Proving something like this is hard to do, but I'd at least try for some retribution."

"Even that won't solve the problem. Etta says there's some people know how to stop it."

"I've heard back East that's true, but it's pretty secretive."

"Even if that could be done, I don't know if I could. And I've been thinking a lot. If there is some way I can take care of it, it will be someone kin to me. A baby has to love its mother, doesn't it? My mama is dead and my papa abandoned me...." Anna fought to keep her lower lip from trembling.

This time, Etta took her hand, "Oh, honey child, I love you, and I know Miz Margaret feels the same way."

"Yes, I know. I can feel it, but what happens now? I don't see how I can stay and do my work here, so I don't know what I'll do."

Margaret pinched her lower lip, thinking. "Anna, you know I'll do everything I can. Mother will be on my side, I think, but I won't mislead you. Father may be a problem. At least we have some time. Let's all have a cup of tea and put this to rest for now."

"One more thing," Anna said. "Promise me that no one will know except the three of us, as long as it's possible."

Etta and Margaret both promised in unison.

The next morning, after a first breakfast in the cookhouse for the three women, Margaret went to the stables to find Ike. She found him in the tack room oiling some harness. He leaped to attention and wiped his hands on the rag he was using.

"Yes, Ma'm, Miz Margaret. What can I do for you?" he said.

"Good morning, Ike. I'd like to take the little buggy out for a while, with one of the trotters. If all works out right, I might be using it two or three days a week, for most of the day. I may have some regular business in Sycamore. Etta can fill you in."

"Yes, Ma'm. Right away."

She smiled. "Take your time. I'll be inside and you can bring it around front." She went back inside the cookhouse where breakfast dishes and utensils were already cleared.

"Etta, is it all right if Anna takes a ride with me down to Sycamore? You can hold off doing the closing down of the rooms until she's back to help. We have plenty of time."

"Why sure. Be good for her to get out. I'll find somethin' easy to do."

CHAPTER 25

Ben Archer was eating his breakfast when he heard a commotion outside. Bone was baying and there was the sound of a horse's hooves. Before he could react, there was the sound of boots clumping on the porch and a pounding on his door. He opened it to see Ferd Harvey, sweating and red-faced.

"Your goddam mule is in my corn! I'll shoot the sonafabitch if you don't' get him out right now!" He shouted.

"I'll come right out and get him, Mister Harvey. Sorry about that." Ben replied.

Ben grabbed his hat off a peg by the door and followed Harvey off the porch. "How'd he get in?"

"He must 'a knocked down the fence."

"I'll get a rope and go after him."

Ben's mules were docile creatures, if a bit stubborn about getting their own way. Ben was able to conceal the rope and walk up to him and make the capture. The mule had knocked down some of the crop, but had done little damage, since the corn was mature and ready for harvesting. Ben led him back the way he had come in by following his meandering tracks back to the fence. Sure enough, one of the rotted top rails was down, making it easier for the mule to clamber over.

Ben took the mule back to the pasture behind the barn, then carried a couple of new rails, cured from the past winter, back to the break and repaired it. He'd left Bone tied up behind the house.

He walked through the cornfield to the Harvey place and knocked on the front door. The hounds were gone, so he wasn't challenged. Ferd Harvey yanked the door open. Ben saw Rose and Estelle in the dim background. The brothers must have been gone somewhere.

"Did you get him?" he demanded.

"I sure did, Mister Harvey. He didn't do much damage. But we need to talk about that fence again. We agreed we'd each do half. Well, I did fix up my half, but the mule came over your half. Seems to me, he wouldn't have done it if those rotted rails had been replaced."

Harvey stuck out his chin and looked up at the taller young man. "You tryin' to tell me what to do?"

"Well…not exactly. But I did want you to know the fence needs fixin'. I put in a couple of new rails where the break took place, but that don't fix it all."

"You just mind your own damn business!" Ferd shouted, and slammed the door in his face.

Well, that didn't go too good, Ben thought, as he made his way back to his own place. I wish I had neighbors that wanted to get along. They can't seem to give up on Pa's getting the place…or maybe that's just how they are. Funny, I really like Ferd's sister, Rebecca, and Rose seems like a normal person. Oh, well, everything else is goin' good.

He recalled a conversation with Pa about the Harveys when he'd gone to fetch Goldie back home from her matchup with Pa's bull. Goldie put up her usual protests at being led by a rope and halter, but she was back producing milk. She'd soon run dry, however, getting ready for her next calf around February. Pa said he'd heard the older Harvey brothers, Ferdinand and Clyde, were rumored to have ridden with the guerilla group headed by Alf Bolden during the Civil War. They were never charged with it, but it might have ruined their outlook on life as regular citizens. "Who knows for sure?" he'd said. "If true, it might explain a few things."

Ben let his thoughts go to the approach of winter. Enough rain had fallen during the summer for the hay crop to be good. He had the barn loft full and a stack of hay outside to use first, more than enough for his horse, cow, and mules. The old apple tree had produced about a bushel. They weren't great, but would produce some applesauce. It would soon be time to get in the corn and do fall plowing for next spring's crops. Then he could start working the wood again. Hacking ties won't make a body rich, but it'll help. And I already have enough seasoned wood for winter from last winter.

As Ben was having these thoughts, Margaret and Anna were approaching Sycamore in the light little buggy, with the folding top up to protect from the sun. Margaret steered the trotter to the right side of the gravel road and pulled to a stop in front of the schoolhouse. It was recess and the younger children were in back of the schoolhouse playing under the trees. The older ones were sitting in groups. Margaret and Anna alighted from the buggy and went inside to find the schoolmaster seated at his desk on the front stage.

Abe Phillips rose and smiled at them as they came down the center aisle. "Well, it's an honor to see you two ladies again," he said.

"Thank you," they both said in unison. Then Margaret continued, "Do you have a few moments?"

"Well, the kids are dying to rush back inside, but I can make them wait."

"I'll get right to it so we don't disappoint them. Recalling our conversation in the spring, I wonder if you might consider having an unpaid apprentice a couple of days a week."

"I think that's a splendid idea." Abe said. "Let's work our way into it. Can you come down on an off day, say Saturday, and make some plans?"

"Certainly. What time?"

"Let's say nine o'clock, here at the school. I can show you what we are doing, and we can go from there." He rose. "Well, I'd better let them come in before they riot." He extended his hand to each in turn and reached for the bell on his desk, ringing it as he walked them to the door.

Margaret was smiling as they left, turning to Anna. "I think we should check out the blacksmith shop and the store. What do you think?"

"Fine with me. I haven't been in a store since I was little and Mama bought me a stick of candy."

"Then I would like to buy you one just like it, for the memory."

As they walked toward the blacksmith shop, George was standing in front, in the shade of the big Sycamore. "I saw you comin' in the buggy and hoped you'd come over," he said as they approached. "Come and sit a spell, if you can." He pointed to the two facing benches.

"We'd like that," Margaret said. "I didn't lie this time. Father and Mother are both away."

George grinned. "So the mice can play?"

"Exactly. Actually, we're not playing. I'm talking to Mister Phillips about helping in the school."

"Great. Does that mean I might have a chance to see you more often?"

"If you play your cards right, it's possible."

George turned to Anna. "And how are you, Miss Anna? Oh, please be seated."

I'm scared, she thought, but she smiled and said, "Very well, thank you."

Anna mostly listened while Margaret told George about her family and her own plans to go into teaching, if Mr. Phillips gave her reason to think she could do it. Anna's thoughts drifted to her mother's burial place on the hillside, so in a pause in the conversation, she said, "Pardon me for changing the subject, but I've never been back to my mama's grave. Did Papa have a headstone put there?"

"We can certainly go look. Do you know, George?"

"I don't think there's a stone, because Pa would be the one to carve it. Let me go ask him."

After George left, Margaret said, "What a great idea to find out. I'm sorry to be so self-absorbed that I didn't ask if you wanted to go there."

"It's perfectly all right, Margaret. I wouldn't have a chance to be here, if not for you."

Homer Zinn came out of the shop, wiping sweat from his brow with a red bandanna. He was an older, heavier copy of his son, with the same wide smile. "Hello, Ladies. Welcome to our front parlor!"

"I told Pa what your question was, Anna."

Homer said, "I'm sorry to say there's no marker, just a little wooden cross that Oley Jensen put there."

"Could I buy one?" asked Anna. "I have a little money."

"Of course you can, Honey. We save up flat stones we find in the creek and you can pick one. What would you want on it?"

"Just her name, I guess, and her date of birth and passing." Her voice broke with the last word. "I'm sorry her last name is so long...more work. And I have a family Bible with the dates."

Homer reached down to pat her hand. "Next time you come, bring it along and we'll set it up."

Henry Guthrie was sitting on the porch in a rocker chatting with Ned Bowman, who was engrossed in carving a piece of wood while they talked. Both old men rose and doffed their hats as Margaret and Anna climbed the steps. Ned nodded and Henry spoke, "Mornin' ladies. How can I help you?"

"We just want to walk through the store and see, thank you," said Margaret.

Henry opened the screen door and followed them inside. "Just help yourselves."

They wandered around inside. Anna was fascinated by all of the goods on display, particularly the bolts of cloth and skeins of yarn in various colors. She knew a time would come when newborn clothing would be needed, if such a remarkable event actually took place. The shoes on display were mostly work shoes for men and boys, avoidance of any attempt to follow ladies' fashions. They drifted to the candy display.

"What kind was it, Anna?"

She pointed to a jar of red and white striped.

"We'll take a half-dozen of those, Mister Guthrie." And aside to Anna, "We'll take a couple to Etta." Then she spotted a small basket of oranges. "Oranges, Mister Guthrie?"

"Yep. River boat brought some up the White. They come all the way from Florida. Ain't cheap."

"Let's have a half-dozen of those, also."

They walked back to the buggy with their purchases and drove to the foot of the hill beside the cemetery. They climbed the hill to Eva's grave, marked by the little weathered cross, Margaret holding Anna's hand. When Anna knelt in the grass now covering the low mound, Margaret backed away a few steps and stood waiting. Anna bowed her head, covering her face with her hands for a few moments, then rose and wiped her eyes, holding herself erect and joining Margaret for the ride home.

CHAPTER 26

September was gone, and the bright blue days of October were waning. The forests had shed their color, beginning to display the gray hillsides of the winter to come. The cycle of harvest was repeated and now complete as it had been for generations. Hay was stacked or in barns, corncribs were full of ears to be shucked and shelled as needed through the winter months. Occasional chill nights called for welcome fires in fireplaces, the scent of wood smoke drifting into the valleys.

Word had reached the community that the president had been assassinated back in September and a new president, Chester A. Arthur, had taken his place. Such news was noted, but it came from far away and had no noticeable effect on the residents of Taney County.

Tom Archer had presided as usual over the gathering of cane and boiling the sap into sorghum. This year, he hauled several gallons down to the store to trade for credit against future purchases. After seeing to a supply for Rebecca Tate, that is, and giving Ben a share for his help with the operation.

Tom and Rebecca had been keeping company since the July Fourth picnic, and it was accepted by the community that a marriage was in their future. They attended services together on Sundays whenever Rebecca felt she could get the girls ready and make the trip in the wagon. Since her niece, Rose, was often helping her, they both endeavored to have her visits fall on Sunday so she could go along, serving as a chaperone when a visit to the Archer home followed. The families took turns furnishing the mid-day meal. Sometimes Rebecca would bring a roasted chicken, or other times, Josie would set a ham to slow-roast in the oven for their return home.

By the natural course of the community grapevine, word reached Ferd Harvey of his sister's involvement with Tom Archer. One late evening, as Rebecca was putting the girls to bed, there was a knock at her door. She'd pulled the latch string, but she had a small peephole in the door. Ferd was standing in the dark on the porch. She opened the door, knowing sooner or later this confrontation would take place.

Ferd barged in, and said in a loud voice, "Just what the hell you think you're doin', Becky?"

"Watch your language in my house and in hearing of girls, Ferd!"

"I'll say what I want!"

"Not in my house. Step out on the porch."

They went outside, Rebecca remembering to put the latch string back out. "Now Ferd, settle down. What is it you want to talk about?"

"You know what it is. You got no business havin' any truck with them Archers!"

"And you have no business telling me what to do, but you tell me one reason why I shouldn't."

Ferd tried a more conciliatory tone, "Look, Becky, before Ma died, she told me to look after you, you bein' just a girl. Now I took that serious. Them Archers may be just after your farm. They already took that Friedrich place out from under us."

"Ferd, I guess you mean well, but I don't see it the same way. There was no underhandedness about Tom buying that farm. You either didn't know about the situation, or failed to take action. As to this farm, I've found Tom to be a decent and honorable person. And I can't see any different future for me and my girls. I know you and Clyde have your own families to look after, but I have to look out for myself."

"Well, me and Clyde have talked about it and we think it's a big mistake. If you do the fool thing and marry this man, we may not see much of each other."

"I'll be sorry for that, but we don't see each other much now. I hope you'll get over it."

Ferd set his mouth in a grim line, shook his head, and whirled around. He clumped down the steps, mounted his horse, and spurred into the night.

On a misty, cool November day, Thomas Archer and Rebecca Harvey Tate drove in a wagon to Ozark, Missouri, for the purpose of joining in marriage. Accompanying them in the wagon were their children, Josie and Oren Archer; and Jennifer and Estelle Tate. The wagon box was half-filled with hay, cushioning and warmth for the children and fuel for the horses while they waited for the return trip. Benjamin and James Archer rode horseback alongside. Rebecca was sad that no one from her family, particularly Rose, would be with her. She had not seen Rose since that conversation with Ferd and knew it was unlikely to happen in the future.

The clerk of the court, a stooped young man with a bobbing Adam's apple, turned pages in a large ledger and inked their names and addresses using a dipped pen. Then he turned the ledger around for them to make their signatures in the correct space, indicating with a blue fingernail. The children gathered close around their parents, Oren and the Tate girls tiptoeing to peep over the counter. Both Rebecca and Tom had brought their family Bibles as the only proof they had of their lineage, but the clerk waved them off. Who cares who gets married? It all pays the same.

Next they found the office of the Justice of the Peace, and filled the small waiting room with their family, the smaller children fidgeting it their chairs, finding reasons to giggle and whisper. Ben and Jimmy stood in a corner, looking solemn. Finally, the male secretary to the Justice came out of a frosted glass door and ushered them in to the office of the Justice, a stern old man with a fringe of white whiskers and thin, unruly hair.

After a short exchange of vows, they were pronounced man and wife. They embraced briefly, conscious of the children watching, then waited while the Justice filled in a flowery marriage certificate. Ben and the male secretary signed as witnesses. The new bride and groom held hands and led their entourage out of the courthouse and down the steps, both feeling a mixture of relief and exhilaration as they began their life together.

Margaret was thrilled to be doing something useful. She worked two days a week for Mr. Phillips, tutoring the slower learners, hearing the small children read their lessons, and grading papers in the evenings after returning home at the end of the day. She loved the children and they seemed to like her. Her application for a teaching certificate had been approved after a glowing endorsement from Mr. Phillips. The future was beginning to take shape in her mind; her only hurdle yet to leap was the coming confrontation with her father. He'd written a scolding letter to her from Washington after finding out from her mother what she had done. So far, there was no schedule for his return.

Another positive advantage of her trips to Sycamore occupied her thoughts most of her waking hours. Many afternoons after school let out she spent some time sitting with George Zinn on a bench under the bare, white branches of the big sycamore. She had found him attractive from the start, but her feelings grew as she found him well-read and eager to converse on almost any subject. On a recent Thursday evening, she had been invited to have supper with his family, a warm and friendly encounter. His mother Irene especially was a welcoming hostess. George had saddled a horse and escorted her home in the evening dusk.

CHAPTER 27

Anna lay on her narrow bed, reading the notes in her journal by the light of a candle on the end table at her head. She could hear the wind outside and the comforting, intimate patter of rain falling on the slanting roof only inches above her. Margaret had given her the small bound notebook when she first learned of the uncertain course of Anna's future. Together, they had inked in the dates by consulting a calendar hanging in the colonel's office. The calendar had a picture of a robust man on it extoling the virtues of "J. W. Bull's Herbs and Iron."

They started numbering the pages with the days of each month in early September when Anna confessed to Margaret her condition. They left an empty page at the beginning and calculated and recorded as best they could the date of conception, leaving out any description of events of that day. Anna tried to excise those memories from any connection to her present state and her future.

She made few significant entries in the early going, but she liked to read her notes from those early weeks. Most were about the routines of keeping the house, but on occasion there were good times, the trip to Sycamore with Margaret was one. And there was another when she returned to place a stone at her mother's grave with the help of Margaret and George.

The notes she made about her feelings gave her some embarrassment with the thought anyone besides herself would ever read them. She smiled to herself as she read, "Etta making me drink great amounts of milk and water. I make so many trips to the outhouse I am wearing a groove in the ground." And another, "my bosoms are tender and growing even larger...."

Best of all were the feelings of the almost undetectable tightening of the waistbands in her skirts. Overall, though, now that the morning sickness was gone, she felt really well and even her spirits were not so low whenever she was able to avoid thoughts of the future. Her favorite page in the journal, and she turned to it now, was that day just past mid-October. "I felt movement. I really did! There were some little tickles in there before, but I thought they were just gas, which happens aplenty. But this time it is real. There is really a little person in there wiggling around. Wait until I tell Etta and Margaret." Best she could figure, that day was about the eighteenth week.

She opened another page and read, "Margaret really likes George, I think. She tells me things they talk about and things he says. He's coming Sunday to take her for a ride in his buggy." A few pages later, "Margaret brings home papers to mark for the students. She goes over them with me to explain what they are about. I still read the books she gives me, and I keep trying to understand numbers."

Reluctantly, she closed the book and blew out the candle, whispering her evening prayers. As she turned on her side to go to sleep, she felt movement. "Good night, baby, time for sleeping," she said aloud.

Ben turned up the collar of his slicker against the light rain as he drove down the gravel road along the bank of Bull Creek. He was hauling a load of logs to his father's place to add to the growing pile. Soon they'd start squaring and notching to add a room to the house. The two families were getting on fine, but Tom and Rebecca agreed that it would be good to have a separate sleeping room for the three girls. Jimmy and Oren could then have the loft to themselves.

He'd been doing double duty looking after his place and now going once a day to Rebecca's farm and feeding her horses. He'd moved her cow over to keep Goldie company, so he now had a surplus of milk for a time. He brought two gallon buckets of it along on this trip, what with five kids to feed at Pa's house.

On his last visit with a load of logs, Pa and Rebecca had asked his opinion about her farm. "Rebecca's in favor of putting it up for sale," Pa had said. "What do you think?"

"Makes sense to me," Ben said. "When you think about putting in all the crops, and stuff, it'll be a little hard to do for the two of us on three places. I reckon you could get a hired hand, maybe. Or you could rent it out."

This time as he pulled into the yard, stopping at the end of the house by the log pile, his whole family came out to meet him. Oren was jumping up and down.

"Hi, y'all." Ben said and they all answered. As he climbed down from the wagon, his new mother Rebecca came up and gave him a hug.

"Thanks, Ben, for all you do," she said.

"Glad to do it. Here, Jimmy, you want to take this milk to the springhouse?"

Jimmy did so, and Ben turned and climbed back on the wagon. Tom joined him. "Somebody make sure Oren stands clear," he said.

The light rain had ceased. They both picked up cant hooks and rolled the top logs off on the ground, then removed the stakes and rolled off the bottom layer.

After Ben pulled the team out of the way, he came back carrying his broad axe. "Pa, I thought I'd spend a little time squaring up. Might not get 'em all done today."

"Anything will help. I've got some lumber for the floor and roof coming from a new mill in Walnut Shade. Oh...by the way, we liked the idea of renting Rebecca's farm until we decide what to do. Found a couple who came in from Tennessee with a family, name of Stotts. We made a deal for shares of the crops. Rebecca says you can have her team of grays, by the way."

"*Really?* Those are fine horses."

"Well, we all work together, anyhow. They'll eat a lot of hay, maybe, but you'll sure use 'em come spring. You can get 'em anytime. The Stotts will try to move in come Monday. We've got to get some stuff out of the house and barn."

Ben worked most of the day squaring the logs. His broad axe was sharp as a razor and because of his tie-hacking experience, he was able to hew flats that looked smooth as saw cuts except for the light part-circles from his notching.

They had a lively noon meal together. Ben could sense the family coming together. Josie helped Rebecca at the stove and in serving the dishes as though they were blood mother and daughter. He worked three more hours, then headed back up the Creek to his own place. Pa assured him he'd work on the logs when he got a chance, admitting, "You'll be able to tell which ones I did. You're really getting good at this."

Margaret had developed a good working relationship with Hank Green. The farm was operating smoothly with harvest done and fall plowing completed. There was little need for hired hands during the winter, just enough for small tasks and help feeding hay to the cattle. Most of the hands had small places of their own they tended when they weren't working for the Madisons.

She ceased sending one of the men to pick up incidentals and the mail from Sycamore, as she could handle that herself on her twice-weekly trips. Hank Green still went to Forsyth or Ozark on occasion if farm supplies were needed.

Usually there was no mail, or nothing of importance, but one morning she found the yellow envelope of a telegram waiting in the pigeonhole. She tore it open to find a terse sentence from her father telling her that her parents would be arriving the fifteenth of November. She sighed, tucked it in her handbag, and thought about it all the way home.

She waited until the three of them had finished eating the evening meal before asking Etta and Anna to sit a moment. She took out the yellow envelope and read the message to them.

"I don't want to make too much of it," Margaret said. "But we all know things are going to change. My father will really be ill with me."

"He ought to be proud of you," Etta said.

"Yes," agreed Anna. "Seems to me things are better now with you in charge."

Margaret smiled. "Thanks to you both, but he won't see it that way. But that's my problem. I do worry some about you, Anna. We'll just all work together to minimize his contact with you."

Anna tried to lighten the mood. "What's that thing called, again, that holds the dress out behind?"

"You mean the bustle?"

"Yes. As I get bigger…" she paused to smooth the apron over her stomach, "I can say I got it on backwards."

All three laughed despite the dark cloud looming over them.

CHAPTER 28

As the day approached when her parents were to arrive, Margaret worked with Anna and Etta to have the house shipshape. They removed and washed all the covering sheets, made up the beds, cleaned and waxed the floors, and applied furniture paste to the mahogany furniture, raising it to a high shine. One entire day was devoted to washing windows.

Etta said privately to Anna as they took a short break. "He can't find anything to complain about, but won't surprise me he think of sumpin'."

"Etta, do you think they'll take note of my stomach?"

"Don't know, girl. One thing certain as the sun comin' up. It'll get bigger. We just face it when it come."

Margaret sent their most reliable hand to Springfield in the surrey the day before her parents were to arrive on the morning train. She gave him money for a hotel room and stabling for the team, knowing he might sleep in the surrey and pocket the money.

The fateful arrival day was a day she worked at school, so she talked about it to Abraham Phillips after school.

"Abe, you know my situation. I can't predict what will happen. I'd better not take any papers home to grade, but I'll do my best to come back."

"I know you will, Margaret. You've been a breath of fresh air, and I hope we can continue. I'm going to recommend to the school board that they hire you on a permanent basis, so you know what might be waiting for you."

"Thanks, Abe. You've been great. I hope this isn't goodbye." Margaret shook hands and walked up the street to the blacksmith shop to see George. She had kept him up to date after the telegram.

"George, I have to go. They'll be getting here pretty soon."

They stood facing each other. "I know, Margaret. I'll be here think-ing of you. God be with you."

She rushed into his arms. "Oh, George. I'll be thinking of you also. In the end, they're not going to tell me what I can or can't do." Since they could be seen by gossips, she gave him a quick, chaste kiss and walked back to her buggy, turning to wave as she drove away. George was still standing where she had left him.

Darkness had fallen by the time the surrey pulled up in the circular drive in front of the house. Hank Green and Ike, the groom, were there as it pulled to a stop. Margaret stood at the top of the steps, Etta behind her. She walked down and to the surrey as her father alighted.

He stared at her, his eyes narrowed. "We will talk in the morning," he said to her.

"All right, Father," she replied. "Welcome home. Anna has laid a cold supper if you are hungry, and they have water heating in case you or Mother desires a bath." Her father walked past her without another word and headed into the house. He looked older to her, perhaps tired from the journey, or maybe it was the dim light from the stars.

Agnes gave her a swift, stiff hug and said, "Hello, Margaret. I hope you are well." She disengaged and hurried up the steps and into her room.

Hank and Etta carried in their luggage the evening before and neither made another appearance. Now her parents were seated for breakfast in their usual formal arrangement at either end of the long table. Nor was there any conversation between her father and mother, but Margaret attempted to converse with her mother. "And how are Aunt Elvira and Uncle Rupert?"

"They're fine, Dear. I had a very nice visit."

"Did you do anything exciting?"

"'Interesting' might be a more descriptive word. Rupert was gone long hours to his position on Wall Street, so Elvira and I were able to spend all our days together. We dined together in the evenings, of course.

The city is growing, with tall buildings going up everywhere. Please pass me another toast."

"I'd like to see it sometime."

"You might do so if you obeyed your parents," her father interrupted from the other end of the table.

Agnes ignored him. "We went to Battery Park, where immigrants are pouring in now that the war is behind us. And the most exciting news is that France is giving our country a great statue to recognize our independence and they plan to erect it in New York harbor. Perhaps we'll go see it someday."

"I'd like that, Mother."

When Etta came in to clear the dishes, Madison said. "Where's the girl?"

"Suh, Anna in the kitchen washin' up," replied Etta.

When the meal was over, Madison said, "Margaret, come into my office."

She followed him in, taking the chair in front of the desk, a change for her from the past several weeks.

Her father jerked his chair out and sat, then stared at her. A flush was rising in his face as he shouted, "Just who do you think you are, young lady!"

She forced herself to remain calm. "I'd like to think I'm my father's daughter. I have no intention to cause trouble and I would like the chance to explain myself."

He was not mollified and spoke through clenched teeth. "Let's hear it then, and it had better be good."

Margaret looked directly at him. "Father, I am grateful for all you have done for me; my education, my worldly possessions. But being a thinking person, which I think I inherit from you, I want to consider my own future. I don't want my future to depend only on 'making a good marriage,' a kept woman who does nothing but attend and host social events and do needlepoint."

Madison's head of steam seemed to reduce a bit. "Is that how you see your mother?"

"To an extent, yes. She's an intelligent woman, but I do not think she is as happy as I wish to be at her age."

"So that's my fault?"

"I'm not saying that, but after she has raised us, she seems at loose ends. I would hope you could encourage her to broaden her horizons a bit. Some ladies in her situation get involved in charity work, volunteering, or other pursuits."

"Ha! Fat chance of that around here!"

"I admit I haven't discussed it with her. But as for me, if you haven't heard, I have been volunteering in the local school two days a week, and I love it. It makes me feel worthwhile and gives me a window into what I want to do in the future."

"You *what?* Well you've had your say and now I will have mine. As long as you are under my roof, you will do as I say and you will *not* be working in that primitive school! You may go."

Without a word, Margaret rose and went to find Anna and Etta to see how they were doing with the change in atmosphere. Anna was upstairs, cleaning and dusting, making up beds. She was wearing a loose apron with ruffles, which did a good job camouflaging her stomach in its current stage at twenty-two weeks.

"Well, Anna, I've had my wings clipped. Father has forbidden my work with the school."

"What will you do?"

"I don't know yet. I may have to wait and see if I can get a full-time job teaching, then I can move out. And how are you?"

"I've had some little dizzy spells, or feel a little faint if I get up too quick, but not bad. Over all, good, in fact. Baby's jumping around quite a bit."

Margaret smiled, "That must be something! You take it easy. Don't do more than you feel like. Lie down for a little while when you can."

For the next two weeks, the Madison household fell into the routine that existed before Perry and Agnes left separately for the east in early September. It could be described as gloomy compared to the preceding weeks. Margaret had gotten a letter from her sister, telling of the wonderful parties she attended and the beaus hovering around. It was supposed to fill Margaret with regret, but it had the opposite effect, reinforcing her decision to stay behind.

The hillsides were dressed in gray, all the leaves, even from the oaks, having fallen. No green from nature was to be seen, except for the dark green cedars and a few patches of winter wheat. Frequent spells of lingering rain and morning fog in the hollows portended the coming of winter. When the weather did clear, nights were cold and the hills shone with frost in the early morning sun.

Margaret was restless, her father watching her every move. When she went riding, he accompanied her, an obvious lack of trust.

Anna was amazed at how fast her body was growing and how it had begun to affect her posture, not to mention the constant need to modify her clothing. She occasionally managed to be seen during the serving of meals, but cleverly used Etta as a screen, avoiding going to serve the table alone. Doing the ordinary housework was hardest, but Etta took over any duty in the Colonel's bedroom and bath, after the incident weeks ago when Anna was accosted by him.

Subterfuge can go only so far, however, in a household of five persons in unpredictable movement about, no matter the size of the house. One early morning, before Etta had come in, Anna was standing at the wood range in the cookhouse. She was building the morning fire as was her duty. She failed to hear Colonel Madison creep up behind her as he had done once before. He put his arms around her waist, then jumped back with a cry, "What the *HELL?*"

CHAPTER 29

E tta came in the back door just in time to hear the explosive burst from Colonel Madison. Oh, my, oh, my, why wasn't I here sooner, she thought. It's just like that other time he came in early and tried to grab her. She saw Anna whirl around, her face inflamed.

"Why do you put your hands on me, Sir?" she demanded.

"Looks like something you haven't been saying much," he shot back. "And don't speak to me in that tone of voice." Then he turned to Etta. "Don't just stand there, old woman. Fetch Margaret. We're going to get to the bottom of this."

He stabbed a finger at Anna. "You! Go into the house to my office. We have a lot to talk about."

Anna hurried ahead of him out the door and in through the kitchen of the main house. She waited in the hall outside Madison's office. Margaret and Etta came down the stairs to the hallway, and Margaret turned and rapped on her mother's bedroom door as she walked by. As they entered Madison's office, he jerked his thumb at Etta and pointed back up the hall. Etta touched Anna's arm as she departed.

Agnes came rushing into the office in a dressing gown, her hair askew. "What on earth is going on, Perry?"

Madison yanked out his chair and sat. He pointed a trembling finger at Anna and shouted, "Take a good look at her. Why don't you ask our whore of a maid?"

"Father, that's untrue and uncalled for! For shame!" Margaret shouted.

"Margaret, calm down and apologize to your father," said Agnes.

"I will not. When Anna was in the woods picking blackberries, she was attacked by a man. She ran from him and fought him, hitting him with a rock. He overpowered her and knocked her unconscious."

Anna stood staring, her face white.

Agnes's face softened, but Madison leered at Margaret. "That's a fine story. And just how do you know it's true?"

"I'd trust her with my life. I know her. Also, she was bruised and her clothing torn."

Madison stared at the three women standing before him. Finally he said in a cold monotone, "Margaret, you've made a botch of things while we were away, defying me. You should have told me about this before I found out for myself."

Anna had heard enough, "Why don't you tell Missus Madison how you found out?"

Madison leaped from his chair and started around it, his face red, "Get that bitch out of my sight!"

Anna whirled and left the room, going to seek Etta. What have I done? she thought. I can feel my baby moving because of the turmoil. No matter what, I will not be spoken of like that.

As soon as the door closed behind Anna, Agnes, still standing, stared at her husband. "Well, Perry, let's hear it. How *did* you discover her condition?"

"I went to check on the coffee and I could see she was that way."

"Well, *I* didn't notice, with that loose, ruffled apron she was wearing."

"Then you aren't observant. She—"

"Did you put your hands on her?"

"Don't be ridiculous! Now the two of you sit."

Margaret, feeling shock, watched the interplay between her parents. When she thought about it, she'd been troubled in the past by her father's gaze following Anna whenever she was in the room.

Madison's face was flushed, but the skin was white around his eyes. He raised a clenched fist, but with the index finger pointing across the desk. "Here's what's going to happen. She's brought shame on this house and she's to be gone by sundown. And you, Missy," pointing at Margaret, "Are to stay away from her. If necessary, by God, I'll lock you in your room!"

Margaret refrained from voicing her anger, and tried to avoid the thoughts churning in her mind. You're jealous. You wanted her for yourself.

Her mother spoke. "Perry, you're being unreasonable. She is a good girl and I see no reason to turn her out. Think of what you're about to do, if indeed she was raped. We should be supportive of her."

"No damn way! You can have your weak opinions, but it doesn't change mine."

Margaret knew he was right. He'd never change his mind. "What do you intend to happen to her?"

"I don't care about that."

"Obviously not," Margaret replied. "But what can she do? She has no place to go."

"She can find her paramour; let him take care of her."

"For the last time, *she has no paramour. She had no idea who he was!*"

"So she says."

"Father, please, for the love of God, at least let me take her down to Sycamore and introduce her to some there in the community, see if I can find a place for her."

"No. Hell no. She walks out the door the same way she walked in it. Looks like you were right in your first assessment, Agnes."

"Perry, Margaret and I will at least see that she has warm clothes and some food to take with her. I will insist on it. Then I can only hope someone with Christian kindness will take her in." She got up out her chair. "I'm going to dress."

Perry Madison said nothing as both Margaret and her mother left the room, closing the door behind them.

When Anna left the office after her confrontation with Madison, she ran down the hall and out to the cookhouse to find Etta. She was trembling inside with anger, but worried about what would become of her. When she entered, Etta turned and came to embrace her. Etta had been crying and as she released Anna she stepped back and wiped her eyes with the hem of her apron.

"How bad is it, child?" she said.

"Let's sit down. I feel weak."

"Sure thing, Honey. Let me get you coffee."

"He's throwing me out, Etta. He called me bad names. Maybe I shouldn't have, but I called him out in front of his wife. Groped his hands on me is the way he found out. I'm disgusted by him and so mad I couldn't help myself. I had to speak out. But now I'm scared. I don't know where to go."

"Oh, you poor thing." Etta said and put her hand on top of Anna's.

Margaret burst into the room and ran to Anna's side. She put her arm around Anna and kissed her cheek. "Oh, Anna," she said. "I'm so sorry and I don't know what to do. My father is not a nice man."

"Of course I agree. But I know there is nothing you can do. Please sit with us. My papa always told me I should learn to hold my tongue. I just couldn't...with the bad names he called me."

Margaret pulled out a chair. "I don't blame you. Mother stuck up for you, but there's no changing him. He said he will lock me in my room so I won't try to help you. Mother said we'd do what we could to prepare you, though."

"She's been nice to me lately. Tell her when you can that I appreciate it. I suppose I'm to walk out of here today."

Margaret nodded her head. "Sadly, I suppose so. Look, while I can say it; if you can get to Sycamore, go to George Zinn and ask for help."

"I'll think on it. My condition is not something people believe in."

"Please try. He's a good man."

"What can I do?" Etta said. "I feel like I'm losin' my own child."

"Mother suggested a supply of food. It can't be heavy, but maybe it'll last for a little while."

Etta jumped up. "I'll get right on it."

Anna went to her garret room and gathered her meager belongings: her cigar box with trinkets and the money Agnes had given her; her mother's Bible; knitting needles, and her quilt. Margaret came up into her room with a carpet bag, a heavy woolen coat, and leather boots. "Let's see if these fit you," she said. "And then let's plan together what else. You can have anything in my closet."

"Oh, thank you Margaret," Anna sobbed. "You have been so nice to me. No matter what happens, I will see you again."

"We surely will. I'll find you when I can." She embraced Anna. "Oh, there's one more thing. I'll have to run to the tack room and get it. It's an oilskin jacket in case it rains before you get to shelter."

They hurriedly packed all she might need, keeping in mind she must carry it. Extra woolen stockings, underwear, a change of clothes, soap, all went into the bag. They rolled the quilt and laid it between the handles of the bag. When all was done, Anna looked at Margaret. "I guess there's no need to wait. I'll go while there's daylight. Can I ask you something? I don't know your middle name."

"It's Mae. But why?"

"If my baby is a girl, I will name her for my mother, Eva. But she will have your middle name if that's all right."

Margaret's eyes welled with tears and they overflowed down her cheeks. "Of course it is. It would be an honor for me."

They descended the stairs to find Perry and Agnes in the front hall, both staring coldly into space and standing apart. Etta hovered up the hall toward the dining room. When she saw them Etta hurried to intercept her before they reached the front door. She threw her arms around Anna, and whispered, "Don't forget me, girl. I be praying for you every day to the Lord above."

"I'll never forget you, Etta. Thank you," she whispered back.

Etta thrust a small cloth bag into her hand and hurried back up the hall, her apron up over her head.

Madison stood aside with his hands in his pockets as Agnes came to embrace Anna. "I'm truly sorry, Anna. I wish you Godspeed." She slipped a small envelope into Anna's hand and Anna thrust it into the pocket of her coat.

Margaret stepped up and embraced her again, "God be with you Anna until we meet again, *my sister*." Whispering the last two words.

As Anna stepped out into the cold November day, she heard Madison say, "Now, Margaret. Up to your room."

CHAPTER 30

Margaret rushed to the window seat beneath her west-facing window. She looked down at Anna walking slowly down the gravel drive, her figure fore-shortened by the view from her high perch. She watched as Anna trudged to the foot of the hill and turned to look back at the house. She looked up at Margaret's window and raised her hand in farewell, then turned and increased her pace. Margaret waved back, knowing that Anna could not see her do so.

The fields along the road were fallow and gray. The hillsides across the way, above the course of Hanson Creek, were also gray, lined with the black trunks of barren trees. The dreary scene, lit by a weak winter sun, was in keeping with Margaret's mood as she watched the receding dark figure walking down the gravel road until it disappeared from sight.

Anna walked until she came to the first ford. She stopped and thought about her choices, and concluded that she had none. I can't go into the settlement and ask for help from almost strangers, not in my condition. I am an outcast orphan, carrying a child from an unknown man. I don't feel ashamed, even though society will probably feel I should be. It is a comfort to know there are people who care for me, but they can do nothing now. It's up to me to fend for myself. I have warm clothing and food for now. Best try to find a place to spend the night and then think about it tomorrow.

She remembered the large boulders where she picked blackberries. With all the leaves that have fallen, perhaps there will be a place to sleep. She made her way up the bank of the creek until she found stepping stones allowing her to cross. On the opposite bank, she stopped and thrust her hand into her pocket to warm it. She found the envelope passed to her by Agnes. She took it out and opened it. Three coins were inside; two large silver dollars like those in her cigar box. The other was gold, unlike anything she'd seen before. It was smaller but said "ten dollars" on it. Ten dollars! There was a picture of a lady on one side and an eagle on the other. It was beautiful and shiny and had a date "1880" on it. This will be for my baby, a gift from one who didn't believe in me at first, but changed.

Anna looked up at the silvery sky and at the high, thin mares-tails clouds. Papa said that meant rain was coming in a day or two. She trudged up the hillside to the rock outcropping and found her thoughts were correct. Dry leaves were knee-deep among them. There would be no roof overhead, but at least there was shelter from night breezes. She picked a spot between two of the larger ones, each nearly the size of her garret room. She set down her bag and used her feet to rake more leaves into a large pile between them, then spread her quilt down over them to make a proper nest. She thought of the robin she had watched build a nest on a ledge on the back porch of the house.

When she sat down to rest on a smaller rock, she realized she had had nothing to eat all day. Baby was moving, reminding her she must think of nourishment. Etta had provided food for her and she ate buttered bread and a thick slice of ham, drinking milk from a pint jar. It made her feel much better. No telling where food will come from after this is all gone, but I'm going to do what I have to do, she said to herself. She walked down to the creek when she had finished and rinsed the jar and filled it with creek water. After that, she determined to stay the afternoon and night, and wait until morning to move on…wherever she decided to go.

Night came and she repeated her meal of earlier in the day, filling her jar again. She had spent most of the day reading from the Bible, by coincidence reading about the Israelites wandering in the desert. I hope it doesn't take me that long! she had thought to herself, amused. Now, weary from tension, she lay down to sleep in all of her clothes, and felt warm enough. She was wearing woolen drawers and shift, with pantaloons, two petticoats, a skirt, and heavy sweater. Then there was the warm coat Margaret had given her and the oilskin jacket over that. She put a knit cap over her head, wrapped herself in the quilt, and went to sleep, warm and comfortable.

Morning came and she awoke with a start, bewildered for a moment with her surroundings. Her nose was cold, but otherwise she had stayed comfortable even though she saw rims of frost on the leaves around her. She rose and brushed the leaves from her clothing, then went a short distance away to sort through the layers of clothing to relieve her urgent bladder. After washing in the creek and another meal of bread and ham, she knew decision time had come.

Several thoughts had roamed her mind during the morning. There was the prospect of seeking mercy in Sycamore, there were caves in the area, but she didn't know where they were. One question kept coming back to dominate her mind: what happened to the home I grew up in? Papa had left, probably sneaking away in the night. Was it empty and abandoned? I am going to go see...if I can find my way. She shook leaves out of her quilt and did her best to straighten her clothing and comb debris out of her hair.

By dead-reckoning, it should be over the ridge behind her. Papa had gone a little west down to Bull Creek, down the creek south, then east up Hanson Creek. It would make sense, it seemed, to cut across, in a northwesterly direction. She picked up her bag, and with a silent prayer, started walking uphill. A high gray overcast had moved in, and she was motivated to find shelter before bad weather would arrive.

Anna walked most of the day, crunching the fallen leaves underfoot, careful to keep from falling in the steeper parts. Occasionally she would find a game trail going in the right direction, making progress easier. Eventually, she was able to reach a downward slope and see across the wide valley she assumed was the course of Bull Creek. The sun was lowering in the west, a bright spot showing through the cloud layer. And there in the distance was a notch in the ridge she recognized. Below her, toward that notch, had to be Papa's farmstead.

She sat on a fallen tree trunk to rest and think. A squirrel was chattering high in the oak tree above her. A shagbark hickory nut hull landed nearby, neatly gnawed open. She brought her thoughts back to the problem. I can't just go walking up to it. What if someone lives there? If they do, I'll have to think of something else. What I must do, if I find it, is look at it from a distance and see what the situation is.

At last, Anna was sitting on a stump in the edge of the woods, screened by some small cedars, looking down at her home place. The slope of the ridge rose behind her. Tears welled in her eyes as she thought of her mother and her tragic loss. Gradually she had recovered some happiness, thanks to Margaret and Etta, only to have it shattered. Now it looked like her plan was spoiled again. Beyond the rail fence in front of her, two mules, three horses, and two cows were scattered in a pasture. There was a haystack by the barn. Just beyond that, a thin thread of smoke rose from the fireplace chimney. No doubt it was occupied. Well, I spent a night in the woods before. I can do it again. It's almost dark so I might as well stay here in the cedars, in a bed of leaves.

Anna made her bed as the night before and ate more food from her sack, this time a slab of cold roast beef and a boiled egg. Across the way, there was a light showing in the log house she knew so well. She imagined a family having supper by candle light, a fire burning in the fireplace, and going to sleep in warm beds. She watched until the light went out, then wrapped herself in her blanket to try to sleep. In spite of her restless emotions, she dropped off to sleep.

She was awakened by the cold touch of raindrops falling on her face. What shall I do? She got up and shook out her blanket, rolling it up to keep it from getting wet. Maybe I can sneak into the barn. I hope there isn't a dog running loose.

She walked across the darkened pasture and reached the barn, circling around to the other side to the entrance she knew. As she reached the door, a hound bayed and came running out toward her. She squatted down to make herself less threatening, and spoke softly, "Hi, doggie. Come here. I have something for you." She made kissing noises and held out a piece of roast beef.

Bone quit barking as soon as she spoke and went up to her. He wagged his tail and sniffed her hand, snatching the beef and swallowing it in a couple of bites. Anna stroked his head and scratched his ears, then entered the barn. Bone stared after her, then trotted back to the porch to lie back down.

CHAPTER 31

Ben Archer had just dropped into a deep sleep, dreaming it was springtime and he was fishing in the clear waters of Bull Creek. Suddenly he was jerked out of the dream by the baying of his dog. Warm in the comfort of his blankets, he debated whether to investigate. Better do it. Might be something after the livestock. He got out of bed, but Bone had stopped barking. Might just be some small animal. He padded across the plank floor and opened the front door. Bone was trotting up the front steps headed for his shelter.

"What is it, boy?"

Bone wagged his tail, but went back to his bed inside the box.

"Must have been nothin', I reckon." Ben noted the rain falling from a dark sky. He went back inside to his own bed.

Anna found the vertical ladder that led to the hayloft. She slowly climbed to the top, stepping into the soft hay. It had the fragrant smell of greens cured in the summer sun. Breathing deeply with relief, she moved to a corner away from the ladder to spread her blanket. Rain began to beat with a stronger tattoo on the shake roof overhead. Giving thanks to God for her good fortune, she was soon asleep.

Ben got up in the early morning light. Rain had slackened, but was still falling gently. He made coffee and stirred cornmeal into boiling water for cornmeal mush. He liked it with milk and a little sorghum stirred in. He scraped some table scraps from last night's supper into Bone's dish and went back in for milk buckets and his jacket.

Whistling a hymn to himself, he strode toward the barn. Bone ran ahead to the side door, wagging his tail. He stood expectantly at the door, trying to stick his nose in the gap where it met the framing.

"What're you after there, silly dog?" Ben said. "You after a big ole mouse or something? C'mon."

Bone gave up and followed him around to the other side of the barn where the cows were waiting to be let in to their stalls. He'd put a measure of coarse ground wheat in their feedboxes, and when he opened the door they rushed in. He latched the stanchions against their necks to keep them in place.

"All right, girls. Let's get to the milkin'," he said. "You first, Goldie. Whatcha got this mornin?"

Anna was startled awake by the sound of a man whistling loudly, then talking to the dog. She jumped up and crawled to the peak of the barn where there were plank doors for pitching out hay. She could see through the crack between them. She saw a tall young man with yellow hair and no beard striding along carrying two buckets. He must be coming to milk.

Sure enough, soon she heard him talking to his cows, then the sound of milk streaming against the side of the metal pail. I've made a mistake, she thought. I'm stuck up here until he leaves, and I'm getting pretty desperate to visit that outhouse. I'll just have to grit my teeth and wait. What if he climbs up here? What would he do to me? Are all men like that one in the woods? I need something to fight with. I think he's using the hay outside first, so maybe I'm safe. I hope he leaves pretty soon.

She crept slowly over to the side the stalls were on. There was an opening she could peer through, beneath the shed roof. She watched him finish the first cow, his milk pail filled with foaming milk. A barn cat appeared and he poured some milk in a shallow dish for it. He set the pail on a shelf out of reach, and went to the next cow. She heard him say, "All right Bessie, your turn. Let's see if you can beat old Goldie."

He finally finished and left with both pails, headed toward the springhouse. She hurried to climb down the ladder and found a battered feed bucket in a corner. An old homemade pitchfork leaned against a wall. She took both back up into the loft and used the bucket to ease the cramps in her stomach. She thought of her recent past and Gertrude Madison. Now I can be just like her, but I don't have a servant girl to empty this for me.

The pitchfork was not very long, so it would work well for defense. It had been made from a piece of oak with a natural bend. The bent end had been split in thirds, with rawhide binding at the split, and the three tines steamed and wedged apart, then rounded and sharpened. Hardened by age, it looked dangerous.

She ate another boiled egg and piece of bread, realizing that her supply was getting low. She drank the last of her water. He was going to have to go somewhere, or she'd have to wait until after dark, when he was asleep. Long term, she'd need to find a way to wash clothes and wash herself. For now, she waited and watched. The question now was whether there was a wife, or other people living here. The man was young, not much older than her brother, Evan, now long gone.

He soon came out of the springhouse and came back around the barn. She went to the east gable and peeked through the crack between those doors. He walked out in the pasture and banged on a pan of feed. All five horses and mules came running. They followed him into a corral and he closed the gate. After a little while, he was driving away in a wagon pulled by the two mules, her friend from last night trotting alongside. He was headed for the woods across the pasture.

The time had come to find out if this could work. Anna straightened her clothing and combed out her hair, braiding it and coiling it into a bun. She put a woolen scarf over her head and climbed down the ladder, bringing the bucket with her. The only way to go is the direct approach, she decided.

She left the bucket for the time being and marched right by the house and up to the front door. She felt confident by the fact that no one else had come out for a trip to the outhouse after a night's sleep.

Anna knocked on the door, holding her breath, breathing a silent prayer. There was no response, so she pulled the leather latch string and stepped inside. She wasn't fully prepared for the feelings that overcame her as she thought back to standing at that stove, laughing with her mother. The interior had changed, yet was still much the same—different table, washstand in a different place, a different kitchen cabinet. But it was the only real home she had ever known. I have to get busy, she said to herself. She hurried to the bedroom where her mother died and stood silently, staring. Then she noted that the bed where she had slept was still there, behind a different curtain.

What I need now is food. Will it be stealing? It will be, but when the time comes, I will pay for it, even if it takes all the money I have. She went to the stove, lifted a lid with a handle and slipped a few thin sticks of wood on the dying embers and opened the chimney damper a bit. The kettle was still full of hot water so she went to the washstand and filled the tin basin with hot water. It really felt wonderful to soap her hands and face clean again. Refilling the kettle from the full bucket, she carried it back to the stove and set it to heat again.

The only food that came easily to hand was a bowl of mush and some extra slices of fried ham. There wasn't time to reheat it. No telling how long he'd be in the woods. It really tasted good; some nourishment for the baby. She washed the bowl, dried it, and put it back in the cabinet. There were several tin plates and cups, so she took one of each just in case, plus a fork, spoon, and small knife from the drawer. It was time to clear out, so she took a quick look around and scurried out the front door. She took her bucket and used the outhouse, then checked out the smokehouse and springhouse. There was a smell of cured meat in the smokehouse, with two sides of bacon, two hams and a pork shoulder hanging on hooks. In the springhouse, she found a five-gallon crock of sauerkraut, a crate of turnips, a crate of potatoes, and nearly a bushel of apples. The morning milk was covered and cooling, so she drank as many cups as she could hold. Taking her "purchases" with her she climbed back into the loft. Then a thought: She went back down with her jar to fill it with water for later. As she was leaving the springhouse, she heard the wagon returning, but she made it back to the barn in time. Next time, I'll check the henhouse. Eggs can be eaten raw.

Ben drove the wagon around the side of the barn and in front of it where he split wood. During last winter's work in the woods, he had cut shingle-lengths of straight-grained oak and left them to season. Now he hauled them in to make split shingles for Pa's room addition. As he came close to the barn, Bone ran ahead, sniffing at the side door just as he had this morning. Then, nose to the ground, he ran around to the front of the house and barked once. In a few minutes, he came back. Ben watched him trail to the outhouse, bark again, then to the smokehouse and springhouse.

"What the heck are you doin', you silly hound?" He said, laughing to himself. Shaking his head, he climbed down and unloaded the cuts of wood around a grooved log and the stump where he split wood. As he drove back around the barn to unharness the mules, he noticed Bone with his nose to the barn door again. Strange, he thought.

CHAPTER 32

Anna watched through the crack between the doors as the man went to work. He took off his coat and rolled up the sleeves of his flannel shirt to his elbows, exposing faded red underwear. He took one of the pieces of wood and set it on the stump, took a one-bladed axe and placed it carefully near the edge. Then he whacked it with a club and split off the side. He didn't swing the axe overhead like Papa did when he split wood. He kept doing the same thing for several of the cuts, squaring them up. Then she remembered something from her childhood. When she was a little girl, her papa took her with him in the wagon across Bull Creek and up in a hollow in the woods. An old man with a long gray beard was doing the same thing. He was going to make shingles. Papa had built the chicken house and needed them for the roof. The old man showed her each step and gave her a shingle of her own to take home.

She was sitting in the hay and something brushed against her shoulder. She jumped up, then saw what it was. It was the black and white cat she had seen that morning. "I'm sorry, kitty," she whispered. She sat back down and stroked its fur and it rewarded her with an arched back and a purr.

Anna continued to watch as the man split off pieces about a thumb width until he had a stack. Then he picked up another tool, a long blade with a vertical handle. She even remembered the old man called it a "froe." Now she watched the same process. He set each piece on end in the groove of the log, put the froe in the middle and split it into two thin shingles by hitting the froe with a smaller club. She watched him work all morning; the dog sitting on his haunches and doing the same. Neither of us have much else to do, she thought.

Finally, he stopped and wiped his brow with his sleeve and said to the dog. "C'mon Bone, let's get some dinner." He slung his coat over his shoulder and walked around toward the front of the house.

Anna went back to her corner and peeled a turnip and ate it, along with a helping of sauerkraut, an apple, and the last stale slice of bread from Etta. I wonder what Etta and Margaret are doing now, she thought. I've been gone only a couple of days, but it seems much longer. I hope that evil man has not been mean to Margaret. She felt drowsy, so she wrapped herself in the quilt and settled down for a nap. The baby was moving around in its nest at the same time, also getting settled.

Ben went into the house to "scare up" something to eat, as he would put it. He had some mush left from breakfast, so he could slice it and fry it along with heating the leftover fried ham. He stoked up the fire, added a spoonful of coffee to the old grounds in the pot, filled it with water and set it on to heat. Now where's that bowl of mush? he thought. It was in that little bowl with the blue rim. I put a dish towel over it right here on the cabinet. Am I nuts? And where's the ham? Was that yesterday instead of today? The bowl is in the cabinet and no mush. Maybe I'm going crazy, but that won't feed me. Guess I'll fry a couple of eggs and get back to work.

And work he did all afternoon, methodically splitting out shingles until he had converted all the wood into its final product. He was supervised by Bone who sat watching each movement with interest. He was also observed from the loft of the barn. Anna awoke and listened to the steady sound of his work outside. She stayed wrapped in her quilt and began to fret about finding more food if he didn't leave the premises again. She decided to sleep as much as possible in the afternoon, and use nighttime to obtain more. She began to have doubts about the long-term plan. I need a better way to wash myself and my clothes and maybe cook myself better food. It doesn't feel good not to be clean and my baby needs to have good food from me. Well, it depends on how things go for the next few days. She drifted off to sleep.

The noise of the evening milking woke her up again, the man talking to the cows, then the cat. He was whistling again. I wonder what his situation is. How did he come to live here? What will he do if he finds me?

Evening ritual was the same as the morning, but after milk was put away, he went to the haystack at the other end of the barn and forked hay into a rack across the fence where the horses were, then filled a smaller one in the corral where the milk cows were let out.

Anna waited patiently until darkness fell, but the rain clouds had cleared and a quarter moon provided some light. It seemed a long time before the window in the house went dark. She waited a few more minutes, then slipped outside with her bucket to go to the outhouse. Bone barked once, then ran around the house to catch up with her, wagging his tail. Thankfully, she'd thought to save a small piece of meat for him and he gulped it down.

He accompanied her as she made the rounds to drink her fill of milk, gather more turnips and apples in the bag Etta had provided, and venture into the henhouse. About a dozen hens were roosting in the darkness on poles a few feet off the floor. They shuffled and stirred as she crept in and felt in the nest boxes. She came away with three eggs.

Bone escorted her back to the barn and she went back to the loft to eat an apple and a turnip. Then she broke the ends of two of the eggs and sucked out the contents. Anything for the baby.

The day Anna was sent away, Margaret sat for some time at her window, long after Anna disappeared from sight. She tried her door, but it had been locked. Any semblance of unity in my family has been lost, she thought. Through the long afternoon, she paced the floor and wondered where Anna was and what would happen to her. She tried to read, but couldn't concentrate. Before suppertime, she went to her desk and wrote two short messages. The first was to Abraham Phillips:

Dear Professor Phillips,

My father has returned from Washington and is quite upset that I have attempted to apply myself to teaching. For the time being he has forbade me to come to Sycamore, so I regret that I will not

*be seeing you until I can either persuade him to change; or decide
to take myself away from my family.*

  With deepest respect and regrets.
  Sincerely,
  Margaret Madison

She was unsure whether the second was proper, but decided to write it
anyway, to George Zinn:

Dear George,

*I hope you will not deem me too bold for writing, but I must
explain why you will not see me until I can sort out our family
situation. Since my father's return from Washington, he forbade
me coming to Sycamore, as he feels teaching is unworthy of our
family. Of course I disagree, but must abide by his wishes for
the time being.*

  *He also sent Anna away without allowing me to assist her
and no plan for her future safety or sustenance. If there is anything you can do to find out where she is or how to assist her,
please try to get word to me. She is as dear to me as a sister, and
I am greatly concerned.*

  *I have enjoyed our time together and hope I can resolve this
problem.*

  With my kindest thoughts,
  Margaret

She folded both sheets of cream-colored bond, and sealed them with wax
seals. She would have to get them to Hank Green to see if he would deliver
them. Just as she finished, she heard a key turn in the lock and she went
to the door and opened it. Etta was standing there, her face set in sorrow.

"The Colonel, he send me to acks you want to come downstairs," she
said softly.

Margaret embraced her. "Oh, Etta, I don't know what to do. I'm so
sorry."

"Me too. Not you fault. He and Missus neither comin' to eat. Say they want trays. I'm fixin' 'em, but if you want, you and me can eat in the cookhouse like before."

"I'd like that, Etta. I'll be right down."

Etta left and Margaret tucked the messages in her bodice and followed her. They had a quiet meal together, the only topic of conversation being thoughts about Anna, and dismay about what could be done. Margaret told Etta about her messages, and Etta praised her for trying. "If me or Ike gets a chance to hear from anybody, we let you know."

Margaret went to the barn to find Hank Green in the farm office writing up a list of supplies the farm needed. He promised secrecy and prompt delivery of the messages.

In the days that followed, there was no news from any quarter. Margaret moped about the house, forbidden to go for a ride, a virtual prisoner. It appeared that her mother was essentially the same. She saw no contact between her parents and there were no more family meals at the big mahogany table.

CHAPTER 33

Anna was cold during the night and added all the layers she could; the coat, slicker, knit sweater, and extra socks. With the quilt around her, and burrowing deeper into the hay, she was able to sleep until early morning. She stayed wrapped for warmth through the now familiar cow milking, talking, and whistling of the man. As soon as all was quiet, she used her bucket, then huddled to watch the house. Smoke rose straight up from the chimney in a strong column, and she thought about how wonderful it would be to sit in front of a roaring fire as she had done as a child. The roof top and all the surrounding grass was glistening with heavy frost in the early morning sun.

After a time, the man came back out toward the barn dressed in nicer clothes; black pants and boots, white shirt, newer hat, and leather coat. He walked around the barn and whistled at the horses. She went to the other gable and saw him catch the saddle horse. A little later, back to the front, she saw him ride away, down the lane she knew led down toward Bull Creek. The dog, Bone, trotted along behind.

I wonder if he is courting, she thought. He is nice-looking and it makes sense he would be thinking in that direction, since it appears he lives alone. Oh, wait. It's Sunday. She counted on her fingers. It *is* Sunday. He must be going to Service in Sycamore. That gives me lots of time.

She sprang into action, getting clean underwear out of her bag and taking her bucket down the ladder and going to the outhouse. She went to the house, boldly lifting the latch and going straight to the stove. She opened the draft and the damper and filled the firebox to get a roaring fire going. She poured water into the largest pan she could find and put it on the stove, along with the kettle, and made plans for a sponge bath and breakfast.

Ben rode directly to Sycamore and met his family at the schoolhouse church. There was a good crowd in spite of the cold weather. It was the one time in the week when farm chores were put from the minds of the citizens along the creeks and in the coves. They followed scripture about work pretty strictly when it came to the Sabbath, including the part from St. Luke which read, "Which of you shall have an ass or an ox fallen into a pit, and will not straightway pull him out on the Sabbath day?" Almost any farmer could have that sort of thing happen.

After the service, everyone circulated and caught up on any news in the area. Ben looked for George, but he hadn't attended. Must be sick or something. He was invited to the family dinner at the farm, so Oren begged to be hoisted up behind Ben's saddle for the ride there. For Ben, it was great to be back with his family and enjoy a roast chicken dinner prepared by his new step-mother. She made fresh biscuits, mashed potatoes and gravy, and steamed cabbage—much better fare than his pot of beans, or boiled turnips and hominy.

Anna was safely back in her barn loft hideaway by mid-day, feeling much better after good hot food. She'd found more eggs to scramble and there was ham to fry. She'd boiled a few potatoes at the same time as she heated wash water, so she'd have some for later. There was a set of shelves in the back room where her parents had slept, and there was a good quantity of fruit in jars: apples, blackberries, strawberries, and gooseberries. She opened a jar of apples and ate part, taking the rest for later.

She found some wire and strung it across the corner of the loft to hang the underwear she'd washed out after using her bathing water. She liked the fresh smell of the soap Margaret had given her and her hair felt clean for the first time since she was banished from the Madison household.

It was a challenge cleaning up and leaving everything just as she had found it, including refilling the water bucket. Now, as she reclined on the quilt, baby was moving again. She placed her hand on her stomach inside her coat and could feel faint little twitches.

Maybe I can make this work for a little while, she thought, but it will be several months before the baby comes. Is that realistic? It is also boring during the times I have to stay in the loft. Reading the Bible can last for only a while. What I really miss, besides being with Etta and Margaret, is feeling useful—doing work and having the satisfaction of doing it well. With these thoughts, she drifted into sleep.

It was mid-afternoon when Ben rode back into the lane beside the house and back to the barn to unsaddle his horse. The day was bright and clear, but cold, even with the sun still high in the west. He looked forward to stirring up a good fire in the fireplace. Bone immediately went into the same routine he had seen before, nose to the ground, trailing all over the backyard to the various outbuildings. Ben ignored him and rode around the back of the barn, putting Charger in one of the stalls and rubbing him down with a burlap bag while Charger crunched on the oats in his feedbox.

As he started back around toward the house, Bone was headed toward that side door to the barn again, this time more excited than usual. As he approached it, he gave voice to several long howls, rearing up and putting his paws high on the door.

"What ya got, boy?" Ben said. "Got a coon treed in there?" He rubbed Bone's neck and Bone dropped to all fours, still wagging his tail furiously and sniffing the edge of the door opening.

"Well, let's see what ya got."

Ben opened the door and Bone squeezed through ahead of him and went straight to the ladder, standing on hind legs again and barking.

"All right. Down, boy. You ain't gonna be happy until I take a look, are ya?"

Ben climbed up the vertical ladder and as his eyes cleared the opening into hay, he was astounded by what he saw. There, a few feet away, stood a girl or woman with a determined look, holding a pitchfork pointed in his direction.

"Don't come any closer!" she said in a loud voice, but there was a tremor of fear.

"Don't worry, but I'm climbin' on up so's I don't have to hang here." He climbed to the top and stared in disbelief. "Do you mind tellin' me what you're doin' here?"

"What are you doing in my house?"

"*Your* house? Oh, you're that Friedrich girl, ain't you?"

"I had no place else to go."

"Now don't be afraid of me. My name's Ben...Benjamin Archer. My pa bought this place. What do you mean, you have no place to go?"

Anna's composure began to crumble and she was angry at herself when tears began to leak from her eyes. Her words came out in a rush. "My mama died and my father went away and he wouldn't let me go with him and I worked for the Madison family but he put me out..." Her words turned into sobs, much to her shame. *Why am I being such a weakling!*

Ben didn't know how to respond. "Well, hey. You can keep that pitchfork if it makes you feel better, but you have nothing to worry about from me. I lost my mother, but I have a sister and a new step-mother. Ain't no way I'd hurt a woman.

"Tell ya what. I'm gonna climb back down and wait outside the barn. You get yourself together, bring your fork, and come to the house. I'm fixin' to crank up a good fire. We can sit ten feet apart and you can tell me about it. We'll try to figger what's best for you."

"I don't trust anybody."

"Don't blame you a bit. You don't know me. But I know me, and I'd die before I'd cause you more trouble than you have now. All right, I'm gonna wait outside."

Anna felt ashamed of her loss of control. I've told myself I'll be strong and there I was bawling like a baby. It has been a strain, though, trying to hide. And it was a shock being discovered, thanks to the dog, Bone. He, Ben, was really surprised, but he seemed not to be mad. In fact, he seemed nice about it in a way. Now I don't have much choice but to talk to him. I feel foolish taking this hayfork with me, but he said it was all right.

Anna straightened her clothing and brushed the hay out of her hair and off her clothing. Then she put on her boots and coat and climbed down the ladder and went outside, fork clutched in her hand. She'd taken three dollars out of her bag and put them in her pocket. As soon as she stepped out the door, Bone came running up to her wagging his tail and trying to lick her hand.

"So now you're nice to me after giving me up," she said to him.

Ben was ten feet away as promised, and smiled before he turned to lead the way to the house. Anna followed at the same distance, her mind churning with thoughts about the talk to come. Do I have to tell him everything? Will he want to turn me in to the sheriff, or tell everyone about me?

He went inside and left the door open for her. Bone had been trained that he was not to invade that space so he stopped and watched the door close behind Anna.

Ben had already set the fire screen aside and was reaching for the poker. "You can take that rocker over there if ya want...uh, do ya mind tellin' me your name?"

"I'm Anna. But before I sit down...I have stolen some of your food. This may not be enough." The silver dollars clinked as she laid them on the table.

"Now you put them back in your pocket. What's a couple of apples or whatever." He smiled at her again. "I will say, when that bowl of left-over mush was gone, I thought I was goin' plumb crazy."

Anna left them lying on the table and went to the rocking chair on the other side of the fireplace, leaned her pitchfork against the log wall and sat down. Ben had stacked logs on the glowing embers and flames started to lick the seasoned oak as he set the fire screen back in place. He pulled out a chair, took off his hat and coat, placing them on another, and sat down. He looked into the growing flames, then turned to face her.

"Well, I never expected to be here like this on a Sunday evening, but here we are. When ya get warm enough, you can take off your coat," he said.

"I thought I could hide. Now it doesn't make much sense, but I didn't know what else to do. What are you going to do to me?"

"I surely don't know. What do ya want to happen? I ain't a mean person." He ran his hand through his thatch of blond hair. "Why don't ya tell me how you got in this fix?"

Anna drew a deep breath and stared into the fire, trying to decide what to do. I can't see that I have much to lose to lay out the whole story. He's either going to believe me and treat me with mercy, or he isn't. What I say may help...or not.

"Here's how it all began," she said.

CHAPTER 34

"Everything started going wrong when Mama was killed by the horse. Before then it was not so bad. Papa was stern, never happy, but Mama was nice to me and so was my brother Evan. But when she died..." Anna stopped, taking a deep breath and gazing at the fire.

"I was at the buryin'," said Ben. "I saw you there."

Anna looked at him. "You were there? I didn't know. I was in a daze. It was after the burying that everything changed. Papa never said what he planned. He hauled me up to the Madison place and showed me to this man, the 'Colonel' they call him, like I was a heifer for sale...."

She went on to explain her embarrassment, then the surprise that her father and brother were leaving and she couldn't go. Then she told about being bewildered when she was delivered to the Madisons and left there. She talked on and on with little interruption, telling how she settled in to her duties there. She described her relationships with each of the members of the household as the months went by...some good, some not so good.

"Now to the hard part," she said. "I'm not sure I can talk about it, or if you'll understand." She stopped again. Flames were leaping high in the fireplace, and the logs shifted in a shower of sparks.

"How about I put the coffee on?" Ben said. "I also got a pot of beans soakin' and I'll clap them on the stove, too. We can eat after bit."

"I saw them when I was snooping in here this morning," Anna said. "I need to go out back for a minute. I promise I'll come right back and finish my story."

Ben nodded. "Sure." After she left, he thought to himself, I don't know what's going to come next, and I sure don't know what to do.

"This next part is the hardest part," Anna said. "It's not something that people talk about with strangers, especially a woman to a man. You'll have to forgive me. It's embarrassing." She stood and unbuttoned her coat, draping it over a chair. "You can probably note what my problem is, but it isn't what you might expect."

"Yes," Ben said quietly, "but you go right ahead. It's just the two of us here."

"I was out in the woods picking blackberries and a man attacked me. I ran, I hid, and I fought back when he caught me. I hit him with a rock, but he knocked me unconscious..."

"Too bad somebody didn't shoot the sonofabitch, s'cuse me, with a shotgun. Do you know who it was?"

Anna sat back down in the rocking chair. She shook her head. "No, but I'd know him if I saw him again."

"I hope I'm around when you do. That's the lowest form of life, takin' advantage."

"It's what caused me to be kicked out of the Madison household. The rest of the family might have kept me, but Colonel Madison was in a rage and banished me from their house. Said I'd brought shame—"

"Sounds like another one needs a horse-whippin.'"

"So here I am. Are you going to turn me in?"

"I'm not doin' nuthin' you don't agree to. You've had enough to deal with. I'm tryin' to think of something. Pa just got re-married and his new wife has two girls. I've still got a sister and two brothers at home. They're jammed up, or they might take you in..."

Anna let silence hang in the air, then said, "When I was at the Madison's, I worked for my keep." Another pause. "If...if I cook and clean and do chores, can I still sleep in your barn? I know it would have to be a secret, since we're like we are...two single people...."

Ben looked at her as she spoke, then put his elbows on his knees and stared at the floor. After a short time in thought, he sat upright and turned to her again. Her face was set in a worried frown. "Here's the thing, Anna. You're right about the two of us and people gossipin'. I think everything you said makes sense except one thing. Goodness knows I'm not good at cookin' and keepin' house. But I ain't about to have you sleep in a dang barn in the winter, not in your condition. How about this? Now don't interrupt me 'til I finish. How about you take that room over there and I build a door on it that you can latch from the other side so's you feel safe, and you sleep in there—"

"I couldn't take—"

"I believe I said don't interrupt me."

"Sorry."

"What would be wrong with that? There's a bed in the part-loft where I bet your brother slept. That'll be fine for me. I'm goin' down to my folks' tomorrow morning to take those shingles. I'll go on to Sycamore and talk George out of some of that nice casket lumber and make a door by tomorrow night."

"You'd do that?"

"I would. You see, I got a sister, Josie, and I keep picturin' her in a fix, and what would I do for her. Now you can talk."

Anna found that she could not talk, not for a few moments. She began to cry and covered her face with her hands. Finally she was able to say, in a weak voice, "You are the kindest person I have met."

"Naw. It's just what a body ought to do. I can't claim to know much of the Bible, but I do remember where it talks about helpin' others...that part that says something like '...whatever you did for the least of these brothers and sisters of mine, you did for me.' You heard that one?"

"Yes, I have," she said softly. "But I didn't know I'd ever see it happen."

"Now, for tonight. You go get your stuff out of the barn. I'll flip that mattress in there and put on clean bedding I had extra for if any of my family came to visit. I'm gonna sleep in the hay tonight, roust out early anyway. When you go to sleep tonight, just pull the latch string, so you'll feel safe and get a good night's sleep."

"That doesn't seem fair."

"'Course it is, cause it's me decidin'."

The plan was put into effect, with both Ben and Anna deep in thought about the awkwardness of their new situation. Many details would have to be ironed out as they went along. Anna was still wary and Ben still determined not to let her feel threatened in any way. He was pleased to see that the pitchfork was still leaning against the wall by the fireplace. He smiled to himself at the image of her brave stance with it when he first discovered her.

By the time they got everything organized, it was evening. Ben went out to milk the cows, and when he came back in the table was set for two and Anna was at the stove. She pulled a cast iron skillet out of the oven filled with golden brown cornbread.

"Wow. You didn't waste any time." He said.

She said, "The beans are done, too."

It was a silent meal, for the most part. Finally, Ben cleared his throat and asked. "If ya want to look around and make a list. I can get anything the kitchen needs when I'm out tomorrow."

Anna had waited for him to ask. "It'll take a while to know. Could use more baking powder. I didn't see much flour. I make bread, but I need some sour dough starter. Do you have any?"

"No. I've done cornbread, but not this good. I'll ask Becky—that's my step-ma—or I'll find some someplace. Let me know in the mornin' if you think of more."

"I will. And use that money there."

Ben lay in the loft, trying to go to sleep. He'd changed out of his Sunday clothes before milking and moved the rest of his clothing out of the shed bedroom, carrying them up to the loft. Now, fully dressed in tomorrow's clothes and wrapped in quilts, he thought; this ain't half bad. My problem with going to sleep is wondering what I just did. Hope it's not stupid. When I look at Anna, she seems like a sister in need of help and I think of how it would be for Josie to be in a fix like that. Anna's a little older, probably nearer the age of Rose Harvey. She's right about keeping it a secret. I've heard of people "living in sin," as they call it, where some men have gone in wearing masks and taken folks out and whipped them with switches. Seems to me that's playing God. We ain't going to be living in sin, but it might look like it to outsiders.

Ben had finally dropped off to sleep, and now awoke in the early dawn. He brushed bits of hay from his clothes and climbed down to ground level.

Nothin' like being close to your work, he thought, as he walked around to the other side of the barn to let the cows in. He retrieved the milk buckets from the springhouse, and set to work. A pretty fair column of smoke was rising straight up in the cold morning air, so it made him think Anna was up and around. As he finished with Goldie and walked around to start on Bessie, his question was answered. Anna was headed for the outhouse, Bone in close escort. From that day forward, it was his routine every time she went, which was frequent. He would sit on his haunches and wait, eyes on the door, sometimes perking up his ears, until she emerged and he could escort her back to the house. Ben smiled to himself. *Looks like I've lost my dog.*

After he finished with milking and had put hay out, he headed for the house. The latchstring was out, so he knocked on the door and went in. Anna was at the stove, stirring a pot of something. She poured a cup of coffee and set it on the table across from her. "I hope you were able to sleep."

"Yes, it was just fine. How about you?"

"At first, it was hard because of the memories, but I thank you for the bed. I didn't make much breakfast, but I opened a jar of applesauce, fried some eggs, and made some mush...to make up for that I stole," she said with a slight smile. "Is there anything I can do while you're gone?"

"Well, I don't want to take advantage, but if you want to, you can skim some cream and churn it. You know where it is, I think," he said, with a smile of his own. "I'll take some of the extra milk down to the family, but drink all you want."

Ben hitched the team of gray Percherons to the wagon and pulled around front, loaded the stacks of shingles, and headed down the valley. They moved at a brisker pace than the mules, so it wasn't long before he pulled in to the farmstead. The new room was beginning to take shape. The foundation stones had been leveled and three courses of logs had been notched and laid. Pa was already out working on it when Ben drove up.

"Hey, Ben," he said. "Thanks for the shingles. They'll go a long way. I've got a few split so far, so we'll see how many more we need."

"You're welcome. I'll run this gallon of milk inside. The cows are startin' to taper off a little, especially Goldie. I may have to come and borrow some back in a few weeks."

"That'll be good."

When Ben went inside, Josie and Becky were working side-by-side finishing up the breakfast dishes. Josie was surprised when Ben came and hugged her.

"What's going on, Ben? Why'd you do that?"

"I've just been thinking how you filled in for Ma and worked so hard. Thank you. And now, you, too, Becky. I'm glad you're in the family."

They both looked some taken aback, and both murmured their thanks.

"And, oh, Becky. Do you have any sourdough starter you can spare?"

"Sure. I'll get you some. I didn't know you baked bread. Do you know how to feed it and keep it alive?"

Now it was Ben's turn to look embarrassed, especially when Josie looked at him with wonder. "Sure, sure. I know how."

Ben was successful in Sycamore, buying flour at the mill and baking powder at Guthrie's store. He went to see his friend George at the blacksmith shop and explained what he wanted.

"You're sure you're not going to bury somebody?" said George.

"Not right now. I'm still trying to fix up a few things at the Friedrich place. I'll need hinges and a hasp, too."

"Speakin' of Friedrich, Ben, I need to tell you something to keep private. I got this note from Margaret, told me Madison ran off the Friedrich girl— remember the one I told you came here once, the good-lookin' redhead?"

"I seem to recall."

"Well, he went nuts, I guess. He won't let Margaret out of his sight to come back to Sycamore to help teach. She asked me to check around and see what happened to the girl. Seems they were close. Wants to know if she's safe and if she can help her in any way."

"I'll sure keep an eye out for her, George."

"Thanks, my friend."

Ben got back home in the early afternoon and unloaded his purchases on the front porch before unharnessing the horses and turning them loose. He came back to the house and found Anna taking a pie out of the oven.

"What ya got there, Anna?" he said.

She was still unsmiling, with a look of worry on her face. "It's just a blackberry pie."

He walked across the room, but stayed on the opposite side of the table. "That's just fine, Anna. But let me say something. I can see that you really want to do a good job, but don't feel like ya got to knock yourself out. I ain't a fancy person like them Madisons, so just you make sure you take good care of yourself."

He saw her lips quiver, and she said quietly, "Thank you. I just don't want you to change your mind."

"I ain't going to. Now, is that those beans warming on the stove?"

It was, so he ate a quick bowl, plus cornbread with fresh butter churned that morning. He also enjoyed a glass of buttermilk before setting to work on the door. Anna had filled both wood boxes while he was away and had made plans for their evening meal. As soon as he gave her the small crock of starter and the flour, she set right to work mixing a batch of bread dough to percolate overnight.

He had the door finished and hung by suppertime, when Anna had prepared ham and fried potatoes with a serving of sauerkraut. During the meal, he told her about Margaret's message to George.

"It's good of her to think of me," Anna said. "But I don't know that it changes anything. She can't do anything as long as her papa is like he is. Maybe I should find a way to tell her that I'm all right without saying where I am."

"I think so, too," Ben said. "Next time I go down, I can put a note in their mailbox, maybe. And thanks again for what you're doing. The food is really good."

"You're welcome. It's little enough for what you've done for me."

CHAPTER 35

Thanksgiving Day was not a big day of celebration in the Missouri hills, but a time when families usually gathered to visit. On this day, however, travel was discouraged by the year's first snowfall. Accumulation was not heavy, but driving wind and cold temperatures made it a day to stay home by the fire.

The three members of the Madison family gathered at the long table for a noon meal of roast chicken with dressing and a sweet potato casserole. Etta also served green beans from those she and Anna had put up in the summer. She baked a pumpkin pie and topped it with whipped cream

It was a dreary meal with little conversation and no mention of Thanksgiving, a feeling distant from all those present. Margaret thought instead of the note she had received yesterday from Hank Green. She knew the handwriting the moment she saw it, and had rushed to her room to tear open the seal. It read:

> *Dear Margaret,*
>
> *I had to get word to you as soon as I could. I hope you have not worried about me too much. I am safe and have shelter and food, so I will be fine. It is best if you do not try to find me because it might cause more trouble for you and for me. As soon as I can do so and be safe, I will contact you again.*
> *With affection,*
> *Anna*

Margaret was glad to receive word, but puzzled by the content of the note. I can't imagine where she might be, she thought. It sounds like some family might have felt sorry for her and taken her in, but it doesn't make sense she couldn't tell me where she is. What harm could it possibly do?

Ben had gotten back to working in the woods, using the one-man cross-cut to cut down trees and work them up into finished product: lengths for railroad ties, fence rails, and fireplace wood. He had been taking the shotgun along because of a large covey of quail in the area. He'd managed to get four of them for Thanksgiving and Anna fixed them for dinner, after Ben told her what the day meant.

Anna was becoming more secure and comfortable around him, and during the meal, she said, "Ben, I want to say again that I am *thankful* that you have taken me in. Otherwise, I don't know what would have happened to me."

"Well, Anna, I have to say the same thing. My life is a lot better since you're here. Seems like before, I didn't get much work done for tryin' to feed myself and stuff like that...and not very well, like you're doin'."

Anna looked a little embarrassed. "I'm glad you're happy with it. Now, as soon as we finish and I clean up, can we talk about a few things?"

"Sure. I'm not doing anything out there today, except milk and feed, of course."

A little later they were seated in rockers on opposite sides of the fireplace. Ben had stoked up the fire and the house was warm.

Anna cleared her throat and spoke. "This may not be something you want to talk about, but I don't know much about what's to come. I've been trying to figure what to expect. People say a baby takes nine months, so I guess that's right."

"I wouldn't know. I wish you could talk to Rebecca. I know a cow is supposed to take around two hundred and eighty-three days, but that don't help, I reckon."

"I hope not! But that may not be too much different, I guess. Anyway, nine months would put it toward the middle of March. Seems to me I need to start making things for it to wear. I can knit and I can sew, but my problem is I don't know how big a baby is to start with."

"You've never seen one?"

"Not that I remember. We almost never went anywhere. A woman came by once with a baby, but it wasn't new-born. At least I hope not."

"Well, I saw Oren when he was born about five years ago, but I don't remember exactly."

"How big do you think?"

He held his hands apart, like a fisherman describing a catch. "He wasn't very big, and he was wrinkly and pink. Well...let me see. Maybe about the size of a possum...except better lookin' and no tail. And of course possums have fur."

Anna smiled. "I would hope a baby would be quite a bit different."

"That may be a little too big. Maybe like the cat? Thing is, they have a big round head for their size."

"Thank you for that!" Anna said.

Ben turned red, and Anna laughed, the first time he had heard her do so. Then he saw the humor in it and laughed himself. "Sorry about that. Not the right thing to say."

"Well, I need to make a list of stuff I need and hope you can get it for me. I have a little money Missus Madison gave me when I left and we can use that."

"Hey! I got an idea. Ma had a trunk she kept baby stuff in, I think. Now, I don't know if it's still there, but I could sneak in when they're gone and see what I can find. I'll skip Sunday meetin' this Sunday."

Ben saddled Charger and rode to his family farmstead on the following Sunday morning. The sun had come out and melted the snow, but it was still a brisk day. He timed his arrival to be sure they had left for Sycamore.

It gave him a strange feeling to invade their house while they were away, but he convinced himself it was the only way to get Anna what she needed without giving away their secret. He tied Charger behind the house, then went around to the front door. As in most of the community, the door had no lock. He hated to snoop all over the house, so he went first to the bedroom of his parents. Sure enough, there was a battered old trunk under the bed. It was leather-bound, with brass corners and latches.

He dragged it out and opened it to find the tray on top held mostly papers, a Bible, and old pictures, including the tintype of his father in his Civil War uniform. It had been on the mantle last time he saw it. Getting back to his mission, he lifted out the tray and found what he came for. He took out tiny knit boots, a flannel nightgown, and what looked like undershirts. Digging a little deeper, he pulled out a little velvet dress with lace trim, probably saved from when Josie was a baby. There was a matching bonnet. All of the items were amazingly small, but Anna should be able to use them as patterns. He found a stack of folded squares, which he took to be diapers. Why did she save those? He decided to take all of them. It made him think to look again in the top tray. Sure enough, he found a few safety pins, those neat gadgets that weren't too common. Except for the diapers, he took only one example of the other items, folding them neatly and carrying the stack back around to his horse. He stowed them in the saddlebags, rode back by the new room addition, noting that it was getting close to adding the roof. By the looks inside the house, they really needed it.

When Ben rode into his own yard, he didn't wait to unsaddle his horse, but tied him out front like a visitor and clumped up the steps with his prizes. When he burst into the room, he was hit by the aroma of fresh-baked bread, which Anna was just drawing out of the oven.

"Wow, does that smell good!" he said.

She turned and saw the bundles under his arm. She almost smiled again. "And that looks good. A success?"

"I think so. Got a few things."

She'd set the pan down on the end of the table. He didn't have loaf pans, so the loaves were rounds of golden beauty.

"Don't suppose you'd like a piece of bread with butter, while we look?"

"I can stand it."

Ben started unfolding and laying out the clothing on the table. He noted the three silver dollars still lying there, tokens of atonement for what she considered her wrong-doing. We can use 'em for the baby, he thought

After they had both enjoyed a slab of fresh bread with butter, he said, "While you look this stuff over, I'll put Charger away."

After they finished the noon meal, Anna spent some time checking the various garments, feeling the fabrics and making a list of yardage, including skeins of yarn. She had a tape measure in her sewing stuff, so she made sketches in her notebook. When she was finished, she went over the list with Ben and had him feel the fabrics also, including her one other skirt. There'd have to be some modifications to her own sparse wardrobe.

"Do you have scissors?" she asked.

"No. I do have shears to clip manes or shear sheep, which I don't have any," Ben replied.

"Well, if there's enough money, you might get some. Here's all the money I have." She laid more silver dollars and the gold piece on the table.

Ben's eyes grew wide at the sight of the gold. Each of the silver dollars equaled a wagon load of railroad ties, cut, hacked, and hauled. "That'll be way more than enough. I'll take care of it next time I go to Sycamore."

CHAPTER 36

Tom Archer came in from the morning milking and feeding and sat at the table having a cup of coffee. Rebecca and Josie were cleaning up the breakfast dishes. The two little girls, Jenny and Essie, were playing with their rag dolls. Jimmy was sprawled on the floor in front of the fireplace after helping his father, and was now playing a game of checkers with Oren, leaving a few juicy jump opportunities for his little brother.

"Becky, I'm a little concerned about Ben," Tom said. "He usually comes to meetin'. I think I'll ride up and see how he's doin'. I should be working on the roof, but I ought to be back in time to work on it this afternoon."

"I think that's a good idea, since he's all by himself."

"Can I go?" said Oren

"Not this time, Son. It's still cold out and I aim to travel fast."

Anna had spent the morning making a batch of hominy, boiling the shelled corn in lye water, removing the skins, boiling and rinsing through three repetitions, until plump white kernels remained. The ash hopper her papa had built was still in the yard and ashes were still being added. The bucket was filled with lye water from past rains. Her project was completed in time to have some hominy with the midday meal. She'd found several jars of meatballs preserved in lard, so she planned to have some along with sauerkraut.

Ben had gone to the woods to haul in another load of fireplace wood he'd cut the previous week. Anna heard him arrive to unload out back. Without giving it a thought, she felt happy to hear him clumping up the steps to come in, and looked forward to seeing him.

"Hey, Anna. Stuff smells good in here."

She turned from the stove to smile at him. "It'll be ready in a little bit."

She had just turned to the cabinet to get out the dishes when they heard the sound of hoof beats outside. She turned with a start. Ben rushed to the one front window to look down the lane.

"Oh, my. It's Pa!"

"*What'll I do?*"

"Guess you'll have to hide."

Anna gave a panicked look about the room, snatched up some socks she'd been darning, and scurried into the bedroom. She closed the new door and latched it just as Tom Archer walked in the front door. Ben was standing at the stove.

"Saw smoke from the chimney, so I just came on in. How're ya doin' Son?"

"Real good, Pa. Dinner's about ready. Have a seat."

"Looks like I'm just in time. We missed you yesterday, so I thought I'd come for a visit. You all right?"

"Oh, yeah. Just got around a little slow yesterday."

When Tom saw the food Ben brought to the table, he asked, "Where'd that hominy come from? And the bread. Are you bakin' bread now?"

"Yep. When you live alone, and you like to eat, you just have to do some stuff."

"And this looks like a lot for one. How'd you know I was coming?"

"Didn't. It's just easier to cook two meals at once and warm it up for supper."

Tom shook his head. "You surprise me."

After a few more bites, Tom looked toward the bedroom. "Hey, you put in a new door."

"Yeah. I can close it off and sleep in the loft. It's warmer that way."

"Makes sense. Say, do you suppose you could give me a hand tomorrow, putting a roof on the new room? Rafe Johnson's coming."

"Sure. Right after chores."

After Tom left, heading over to Rebecca's farm to check on the Stotts, Ben knocked softly on the bedroom door. "He's gone, Anna."

When she came out, he said, "I'm sorry it worked out that way. He ate the meal you'd fixed."

"It's all right. There's more I can eat. I heard you take credit for my cooking." She smiled.

"I guess I did. He seemed kinda surprised." He smiled back at her. "I do plan to go help him tomorrow. That'll give me a chance to go on to Sycamore and get the stuff you need."

The next morning, Ben did the morning chores, then built a fire under the iron kettle outside so Anna could do a washing. He made several trips from the spring with buckets of water to fill the kettle and rinse tub. After breakfast, he told Anna he'd see her late in the evening. "You be careful now, Anna, ya hear? Don't overdo it. I'll take the team and wagon and I ought to be back not too long after dark. You pull in the latch string after I leave, and there's a shotgun there if you need it. I'll make Bone stay behind to keep watch."

Anna stood by the big iron pot, carving flakes of soap into the water while waiting for it to get hot. She thought about where she was and what had happened. I used to be just a kid, she thought, never thinking about things, particularly the future. Now I'm not a lot older, really, but everything changed when Mama died, then it changed again when Etta told me what was happening to me.

Now I feel like a grownup and all I think about is the future. I'm so lucky to be here right now, but what will I do when I have a child to care for? There was a time in the past when Mama took care of me and she'd give a hug and make me feel safe, but that memory is fading into the past. For a while, Etta and Margaret were almost like family to me, but now that is gone. Ben is being nice to me, but I think it is because he feels sorry for me. I don't see any way I can stay here for long in a situation like this. I've never thought about boys or men in connection with a future of my own, but I can see that Ben would be a good man for someone.

Her thoughts continued as she carried baskets of wash out of the house. It was cold, but above freezing so the clothes should dry on the line without a problem. She threw the bedding and her underwear in first and stirred with a wooden paddle until they were clean. She fished them out and into the cold water in the galvanized tub. They'd warm the water a bit, so her hands shouldn't freeze when she wrung them out. Some of the outerwear, particularly Ben's overalls, would need scrubbing on the washboard...

Tom Archer was surprised when his son arrived with the team and wagon. "That's a powerful way to haul a hammer down here, Son."

Ben laughed, "It's a really heavy hammer! Naw, I'm goin' on to Sycamore for a few things when we get done here."

Rafe Johnson brought his oldest son, Matthew, and the four men spent the day working on the roof, helped some by Jimmy and Oren, at least by intent. They got the rafters up, the stringers on, and most of the shingles before Ben had to leave for Sycamore. He got to Guthrie's store before Henry closed down to walk across for his supper. When Ben handed him the list, he expressed surprise.

"You takin' up sewing, young Ben?"

Ben looked embarrassed, but rallied. "It ain't for me. I was comin' down so I got orders from others."

Henry looked at him for a few beats, then headed toward the dry goods shelves. "Well, let's see if two men can make any sense out of what you want."

Henry measured and cut, Ben feeling the cloth available, making selections. When they were all finished, Ben said. "Ya know, it ain't long 'til Christmas. Don't know if I'll get back. How about makin' up a bag of hard candy and such, enough for five kids? Also, are those women's shawls over there?"

"Yep. Some of the women, 'specially those with sheep, spin yarn and knit 'em up to sell."

"I'll pick out one of them, also."

"Gotcha a girl?"

Ben replied too quickly. "No, no. It's all family."

In the short days of winter, it was long after dark before Ben got back home. After he left Guthrie's, driving back up Bull Creek, he found himself looking forward to getting to the log house, hurrying through chores, and seeing how Anna had spent her day. It's completely different now, he thought, from how it was before. I wonder what will happen to us after the baby comes. Surely she's gonna stay at least that long. Where will she go? If she goes, what will life be like for me? Can I go back to the way it was?

CHAPTER 37

A cold winter rain was falling as a lone rider traveled down the wagon road on the east bank of Bull Creek. He was wearing a black hat pulled low and a heavy black duster that also covered the saddle. He had ridden most of the day, first by mail coach, then the rented horse from Ozark. He forded Hanson's Creek and headed up the creek to his destination.

He rode into the circle in front of the Madison house and dismounted, wrapping the reins around the hitching rail. He mounted the steps and shook the rain from his coat before rapping on the front door. He heard footsteps padding down the hall inside and the door was opened by the black maid. "Good evening. I'm here to see Colonel Perry Madison." He thumbed aside his lapel. "Marshal Elbert Strong."

"Yes, suh. I go see if he in." She closed the door.

Strong removed the wet, heavy coat and draped it over a bench while he waited. Some of the moisture had seeped through into his coat and he shivered. Several minutes passed. Finally he heard the rattle of the door being opened. Madison stood in the light of the hall. His face was white and pinched.

"What are you doing here?"

"I'm here to serve you again to come to Washington."

"I thought we were through with all that! What with the president being shot and Arthur taking office."

"I reckon not. Committee got together for final conclusions, and they desire you to attend."

"Step inside. It's late and I have some things to attend to." Then over his shoulder, *"Etta!"*

The maid came back down the hall. "Suh?"

"Get Ike in here." Then to Strong. "We just as well go to my office. I'd suggest we depart first thing in the morning. We have a small bunkhouse that's empty. There's a stove in there. I'll get the maid to bring you some food."

"I believe it best we start out now."

"What's a few hours? I can't just up and leave without talking to my foreman. I have a business to run."

"Well…against my better judgement…" Strong was wet and cold and thought a night's rest wouldn't hurt.

When the groom and maid were given their instructions, Strong listened. It all sounded logical, especially when he gave instructions for the surrey and driver to be out front at six o'clock the next morning.

Nearing midnight, rain was still coming down in swirling gusts as two riders rode out south on the Madison spread. One was upright, his feet in the stirrups, but the other was draped over the saddle, a rope securing his head to his feet under the horse's belly. After the marshal retired for the night, Colonel Madison countermanded his order for the surrey, telling the groom, Ike, that they'd decided on horses instead.

A simple sedative of a bottle of whiskey left in the bunkhouse, and a silent, late night entry with a hammer is all it took to solve the problem. Took some doing to wrap a grown man into a raincoat and carry him to the stable, but it's amazing what a person can accomplish if they're motivated.

I could see the writing on the wall, Madison thought. If I'd gone back there, good chance I wouldn't be coming back. Best do it this way. My family's come apart anyway, so it's time to start over somewhere else. Need to make a withdrawal first, then a deposit. He smiled to himself.

Madison rode down a dark game trail toward a little used hillside strewn with large boulders. He dismounted and tied his horse to a sapling. He removed a small entrenching shovel from a saddlebag. I hope this one is better than some of that stuff we procured, he chuckled. Going to a well-remembered waist-high chunk of limestone, he raked the wet leaves aside and began to dig at its base. In a few minutes he withdrew a leather valise. It was packed with wet leather bags. He opened one and poured a stream of gold coins into his hand, pleased with their heft and the way they seemed to glow in the darkness.

With all of the gold transferred to his saddlebags and the valise buried, he rode on, leading the other horse. Soon he came to a deep ravine filled with cedars and made his deposit. The body and the saddle, blanket, and bridle were concealed deep within the thicket of brush. Now, he'd have a spare horse to give Devil a rest. He'd be moving fast to put as many miles behind him as he could before daybreak. Needed to ford the White and head south, maybe hit New Orleans. A name change and a ship to Panama ought to do it...head to California on the other side; start a business.

The rain would wash out his tracks.

Margaret came down the staircase to a quiet house. Mother was probably still sleeping and Father had said at the evening meal that he had to go to Washington again. Maybe he left early. She walked through the dining room and kitchen and went out to the cookhouse. Etta was at the stove, putting a kettle on to boil.

"Good morning, Etta. How are you?"

"Fine, Miss Margaret. You like coffee?"

"I sure would. Did Father leave early?"

"That a funny thing. Ike, he say the colonel tell him he don't need no surrey, then Ike say they both gone and both they horses. Mus' been awful early, 'cause he didn't hear nuthin'."

"That does seem a little strange. Maybe the marshal changed his mind. He wanted to leave last evening according to Father. It was a miserable night with the rain. It's just now slacking off. Oh, well, who knows? I guess I'm out of jail now."

Etta chuckled. "S'pose this means you goin' back to Sycamore."

CHAPTER 38

November moved into the past, and the weeks of December marched on, headed for Christmas. Anna still wrote regularly in her notebook, describing the passing days and the wonder of her changing body with the anticipation of what was to come. As she grew larger, she also noted changes in the baby inside her. He or she now seemed to be on something of a cycle, having waking active periods of times followed by peaceful naps. It made her smile, trying to imagine the tiny creature growing in the comfort of her protection.

Not only was her stomach swelling, her feet and hands were swelling also. She noticed it when she put on her boots to go outside, which was often. She had her own cycle, goodness knows, not only night and day, but drinking water and going to the outhouse. She suffered some from back pain, but there was always work to do—and there was sleeplessness, but maybe that was part of her situation.

Anna refrained from writing about Ben since there was no way to know what might become of her notebook. She continued to think of him as a kind and good man who was sincere in taking care of her. And he worked hard. He was always there to lift anything heavy, and he had forbidden her carrying wood as she had done when she first arrived. He continued to respect a personal space around her as she had demanded that first day when she threatened him with the pitchfork. He had never touched her anywhere, not even her hand. She admitted to herself there were times that it would be nice to be greeted with a hug when he came in at the end of the day. But that might spoil everything, since the future was so uncertain.

Ben continued to work in the woods when weather permitted. There'd been only a few rainy days the rest of November and in December, and no more snow. It was cold, and all the animals had grown their winter coats. After Christmas, he would set out his trap line. There was a small creek at the foot of the property that his spring fed into which should have some mink and coon traffic. For muskrat, he'd need to see about a few traps on Bull Creek.

Life was certainly different with Anna around. She held down the home place, cooking, cleaning, and making the place welcome to come in at the end of a cold day. He noticed the changes in her, but refrained from saying anything. She had an erect posture when he first encountered her but now she walked with a little backward lean to balance the bump in front. He'd spent a lot of time thinking about that bump, and wondered if he dared talk to her about some of those thoughts. She worked every night and at times during the day knitting and sewing to make ready for the new arrival, although it was still months away.

Ben had managed to shoot a wild turkey for Christmas. It was a small hen—too much for two people, but a symbolic feast with leftover food for days. Anna had started it to roast in low heat for all Christmas morning. Ben had also brought in a small cedar tree the morning before and they had decorated it with popcorn strings, colored yarn, and strips of colored cloth trimmings from Anna's sewing. Ben had ridden down to see his family on that afternoon to give his bag of candy to the family. His father urged him to come down for Christmas day, but he declined, saying the day was more for the smaller children. Tom was puzzled, but didn't press the issue.

When Ben came in from the morning chores and washed up, they had a breakfast of bacon and eggs. Afterward, he climbed up in the loft and brought down a package wrapped in brown paper.

"Anna, I got you a little something when I was down at Sycamore. I hope you like it."

"Ben, I didn't expect anything." She took the package and began to unwrap it.

"It's probably something you could make yourself, but—"

"It's really nice! Thank you!" She wrapped the black wool shawl around her shoulders. "It's warm…and I never had a present so nice." Tears welled in her eyes. She wiped them away with the back of her hand

and dashed back to her bedroom, causing Ben to worry that he'd made a mistake.

She came out smiling, holding a bundle of blue knit. "I'm making this for you, but I don't have the fringe on yet. It's a scarf." She handed it to him.

"Why thanks, Anna. That's real nice. That'll keep my neck warm when I run traps."

They stood looking at each other, both a little ill at ease. Then Ben decided the time was right for a talk. "Anna, we got some time before dinner. Can we sit and talk a bit? I've been thinkin' about a few things."

She looked worried. "Yes...all right."

Ben led the way to the rockers in front of the fireplace, pulling his over closer to where she usually sat and turned it to face her.

"I don't know how to start, but I been thinkin' and studyin', worried about how to talk to you about this." He cleared his throat. Anna sat staring.

"When I was a kid in school, there was a couple of kids over the years that didn't have a normal life with a ma and pa. Well of course everybody has a ma and pa...but what I mean is, well, they was from a ma with no pa around and he wasn't dead." Ben felt heat rise in his face, and he began to question his own judgement.

"What are you trying to say?" Anna demanded.

"What I'm trying to say is, the other kids was mean to those kids, teased 'em and sometimes called 'em names and not good names. And the teachers even sometimes seemed to treat 'em a little different...leastways, it looked that way."

"So what you're trying to say is my child will have a hard time."

"I would hope not, but the thought of it bothers me a lot."

"Well, what do you expect me to do about it?"

Ben thought to himself, well here goes. He started talking and rushed to say all he could without stopping to breathe. "I think we should get married. You could take my name and the baby could take my name and you wouldn't have to be a real wife and you could get out of it later but the baby wouldn't know and it wouldn't have to think there was something different about it—"

"*Wait, wait, wait.* You'd do this out of pity for me, is *that* what you mean?" Anna jumped up and ran toward the front door, grabbing her coat from a peg, stuffing her feet into her boots, and running out into the cold.

Ben leaped to his feet also, but hesitated. Oh, Lord, what have I done? Am I stupid, or what, to bring this up on Christmas Day? He went to the door and donned his own coat and boots to go and find her.

She was where he thought she would be. He climbed the vertical ladder to the hayloft, and sure enough, there she was. She was lying in that far corner where she'd first stood her ground with a pitchfork. He climbed all the way to the top and stepped into the hay. She stood and looked at him in the dim light.

"Anna, I'm sorry I said the wrong things and made you unhappy— 'specially on Christmas Day. Can we talk about this?" He waited before continuing. "I know I don't know nothing about how to say things, but I sure didn't mean to hurt your feelin's. Will you say something to me?"

She said in a soft voice he could barely hear. "I don't feel good about pity and I don't feel good about charity. I wish I could do for myself and my child, and it makes me feel bad I can't."

"Anna, Anna. You've given me more than I've given you. You don't realize what it was like for me up here all by myself all the time. I didn't say what I did out of pity. I was just thinkin' about that little one to come. A baby don't have no say in things when they come into the world. They don't know nothin' and they just expect to be taken care of. It really bothered me to think it wouldn't have the best we could give it."

Anna came halfway across the loft, balancing in the soft hay. He could see the glisten of tears on her cheeks. "It made me feel bad. I know you weren't being mean, but it hurt me. But you're right. A baby is better off if it sees a papa and mama, even if it's pretend. I'll do what you suggest." Then to herself, she said, I never thought much about the future, but I guess every girl thinks about marriage someday, but false promises make it not mean much. I don't think he understands.

"Well, good," Ben said. "It won't be real, so like I said, you aren't obligated. We ain't so much as touched hands, and we agreed we'd be like sister and brother or this wouldn't work. We're both really young and what I said was all I could say without bein' too forward. I really do like you and I want to do the best for you and the little one."

"I know. I know, Ben. And I'm sorry too for the way I acted." She walked toward him.

Ben stepped forward and took her arm, the first time he had done so. "Can I help you down?"

"I'll manage. All right?" she said.

"That's just fine. We've just got to make things right for that little one. Now let's go in the house. And don't you be climbin' ladders any more, ya hear?"

CHAPTER 39

On mid-morning of the third day after Colonel Madison went away, Margaret sat at his desk opposite the overseer, Hank Green. Hank was briefing her on the farm status, since her father had been running things for the last few weeks. The office door was open and Etta reached in and knocked on it.

"Miz Margaret, theys three men on the porch askin' for the Missus, but I thought you might want to come."

She and Hank rose. "You did right, Etta. I think she's napping. Hank you might come along."

When she opened the door, she recognized Sheriff John Horton. Two men were with him. "Yes, Sheriff?"

"We need to speak with you Miss. Kin we come in?"

"By all means." The three men trooped in, wiping their boots on the mat. Margaret indicated the door into the little-used parlor with its carved Victorian furniture.

"Be seated, Gentlemen. I'm Margaret Madison. My mother is indisposed at the moment. This is Hank Green, our overseer."

"Pleased to make your acquaintance, Miss. This here's Ed Bain, sheriff of Christian County, and Dooley Smith. He owns a livery stable in Ozark."

"What's this about, Sheriff?"

"Well…it's about your father—"

"Has something happened to him?"

"We don't rightly know, Miss. He was expected in Washington yesterday and they sent a telegram, asked me to check on him. Do you know his whereabouts?"

"Why, no. He left in the early morning before we were up."

"And another thing, Mister Smith, here, rented a horse to a U.S. Marshal and he ain't brought it back yet."

Margaret brought both hands to her face. "Oh, my! This sounds awful!"

Sheriff Horton had rested both forearms on his knees and now rotated the brim of his hat through his hands as he looked at her. "I reckon it don't look good. Did anyone see them leave?"

Hank spoke up. "I wasn't here until after they were gone. Old man Ike takes care of the horses. We can ask him."

"Let's get him in here. And while he's comin' let me ask you a few questions, Miss Madison. Were you aware of the marshal's arrival?"

"Yes. He came right before the evening meal. Father spoke of his plans to go to Washington again. He gave the marshal a room in the bunkhouse and sent supper to him. As you may know, it was raining and cold."

Ike rushed into the room followed by Hank Green. He whipped a battered cap from his head and bowed slightly, looking uncomfortable.

Horton rotated his chair to face him. "Understand you look after the horses."

"Yes, Suh, Mista Sheriff."

"Tell me what happened the evening the U.S. Marshall got here."

"Yes, Suh. He went to the bunkhouse with his saddlebags, and I put his mare away and took care a' her. Colonel, he say he might want the surrey the next mornin' but later he tell me they take horses."

"You hear anything in the night or the next morning?"

"No, Suh."

"Were the horses gone?"

"Yes, Suh, Colonel's horse and the marshal's mare."

"What does the colonel's horse look like?

"He a big black stallion, name Devil, and he ack like it. The little funny saddle Colonel like still here, but a reg'lar saddle gone."

"All right, you can go, but let this man go with you if he likes, look around." Then to Smith, "Dooley, you can look around it you want to, and go on home if you don't find nuthin. Me and Ed will see what we can find out."

Horton put the edge of his hand under his nose and stroked his mustache down over his upper lip, like one would pet the head of a dog. "Miss Madison, do you know why the marshal came to fetch your pa?"

"No Sir, he never talks 'business,' as he calls it, with women. We're not capable of understanding complicated things."

"You don't sound too happy about that."

"I'm not."

"Do you s'pose your ma knows anything?"

"She's less likely than I am. If you want, I'll see if I can get her to talk to you."

Horton shook his head and looked at Sheriff Bain. "No, that's all right. Ed?"

"No. I think we can report in and see where to go with this."

They rose, shook hands with Margaret, and departed. Margaret followed them to the porch and watched them ride away. I have a feeling I'll never see Father again, she thought. I wonder what will happen to this place, and to Mother. Only time will tell.

Two weeks later, one of Hank Green's hired hands, cutting wood in a cove a mile from the farmstead, saw vultures circling and went to investigate. He expected to see the carcass of a stray cow or a deer, but found something far different. It took a day to get the sheriff out to look at his find. After Sheriff Horton viewed the scene, now disrupted by animal denizens, he rode up to the house, dreading what he must do.

It was just before suppertime, and the maid answered his knock drying her hands on her apron. Etta opened the door without speaking.

The sheriff had already removed his hat. "I need to see the missus, and better get Miss Margaret also."

"You can step inside, while I fetch 'em," Etta said and departed down the hall.

Agnes Madison walked down the hall, head erect, as she had been taught in finishing school so many years ago. However, Sheriff Horton saw that she had aged since he last saw her some months ago.

"Sheriff Horton," she said. "So nice of you to drop by. What may we do for you? Oh, and please step into the parlor where we may talk. Would you like coffee or tea? Perhaps something stronger?"

"No, Ma'm, you're very kind, but we do need to speak."

Margaret nodded at the sheriff, and the three of them sat in the velvet chairs.

The sheriff assumed his usual position, leaning forward, running the edge of his hat brim around and around through his thick fingers. "Uh… Ma'm and Miss, I have bad news. Just as well speak right out. We found the body of the marshal that was here, in a holler to the south a mile or two."

Margaret gasped, but her mother said, "Well, that's too bad. Of course I didn't know the man, but it's always sad when someone passes on. I assume my husband is all right?"

Sheriff Horton glanced at Margaret and cleared his throat. "Well, Ma'm, we don't rightly know, but there was no evidence anything happened to him at the same time."

"Well that's good," Agnes said. "He was headed back to Washington, you know, so you'll probably find him there. He's helping the President on some matters."

The sheriff rose and Margaret and her mother did as well. "Well, thank you for your time. I'd best be goin'."

"Thank you, Sheriff Horton. Please come again," Agnes said. She smiled and walked out of the room.

Margaret said. "I'll see you out." She followed him out onto the porch. "He killed him, didn't he?"

"Looks that way to me, Miss. I'm sorry."

"Any idea where he went?"

"No clue. We already know what both horses look like, also the man. Your pa's is a Tennessee Walker, as I recall. We'll get the feds on it."

"Correct. And I need to put a hold on the bank account in Forsyth if I'm not too late. We have a farm to run."

"I understand. I'll get aholt of Webb as soon as I get in tonight, but you'll have to come in, see a judge. I doubt the Colonel will try that 'cause it'll give away where he's at. He prob'ly had a stash somewhere if he thought this might happen."

"I hope you're right. In any case, I'll leave at first light tomorrow morning and see what needs to be done."

Days passed before federal authorities got into action to pursue the cold trail.

CHAPTER 40

Ben drove the team of grays up the mail road on the west side of Bull Creek, headed north toward Ozark. Anna was beside him on the spring seat, the most intimate contact they had had since he found her in the barn loft. She was bundled in the coat Margaret had given her and wore a knit cap, with the black wool shawl over her head, wrapped around her neck and shoulders. Ben glanced over at her. Only her fair face was exposed, now pink in the cold wind, her expression set in concern.

"Anna, they ain't gonna shoot us."

She turned to look at him, "I just wish it was over with."

"Not every day ya get married," he said.

Anna didn't reply. It wasn't something to joke about. She adjusted the quilt over their laps and stared straight ahead.

After a couple more hours, they were standing before the same clerk Ben remembered from his father's marriage the year before. The young, stooped man had stringy hair hanging over his ears below the band of a green eyeshade. He peered at Anna. "How old are you?"

"Sixteen." *Almost*, she said to herself.

"Any proof? Are your parents here to vouch for you?"

"My mother is dead and my father abandoned me."

He stared at her, leaning over the counter to look her up and down. He frowned. "Well…"

He looked at Ben. "How about you?"

"Eighteen." *Almost*, he said to himself.

"Normally we'd like to see some paper, but looks like a marriage needs to take place."

He reached for his dip pen and scratched their names in the register as they spelled them out for him. Then he picked up a certificate from a stack and filled it out as they gave him the information, then dusted it with sand and passed it over the counter, holding out his hand. "Two dollars."

Ben paid him and they went to find the Justice. It was a repeat of his father's marriage to Rebecca, so he knew where to go. Anna was looking bewildered. She was overheated in the coat and wraps, but liked the concealment.

When they were before the Justice, despite his stern appearance, he was kind to them, sensing Anna's discomfort. When they spoke their responses, hers in a soft voice, he pronounced them married, then said, "This would be a good time to kiss your bride, young man."

Ben hadn't kissed a girl since grade school, and that was on a dare and it was on her cheek. He wrapped his arms around Anna and bent to kiss her firmly on the lips. She looked startled, then closed her eyes and responded, surprising them both.

As Ben hurried the team back toward home, Anna sat silently beside him, but her mind was churning with what had just taken place. Married? *Really?* And what happened there at the end? I've never kissed anyone except my mother and it wasn't like that at all. Why did I act that way? Ben probably did it because that old man told him to.

Ben was also silent, lost in thoughts of his own. We did this just to make sure that baby saw two people taking care of it, but now I really feel responsible to take care of both her and the baby. Legally, she really is my wife. I don't know how it could be brought up with her, but the thought of her going away when she's able sure don't sound good. I've been kidding myself about her. She's the best-lookin' girl I've ever seen, and she's nice besides. I'm glad that old Justice said what he did. No way I'd a' had the guts to kiss her otherwise. And she didn't seem to mind. It gave him a warm feeling inside.

"Anna, we'll get home late. I'll have to change clothes and scoot right out to the barn, take care of things."

"I know. I'll get the fires going and find us something to eat."

"Good. Uh…are you all right? I mean about today."
"Yes. We did what we set out to do."

Weeks of winter weather passed by; some snowfall at times, followed by sunshine and thaws. After their return from Ozark, they settled into the routine they had developed before their appearance before the Justice. They worked together with an unforced politeness and caring, as they had done from the beginning. There were times when one or the other would gaze at the other, then look away if they were noticed doing so.

Ben ran his trap line in the early mornings before chores and Anna always had coffee waiting for him when he came in, sometimes hearing him stamping snow from his boots on the porch to announce he was home. After coffee, he'd tend to the cows and horses, come in for breakfast, then skin his catch and stretch the furs. After that, he'd spend most days working in the woods, sometimes spending the day without coming in for a noon meal, by prior arrangement, of course.

In the evenings before bedtime they sat by the fireplace, Ben usually shelling corn, repairing harness, or some other chore. Anna continued to sew and knit, manufacturing little garments for the little one to come. They were both amused by the little undershirts, made from red flannel. Ben could find no suitable cloth, so he brought home a new one-piece suit of men's underwear to take apart.

Anna was lonely on those days Ben stayed out all day. She often thought of Margaret and wondered what was happening in the Madison household. She was eager to be with Ben, even in the polite separation they maintained. It would have been a comfort to discuss the changes in herself with someone as the weeks went by but she had to content herself with writing in her journal. In mid-January the baby was growing to the point that the skin stretched over her expanding stomach felt tight and itchy. As she continued to expand she experienced heartburn and shortness of breath. An occasional loud burp would slip out, embarrassing her, and Ben would look over and smile.

On a Sunday in late January, Ben came home from a church meeting with news that caused them to discuss changes in their exile. He hadn't been going regularly, but thought he'd better put in an appearance. As soon as he took care of the horse, he came rushing in the front door. "Got some news, Anna," he said.

She rose heavily from a rocking chair. "Hi, Ben. What is it?"

He rushed over by the fireplace and they stood facing each other. "Talked to George Zinn. Get this: Colonel Madison has flown the coop. Seems a marshal came to take him back to Washington. The next morning both were gone, then they found the marshal dead in the woods a couple of weeks later. Everybody thinks the Colonel did him in and is on the run."

"My goodness! I guess that means Margaret is free to go back to work in the school."

"She's done just that. And George don't gossip, but he thinks her mother isn't well, so Margaret's running the farm. What's more, she's been ridin' all the coves and hollers asking folks if they've seen you."

"Oh, my. It's not fair to her, keeping secrets."

"That's what I thought about all the way home, and I hope you don't mind but I talked to my folks about comin' down for a visit tomorrow without sayin' why." Ben reached for her hands. "Anna, I think it's time we talked to them and to Margaret. But now that we're standing here, there's more I want to say. I ain't very brave when it comes to this..."

She looked up at him with eyes wide, lips parted. "You can say anything you want to, Ben."

Ben swallowed, and felt tears form in the corners of his eyes. "I tried to make light of that gettin' married for the baby's sake...and that was all true, but fact is, I don't want that to be all of it. I want to be with you, not just the baby. I was afraid to say anything before...upset things, you know?"

Anna stepped closer to him. "I've been waiting and hoping, but I was afraid you wouldn't want a damaged person."

"You ain't damaged. You didn't do a thing wrong. I like the way you are."

"Why don't you kiss me again without that old man telling you to?"

Ben smiled and took her in his arms, doing what he'd wanted to do since that day in Ozark. They held each other for some time, until he whispered, "We'd better let you sit down."

"I don't want to, but someone's acting up."

Ben guided her to her chair and pulled up his own, facing her.

"We need to think about what we'll tell my folks."

"What will they think?"

"They're gonna love you. Pa and Rebecca are both the best."

"Good. Why don't we tell them the whole story, just as it is?"

"I agree. But maybe we can all tell outsiders we got together and married like most folks do. We don't need the gossips and wagging tongues lookin' crosswise at us."

"Margaret knows different, but she'll go along. Will she ever be surprised!"

"Maybe we can go on to Sycamore and catch her at the school."

CHAPTER 41

Tom Archer looked out the front window and saw the wagon approaching. He called out to Rebecca, in the kitchen area drying dishes and putting them away. "Becky, come here. He's comin' and he has a girl with him!"

Rebecca rushed to the window. "Well, now we know what he wants to talk about!"

They both moved away from the door and waited in the kitchen area. Then there was a knock at the door and Ben opened it and walked in. He reached behind him and led a young woman in. Tom and Rebecca came forward and Ben began the introductions.

"This is Anna. Anna, meet my pa, Tom, and his wife Rebecca."

"Nice to meet you, Anna. Sorry about your Ma," Tom said.

Rebecca came forward and hugged Anna. "Welcome, Anna," she said.

"I'm pleased to meet you both," replied Anna.

Oren came running and hugged his brother's thigh. Ben said, "This is my brother, Oren, and that's Estelle hiding behind her ma's skirt." Anna nodded and smiled at them.

"Is this your girlfriend?" Oren said.

"You might say so," Ben replied.

Anna had dropped the shawl from around her head and Tom saw a girl of striking good looks with a cascade of red hair, fair complexion with a sprinkling of freckles, wide gray-green eyes—and pregnant. "Take off your coats and come sit down," he said. "Oren, you go out into the new room and play. We have coffee on. I believe you said you wanted to talk."

"Do I hafta'?" Oren said.

Tom just pointed toward the room and Oren slouched out, dragging his steps. Essie went back to the corner with her doll.

When they were seated at the kitchen table, with fresh coffee poured, Ben said. "I reckon we have quite a story to tell. We want you two to know every detail, why things happened as they did, and we want your advice about how we handle the community gossips.

"Let me give you the first shocker, then Anna can tell her story. We're married, and I'm proud to call Anna my wife."

"Well, I guess it is a surprise," said Tom, but he rose to reach across the table to shake Ben's hand. Congratulations, Son, and welcome to the family Anna. I can't wait to hear the rest of the story."

Rebecca came around the table and sat beside Anna on the bench, putting her arm around her, and kissing her on the cheek. "We're happy to have you, and you'll like the family you married into."

Anna talked on and on, starting her story with the death of her mother and the abandonment by her father, essentially selling her to the Madison family. She spoke about and answered questions about the various family members.

"I hear tell Madison might have killed a federal marshal," Tom said.

"It wouldn't surprise me," Anna said, and she spoke delicately about his unwanted attention and his tyrannical treatment of his family.

The hardest part of her story was a brief description of that pivotal happening in the woods, bringing an expression of horror to Rebecca's face. She told about how naïve she was and of the kind treatment of the maid, Etta. They listened with rapt attention as she talked of her exile into the cold and her journey to the only shelter she knew.

Ben interrupted to tell of his puzzlement at Bone's behavior, the missing mush, and then the discovery in the hayloft. "You want to talk about surprise!" he said.

"Ben saved my life," Anna said, then she broke down in tears. Rebecca ran around the table again and held her in her arms, herself in tears.

After Anna regained her composure, she continued. "Ben gave me complete safety and respect. He built a door with a latch and moved out of his bedroom. He never once touched me until we were married. That's a story in itself."

Ben broke in. "I was afraid to tell Anna how much I cared for her, but there was one thing that had to get settled. It wasn't fair to the baby to be born without two parents. I considered it my baby from the time she came into the house. So I suggested we marry for that reason alone."

Anna smiled at him. "And I agreed, but I was put out that he was just doing it out of charity. You see, I'd begun to respect and care for him, also."

Rebecca, still sitting beside her, said, "Well, all's well that ends well. For the benefit of the community, you're two people who fell in love, got married, and are expecting a baby."

"I agree," Tom said. "Now, what can we do to help?"

"Well, there's a couple more things," Ben said. "We need to catch up with Margaret and talk this out, so we may go to Sycamore from here and see if she's at the school. And the other thing I was dishonest about. I sneaked in here one Sunday morning to look in Ma's trunk for baby clothes—not to take them, but to use as patterns. Neither of us knew how big a baby is. Anna's been sewing and knitting, getting things ready—"

"I can help with that," Rebecca said. "I still have some baby clothes—for no good reason until now."

After the noon meal, Ben and Anna were once again in the wagon, headed for Sycamore. They'd forded Hanson Creek and were nearing the settlement. Essie and Oren had huddled around Anna, showing her things and talking to her, becoming acquainted in the manner of small children. Ben had talked privately with Tom about the problems with the Harveys and the fence line. "They seem to want to see how far they can go. It's rotting into the ground. I've added a few rails in the worst places on their part, but it needs rebuilt."

"How about I come up and we can try to talk to Ferd again? Rebecca can visit with Anna and tell her a few things."

They'd agreed on two days later. Now, as they drew nearer to the schoolhouse, Anna said, "The afternoon recess should be pretty soon. That looks like her buggy over there under the trees. Why don't I wait by it and you can go tell her someone would like to see her. I'd rather not have the children gawking at my condition."

That's what they did. As soon as they saw children streaming into the back yard, Ben ran over to the school house and came out with Margaret following. When she saw who was standing by the wagon, she burst into a run and enveloped Anna in an embrace. Ben saw from a distance, the laughing and the brushing away of tears. They were still clasped tightly together when he walked up in time to hear Margaret say, "Anna, oh Anna. You have your bustle on backwards!"

They both giggled and Ben thought, Must be an old joke.

Anna saw him return and said, "Margaret, this is my *husband*, Ben Archer."

"Your *husband?* You're *married?*" Then she turned to Ben, her mouth hanging open. "I remember you. You rescued me from the rain."

"That's me. Nice seein' ya again."

"We have to talk," said Margaret. "I'll run and tell Mister Phllips. We can sit in my buggy. *Oh...Oh...Oh!*" She was dancing up and down.

"I'll leave you to it, Anna," said Ben. "I'll see if I can find George."

Ben heard the ringing of hammers on anvils as he approached the black-smith shop. George and his father were both going at it, alternating blows sounding like music with a staccato beat. It stopped as Ben blocked some of the light from the doorway. "Ben!" yelled George. "Come in." He dashed the andiron he'd been hammering into a tub of water.

"Hey there, Ben," said Homer.

"Hi to both of you. Hope I'm not stopping your work."

George walked over and removed his glove to shake hands. "Time for a break, anyway. Let's go sit outside."

George put his coat on and they sat on the bench. "What brings you to the city of Sycamore?"

"I'll get right to it. Get hold of yourself. You know that Friedrich girl you described awhile back as a 'looker'?"

George stared at him.

"She and I are married."

"Married? George slapped him on the shoulder so hard he nearly fell from the bench. "You're kiddin' me, ain't you?"

"Absolutely true."

"Well, congratulations. I'll see if I can clap my mouth back shut. Tell me about it."

"Did Margaret tell you what happened to her?"

"She did, but swore me to secrecy."

"Well, I'll ask you to do the same. The first time I saw her since her ma's buryin', I found her hiding in the loft of my barn..."

Clouds were rising in the west and a cold wind had come up as they drove along the wagon road up Bull Creek. Anna was huddled next to Ben, the shawl around her head and shoulders. They compared notes about their separate conversations. "It was so good to see Margaret again," said Anna. "She's worried about what might happen to her family. Her mother doesn't seem to think straight. She did manage to freeze the bank account so the farm can operate. She thinks the government might take everything away."

"What'll she do?"

"She's already lined up with a teaching job. She thinks her mother may go back to New York to live with her sister, Elvira."

"What did she say about you?"

Anna smiled, her eyes bright. "She went on and on about how relieved she was and how she wants to help if she can. Says to get word to her when it happens. She also said nice things about you...and no, I won't say what they were."

Ben smiled back at her. "You should have heard George, but I won't tell you, either." Then on a more serious note, "Do you think they'll keep the details to themselves?"

"I think so, but I'm past caring. Can I ask you something?"

"Sure."

"Do you think the baby might grow up mean like that...that...."

"I don't think so. It's growing in your body and living off your blood. It'll have you for a mama. No, it's gonna be a good person like you."

CHAPTER 42

Tom and Rebecca came for their visit on the first day of February, normally Missouri's nastiest month. True to form, it was cold, with gusty wind and powdery snow swirling in eddies around the log house as they drove into the yard. Ben rushed out to greet them and ushered them in to the warmth of the fire. After greetings were exchanged, Ben said, "You get comfortable. I'll put the horses in the barn."

Tom and Ben bundled up in their coats and set out to walk across the fields to the Harvey place, rather than go around by the road. Rebecca set the children to drawing pictures on their slates while she joined Anna at the kitchen table, both with mugs of coffee.

"Well, I'm sure you must have some questions," Rebecca said.

"Everything," said Anna. "It's all new and I don't know what's normal. I feel like a cow, my belly is so big. The skin's tight and it has marks on it. Funny thing is, lately it seems to be lower down."

"Those are called 'stretch marks' and they may stay, maybe fade a little. And the lower down part is probably just because your time is getting closer."

"What'll happen next? I'm scared, but I want to get it over with."

"When the time comes, you'll start getting labor pains, or your water may break."

"Tell me more. I don't know anything."

"Well, the baby floats in water, and sometimes the membrane will break first and it'll come out like a river or just a dribble down your leg. Don't be afraid. It's normal. Then the labor pains start, sort of like cramps. Or the pains could come first, then the water. Does Ben know the midwife?"

"It's the same old lady that came when Mama died. We talked about her."

"Good. And when he can, he can come and get me. I'll do anything to help, before and after the baby comes."

"Oh, thank you. As I said, I've never even seen a tiny new baby. I'll get some of the things I've made and you can tell me if they'll work."

"I also brought you some things. It needs to be a girl. A boy might not look good in little dresses."

They both laughed.

Anna paused, looking uncomfortable. She glanced at the children, then said quietly to Rebecca, "I don't have a mama now. Can I ask you something?"

Rebecca patted her hand. "Of course you can."

Anna said, almost whispering, "I think I know what married people do. But the way I am now, and what happened to me, I don't know what comes next."

"Oh, honey. Nothing needs to happen anytime soon. Just be kind to each other as you have been. Stay close to each other, and nature will take its course. When I was a new married girl I knew nothing. It all worked out."

"Should we sleep together?"

"It would be a nice idea for both of you. It'll get you used to being close. After the baby comes and time passes, everything will be all right. From what I've seen of him, he'll be kind to you. He's probably more bashful than you are." She smiled at Anna.

"Thank you, Rebecca. You make me feel better."

As Tom and Ben approached the Harvey house, three hounds came out from under the porch, barking and snarling. One was a blue tick, one a redbone, and one an ugly brindled mix. They ignored the dogs and stepped up on the porch to be met by Ferd Harvey, shotgun in his hands. His face above his bristly beard was red. "You Archers get off my property!" he shouted.

Tom held up his hand. "Now Ferd, we've known each other for a long time. No need to talk that way."

"You've got your nerve, stealin' that property then takin' after my sister. Now git!"

"We need to talk about the fence."

"We ain't talkin' no fence. We ain't talkin' nuthin'."

"Well, sorry you feel that way. Come on, Ben. We just as well go." He turned and led the way back down the steps.

As they walked away from the house, Tom said. "That didn't go very well. Looks like the next thing is to try to get the law involved."

The spitting snow had stopped, but it was still cold and windy. Tom and Rebecca were on their way back home, huddled together with a blanket wrapped around them, with the little children wrapped up in the back of the wagon. Tom asked, "Well, what do you think."

"About the kids? It was sweet. Anna wanted to ask a few mother-daughter questions...not just about the baby coming. They're going to be just fine, I think."

"Different kind of courtship, ain't it?" Tom said.

Two weeks later, on St. Valentine's Day, Ben loaded the wagon with wood and set out to find the way to Ma Bright's cabin. He took no notice that the day was any different, but he had noticed that Anna had been closer to him since he folks' visit. It was a nice feeling. She'd even asked if his bed up in the loft was comfortable and said that now they were married, the bed in her room was big enough for two. As he forded Bull Creek and headed up the holler where Ma Bright's cabin was, he thought on what he should do. He knew his ma and pa always slept together. The idea of it filled him with wonderment. Of course she was now awful big and uncomfortable, but after the baby, well...

The cabin was right where Pa said it should be. It was small, but in good repair. Folks with no cash money did what they could to keep her going. That was one reason for the load of wood, but he had money, too, for when the baby came.

Smoke rose from the chimney, so she must be home. He stopped in front and climbed the steps to the front porch, knocking on the door.

She opened it and he saw her up close for the first time. She was tiny, with strange black and white hair, wrinkled countenance, and piercing black eyes. "What is it?" She said.

"Ma'm, I'm Benjamin Archer, Tom's son. I'm married to Anna Friedrich. You tended her ma when she got kicked by a horse."

"I remember," she said, almost in a whisper. "Is she sick?"

"Not exactly. She's gonna have a baby pretty soon, so I wanted to find the way over here, so's I'd know. I brought you some wood."

"I could use some, with this cold. Do I need to come now?"

"No, I don't reckon. She talked to Rebecca, Pa's wife, about things. I'll just unload this wood if you tell me where you want it, and I'll pay, too, when the baby comes."

Ma had him put some on the porch and stack the rest at the end of the cabin by the fireplace. She thanked him, gave him a biscuit with some ham in it, and he headed back down the hollow.

Ben went out the next morning to see if he could coax a little more milk out of Bessie, Goldie long since gone dry. In fact, it should be time for Goldie to birth a calf, if his figuring was correct. He decided to check on her and found her in the edge of the woods, circling and straining, tail in the air. What do you know, he said to himself. Good timing. He hurried back to milk Bessie, then rushed in to the house. "Anna, guess what."

She turned heavily from the stove. "What?"

"Goldie's havin' her calf. Would you like to come out and watch?"

Anna stroked her protruding stomach, and slowly shook her head. "I don't think so. I'll come and see the calf after it's born. Here's you some coffee to drink when you go back out."

CHAPTER 43

February was drawing to a close, with the snow of a week before now melted except for patches in the shade. It was still cold with March winds stealing in a few days early. Ben had started thinking about spring plowing just weeks away, and had pulled his traps so he could concentrate on helping Anna with her more rigorous chores. He was now helping in the kitchen and doing the washing. For some time now, he'd forbidden her from carrying water or stoking the fires.

For her part, all she could think about was the trial of the birth to come. She'd forgotten what it was like to have a normal body without the aching back and swollen ankles. When the snow was on the ground, Ben walked her to the outhouse, holding her elbow to steady her. At night he urged her to use a bucket.

Ben and Anna were able to overcome their shyness when he moved from the loft into the bedroom. After a time of leaving space between them, they soon found comfort sleeping spooned in close contact, especially when winter cold intruded and the fires died down. Ben was thrilled when she invited him to put his hand on her stomach and he felt what seemed to be a tiny foot skating across the inside.

On the first day of March, Anna felt a twinge in her back. For the last couple of days, the baby seemed to be moving more than normal and not in the same routine. She was standing at the kitchen stove, frying potatoes for the noon meal. Ben was washing bedding and clothes in the big iron pot outside. It started like Rebecca said it might. She felt water start running down her leg. She stepped back and the flow increased until there was a puddle at her feet. She pulled the pan from the burner and hurried to the front door, dribbling puddles behind her. Throwing it open, she leaned over the porch railing and yelled. "Ben! Ben, come quick!"

Ben's hat flew off as he came running around the house and up on the porch. "What is it, Anna?"

"The time's come." She held the door open as he charged inside.

"Thought that might be it. How d'ya feel?"

"Not bad. Just leaking water…oh!" she grimaced. "Spoke too soon. Had a cramp."

"Let's get ya in bed."

"In the little bed behind the curtain where I used to sleep. Get a couple of towels."

Ben led her gently to the bunk. "You just rest easy. I'll get the wooden bucket and a glass of water." He scurried away and was soon back by her side. "Do you need anything else? I'll hitch the team and get goin' for Ma Bright."

"No. I'll be all right. Hurry back."

"I hate to leave ya. Uh…Anna? I love ya."

She smiled up at him and looked as though she could cry. He squeezed her hand and was gone.

Ben slapped the reins and hurried the grays up the narrow lane leading to Ma Bright's cabin. He kept them at a trot and the old wagon groaned and bounced over the rocks and ruts. I've been gone too long already, he thought. Don't know how long this takes. Hope Anna's all right. Just a little longer and we'll be there. Can't wait to get the old lady back to help her

When he rounded the last bend and saw the cabin, his heart sank. No smoke rose from the chimney. Maybe she just let the fire go down. He tore around the circle in front of the cabin, jammed the brake lever forward, and jumped to the ground. He leaped onto the porch and pounded on the door. Nothing happened. "Miz Bright!" he yelled. When there was no answer, he pulled the latch string and went inside. In the dim light, he could see there was no fire burning in the fireplace. The cabin was empty.

Anna was in pain. Her lower back hurt and from time to time she had severe cramps that caused her to cry out. Please God, she said. Help me. I'm afraid. When will Ben come back? Oh, please, Ben, I want you here.

She was unable to stay lying in bed. She found it helped to get on her hands and knees from time to time. It seemed to ease the back pain. But those cramps that kept happening made her try different positions, on her side, sitting up, even standing. They were sort of like cramps when you ate too many green apples, she thought, but much, much worse.

Finally she heard the sound of the wagon approaching and got back in the bunk as she was when he'd left her. She heard it pull to a stop, and Ben burst in the door, running straight to her side.

"I'm sorry, Anna. She wasn't home. I was afraid to go anywhere else without checkin' on you."

"What'll we do?"

"Don't know. I guess Miz Johnson is closest, but that 'ud take a while. If the Harveys were normal people, I could go there."

"O-o-o-o-h-h-h!" Anna replied, rolling back and forth.

"I hate to leave you."

Anna was gasping for breath and sweat ran from her face. She gave a small smile. "It comes and goes." She took a deep breath. "I don't like to be compared to a cow, but you have helped them, haven't you?"

"Many times, but—"

"Then we'll do it ourselves." She was wracked by another pain and stifled her urge to cry out.

"Ben, will it bother you to see me? It'll have to happen."

Ben looked embarrassed. "Prob'ly. But we'll do what we have to."

"You can go get my nightgown."

Ben hurried to get it, and brought fresh towels for her to lie on. Then they both had the same thought. Strange though it was, there was going to be another person living with them. Ben got an empty drawer from the chest in the bedroom. He took a small blanket and folded it tightly to fit the drawer and he placed it on a trunk he carried in from the bedroom. Rebecca had brought baby blankets to add to the ones Anna had knitted.

Ben left her side for only minutes at a time. He brought a chair to sit by the narrow bunk, and held her hand when the pains came.

"When you want to, just let out a holler," he said. "Nothin' to be ashamed of."

Anna found that it helped.

Ben's instincts were good. "I think it'll take a while. Try to relax and don't push too hard yet. Lay on your side and led me rub your back."

"Thanks. It feels good. But when the pains come, it's hard not to strain... o-o-o-h-h...here comes...another one!"

Hours went by. Anna was growing tired and Ben was worried. He began to wish he'd gone for help, but it was too late now. She couldn't think of eating anything, but would drink a little water. He left her only to keep the fire going and to keep water heating on the stove. Sometimes she wanted to sit up for a few minutes, or lie on her side, or even get back up on her hands and knees.

Between the pains, as Anna lay sweating and breathing hard, she felt like talking.

"Rebecca said to have a knife and some string ready to tie off the cord and cut it."

"Got that already, Babe."

"Good. And she said sometimes they have to slap the baby to get it started breathing. And she said you'll have to wash it."

He squeezed her hand. "That figgers. I'll be ready."

"And I'll bleed some, so don't worry."

Another pain came, stopping the flow of conversation.

As the sun descended in the west, it cast orange light through the front window. The pattern of pains changed, coming closer and closer together.

Anna said, "What if it won't come out? I'm scared."

"It'll be all right. Just hang in there. You're doin' good."

Anna lay back, her head and shoulders propped up on several pillows. Then she raised her head with a grimace of pain. "Ben, it's happening, now. I can feel it changing." She brought up her knees and lifted the gown up to her waist. "Can...you see..." She was overcome with another spasm and couldn't help pushing until her face turned red.

She reached for Ben's hand and clung to him. He felt no embarrassment after all, but was struck with wonder at what was about to happen. Please help us, God, he prayed silently.

Beneath the patch of dark red hair, her body was beginning to open slightly. She continued to strain, taking deep breaths and grunting with the effort. At last, he could see the very first of the crown of the baby's head. He could already see fine, wet red hair. Different from cattle, he thought. First thing you see of a calf are its front hooves, something to get hold of and help. Now I don't know what to do to help.

"You're doin' great Anna. I think it's startin' to show."

"Oh, Ben. It hurts!" She cried out in pain again.

"I know, I know. It's coming. You're doin' good!"

Soon the entire crown of the head was beginning to emerge, her body opening and stretching tightly, beginning to tear, with blood trickling down. In one last great push by Anna, the baby practically popped out into his large hands. He quickly wiped its face with a towel and turned it face down in his hands and patted its back.

Anna felt a great sense of relief and exhaustion. Then she heard a tiny cry. It was not angry but more like the mewling of a cat. A baby!

Then Ben practically shouted. "Oh Anna, Anna. We have a baby!"

"What is it? What is it?"

"Didn't look. Oh my love. It's a girl. Praise the Lord!"

He packed a folded cloth between Anna's legs to staunch the bleeding.

He wrapped the towel around the tiny bundle and placed it on Anna's breast. Anna opened the towel to look. The baby was wet and slick, streaked with blood...and pink and beautiful. She clasped her child to her. She looked up to see Ben crying and sobbed uncontrollably herself. Her little girl joined in with her own chorus.

Ben tied and cut the cord, then fetched a pan of water and a washcloth. He gently took the baby again and washed and dried her with the towel. Then he laid her on the foot of the bed and pinned a band around her middle as Rebecca had instructed. Next he pinned on a diaper, his first attempt since Oren was a baby. As small as the diaper was, it enveloped the little body so that only the legs from the knees down protruded.

"Anna, she's a cutie. All ten toes and fingers. She ain't opened her eyes yet. Maybe waitin' to see her mama."

"I want her again."

"Just a second." He put a red flannel jacket on her and gave her to Anna.

"Ben, you're really something. I bet most men couldn't do what you do."

Ben shrugged. "Had to be done."

Anna took her first step as a new mother. She untied the top of her gown and moved the little one's mouth to a nipple and she began to suck! "Ben! Ben! Look! She's eating!" She began to cry all over again. "Oh, oh, she opened one eye a crack!"

Ben was struck by the beauty of the scene; Anna with her tousled red hair, her creamy skin, holding the tiny pink child to her breast, the breast with a roseate aureole and nipple. He was so thankful that they had found each other, unusual though their meeting was.

Ben got one of the soft blankets Rebecca had brought and tucked it in around their little girl. "That's really something, how they know to do that. Anna, the after-birth will probably clear out pretty soon. Let me rub your belly a little and see if it helps settle down."

"She's asleep. You can bundle her and put her in her bed, though I hate to give her up."

In a few minutes, she experienced minor contractions and expelled the placenta. Ben put it in a bucket.

"What will you do with it?" Anna asked.

"I'll dig a deep hole and bury it out by the garden, put some rocks over it. Just be glad you ain't a cow."

"Why's that?"

"They eat it."

Anna shuddered. "Ugh! They don't!"

"They do."

"*Really?* Why?"

"I reckon it's so's wild animals don't come around and find the calf."

"Well, that's not the only reason I don't want to be a cow, but it's a good one."

Anna was weary and sore, but so thankful her ordeal was over. And the baby! She found it hard to believe it wasn't a dream; a child of her own to hold and to love. And Ben; he was so steadfast and dependable. He had brought her warm water and cloths to wash with and a clean gown to wear, then helped her to their bed. The little bunk was a mess and Ben set about cleaning up.

As she slept, Ben went out in the freezing darkness and milked the cow and fed the animals, then came back inside and ate some of the cold food Anna was preparing when the first signs arrived to announce Eva's birth.

CHAPTER 44

The sun was shining with a hint of spring in the air. March wind had abated during the night, so it appeared Rebecca would have a comfortable ride back up the creek road, if she chose to come back with him. Ben hurried the team along, trying to stay awake. It had been a long night with Eva Mae asserting her role as the center of the new small family. She had awakened several times during the night, demanding to be fed. Ben couldn't manage that part, but each time he helped Anna to the rocking chair, changed a diaper if needed, and kept the fire stoked. Despite the loss of sleep, both he and Anna were drawn close with their pride at being a family.

By candlelight during one of the changings, they both stood over Eva and marveled at her perfection. "Look," Anna had said. "You can still fold the top of her foot against her shin, like she was in the womb. And look at her tiny, tiny fingernails!" As Ben drove along, he smiled at the recollection.

Rebecca indeed jumped at the chance to help with the newborn for a couple of days. Tom made plans to come for her, promising to bring the children with him. The promise was mainly for Josie, who would have to step back into the role of taking care of the household, now increased by her two little stepsisters.

Rebecca hurried into the house behind Ben and both tiptoed into the silence toward the back bedroom. Ben peeked in to find Anna and Eva both asleep. He held his finger to his lips, but beckoned Rebecca to follow him to the makeshift drawer-bed where Eva slept. Rebecca smiled, but her lips trembled as she gazed at the angelic face. Eva moved her lips in a sucking motion in her sleep, apparently a pleasant baby dream.

They withdrew to the kitchen area, and spoke in whispers. "Rebecca, I moved the mattress from the loft bed to the one down here behind the curtain for you. I've taken that one out to wash."

"Good. I'll bring my stuff in and wait for Anna to wake up. You can bring the cradle in."

"I'll do it, and thanks. Then I'll put the team away. I've got a batch of washing to do that I started before the baby came. Give me a holler if you need anything."

Ben went about his chores, building a fire under the big black wash pot and setting the towels and ticking from the birth bed to soak in a tub of cold water. Rebecca went to work putting the kitchen in order and getting out fixings for the noon meal, all done quietly. Anna woke up when she heard whimpers coming from the baby and she carried Eva into the kitchen to embrace her mother-in-law.

The four settled into a routine for the next couple of days. Rebecca relieved Anna of the household chores while she recovered, and helped with the baby when Anna napped. Ben urged Rebecca to sleep-in during the night feedings, since they had to wake up anyway, then she could give Anna some rest during the day.

Eva proved to be a good baby, sleeping well in her borrowed cradle between feedings. She greedily drank her mother's milk, and from it produced a surprising number of dirty diapers. Ben took on the task of washing them. He said to himself, I reckon if I can muck out the horses' stalls, this is no problem. With Rebecca there, he managed to put in two good half days of plowing, the weather staying mild.

Tom brought the rest of the family up on Saturday when the kids were out of school. It was a joyous gathering around the youngest member of the family, but particularly for Anna, who only a short time before felt alone and unloved. What a change it was from those days in exile, hiding in the cold attic of the barn. Now she had a family who cared for her.

Little Eva was passed from one grandparent to another, but Josie was the most interested in holding her niece. The little girls, Jenny and Essie, didn't leave Eva's side until they were called to eat the meal Rebecca had prepared, a big pot of navy beans with ham, cornbread, and lots of fresh milk from Goldie, now with her own new baby. Jenny and Essie were amused and pleased that they were now aunts. In the afternoon, the time came for the family to go home, leaving Ben and Anna to their new life together. Rebecca promised to get word to Margaret, who had started coming to Sunday services.

The following morning, a clear Sunday, Ben and Anna were having break-fast, discussing the family visit. "I'm so happy, Ben. I never dreamed life could be so good after losing my mother the way it happened."

"Well, you can tell they all love you, just as I do. Things are shapin' up—"

Just as he spoke these words, there was the loud *boom!* of a shotgun, and the bray of a mule. As Ben jumped to his feet, they heard the thun-der of horses' hooves from the direction of the pasture.

Ben grabbed his hat and the Winchester and ran out the front door. The horses and mules were galloping toward the back corner of the field. Both cows were following, their udders flopping from side to side as they ran. He hurried after them and found them huddled together, the horses' heads held high, nostrils dilated, the whites of their eyes showing.

"Steady guys," Ben said as he approached. "What the heck's goin' on?" As he drew closer, he saw that one of the mules had scattered spots of blood on his rump, some of the blood trickling down his leg. He shook his head. The mule clambered over that dang fence again and one of them shot him. Now I guess I gotta go talk to 'em. I've about had it with this business.

Ben went by the house and stuck his head in the door. "Anna, I gotta go to the Harveys and talk about this. One of the mules got out and I believe they shot him with a shotgun."

"*What?* Will he be all right?"

"I reckon so, but it ain't how a neighbor is supposed to act."

"You be careful. I don't trust them."

"Me either. I'll leave the Winchester here."

"You sure?"

"Yeah. I'll try to keep things cool."

Ben back-tracked across the pasture until he found a single set of tracks coming from the direction of the Harveys, the tracks far apart with evidence of the caulks on the shoes digging deep. Sure enough, they came from the decaying rail fence, and on the other side were more tracks. The Harveys had started spring plowing with several furrows ringing the field. In the middle of the field some downed cornstalks were still scattered about, with the possibility of some nubbins of corn to be gleaned by a stray mule.

He came to the gap in the fence, where the rotten rails and the riders had collapsed. He sighed and trudged on toward the Harvey house place. As he drew nearer, he saw Ferd and his two older sons, Bob and Clint, waiting for him. Clint cradled a double-barreled shotgun in his right arm.

"Thought you might show up," said Ferd. "That damn mule of your'n don't know where he belongs."

"A fence would keep him out. It needs fixin'. People are supposed to think for a mule, not the other way around."

Ferd's face reddened. "Whaddya mean by that?"

"I mean the fence needs to be put right. I'm tired of talkin' about it."

Clint stepped forward and shoved the muzzle of the shotgun against Ben's chest. He pulled back one of the hammers. "We can fix that. How about this here doin' a little talkin'?"

Ben stood his ground. "I said I'm through talkin'. I'll just build my own fence."

"You ain't gonna like what happens if you do," said Ferd. "Clint, you can ease off. We'll take care of this later. But there ain't gonna be no devil's lane by my property, I can tell ya that."

"Sorry you have to feel this way," said Ben, and he turned and walked away, feeling tension in the middle of his back, the spot where a shotgun blast would strike if it came.

When Ben came into the house, Anna rushed to embrace him. "I was so worried," she said, almost in a whisper. "Now that we've found each other, I couldn't bear it if anything happened to you."

Ben said, "It'll be all right." He held her to him and kissed her, then he led her to the kitchen table and pulled out chairs.

"What's wrong with those people?" She asked.

"Well, they didn't seem to be happy folks before, but there was several things set 'em off. When your Pa left, I think they thought they could just kind of slide in and take over this place. It has a lot of timber they don't have. Pa didn't think much about it, but he bought it from the bank by takin' over the loan. He had it in mind to give me a start. It really made 'em mad, for no good reason. Then their sister got widowed, and who should marry her but my Pa. Well, in Ferd's eyes it was a play for Rebecca's farm. He's wrong, but it makes him about as mean as a bear with a sore tail."

"He has some grown boys, too, doesn't he? I didn't pay much attention when I lived here but it seems like Papa talked about them."

"Yes. Clint is the worst. He's tried to push me around a little, but I haven't taken the bait. Bob's better, but he just goes along. They have a little brother, and a sister maybe close to my age that I know from school."

"What'll we do?"

"I think they don't fix the fence on purpose, just to provoke me. I don't see much choice but to just build the fence for myself on my own side to keep in my stock. I'll talk with Pa. It could be a source of more trouble as Ferd has already said. Folks call it a 'devil's lane' when there's two fences side by side."

"Why?"

"Hurts their pride, I reckon."

"They should just fix the fence."

"Sure. But they don't want to, as I just said. But try not to worry."

CHAPTER 45

Tom Archer was setting the morning milk to cool in the spring-house when he heard the sound of hoofbeats on the lane. A horse whickered, answered by his horses from the lot behind the barn. He stepped outside into the light drizzle, as Ben reined Charger to a halt.

"Mornin', Pa," Ben called.

Tom walked to meet him. "Hey, Ben. What brings you out on a day like this?"

"Got a problem."

"Climb down and let's go inside. I'm done takin' care of the milk."

When they were inside, seated at the kitchen table with coffee, Ben began. "Them Harveys are actin' up again." He went on to describe the incident with the mule being shot.

"Pa, I was scared when Clint shoved that shotgun against me."

Tom shook his head. "Don't blame you. That's crazy stuff."

Rebecca had joined them and she said, "I'm so sorry, Ben. It makes me ashamed of my family."

"Not your fault, Rebecca," Ben said. "But what do you think I ought to do?"

Tom took a deep breath, then a sip of coffee. "Well, there's got to be a fence. We've talked to them more than once. You've patched the fence on their end when you didn't have to. Here's what I think. I'll go talk to the sheriff and tell him what's goin' on; see if he'll get into it. If he don't, we have a right to build on our own place to keep your stock in."

"All right, Pa. I'll wait 'til I hear back from you."

"I didn't want to interrupt," Rebecca said. "But how're that sweet baby and that sweet mama in your house?"

Ben smiled back, "They're both doin' good, thanks for askin'."

It was four days later that Tom Archer rode up in mid-afternoon to see Ben, who was unloading split rails in the back lot by the barn.

"Hey, Pa," Ben said.

"Good to see ya, Son," Tom said as he swung from the saddle. Beauty shook herself and snorted to clear her nostrils, then blew a loud, blubbering breath out through her velvet lips.

"News from the sheriff?"

"Yeah. That's why I came up. He thinks it won't amount to nothing. Don't know if I agree with him, but I hope he's right. He said you did the right thing, not takin' a gun along. Things are calmer that way."

"That's what I thought. I can't see somebody startin' a gunfight over a fence. They do seem to be spoilin' for a fight, at least that Clint does. There've been a couple of times he's tried to provoke me but I didn't fall for it."

"Well, if we do decide to go ahead, I'll come up and help. And I think Rafe and Matthew would come, too. The faster we get it up, the better."

"I appreciate it. I don't see much of a choice but to get it over with and make sure my stock stays over here where they belong. The mule's all right, but he'll carry some shot around. I think it was probably a turkey load of BBs, scattered enough that he caught only a dozen or so."

Tom shook his head in disgust. "What a thing to do. Well, let's talk about something better. How about I go see your pretty girls?"

Three days later they assembled at Ben's to start building fence. It was a bright, clear morning, with the promise of spring. Ben had loaded his wagon with fence rails from the pile he had accumulated from two seasons of work in the woods. Tom arrived first and he and Ben began loading his wagon with additional rails, along with the few tools they'd need; primarily axes and sledges. Rafe Johnson and his eldest son, Matthew, arrived while this was in progress and they helped finish the load.

"Well, are we ready to build fence?" said Tom.

"I reckon so," Rafe replied.

"I sure thank you for comin'," Ben said. "And I hope there's no trouble."

"Them Harveys is always lookin' for trouble," Rafe said. "Don't know that they've done much since the war, though. They mostly just don't amount to much, the menfolks, that is. Hard to believe they're kin to that Rebecca of yours."

"She doesn't say much about them, but she sure isn't proud of them."

When they were loaded they drove the teams across the pasture behind the barn to the center point of the fence where Ben's half ended and the Harvey half began, the men walking beside the wagons. Here the open pasture gave in to some scattered trees and clumps of brush.

"This is it," Ben said. "You can see my half is about new. There's also a bunch of my new rails on the other half, but I refused to rebuild the whole thing. Now I'm ready. I don't know exactly where the property line is, so we'll move in a few feet."

They all nodded and began to lay out the tools and unload rails.

Ben laid out the first rail, interlocking its end in the newer fence he'd built and angling it toward his side from the old fence, leaving room to walk between the two. He staked it down, and Tom brought the next rail to start the new line. Rafe and Matthew followed with more rails and the first sections of the zigzag fence began to take place, the fence four/three rails, or a little over waist high. It had to be laid up several sections at a time, since the ends overlapped the previous section rails.

"That oughta keep that mule in," said Rafe.

"Once they get out, it's harder to keep them in," said Tom. "Although gettin' shot might make him stay home."

They had been working perhaps a half hour, when they saw the Harveys approach in the distance.

"Here comes trouble," Tom said. "Ferd and his three boys. He should'a left the young'en at home. Not a good lesson for a kid, seein' they've brought guns with them."

"Well, we're not armed, so I doubt they'll try anything," Rafe said. "They just want to look tough."

They kept working as the Harveys approached, the three men abreast, Ferd in the middle. Young Buford trailed behind, one of the hounds walking beside him.

As they drew closer they came to a halt. Bone trotted over to the other hound and the two circled each other. Bob and Clint raised their shotguns across their chests and Ferd spoke, "What the *hell* you'ens think you're a-doin'?"

"We're here to build a decent fence to keep the livestock in," Tom said.

"That ain't the way to treat a neighbor, trying to make him look bad."

"Ferd, we had an agreement and we've talked about it and it didn't get done. Now if you look bad, it ain't our fault."

"Just 'cause we ain't got to it, you got not right to show off and make a devil's lane. Just 'cause you was a big shot Yankee yella-leg in the war don't mean you get to do what you want."

"The war's been over for quite a spell, and I know how you and you brother spent those years. That's all in the past, as far as I'm concerned. Now we need to do the right thing by each other."

Clint raised the shotgun and aimed it at Tom's feet.

"There's no call to start trouble," Tom said. "We've a right to build what we want on our property and we're goin' ahead."

"Property you stole out from under us," said Ferd. "Clint, you can go ahead and show him what might happen."

They were all shocked by a shotgun blast, exploding dirt and rocks on Tom's boots and lower legs. Tom didn't flinch, but stared back at Clint. "You'd better not start something that'll cause you grief, young man. I've seen plenty of your kind." He looked at his companions, then turned to Ferdinand. "Ferd, we'll leave for now, to let things calm down. But I will tell you, we're goin' to have a decent fence between properties, and you know that's the right thing. If you want to build it, we're happy to let you. If not, we'll be back to build it ourselves."

Ferd merely stared at him.

Tom turned around. "We'll, men, let's gather up and get out of here."

Anna heard the shotgun blast in the distance. She wrapped a shawl about her shoulders and bundled baby Eva close to her breast. She stepped out on the porch and looked anxiously toward the fence line where she knew the men were working. What shall I do? she thought. Surely, it must be nothing, but there are four of our men over there, including my precious new husband.

Shortly, she heard the wagons coming back toward the house and felt a sense of relief when she saw two men in each. When they drew into the gravel drive, she ran to the first one to meet Ben and Matthew. Ben handed the reins to Matthew. "You can go on back. I'll be right there." He jumped down and embraced Anna with the baby between them.

"Everything's all right, Anna."

"I was so worried when I heard—"

"It was just that Clint showing off."

"Well, I don't like it. I'll put coffee on if you all want to come in."

When they were seated around the kitchen table, Tom spoke first. "What do you think, Rafe?"

"Hard to say. I don't think much of the old man and what he did in the past, but that son of his is a bit crazy."

"Ben?"

"I don't know, Pa. As you know, Clint's tried to pick a fight before. Seems to me, though, he'd be foolish to do anything in front of witnesses. Would it help to let word leak out?"

Tom took a sip of coffee. He drummed his fingers on the table. "It didn't do much good to talk to the sheriff. I may see what Oley Jensen thinks, since he's the nearest thing to a preacher around here."

"Sounds good," said Rafe. "We'll be coming to Service this Sunday. Maybe by then the whole thing will have cooled down, anyway."

Anna was standing near the stove, holding the sleeping baby. "If I can say so, Ben, I'd like to go on Sunday, see if Margaret is there."

Ben looked up. "If you feel up to it, we'll go."

"That settles it," Tom said, getting up.

"Pa, would you like to leave the team and wagon? Ride my horse home?"

"Guess we'd better unload it. Might need it in the next couple of days."

CHAPTER 46

Anna confessed her anxiety as they approached Sycamore for Sunday services. "What will they think of me, my age with a baby already?"

"Not that unusual," said Ben. "It's all in your own mind. Folks who come to Service are generally good people. They'll welcome you and love you, not to mention that little bundle you're holdin'." He smiled down at Eva, snugly wrapped in her best blanket.

"I hope you're right. I hope there's been no gossip."

"Well, if there is, it's on them. We know what the real story is."

Ben was right. As they joined the other families streaming in wagons and buggies toward the schoolhouse, there were smiles and waves. When they drew close, Margaret came running toward them, skirts held up so as not to trip.

She arrived as Ben climbed down to tie the team to a tree. "Oh, Anna!" she shouted. "Give me that baby this instant! And get down here for a hug!"

George Zinn had followed Margaret at a slower pace and arrived in time to join Ben in watching the reunion. "Let me see that baby, too," he said, "then we'd better get on in to the schoolhouse."

The four found seats near the back, in case Eva decided to create a fuss. Oley Jensen took the podium and began the service with a lengthy prayer, imploring God to provide good weather for the crops and thanking him for health and happiness on behalf of those who had those benefits. Then he said, "Jewel, if you'll crank up that peeanner, we'll sing 'Amazing Grace'."

Eva woke up during the hymn and joined the chorus to the extent that Anna carried her outside. She missed the opening of Oley's sermon.

Oley cleared his throat and began. "I hear tell of some strife in some parts of our area, so I'm gonna speak on the commandments of our Lord. Not all of 'em, just a couple. Let me refresh your memories, for you'ens that might need it."

He perched wire-rimmed glasses on his nose and consulted a worn Bible. "In the book of Mark, Jesus was bein' quizzed by the scribes and they asked him which is the first commandment of all. Jesus must'a said, that's easy. 'Thou shalt love the Lord thy God with all thy soul, with all thy heart, and with all thy mind, and with all thy strength'. Now if we all was to do that, the rest might not even be needed, but bein' sinners, you know we just don't do it.

"Anybody recollect what the second most important one was? I won't embarrass you by askin'. It was 'Love thy neighbor as thyself.' Jesus said these two are the most important of all. They went on to talk about other things, but not the other eight commandments, though they're important, too, of course.

"So if you're havin' trouble with a neighbor, it's purty clear what the Lord asks of you..."

Ben heard these words, but his thought blurred the sermon that continued with further examples and exhortations to "get along." He seems to be talkin' right at me, since I know Pa told him about the fence. But who in the world would love somebody that acted like them Harveys? I don't see any way I can. They'd laugh at the idea and just get meaner. No, I'm gonna go ahead and make sure there's a good fence. I always heard "good fences make good neighbors," like Pa said to Ferd. That may not be a commandment, but it sounds good to me.

Later in the afternoon, Ben and Anna talked about the morning. Anna was pleased that Ben had been right. During the short social gathering after church, she had been welcomed with open arms and baby Eva admired by all without a hint of condemnation. They'd gone on to have dinner with the Archer family with happiness pushing aside the cloud of concern hanging over Ben and Tom. They'd had a chance to talk privately and Tom agreed with Ben's thinking. The subject of the sermon was all well and good, but they couldn't see how it applied to their problem. Tom thought the Harveys were mostly talk and bluster, so they agreed to go back the following day and resume work on the fence. Tom had to go into Sycamore the next morning, but would get up there some time after noon.

"I'll ride over this afternoon and see if Rafe and Matt can come again," said Ben. "If not, we'll do what we can."

The wagons were loaded and ready by mid-afternoon. "The days are longer now, so we should be able to get in a few hours before sunset," said Tom.

"You think they'll cause trouble?" said Rafe. "I see you brought your shotgun this time."

"I don't think so," said Tom. "I don't intend to start anything, but I'd sure hate not to be able to defend myself."

Rafe smiled. "I had the same thought. I brought my old Springfield. I see Ben has the Winchester."

Tom shrugged. "Just as well be ready. I may have been thinking backwards. Maybe if they see we're armed, they'll be less likely to do anything. Who knows?"

They trundled out to the fence line in the two wagons to where they had left off a few days earlier. Bone gamboled alongside, sniffing the ground, reading the actions of wildlife from the night before. As they creaked to a halt, all four men jumped to the ground and started unloading tools and a few rails to begin. Weather was cool and clear, but clouds were gathering in the west, partially obscuring the declining sun. They leaned the guns against some scrub bushes out of the way.

As before, Ben took the lead, laying out the fence line with the bottom rails, staking them in place. The other three followed behind, adding rails and riders to carry the top rail, the way Tom liked to do it. The work went fast with four men working, and they had to keep moving the wagons.

As they moved along, Ben would occasionally retrieve rails he had placed on the old fence. "Just as well use these. They're doin' no good over there; like a saddle on a dead horse."

"Things are goin' good," Rafe said, looking toward the Harvey place. "Maybe they've decided to give it up; they ain't home, one or the other."

"I hope so," said Tom. "At this rate, thanks to all the good rails Ben made, we should be able to finish with this in another full day." He glanced toward the west. "We've still got maybe two more hours. Wait a minute...who's that over on the lane?"

The others looked toward the lane that bordered the field a hundred yards or so away. "Two or three men," said Rafe. "Don't recongnize 'em from here, but it ain't the Harveys."

Tom groaned. "I bet it's some snoops from around here. I talked over our situation with Oley at the mill this morning, after his sermon yesterday. I bet somebody overheard, or he talked too much. Well, it don't change anything."

They went back to work, ignoring their audience. After another half-hour and more rails in place, Bone raised the alarm, baying and staring toward the Harvey place. Sure enough, three men appeared, starting to walk across the fallow cornfield in their direction.

"Well, here they come again," said Rafe.

Ben walked back to where the guns were and carried them to a bush closer by. Tom glanced at him without comment, then turned back to watch the approach of the three men. They'd left the boy behind this time. As before, the two younger men were carrying long guns, framing their father, who appeared to be wearing a sidearm.

Tom stood and watched them draw closer. When they were about thirty yards away, he called out, "That's far enough, Ferd! Stop and say your piece."

They did stop, but Ferd replied, "Ain't up to you to give orders. We come to put a stop to this."

Ben eased his way toward the guns. Tom said, "Ferd, you and your boys don't want to stir up trouble."

Ferd drew the long-barreled revolver and waved it in the air. "Ain't me causin' trouble."

"Well, we have to have a fence, so we're goin' ahead." As Tom replied, Rafe walked slowly toward Ben and the guns.

"I see ya been stealin' rails off our fence."

"Rails Ben put there. He just took 'em back."

Without warning, the confrontation erupted in gunfire with tongues of flame and clouds of smoke. In but a few short moments, Tom Archer was down and Clint lay sprawled on his back, his shotgun several feet away. Ferdinand Harvey was holding his right arm, blood flowing down his dangling forearm. Both Ben and Rafe had been hit by shotgun pellets.

Ben ran to his father, who was writhing on the ground, holding his left side with his right hand, blood leaking through his fingers. Rafe went to check on Ferd and Clint.

"Pa, are you hurt bad?" Ben cried.

"I'm all right, Son. Just got me in the meat of my side."

Ben took off his work jacket, and tore off his shirt. "Let me bind it up."

As he did so, Tom asked, wincing with pain. "How are Ferd and his boys?"

"Ferd and Clint are down. Bob ran away. Rafe's checking on them." He looked in that direction. "Looks like Ferd's settin' down and Rafe's workin' on him. Clint's down for good, I expect."

Clouds of smoke still drifted among the trees. The distinctive scent of gunpowder filled the air. Matthew approached, white and shaking. "Is it over?" he said.

"I think so, Matt," Tom said, now sitting up. "You can go see if your Pa needs help."

The whole sequence had taken place in less than a minute. After binding his father's wound, Ben went to check on the others. In the distance, three men were walking across the field from the direction of the lane.

Both he and Rafe were bleeding, but not seriously. We'll see to that later, Ben thought. Rafe was wrapping a piece of his shirt around Ferd's right arm, Matthew standing over him. Ferd was slumped over, looking at the ground.

Ben walked over to see about Clint. He lay on his back, arms flung overhead. He was staring at the evening sky, mouth open, blood trickling from a small round hole in the middle of his forehead. With the release of tension from the adrenaline in his system, Ben began to shake. What have I done? he thought. It happened so fast and all I saw were his eyes on me and the black twelve-gauge muzzle bores. I saw his forehead in my sights and squeezed the trigger. I didn't really think about it. I hope God will forgive me.

As he started back to his father, he glanced toward the Harvey place and saw Rose and Buford running toward them, their ma right behind. Oh, my, what will we say to them?

By the time he got back to his father's side, the three men were standing over him.

"What the hell happened, Tom?" asked Ezekiel Peake.

"What are you doing here, Zeke?" Tom replied.

"Well, we wuz down't Sycamore and heard tell there might be trouble."

"Did it work out well for you, then?"

"Now, Tom, don't be that-away. We jest thought we might be able to help."

"How about you, Hannibal, and you, Preston?"

"Well, me and Press was headed up this way, anyway," Hannibal Montgomery said, looking down at the dirt.

Tom took a deep breath, and winced. "Well, I don't mean to be hard, but I don't feel good about it. I think we got one dead, and for no good reason—"

He was interrupted by a loud wailing. Estelle Harvey had fallen to her knees by her son and her husband.

"You fellers might go see what you can do for the Harveys. They have more trouble than we do," said Tom.

Ben looked toward the west, where a blood-red sunset shone through the bare silhouettes of the trees. In his state of mind, it looked like it could be the fires of hell.

CHAPTER 47

T om Archer had lain back down, still in pain. Rafe and Matt
had joined them. He'd been thinking about what to do. "Here's
what I'm thinkin'. I believe that pistol bullet is still in me, so I
need to get it dug out. I hate to say it, but I need to get to the doctor in
Forsyth. Any ideas?"

"I need to drive you in, Pa," said Ben. "I need to turn myself in to the
sheriff 'til this gets sorted out."

Rafe spoke. "Me and the boys, Matt, Mark, and Luke, will see to your
livestock—both your places as long as it takes."

"Thanks, Rafe. And Ben? I think Anna and the baby need to stay
with Rebecca."

Ben nodded. "Rafe, do you think we ought to offer Ferd a ride in to
Forsyth with us?"

"I'll go see, but I doubt he'll go. Bullet didn't hit the bone and went
on through."

They unloaded Tom's wagon and headed back toward the house. Tom
was lying in the wagon box. As they cleared the fringe of scattered trees,
they saw Anna running toward them in the fading light, her red hair
streaming behind her, clutching the bundled baby in her arms. Rafe was
driving the team, so Ben jumped down and ran to meet her.

It was a gentle collision, with the baby in her arms, Ben supporting
them from falling. He could see Anna was crying. "It's all right," he
said.

"B-but Ben, you're bleeding!"

"It's just a few pellets. Now me and the mule are just alike."

"Don't tease at a time like this! What happened?"

"Shootin' started and it ain't good. I'll tell you all about it when we get to the house."

"Anybody hurt bad?"

"Clint's dead, and Pa's got a bullet in him that needs to come out."

"*Dead?*" That's one of the Harveys?"

"It is. He's been a trouble-maker."

As they talked, they turned toward the house and the wagons caught up with them.

"Here's what we decided," Ben continued. He laid out the plan for her. When he got to the part of turning himself in, she stopped.

"You're the one who shot him?"

"I'm afraid so, Darlin'. I hate it, but there wasn't much choice."

"Oh, my! What'll happen?"

"We'll see, but it should be fine."

"You're not just saying that?"

"No. It'll be all right."

Ben drove the team up the dirt main street of Forsyth in the predawn darkness. It would be at least another hour before dawn, maybe later with that cloud cover. It was a new town of frame and clapboard buildings, since it had been burned to the ground by the Union Army back in '63. They must have started building it back about the time I was born, Ben thought. Course we lived in East Tennessee then, while Ma waited for Pa to come home. I heard that the brick courthouse down on the left was gutted and rebuilt. Guess I might be seein' the inside of that pretty soon.

Only a few lights were showing in some upstairs windows. Early risers or those afraid of the dark. Good thing the doc's house is on this side of town. Ben reined in in front of the two-story house, which was all in darkness. It had a picket fence along the street with a walkway of flat limestones leading to a porch that wrapped around two sides of the house. There were rocking chairs and benches for those waiting to see the doctor at his clinic on the first floor.

Ben stepped back in the wagon box to check on Tom. Last time he'd looked, Pa was sleeping, his face gray and set in pain. They'd put one of the shuck mattresses in the box and bundled him in quilts. "We're here, Pa," he said softly.

Tom blinked awake. "Where?"

"At the doc's in Forsyth." As Tom started to stir, Ben said, "Just rest easy, if you can. I'll see if I can rouse him."

Ben ran up the walk and knocked on the door. Nothing happened. He knocked harder and waited. Finally, after he pounded on the door loud enough to shake the building, a faint light showed through the curtains next to the door.

The door swung open and a small man in a nightcap and long gown peered at Ben. "What's going on, young man?"

"My pa's got a bullet in him, needs to come out."

"What's your name?"

"Ben Archer, Sir. My pa's Tom Archer."

"*Tom Archer?* How'd it happen? Well, never mind that now. Where's he hit?"

"In his side."

"Can he walk?"

"I think so."

"Let's get him in here. If you can do that, I'll go get ready."

Tom Archer lay on his back, both hands gripping the edges of the table, a piece of harness leather clinched in his teeth. Doctor Stevenson bent over him in concentration, beads of sweat on his forehead, his spectacles slipping down his nose. Ben stood beside him, feeling helpless at the groans of his father.

"Slide that lamp a little closer," the doctor said, nodding at the small table across from him. "I think I've about got to it."

He was probing deep in the wound on Tom's left side. When he had first removed the cloth wrapping Tom's waist, it had stuck to the clotted blood, starting the flow again. He wiped it away to reveal the small round hole, ringed with bruising.

"Ah," Stevenson said, withdrawing the forceps and holding the bullet up to the light. "Thirty-six caliber, I'd say. Saw plenty of them during the war." He dropped it with a clink into a metal pan.

"We got it, Mister Archer. Now this is going to sting. We'll wash it with alcohol and put a dressing on. Should start feeling better."

Tom spit the leather out of his mouth. "Thanks, Doc. Coulda' been worse."

"Looks like you've had worse. Saber cut?"

"Yeah."

Ben had seen the long white scar across his father's chest.

After Tom was properly bandaged, Doctor Stevenson and Ben helped him lie down on a bunk in the next room.

"Now you, young man. That blood—is it from you?"

"Yes, Sir. I got hit with some shotgun pellets. Should we just leave 'em be?"

"Let's have a look."

The doctor dug out four or five and left about the same number in place. After he was disinfected and bandaged, they walked into the front waiting room. The doctor wiped his hand across his white bristle of a mustache. "Your pa's pretty tuckered out. Why don't you go ahead and take care of your horses and stop back by in a few hours. You're probably beat, yourself."

"I'll do that. I've got to go see the sheriff."

"I figured that. I'll stay out of that part, but I will do this: I'll seal that bullet in an envelope and keep it here. Then I'll testify, if it comes to that, about where it came from."

"That's good, Doctor Stevenson. And let me know what we owe you, beyond my thanks." They shook hands and Ben left.

The town was beginning to come to life as he drove the weary team up Main Street and down a side street to the livery stable. Merchants were sweeping sidewalks and lighting lamps in their shops. He arranged with the proprietor for parking the wagon in back, stabling the horses, and hanging the harness in a secure tack room.

"How long ya gonna need to keep 'em here?" he was asked.

"I don't know for sure," Ben replied. "At least a couple of days, maybe longer."

"All right. Just let me know."

Ben went back and brushed the horses down, then trudged back to Main and left toward the county jail and sheriff's office, carrying saddlebags and the Winchester.

Sheriff Horton turned from the stove with a coffee pot and cup in his hand when Ben walked in. "Good mornin' young feller. What can we do for ya?"

"My name's Ben Archer and I need to talk."

"Oh yeah, I know your pa. Grab a cup and come back to my office." Then to a deputy seated behind a chest-high counter, "Henry, we'll be in back."

Ben followed him past a row of benches and into a corner office. There were deer antlers on the wall and a long gun case full of Winchesters like his and stubby double-barreled shotguns. Ben leaned his rifle against the doorjamb and dropped the saddlebags on the floor.

"Have a seat," the sheriff said, sitting behind a scarred oak desk. "What seems to be the trouble?"

"I came to turn myself in. I killed a man yesterday."

The sheriff sat up straighter. "How'd it happen?"

"Pa talked to you about the Harveys and the fence, I believe. Well, it don't make sense, but it led to shootin' over it, and well—"

"Oh, no." The Sheriff Horton wagged his head. "I didn't think it would come to that. Who's dead?"

"Clint. We didn't either, and we tried to talk sense."

"Shoulda' known," the sheriff said to himself. "Wait here." He walked to the door and shouted down the hall. "Bobby Joe, you and Henry come down here."

Ben heard them clomping down the hall and they came into the room. Both were dressed in denim and wide hats. Handlebar mustaches, gun belts, vests with stars, and boots completed the nearly identical outfits.

The sheriff addressed the larger of the two, a heavy-set man about Pa's age, thought Ben.

"Henry, we got us a dead man, Clint Harvey. Without hearin' anything here, I want you to get on up to the Harvey place, that's Ferdinand, up on Bull Creek, not Clyde. Take a statement from them and look at the body real careful. If they've already buried him, have 'em dig him up. I don't want no dee-tails wrong."

"Yessir."

"Get right on it. Have Sloan watch the desk."

As Henry left, he turned to the other deputy, a smaller, wiry, dark-haired man. "Bobby Joe, get some paper and take down what Ben Archer, here, tells us."

"Before anything else, I need to tell you Pa is over at the doc's in a bunk. I brought him in during the night and Doc took a pistol bullet out of his side. Doc kept it and will vouch for it. Now, you know about the fence problem and the Harveys shootin' the mule, I think. If it's all right, I'll start right with them comin' yesterday to where we were workin'...."

Ben talked on for the next two hours, talking slowly and repeating so Bobby Joe could get it all down. When the sheriff decided it was complete, Ben read it over, making some corrections before he signed it.

"Now, I'd better go check on Pa and see if he's woke up." He started to rise.

"Let's hold on a minute," Sheriff Horton said. "No offense, but we just have your side of the story. I think my duty would say that we detain you at least until Henry gets back and we sort this out."

Ben looked stricken.

"Ya can't take it that way. This is serious. I'll go talk to your pa and see how he tells it."

"There's only one way, and that's the way it happened!"

"I know, I know. But here's somethin' you might not have thought of. What if they come after you for revenge...you know the old 'tooth for tooth'?"

CHAPTER 48

Ben took little notice of his surroundings as he was led into a cell and the iron door clanged shut behind him. He was numb from the events of the day before, and by the weary all-night drive into Forsyth. Now all he saw was the narrow bunk along the wall. He collapsed into it and was soon asleep.

He was unable to gauge the passage of time when he was awakened from tortured dreams by the sound of the door being unlocked. He sat up to see the sheriff standing there with a jingling ring of keys.

"Wake up, young fella, and come out here for a bite to eat."

Ben rose unsteadily. "Thanks, Sheriff. What time is it?"

"It's mid-day. We can talk some more. Your pa's doin' good."

Ben sat at a plank table to a bowl of beans with fatback and a chunk of cornbread.

"Pa's doin' good?"

"Yeah, he's stiff and sore, but Doc says he'll do fine. I talked to him about bunkin' in with you this evenin'."

"You're going to lock him up?"

"Yep. Same reason as I told you. Henry should be back tonight and we might get a better idea of how things stand."

Tom Archer was escorted in to the jailhouse and brought in to stay with Ben in the same cell. Ben hugged him gently, noting that he looked older than before the shooting. "Hey, Pa. I'm glad to see you. Sheriff says we're safer here, just in case."

"It's what he told me, too. Are you doin' all right?"

"Yeah, Pa, but I wish it hadn't happened."

"Me, too."

After they'd had their evening meal and were in their bunks, they heard sounds and muffled conversation coming from the front, but were unable to make out what was being said.

Deputy Henry Jeffrey rode in late at night and was giving his report.

"Just give me the short version and we can talk again tomorrow," Sheriff Horton said.

"They hadn't buried him yet, but he was wrapped up waitin' for the box to be built. I made 'em unwrap him so's I could have a look. Wasn't no doubt. Just one bullet right between the eyebrows."

Horton nodded. "Anybody else?"

"Ferd had one through the right arm."

"What'd he have to say?"

"Claimed they was just out huntin', him and the boys, and they happened by to see what was goin' on. Said the Archer boy drew down on them with the Winchester and started shootin'. Natcherly, he says they just tried to defend theirselves."

"D'you believe that?"

"No."

"I don't either. But I guess it ain't up to us. Wasn't the older boy there?"

"He was. I made him stay away while I talked to his pa. I couldn't get much out of Bob, except he'd been coached to say they was out huntin'. As to who shot first, all I got was 'it all happened fast.' He says he didn't shoot. Ferd's brother was there and they was makin' hints about gettin' even, without directly sayin what."

"I figgered as much. You go ahead and get some rest, Henry. We'll double up nights until we see this through. We can see what the prosecutor says, but it looks like a trial will have to happen. We'll need to talk to Rafe Johnson and his boy and them three yahoos Tom Archer said had come to watch. I'll see you tomorrow."

Tom and Ben spent a restless night. The town and the jail were quiet, but they talked into the night about what was to come. They received a pleasant surprise, however, when Deputy Duke came back in late morning and unlocked the door; told them they could come out front to see some visitors.

When they entered the booking area, Anna and Rebecca rushed to embrace their husbands, taking care for their wounds. Margaret and George stood back, Margaret holding baby Eva.

Anna looked up at Ben, tears flowing. "Are they going to keep you here?"

"Yes, Darlin'. Sheriff says it's for my own safety. He don't treat me like a criminal. Question is, how are you?"

"Aside from worry for you, all right. George is bunking with the boys and helping out. Rafe and Matthew have been coming to take care of the livestock. Is there danger for you?"

"I doubt it. But two of the deputies are here all the time just in case."

Nearby, Rebecca asked Tom, "Are you going to have to stay here?"

"At least for a while. We'll see what the schedule is. I have to lay around anyway while this heals some."

Ben and Anna went to the other couple. Ben shook George's hand. "Thanks, George. It takes a lot of worry away."

"Glad to do it. Sorry for the trouble."

"And Ben," Anna said. "We all came in Margaret's surrey."

"Thanks Margaret." Ben smiled at her. "Paid me back for that wagon ride in the rain a couple of years ago."

Margaret laughed. "You can bet I would have done it anyway. Want to hold Precious?"

"I surely do!"

After their short visit, George had agreed to get the team and wagon from the stable and drive it home, while Margaret drove the surrey. They all said reluctant goodbyes. The women had brought baskets of food, including two apple pies which Tom and Ben shared later with their jailers. Peace must have reigned over Forsyth in recent days, as there were no other prisoners in the jail.

Tom and Ben spent the rest of the day resting and contemplating the nature of the possible trial to come. As before, when mealtime came, they were allowed to come out into the booking area to eat. Deputy Sloan gave them a checker board to pass the time until bedtime.

Ben was awakened from a sound sleep by raised voices and the sound of horses' hooves. "Pa, wake up! Somethin' goin' on outside!" He said. He stood on his bunk and peered through the small barred window. Tom sat up in bed.

"Pa, there's a bunch of men on horseback with bandannas over their faces and they've got guns and mullen torches. Must be eight or nine of 'em!"

Just as he said that, Sloan unlocked their cell door. He was carrying two of the stubby shotguns and a Winchester rifle. "We got some troublemakers out front. Sheriff and Jeffrey are takin' care of it, but just in case…"

"Thanks, Jake," Tom said, rising stiffly.

"I'll leave the door unlocked."

Sheriff Horton stood on the board walk in front of the jail, a shotgun in his hands and the Colt Peacemaker on his hip. Henry Jeffrey stood beside him.

"You fellers lookin' for trouble, I got this Crowd Buster ready to give it to you." He lifted the stubby shotgun. "Both barrels loaded with double-aught buck."

One man, who appeared to be the leader, said, "We don't want trouble. We came to take the Archers out and ask some questions."

"You won't be doin' that. It's a matter for the law."

"Law works too slow. Hand 'em over, Sheriff, and nobody gets hurt."

"That's where you're wrong, Clyde. Whoever gets this first barrel is gonna hurt real bad."

"What did you call me?"

"By your name. I ain't as dumb as I look. Now get on out of here before we take you down or put all of you in jail. Now git!" He waved the shotgun across the faces of the men, and saw them lower their guns. Those in the back whirled their horses and started back up the street. One by one, those in front followed.

"Well, Henry, I think that about does it. Don't know what them damn fools thought I'd do. Give 'em up?" Sheriff Horton turned to go back into the jail. "What say we have a dram, settle our nerves?"

CHAPTER 49

The courtroom was filled to standing room. It was windowless, being in the interior of the courthouse, so a pall of tobacco smoke gathered at the high ceiling and the air smelled of horses, barnyards, and stale bodies. No one noticed, however, since that was the normal way of things indoors. The crowd was comprised of all men, except for the three women allowed a place to sit. The three had a part in the coming drama; Anna Archer, Rebecca Archer, and Estelle Harvey.

The noisy, waiting audience naturally divided into three groups; for the defendants, against, and undecided. "Undecided" tended down the center, separating the others behind the accused table and the prosecutors' table, respectively.

Deputy Bobby Joe Duke, acting as bailiff, shouted, "All rise!" and a hush fell over the room as a door opened and Judge William Blackburn strode in, taking his place behind the high bench. He was a tall, heavyset man with a tanned square face and a mane of white hair. His face was lined with a stern expression from carrying the weight of justice as he traveled from county to county for major cases. He eschewed judicial robes, but did dress formally in a long black coat, with white shirt and black string tie.

He placed a leather case on the bench, withdrew a gavel, and seated himself. Only then did he survey the crowd. "Be seated," he commanded. As the commotion died, he continued. "As you all know, I'm from out of town, but for now I own this here piece of real estate. What I say goes, and the case will be tried up here, not by you-all out there. Let's get a few things straight. No more smoking in this room. For the love of God, we could all die from breathing this air! No talking or noise-making. That's for outside and it's where you'll be if you violate." He was met with silence and staring eyes.

He turned toward the door he had just entered. "Mister Duff, you may come in and take your place." A young blond-haired man, slight of build, also dressed in a black suit, came in and took his place at a small table.

Blackburn banged his gavel on the bench and said, "This court is in session. Let's get on with it. Gentlemen, uh, and ladies, this young man is Nathaniel Duff. He is proficient in recording these proceedings. He's also reading law, so he knows what it's about.

"Now, you sir," pointing at the prosecutor, "we met yesterday during jury selection, but you may introduce yourself to the court."

A tall man with a noticeable stoop rose to face the judge. He was dressed in a butternut-colored suit with off-white shirt and drooping black cravat. His well-oiled black hair was combed over a thinning scalp. "Thank you, Your Honor. I'm Moses Shelby, Prosecutor for Taney County. I'm here to—"

"Beg pardon, Mister Shelby. You'll get a chance for an opening statement."

Shelby sat down and the judge pointed to the defense table. "You, Sir?"

The man seated at the defense table was young, well-built, well-dressed in a dark blue suit of modern cut. His hair was blond, combed straight back, and its slight tint of red blended into a red beard, closely trimmed. He rose, shot the cuffs of his shirt, and addressed the judge. "Thank you, Your Honor. My name is Charles Kilgore of the Springfield firm of Kilgore McVey Blanchard."

"Thank you Mister Kilgore. Are you ready to proceed?"

"Yes, Your Honor."

"You may be seated. Mister Shelby?"

Shelby shot to his feet. "Yes, Your Honor."

"Be seated. Bailiff, you may seat the jury."

The eight jurors filed in. All were men, of course. All were land or business owners and all early to late middle age in keeping with the required "jury of peers." When they were settled, with hushed murmurs drawing the glare of the judge, he turned to Sheriff Horton, standing by a door to his left. "Sheriff, you may bring in the accused."

Tom and Ben had grown weary of being confined as the days and weeks went by, especially during spring planting time. Anna and Rebecca had managed to visit two or three times and reported that neighbors, led by Rafe Johnson and his sons, had gotten in the spring corn crop at both places. Rebecca said that Jimmy had been a big help to her, maturing rapidly in his father's absence. Eva had grown and now could be coaxed to smile. Ben thought his heart would burst when he held her. How thankful he was to God for sending Anna to him!

Now as they sat waiting in a secure room in the courthouse, he couldn't wait to have the trial over with, believing they must be set free, but worrying nevertheless. He was replaying the episode in his head for the hundredth time just as the door was unlocked. Sheriff Horton stuck his head in. "You-all can come in now."

Tom embraced his son. "It'll be all right, Ben. We'll soon get to go home."

The sheriff walked behind them as they entered the courtroom. They were amazed at the standing crowd, but immediately focused on the two women waiting behind the rail.

Ben and Tom both embraced their wives, leaning over the rail, but the judge immediately rapped his gavel on the bench. "No demonstrations!" he said. "Sit down!"

Judge Blackburn waited until all were seated. He looked at the prosecutor, who was shuffling papers. "Mister Shelby, you may present your charges, and make a short opening statement. 'Short' means not presenting your whole case."

Shelby rose and took the sheet of paper handed to him by his clerk. "Thank you, Your Honor." He walked over and faced the jury. "Thomas Archer and Benjamin Archer are charged with capital murder, in that they did willfully and with aforethought cause the death of Clinton Harvey on March twenty-first, eighteen eighty-two. Benjamin Archer is further charged with assault with a deadly weapon on the person of Ferdinand Harvey in the same incident.

"We will show with testimony of witnesses that the Harveys were out hunting and came upon the Archers and their accomplices, Rafael and Matthew Johnson, at which time they were fired upon by the Archer party without provocation on their part. The Archers were involved in a scheme to embarrass their neighbor before the whole community. This was not in keeping with the way folks are expected to behave. The Golden Rule says…" Shelby droned on, repeating himself. He had been offered assistance out of Springfield, but had refused. Now, the courtroom observers and the judge himself began to squirm in their seats. Finally, he realized he was beginning to double back again and came to a halt. "…and that is what we will prove. Thank you, Your Honor."

Ben glanced over at the seats behind the rail on the other side. Ferd Harvey was staring at him with a triumphant smile.

Judge Blackburn straightened in his seat. "Thank you, Mister Shelby. You may be seated. Mister Kilgore, let us hear from you. Your clients have agreed to be tried together, but I must hear a plea from each separately. Mister Tom Archer, how do you plead?"

Tom rose. "Not guilty, Your Honor."

"And you…" Blackburn glanced at his notes, "Benjamin Archer, how do you plead?"

Ben rose. "Not guilty, Your Honor."

"You may be seated. Mister Kilgore?"

This was Charles Kilgore's first murder case and he was excited to prove himself. His father, Stanford Kilgore, was managing partner of the firm and had assigned him to take the case pro bono to get some experience on his own in this backwoods case he'd heard about. Whichever way it went, there would be little reflection on the firm's reputation. For his part, Charles had chafed at the routines of an associate up until now, so he had plunged into a detailed examination of every facet of the case.

Now, controlling his excitement, he rose, using language he had heard from his father. "May it please the Court, we will show the innocence of the accused beyond any doubt. An extensive investigation on our part indicates that no charges should have been filed in the first place. Witnesses will testify that the first shot was fired by Mister Ferdinand Harvey. Further, we will show that the confrontation on March twenty-first was the culmination of a series of provocative incidents perpetrated by the Harvey family."

He had been pacing back and forth, but now stood before the jury. "Gentlemen, you are charged with finding the defendants guilty *beyond a reasonable doubt.* After you have heard our case, you will not find your task difficult. You will find the defendants *not* guilty, without *any* doubt. Thank you."

The judge almost smiled. "Thank you for your brevity, Mister Kilgore." He pulled a watch out of his waistcoat pocket. "We have a good bit of time before the noon break. Is prosecution ready to present its case?"

"Yes, Your Honor." Shelby shot to his feet and walked around in front of the jury, but he faced the courtroom audience. "We call Mister Robert Harvey."

Bob Harvey walked through the gate and up to the witness stand to be sworn in by young Nathaniel Duff. Duff retreated to his desk and continued to scratch rapid Pitman shorthand notes with a collection of steel dip pens.

Bob Harvey looked nervously at the judge then to Shelby as he approached.

"Mister Harvey, you were present, were you not, on the day in question when you brother was murdered—"

Kilgore jumped up. "Objection!"

"Sustained. Mister Shelby, I take it you've been in court before. I won't be warning you a second time. Jurors, strike that last word from you consciousness. Nothing's been proved yet."

"Sorry, Your Honor." Then to the witness, "You were present at the death of your brother, were you not?"

Harvey replied, practically in a whisper.

"Speak up, please."

"Yes."

"Now tell the court the events leading up to that confrontation."

Harvey went through a rehearsed story about going hunting, and dropping by the location where the shooting took place.

"Now, Mister Harvey, tell us how the shooting started. Who fired the first shot?"

Bob Harvey shifted in his chair. He looked at his family, then at his clasped hands, before looking at Shelby. "Benjamin Archer did."

There was a murmur in the courtroom and Blackburn banged his gavel.

"Will you point to the person just named," said Shelby.

Bob Harvey pointed at Ben with a shaking hand.

"Were you armed?"

"I had a shotgun."

"Did you fire your weapon at all?"

"No, Sir."

"Did anyone else?"

"I think Mister Johnson did, and Ben shot more than once, and Pa did, to try to defend us."

"And was your father wounded?"

"Yes he was. He was shot in the arm."

"Was anyone else wounded?"

"I believe Tom Archer was, but I left right away to go get Ma."

Shelby looked at his notes and said, "Thank you. I have no further questions at this time."

Bob started to rise.

"Hold it a minute, young fellow." said Blackburn. He looked at his watch again. "We just as well take the noon break now. Be ready to go at one o'clock. Now you can go."

CHAPTER 50

Ben and Tom had just a few brief moments to exchange words with their wives before being led away by the sheriff.

"He's lying, Ben," Anna said. "It'll all come out. I've got to go feed the baby. Margaret's taking care of her and she brought Etta with her. I can't wait for you to meet. She was my second mother when mine passed away."

"I look forward to it, too, Love, just as soon's I get out of here."

They were led back to the secure room and locked in with plates of food.

"They won't get away with it, Son," Tom said.

"I know. I can't wait to hear Mister Kilgore go after him, 'cause it's all made up."

Court reconvened on time with the rapping of Blackburn's gavel. "Mister Robert Harvey, you may take the stand. And remember you are still under oath."

As soon as Harvey was seated, Charles Kilgore approached him, standing two feet away. He began, "Good afternoon, Mister Harvey. I'm sorry for the loss of your brother." He waited for a reply, and when none came, he began.

"Mister Harvey, when Deputy Jeffrey interviewed you, he asked you who shot first. That was right after it happened, and you declined to say." He glanced down at his notes. "Your exact words were, 'it all happened fast'. Correct?"

"I reckon."

"How is it you now remember in such detail?"

Harvey shrugged. "More time to think about it."

"Or be coached—"

"Objection!"

This time it was Shelby.

"Sorry, Your Honor. Withdrawn," Kilgore said.

"Since you now remember more clearly, tell us again who shot first and who was shot at."

Harvey looked over at his family and at the prosecutor.

"Take your time," said Kilgore.

"As I said before, it was Ben."

"Who did he shoot?"

"Clint, I think."

"All right. Who shot a shotgun at Mister Johnson and Benjamin?"

"Wait a minute. I guess he shot Pa first."

"That was before or after your father shot Mister Tom Archer?"

"I don't know. Like I told the deputy, it all happened fast."

"Thank you Mister Harvey. No further questions."

The judge looked at Moses Shelby. "Re-direct?"

"No, Your Honor."

"Call your next witness."

"State calls Missus Estelle Harvey."

Estelle Harvey rose and walked forward to the witness stand to be sworn in. Kilgore looked at Tom Archer with a question in his expression. Tom shrugged.

"Missus Harvey, sorry for your loss," Shelby began. "Tell us what happened on the day in question."

Estelle wiped a tear with her thumb. "Well the men folks went out huntin' and pretty soon I heard shots and Bob came runnin'. He said the Archers—"

"Objection!"

"Sustained." Blackburn leaned over toward Estelle Harvey and said in a kindly voice. "Missus Harvey, when you testify, you can't say what other people tell you about something that happened when you weren't there. They have to tell their own story."

"Sorry, Judge. I didn't know that. Can I say he told me that Clint and Ferd had been shot?"

"Yes you can because it's between you and him."

"Well, I went runnin' and to my sorrow..." her voice broke. "My second son was dead." She pulled a handkerchief out of her sleeve and wiped her eyes.

Moses Shelby looked bewildered for a moment, then said, "Thank you Missus Harvey. No further questions."

"Mister Kilgore?" Blackburn said.

Charles Kilgore rose. "No questions, Your Honor."

"Mister Shelby, call your next witness."

"The state calls Mister Ezekiel Peake."

A bandy-legged little man with a grizzled white beard rose and ambled up to the bench, then stepped up to the witness box to be sworn. He sat, then looked from side to side at the full courtroom, sitting up a little straighter.

Shelby began. "Mister Peake, please spell your name for the record."

He looked at Shelby. "Your Honor, I ain't much for letters. I'm just Zeke Peake. Now if you'd get Sarah in here—"

"Never mind, Mister Peake. And I'm not addressed as 'Your Honor.' That's for the judge."

"Yessir."

"Now tell the court what happened on the day in question, when the shooting happened."

"Well, me and Hannibal and Press heard there might be trouble so we went to watch. Sure enough, there was shootin' and such."

"You were there, then. So, getting to the point, who started the shooting?"

"It was that young fella over there."

"Let the record show that he is pointing at Benjamin Archer. Thank you, Mister Peake. I have no further questions."

Judge Blackburn drummed his fingers on the bench, then looked at the defendants. "Mister Kilgore?"

Charles Kilgore rose, buttoned his jacket, and adjusted his cuffs. He walked over in front of the witness and paused for a moment. Peake shifted his eyes and licked his lips.

"Good afternoon, Mister Peake. Thank you for coming."

"That's all right."

"How far away were you when the shooting started?"

"We was down on the lane to the west. I'd say we was about half a furlong."

Kilgore thought for a moment. "A furlong is two hundred twenty yards, so you were over a hundred yards away."

"If you say so. I don't know yards very well."

"Very good. Could you see clearly?"

"Yes, I reckon so. There was lots of smoke after the shootin'."

"I understand. Now I want you to put your mind back to that time and think about the gunshots. Were some louder than others?"

"Yessir."

"Now, think some more and tell me what you heard."

Peake closed his eyes, stroked his beard, and shifted in his seat. After a moment of silence, he looked back at Kilgore, his brow furrowed. "Best I can recollect, there was a pop, and a louder crack, and a boom, and more cracks and pops."

"Thank you, Mister Peake. Would you say that the 'pops' were from a pistol?"

"Objection!" shouted Moses Shelby. "Witness is not qualified to answer."

Peake looked confused. Judge Blackburn said, "I'm inclined to agree. Sustained."

"Then I withdraw the question, but I may ask the Court's indulgence to do some blind testing with this witness later, depending on where this goes.

"Now, Mister Peake, let me ask you to search your memory again. Did anyone fall down?"

"Yessir."

"Who?"

"Well, Tom did and Clint did."

"Who fell first?"

Peake looked confused. "I don't rightly know. There was a lot of smoke…"

"Did you talk to the participants?"

"Participants?"

"The people involved."

"Oh…yes. We all went and talked to Tom a little bit, then we went to Ferd and helped him and his family back to his house."

"Did he tell you how it happened?"

"Objection!"

"Denied, Mister Shelby. Mister Peake, you may answer." said Blackburn.

"Yeah, we talked about it. He told me—"

"Let me stop you there, Mister Peake," Kilgore said. "Why are your friends, Hannibal and Preston, not here?"

"Objection!"

"Over-ruled."

"They're puttin' in their crops and they didn't see nuthin'."

"I have no further questions."

Judge Blackburn looked at the prosecution table. "Re-direct?"

Shelby jumped up. "No, Your Honor."

"Then call your next witness. Mister Peake, you may step down."

Shelby called Ferdinand Harvey to the stand. Harvey strode confidently forward, sporting a large bandage. He emphasized the pain of his injury as he raised his right arm to take the oath and was seated.

"Now, Mister Harvey," Shelby began, "We're going to go through the long chain of events leading up to that fateful day when you were shot and your son was killed."

Harvey nodded, and the spectators shifted in their seats, knowing that a long, entertaining dialogue was coming.

"Well," Harvey began, "Tom Archer thinks he's better than—"

Judge Blackburn rapped his gavel on the bench, not waiting for an objection. "Mister Shelby, advise your witness that we are here to listen to facts, not opinions."

Shelby spoke quietly to Harvey, who nodded. He began again, "The trouble started when the farm bordering me come available, and it was snapped up before I had a chance to buy it…" He continued in a firm voice, telling how much he had counted on it. Then he launched into a narrative about the tragic death of his brother-in-law. He spoke of taking his sister "under his wing" as a family does. Spectators sat forward, intent on his tale of trouble, many with frowns on their faces.

"Then, what do you know, Tom Archer courted her and married her so he could take control of that farm, which shoulda stayed in the family."

"Objection!" shouted Kilgore. "Witness is assuming he knows the motives of Mister Archer."

"Sustained," said Blackburn. "Mister Shelby, I believe you know better. I suggest you counsel your witness."

Tom looked over his shoulder at Rebecca, who had her mouth set in a grim line, her face red.

"Yes, Your Honor. Mister Harvey, let's move to the events of March twenty-first. Tell us in your own words what happened."

"We had an agreement on the line fence. Archer would keep up half and we'd keep up half. They was always pesterin' us about our half; never satisfied. Then they up and started buildin' one alongside our half, stealin' rails off our side. Natcherly it caused hard feelin's. One day, as you've already heard, we was just out huntin' and come across them messin' with the fence. An argument started and got loud and they told us to go away and started shootin' at us. That's when my boy was killed." He wiped a tear from his left eye.

"I'll ask you a direct question. Who shot first?"

Harvey pointed at Benjamin. "That one did! The Archer boy!"

There was stirring in the courtroom and the rumble of lowered voices.

Blackburn rapped his gavel. "I warned you! Another outburst and I clear the court!"

"No further questions, Your Honor."

Judge Blackburn looked at his watch. "Mister Shelby, do you have further witnesses?"

"Not at this time. We'll see if I need to re-direct after cross."

"Mister Kilgore, we could break now, or you may cross-examine."

"We prefer to proceed, Your Honor."

"Then do so." Blackburn poured himself a glass of water from a pitcher on the bench.

CHAPTER 51

Kilgore confidently strode forward and faced Ferdinand Harvey. "Good afternoon, Mister Harvey. I'm sorry for your loss." He waited a few moments. Harvey stared at him without reacting.

"Now Mister Harvey, you have presented quite a tale of ill-treatment directed at you. I'd like to ask you a few questions about some of your statements.

"As to the Friedrich place next to your farm, what steps did you take to indicate your interest in it after it was abandoned?"

"Well, there wasn't time! It was gone before I had a chance!"

"You didn't check with the bank about availability? Did you talk to neighbors?"

"As I said, there wasn't time?"

"Why do you seem to resent the fact that Mister Archer bought it?"

"'Cause he got it and I didn't."

"Let's move on to another subject. During the time after her husband's death, what did you do to help your sister and her family? You said you 'took her under your wing.'"

"Well, me and my brother Clyde did lots of stuff."

"Bring her wood? Put in her corn crop? Take care of her livestock?"

"I don't remember every dee-tail."

"Do you know who now holds title to your sister's farm?"

"Well, I reckon he does." He pointed at Tom Archer.

"We'll let you find out when we present our case," said Kilgore. "Now, moving on to the line fence. I understand that it was in some state of decay. You are aware that Benjamin Archer rebuilt his half, putting in a few hundred new rails, are you not?"

"I don't know."

"Did you rebuild your half?"

"No. Didn't need it."

"Did any of his livestock get into your cornfield?"

"Yeah, his damn mule did a couple of times."

"Through your half of the fence?"

"Maybe, but who knows what a mule will do?"

"Now, Mister Harvey, did you or one of your sons shoot the mule with a shotgun?"

"How else can you teach a mule anything?"

"Please answer the question. Yes or no?"

"Yes."

"There was a confrontation at the fence a few days before the one in question. Correct?"

Spectators sat upright. Shelby looked up from writing notes. Harvey hadn't told him about that.

"Yes."

"Were you and your sons also out hunting that day? Strike that. During that argument, did your son Clinton discharge his shotgun at the feet of Tom Archer?"

"It went off by accident."

"I see. Now, you testified that during the argument on March twenty-first it escalated to the point that Benjamin Archer fired the first shot. Your son, Robert testified that it was directed at you. Is that correct?"

"My boy don't lie."

"And did that cause the wound to your right arm?"

"Yes."

"Did it cause you to drop your pistol?"

"Yes, it did. Bullet went right through my arm."

"So did you then start shooting? With your pistol on the ground and your right arm wounded?"

Harvey finally realized it would take some thinking to come up with an answer.

"I picked it up with my left hand and started shootin' back."

"What kind of pistol is it?"

"Colt Navy. Best gun ever made."

"No further questions," Kilgore said, and walked back to the defense table.

Judge Blackburn turned to his right and said, "Re-direct, Mister Shelby?"

"Just one question, Your Honor." He strode over in front of Harvey. "Are you a good shot with either hand?"

"Oh, yes. During the war, we sometimes had a gun in each hand."

"No further questions, Your Honor. That completes our testimony."

Kilgore jumped to his feet. "Your Honor, may I ask this witness one more question in rebuttal?"

"I'll allow it."

Kilgore walked over in front of Harvey. "Mister Harvey, you brought up your war experience. Where did you serve during the war?"

"Why, right here, guarding the home front."

"Were you in the Union Army or the Confederate Army?"

"Neither one of them. We had our own group."

"I see. No further questions." Kilgore decided it was unnecessary to explain.

"All right, Mister Harvey, you may step down," said Blackburn. Ferd Harvey did so, making his way back behind the rail. Blackburn continued, "Gentlemen, I believe this is a good time to break. Mister Kilgore, you may start your case first thing in the morning." He rapped the bench with his gavel.

Bobby Joe Duke shouted, "All rise!" in his tenor voice.

The spectators did so and the judge left the room. After he disappeared, the room burst into the noise of everyone talking at once with arms waving, pointing and gesturing.

Ben and Tom were able to say a quick farewell to their wives before being led away. Ben noticed some strangers departing and assumed they were reporters from out of town. There was one distinguished middle-aged man who stood near the back of the room and looked in their direction as they were led away.

Rebecca and Anna were fortunate to have been approached by an elderly lady that morning before the courthouse doors opened. She gave her name as Edna Harkness and told them she was the widow of a war veteran, left with a house and a pension. She had heard of the case coming to trial and came to ask them if they would like to stay with her. She'd heard about the young wife and baby.

"God has sent you!" Rebecca proclaimed. "We didn't know what we would do, since the boarding houses are full. We thought we'd have to go home."

"Think nothing of it, Dear," said Edna. "I'm happy to help out."

"We'll pay our board of course," said Rebecca.

"Of course not," said Edna. "Only pay is to let me have a look at that baby. My grandchildren are long grown up."

Now, with the trial over for the day, Anna said goodbye to Margaret and Etta, who were making the long drive back to Bull Creek. Anna introduced them to Edna, who promised to help with the baby until Margaret could return the next day.

Kilgore accompanied Tom and Ben back to their cell and had a brief meeting with them before their evening meal. "How do you feel about it?" he asked.

"Well, it was obvious to me they were all lyin'," Tom said. "But I was there. How about you?"

"I think we're fine once we get our witnesses up there. Here's what I have in mind..." He outlined his planned approach and they nodded in agreement.

"You know best," Tom said. "We appreciate what you're doing for us."

Tom and Ben were ushered into the packed courtroom the next morning, tense with anticipation of what was to come. Ben noticed the same man from the day before, seated near the back of the room. He had but a few moments to speak to Anna. She said, "Ben, a wonderful lady let us stay with her so we didn't have to go home."

"I wondered if you could be here. I'm so glad."

At that point, he had to be seated at the demands of the judge's gavel.

"Mister Kilgore, are you ready to proceed?"

"We are, Your Honor. Defense calls Missus Rebecca Archer."

Rebecca walked sedately through the gate and up to the witness box. Her face was set and she ignored her brothers and their families as she walked by.

"Good morning Missus Archer. Thank you for being here."

"Glad to be."

"Good. Your brother said he took you under his wing at the sad occasion of your first husband's passing. What did that consist of?"

"Well, they helped me with the burying."

"I see. Who supplied you with firewood that winter?"

"Benjamin Archer did."

"And who put in your corn crop that spring?"

"Rafe Johnson and Tom Archer and their boys."

"And one more question. There was speculation yesterday that Tom Archer married you to get your farm. Whose name is on the deed?"

Rebecca smiled for the first time and she looked over at her husband. "Well, my name is the only one on the deed, which is being held by the bank. Tom insisted we keep it that way for my own future security. All of the income from renting the farm goes against the mortgage."

"Thank you, Missus Archer. No further questions." He walked back to the defense table.

Blackburn looked at Moses Shelby. "Cross examine?"

"Uh, no, Your Honor."

"Then you may proceed, Mister Kilgore."

"Defense calls Mister Ned Bowman."

Grandpa Bowman was seated several rows back and he made his way down the aisle with the aid of a cane made from an oak sprout that had spiral grooves from a vine.

When he was seated and sworn, Kilgore said, "I understand you were present at Guthrie's store when an incident took place involving Clinton Harvey."

"Objection! The deceased is not on trial here," said Shelby.

"Over-ruled. Your witness Mister Harvey opened the subject of strife between the families. So that horse has left the barn. The witness may answer."

"Well, it was back in the summer. Ben came out of the store with some stuff just as Clint and Bob stepped up on the porch. Clint said something about his sister and the picnic, then he grabbed Ben's shirt and shoved him over the railing. We grabbed Clint and held him. Ben went in and replaced the stuff that was ruined, came out and said 'good day' and rode away."

"He didn't do anything to Clint?"

"Nope. I says to Clint, 'You made an ass of yourself. Yonder goes one who acted like a man.'"

"Thank you. No further questions."

This time the judge just looked at Shelby, who shook his head.

"Defense calls Mister Rafael Johnson."

Rafe came forward, nodding at Tom and Ben as he passed.

Kilgore began. "What is your relationship to the accused, Mister Archer and his son?"

"We knew each other during the War and settled out here about the same time. We help each other out when need be."

"You were present at the events of March twenty-first, were you not?"

Rafe stroked his fringe beard. "I was, and the time before when we were unarmed and Clint shot the shotgun. Bein' a' accident is hogwash. Ferd said to him something like 'show him what might happen' before he shot at Tom's feet. When we went back, we took our guns along and leaned 'em against some bushes. And as God is my witness, here's the sequence of the shootin'..." Rafe held up a big left hand and ticked off the sequence on his fingers. "Ferd was mad and shot first and Tom went down. Next, I got off a shot at him with my rifle, but missed. Clint shot one barrel of his shotgun. Several of the shot hit me and Ben." He paused and pointed to his temple and neck. "And some on my shoulder. By that time Ben had the Winchester up and I was kneelin' down to reload. Ferd was still shootin' some wild shots. Ben shot him in the arm and he went down. By that time, Clint was drawin' a bead on Ben with the shotgun and Ben shot him."

"How long did this sequence take?"

"Less time than it took me to tell it. Just seconds. But there is no doubt on God's green earth that Ferd Harvey shot first. He was wavin' the gun around and it came as a surprise to us."

"Thank you, Mister Johnson. No further questions."

This time the spectators were all silent and staring, as were the members of the jury.

"Cross, Mister Shelby?"

"Yes, Your Honor." Shelby strode slowly across in front of the bench to face Johnson. He glanced at a pad of paper in his hand. "You've testified that you and Tom Archer are real good friends. Correct?"

"That's right, but if you're tryin' to say I lied, think again. I don't lie for nobody."

"You'd stretch the truth a little to help a friend."

"You don't know me. Ask anybody. And there's three more men here, includin' my Matthew, that can tell you what happened."

"No further questions."

Judge Blackburn took out his watch. "This looks like a good time for a noon break. What does your schedule look like, Mister Kilgore? Any chance to wind up this afternoon?"

"It's possible, Your Honor. I have perhaps four more witnesses planned, but it depends on how things go."

"Very good. Court's in recess." He banged the gavel on the bench, rose, and left the room.

CHAPTER 52

Charles Kilgore had to decide how much repetition his case could stand. He decided that too much was not going to detract from the truth. Therefore, he called Matthew Johnson to the stand as soon as everyone was settled. Matthew earnestly repeated the sequence of the shooting his father had provided, practically word for word. Probably didn't change any minds one way or the other. The only question on cross by Shelby, was, "What were you doing while all this was taking place?"

Matthew looked embarrassed. "I was hidin' behind an oak tree. My gun was too far away and it was over too quick. But I saw it all, and Mister Harvey shot first with his pistol."

That question did the prosecution more harm than good, and set up the next witness.

"Defense calls Doctor Stevenson."

After the doctor had settled in the chair, Kilgore said, "Doctor Stevenson, you brought a piece of evidence with you, correct?"

"I did. This envelope holds a bullet I removed from Thomas Archer the morning of March twenty-second. I sealed it then and signed my name on it."

"Going back to your experience during several years of the War, what was your conclusion of the type of bullet?"

"In my opinion, it is from a thirty-six caliber pistol, which is the caliber of a Colt Navy."

"Thank you, Doctor." Kilgore carried it to the bench and gave it to the judge. "I'd like to place this into evidence for the defense," he said.

"Mister Shelby, you may approach." Blackburn waited until both attorneys were before him. "Now I'll tear open the seal, and you both may examine the bullet."

Both did, and Shelby declined to cross examine. Doctor Stevenson was excused.

Now Charles Kilgore had to make another decision. Should he ask for the demonstration outside to corroborate the "pop" testified to by Peake, or rely on his witnesses. He quickly decided on the latter. Thomas Archer was well-respected in the community and would be a good witness. Benjamin, though younger, had the same openness of character. Some attorneys, he knew, didn't want to have their accused testify with the fear they might be tripped up on some trick question. He decided very quickly, however, he'd have Tom go first, then end his case with Benjamin.

"Defense calls Mister Thomas Archer."

Tom made his way to the witness stand, glancing at his wife Rebecca as he walked past her, in a sense apologizing for what he might have to say about her brother.

Kilgore had not rehearsed his witness, convinced that rehearsed talking points always sounded that way and were less believable than spontaneity.

"Mister Archer, talk us through your relationship with the Harvey family. You've heard various accusations from Mister Ferdinand Harvey."

Tom cleared his throat. "It distresses me to have strife with anyone, particularly a neighbor. We had very little relationship with the Harveys until I bought the Friedrich place. I knew them, of course, but was surprised by Ferd's accusations since there was never any intent to cause them harm. I bought the place since I had a son about old enough to go out on his own and it was available at a good price from the bank.

"That seemed to be the start of the trouble. Ferd was unhappy when we went to set up the deal on the fence, but we reached agreement on it. But the son, Clint, attacked Ben at the pie supper. It seemed to bother him because Ben was eating pie with Clint's sister. We had to drag him outside. Ben never told me about the incident at Guthrie's store. But I was well aware of strife over the mule getting in the corn and went to ask Ferd to build up his half of the fence. Later, there was the mule getting shot with a shotgun.

"As to my dear wife, Rebecca, Ben was the first to come to her aid, since he lived nearby. I went to help out with the crops as it's what neighbors do. Just like this spring, neighbors and friends put in my corn crop while I was held up here, and none of them had an eye on matrimony—"

There was a burst of laughter, gaveled to silence.

"Anyway, I was a widower for some years with children, and here she was, a widow who'd lost her husband, my good friend Charlie. There was no commercial thought of acquiring any farm; just love and admiration."

"Thank you, Mister Archer. Let's turn to the events of March twenty-first. What happened when the dispute heated up?"

"It was as you've heard from Rafe and Matthew. Ferd was waving his pistol around and getting more and more worked up. All of a sudden, he pointed it at me and fired, hitting me in the side. I went down, and can't verify what exactly happened after that. But that 'pop' Zeke talked about? Anyone who's been in combat can tell the difference in a pistol shot and a rifle. And Clint did shoot at my feet to give a warning that week before."

"Thank you. Anything else?"

"No. Except I'm sorry it came to that. Would have been better if he'd talked to us about his suspicions."

"No further questions," Kilgore said.

Blackburn looked toward the prosecution table. "Cross examine, Mister Shelby?"

Shelby walked over to confront Tom Archer. "Mister Archer, you just testified that you don't know what happened after you claim to have been shot. Is that correct?"

"Well, I didn't just claim to have been shot. As to the rest, I heard pretty much the same as Zeke described it, although I was down. There were a few more pistol shots mixed in with what I believe was Rafe's forty-five-seventy, a couple of shotgun blasts, and two from the Winchester. The next to last was one of the Winchester's forty-four-forties and the last a shotgun which may have been Clint's as he went down. That's how I heard it."

"You sound awfully confident. Did someone tell you all that? After all, you were lying on the ground wounded."

"No, but I've been in worse situations and kept a clear head."

"No further questions."

Blackburn picked up his gavel. "Let's take a fifteen minute break." He rapped the gavel. There was the ritual of rising as he left, then the burst of conversation.

When the courtroom was all settled, everyone in place, Charles Kilgore called his final witness, Benjamin Archer, to the stand. Ben walked confidently forward, having just had a few minutes talking to Anna before the judge came in. She told him how important he was to her and how she was there for him and believed in him above all else. He knew it was true, but it still made him feel stronger to hear it. He scanned the crowded room. Many out there were people he knew; many were strangers. He noted the distinguished-looking man he had seen each day. He looked at his father, who nodded, and last at Anna, who smiled at him. I'm nervous, but it should be easy. The truth is the truth.

"Mister Archer, you've heard all the testimony from both sides, but I'm going to ask you to take us to that afternoon and describe for us exactly what happened."

"Well...Sir, I can do that. I've replayed it in my mind a hundred times. I wake up at night and think about it. It's not because I feel like I did anything wrong, because I haven't thought of anything I could have done different. It's just such a shame that things come to that. I'm sorry for Missus Harvey, for Rose and Buford, those in the family who were innocent and lost their son and brother. I'll start with that actual afternoon. If you want all that other background, let me know.

"They didn't just happen by, because they ran us off a few days before when we weren't armed—that time when Clint blasted the dirt in front of Pa. On March twenty-first, the argument led to Mister Harvey shootin' Pa with his pistol. It was the first shot and it surprised us all. None of us had a gun. They was all leanin' against trees or bushes. We right away grabbed 'em, except for Pa, because he was on the ground, and Matthew, who was farther away..."

Ben went on, methodically describing each shot in exactly the same sequence as the court had heard from Rafe Johnson's testimony. Finally, he described the ending shot he fired at Clinton Harvey.

"So you admit that you are the one who killed Clinton Harvey?" Kilgore said.

"I do, and it's just awful to have to even say such a thing. That's the shot I play in my head over and over, but I was staring at the wrong end of a shotgun that had already hit me and Mister Johnson with the other barrel."

"Thank you, Ben," Kilgore said. "No further questions."

Blackburn looked in the direction of Moses Shelby, who had already jumped up and marched forward. "I take it you wish to cross?"

"I do, Your Honor." Shelby had been huddling with Ferd Harvey during the recess and now displayed an air of confidence.

"Mister Archer, you're a good shot with a rifle, correct?"

Ben looked puzzled, but replied. "Yes, I reckon so."

"You won the prize at the July picnic, correct?"

"Yes."

"So we can assume you meant to kill Clint Harvey?"

"No. Not really. There wasn't time to think about it."

"Then tell us how come you were able to place a shot so accurately as to hit the gun arm of Mister Harvey, yet you shot Clint with an accurate, fatal shot."

Ben's face flushed and he squirmed in his seat. "As I already said, there wasn't time to think about it, looking directly at the black bore of a twelve-gauge. It just happened."

"Why not shoot to wound, as you did with Mister Harvey?"

"Objection! "Asked and answered," said Kilgore.

Blackburn thought for a moment. "I'll allow it. You may answer."

"I do believe I've answered. No time to think about it. That barrel could have been loaded with double-aught, which would have killed me, or even a deer slug."

"Let me get to the point. Did you intend to kill him because of his relationship with your wife?"

Ben's face went white and the courtroom burst into loud confusion, overpowering the judge's gavel and Kilgore's shouted "Objection!"

Finally, Blackburn, shouting "Order!" several times, was able to restore reasonable decorum.

The judge pointed his gavel first at Shelby, then at Kilgore. "You two, see me in chambers."

CHAPTER 53

Judge Blackburn, seated at a small desk, his face flushed, practically shouted at Shelby. "Mister Shelby, I'd like to know where the hell you're going with this, and I think Mister Kilgore would also!"

The two attorneys were standing before him, and Shelby said, "I apologize to Your Honor, but it has just come to my attention that Clinton Harvey is probably the father of Ben Archer's child."

"What the hell are you talking about?" shouted Kilgore. "Sorry, Your Honor."

"My thoughts exactly," said Blackburn.

"Ferdinand Harvey just told me about it. He said Robert told him that Clint boasted to him about it and they counted up and it was about nine months before Ben Archer's wife gave birth."

"Christ Almighty!" said the judge. "I don't have to tell you how many layers of speculation and hearsay you're trying to introduce to bollix up this case!"

"It would be a strong motive, Your Honor," Shelby whined.

"And you'd have to provide proof there was any contact and Clinton was the father and young Archer knew about it," replied Blackburn. "I doubt you can do any of that."

"If I can get the wife on the stand and continue my cross with Ben Archer—"

"You already rested your case," Kilgore said.

Blackburn steepled his large hands, his elbows on the desk. "Here's what we're going to do. We're going back in there, and I'm going to close things down. Mister Kilgore can meet with his clients as he sees fit, to find out what he can about this ambush. And you—" He glared at Shelby, "will clamp your mouth shut. If I find out you've talked to

reporters or anybody else except your prime witness—I'll declare a mistrial. We'll resume in the morning, meeting here first in chambers."

Ben was left sitting in the witness chair, and could do nothing to comfort
Anna, whose face was set in pain. I wonder if this is true, that it was
Clint? He thought. If it is, then God forgive me, I don't mind what hap-
pened so much. But how will anybody prove anything? I believe what
Anna told me. She had no idea who the animal was that did that to her.
What a mess this is, to talk about such a thing in public.

He was relieved when the judge and the lawyers came back in and the
judge gaveled the proceedings to an end for the day. The judge called the
sheriff forward and said, "Sheriff, I want you and your deputies to clear
the room of everybody except those at the defense table and the two ladies
behind them. I suspect Mister Kilgore would like to borrow the holding
room for a meeting. You can take it from here."

Kilgore stood with Tom and Ben and their wives, separated by the
rail. "Tom, you'll forgive me, but I'd better meet with the young folks
and get to the bottom of that outburst."

"I understand. Ben, I'll see you back at our 'hotel'."

As Tom started to leave and Rebecca turned to follow, Anna said,
"Wait. Mister Kilgore, I'd like for my friend Margaret Madison to join
us if it's all right. She knows what happened. She's taking care of my
baby."

Kilgore thought a moment. "Sure, that'll be all right. We can always
ask her to excuse us if need be."

"I'll get her for you and take care of Eva," said Rebecca.

When the five of them were seated in the holding room, a deputy outside, Kilgore began. "It's good to meet you Miss Madison. You may
be puzzled about this meeting. What happened last in the trial, the
prosecutor was cross-examining Ben and threw a bombshell, something
about Clinton's relationship with Ben's wife. Of course it was a shock to
Ben, and the courtroom went into an uproar. The judge halted everything and brought Shelby and me into chambers. He closed us down for
the day and offered me a chance to find out what Shelby meant. Supposed

to be something Clinton told his brother. So...here we are. I have to know if there is anything to it. Anything you say to me is totally held in confidence. We'll decide together how to handle it."

Anna looked at Margaret, then at Ben. "I told everything to Ben and also to Margaret. I was working as a maid for Margaret's family. One day nearly a year ago, I was in the woods by myself picking blackberries. A man approached me and scared me with how he acted. I ran, I hid, but he hunted me down. I ran, he caught me and dragged me down. I fought, I hit him with a rock, but...he...he hit me with his fist and I passed out...." Anna swallowed.

Margaret's eyes were filled and tears streamed down her cheeks. She put her hand on Anna's. Ben was holding her other hand.

"I understand," Kilgore said. "You don't have to go on unless you want—"

"I want to," Anna said. She sat erect, took a deep breath, and continued. "I was just kid then, such a short time ago. I was ashamed and cleaned myself up, then I lied to Etta, the housekeeper, and Margaret, saying I fell crossing the creek. For weeks, I tried to put it out of my mind, but I guess you know what happened. I had no idea what was wrong with me, but dear Etta knew."

Kilgore looked down and wagged his head. "Some relationship!"

"Margaret's father eventually found out and threw me out of the house. I could tell how I got there if you wish, but Ben found me hiding in his barn, which used to be where I lived, and Ben, now my husband and my hero, took me in and cared for me." She squeezed Ben's hand.

"I didn't know who that horrible man was," said Anna. "I'd never seen him before or since, and hoped never to think of him as a person because of my sweet Eva. Now I'll have to start over and try to put him out of my mind forever."

Margaret spoke for the first time since Anna began. "I can testify to all Anna said and the condition she was in when she came home that day. I saw her torn clothing and the bruises on her face. That is, if you need me."

Kilgore thought for a moment. "I want all of you to be ready tomorrow morning, but when I get back in the judge's chambers, I think I can handle this. Do you trust me?"

All three nodded.

"Good. We can take care of this."

At nine the next morning, Moses Shelby and Charles Kilgore were standing side-by-side before Judge Blackburn, seated behind his desk with a frown on his face. He looked up at Kilgore. "Well, let's hear it."

"The so-called 'relationship' was forcible rape."

Shelby looked startled.

"Anna Friedrich Archer was working as a maid for the Madison family, up Hanson Creek. Nearly a year ago, she was in the woods picking blackberries when a man approached her. It scared her and she hid; eventually he found her and overpowered her, knocking her unconscious. She managed to hit him in the face with a rock, so Ferd might remember his son coming home that way."

Shelby was speechless, but Blackburn prompted him. "Well, Mister Shelby, how does your so-called relationship sound now?"

"Well...well, how do we know she's telling the truth?"

"One of the Madison daughters is here, and both are ready to testify. And I'll warn you now that Anna Archer, though a good-looking young woman, has been through a lot and has steel in her spine. I'd put her word up against the Harveys anytime. Here's the thing: does your witness want to air dirty laundry in front of the world, all of it hearsay, only to guarantee a loss? I'd suggest a public apology."

Judge Blackburn did not comment except to say, "Well, gentlemen, anything else? Let me remind you that there is a gag rule about this discussion. Anything leaks to the newspapers will find the person responsible back in court and not as an attorney. Let's head back inside."

When the judge and the two lawyers walked into the courtroom, it was quiet as a tomb. They faced staring eyes and silence from the standing spectators as they took their places. The judge needlessly rapped his gavel and said, "Court is in session! We will resume where we were yesterday when we recessed. Mister Benjamin Archer, you may take the stand. Remember you are still under oath."

Ben walked forward and seated himself in the witness chair. He looked at Anna and gave her a small nod. She looked beautiful in the gray traveling dress trimmed in white Margaret had worn those many months ago. Margaret had also fixed Anna's hair, putting it up in a stylish swirl of curls. She looked ready to testify.

His thoughts were interrupted by the appearance of Moses Shelby before him and the words of the judge. "We ended with an objection raised by Mister Kilgore following a question posed to the witness by Mister Shelby. I did not rule on that objection until gathering more information. Before I rule, it is appropriate to have that question read from the record. Mister Duff?"

Duff stood in place and said, "Mister Shelby to the witness, 'Let me get to the point. Did you intend to kill him because of his relationship with your wife?'" He sat back down.

Kilgore rose and said, "Objection!"

"Sustained," Blackburn said. "Mister Shelby, you may continue."

Shelby turned to face the courtroom, observing the uniform disappointment on the faces of the spectators, who were looking forward to scandal. "I withdraw the question and apologize to the witness and to Missus Archer and to the court. I have since discovered the question has no basis in fact, and should never have been asked."

"Thank you, Mister Shelby," Blackburn said.

Shelby turned to Benjamin. "Mister Archer, do you admit you are the one who shot and killed Clinton Harvey and wounded Ferdinand Harvey?"

"Yes."

"No further questions."

"Mister Kilgore, re-direct?"

"Yes, Your Honor." He walked up to face Benjamin. "Benjamin, did you fire in self-defense?"

"Yes, Sir. Pa had been shot and was down. Me and Rafe Johnson had been hit with scattered shot already and the other barrel was aimed at my face. I don't see I had a choice."

"Thank you, Benjamin. No further questions. Defense rests."

Judge Blackburn looked relieved. "Thank you, Mister Kilgore. Gentlemen, are you ready for closing statement?"

Both attorneys stood and said they were.

"Good. Let's see if we can finish by the noon break. Mister Shelby, you're on first."

CHAPTER 54

Shelby tugged at the sleeves of his coat, straightened his cravat, and walked over to face the jury box. The jurors perked up to listen and there was an air of anticipation in the courtroom. This was going to be high drama. Shelby cleared his throat and began. "Gentlemen of the jury, a young man with a life full of promise lies dead in a cold grave with a bullet in the brain, and over *there* are those responsible." He whirled and pointed toward the defense table. "A mother, a father, two brothers, and a sister are mourning their loss, a loss that was unnecessary, all over a fence. A *fence!* I ask you, can a fence be worth such a price? No, it cannot. You have heard testimony that the Harvey men were out hunting and happened by. An argument ensued and the defendants chose to end it in gunfire. Oh, you have heard them deny it, but don't you believe what they say, to excuse what they have done."

He paced across the front of the courtroom, then back to the center, whirling to face the spectators. He raised a fist in the air and shouted, "The Holy Bible says 'Thou shalt love thy neighbor as thyself!' If only the defendants had lived by that word, we would not be here...." He went on to outline the testimony of all of his witnesses, and finally concluded by going back to face the jury.

"Gentlemen, there is only one conclusion you can come to. Make right this deed committed against this family. Find the defendants *guilty!*"

Judge Blackburn pulled out his watch and sighed. "To be fair to you, Mister Kilgore, we'll take an early noon break. Be back in place at one o'clock."

Kilgore met with his clients during their lunch in the holding room. He asked them, "What did you think of his closing statement?"

"Sounded like he was preaching a sermon," Tom said.

"My thoughts exactly. Seemed an attempt to appeal to emotion. I don't intend to do it that way."

"Sounds good to me. If I was on a jury, I wouldn't like it."

When the courtroom was settled, all in their places, Blackburn nodded at Kilgore. He rose and walked forward to the center of the room, then over to face the jury. He quickly scanned their faces, looking each one in the eye before beginning to speak without notes.

"There is no question that a tragedy occurred that day and there is no question that the man responsible for it is in this courtroom. However, he is not seated at the defendant's table but behind the rail on this side." He pointed at the side behind the prosecutor's table. "Mister Ferdinand Harvey and his family suffered a great loss, but he is the one who caused it to happen. He was consumed by jealousy and resentment and it caused him to strike out by attempting to kill the source of his misdirected anger on that late afternoon in March.

"You are all responsible citizens and have been paying attention to testimony; therefore I will not repeat all of it in detail, but let's focus on the key point. Both Johnson men, both Archer men, and even the prosecution witness, Mister Peake, unknowingly, tell the same story: the first shot was a pistol shot, a 'pop', from Ferdinand Harvey's Colt that started the exchange of gunfire. Benjamin fired to defend his father, down from that first shot. He then fired in self-defense, as I would have done and each of you would have done, when his own life was on the line. Mister Archer wounded with the pistol shot, Mister Harvey's wound, the shotgun wounds to Mister Johnson and Benjamin Archer, and finally the fatal shot cannot be made to fit any sequence except that which occurred as described by Mister Johnson and the others.

"With all of the other testimony a clear picture has been presented of the facts leading up to the confrontation that took place that day. I believe you would have no problem finding Tom Archer and Benjamin Archer not guilty. However," turning to the judge, "Your Honor, in light of the over-whelming testimony presented herein, I move for dismissal. Thank you."

Kilgore bowed slightly, and returned to his side of the courtroom. There was a murmur in the crowd. Judge Blackburn rapped his gavel and looked over at Moses Shelby. "Both counsels approach the bench."

When they were in front of him, Blackburn leaned over the bench and said, *sotto voce*, "Mister Shelby, you got anything?"

"No, Your Honor, except we stand by the testimony we presented and it calls for a finding of guilty on all counts."

Blackburn sighed. "I'm tempted to dismiss, but let's see what the jury does. Be cleaner if they decide." He waved them away, then said to the courtroom, "I deny the motion to dismiss, to give the jury a chance to deliberate and reach a verdict."

Then he turned toward the jury and charged them to retire and reach their findings. "I will remind you that a finding of guilty must be unanimous, and reached beyond reasonable doubt. You may reach a finding of a lesser charge if that is your conclusion, as printed in the instructions to be given to the foreman you elect. You will now be escorted to the jury room."

They rose as a body and followed Deputy Duke out of the room. The judge rapped his gavel and said, "Court is adjourned, pending a verdict by the jury. We will send messages to those concerned when their deliberations are complete."

Those in the courtroom all rose and he left the room.

Sheriff John Horton's experience with Taney County juries told him not to try predicting anything. Still, he figured he wasn't taking any chances by being kind to the family of the accused. He had a couple of drunks recovering in cells in the back, so he let Kilgore know that he'd be taking his clients back to the jail, but they could have their families with them in the front processing room. Kilgore thanked him and left for his rooming house. At the Sheriff's office and jail, Horton stationed a deputy outside and barred entrance to anyone except on his personal authority.

Anna and Rebecca were given the freedom to embrace their husbands in the privacy of the outer waiting room.

"I know it will be all right," Anna said. "I don't see how it could go any other way."

"Even if it's in our favor," Ben said, "we'll have to decide what to do. The Harveys still live next to us."

"You're right. Maybe we could move somewhere else."

"We'll have to think on it. Are you going to get Eva? If things go wrong—"

"They won't! But I'll see if the sheriff will let me."

Rebecca and Tom sat quietly in a corner trying to come to terms with the unknown. "I have to believe in the truth," Rebecca said. "I couldn't go on—"

"It'll be all right, you'll see," said Tom. "Remember, they *all* have to think we're guilty, and that just can't possibly be."

"I just wish it could be over."

Tom squeezed her hand. "It will be soon."

Their thoughts were interrupted by the entrance of Anna, holding Eva, accompanied by Margaret. Anna handed their daughter to Ben who immediately talked quietly to her, seeking that infant smile.

As they gathered together, Margaret said. "I came in the big surrey, so when they finally set you free, we can all go home in it."

"Thanks, Margaret. I like your way of thinking," Tom said.

They passed the rest of the afternoon in a state of nervous tension, periods of quiet, periods of talk, pacing the floor in turn. Finally, after six o'clock, Duke came into the room to announce that the judge had called a halt. The jury had not reached a verdict. They'd start again tomorrow morning.

"Oh, my," Tom said. "Guess we'll have to wait another day."

"'Fraid so," said Horton. "I reckon you ladies will have to leave now."

Edna Harkness had extended her hospitality to include Margaret as well. Margaret had caused a large delivery of food supplies to be delivered to the Harkness house to help pay for their keep. The women all went to spend another tense night, while Ben and Tom were returned to their cell.

The next morning the sheriff allowed the Archer family and Margaret to take up station again in the outer waiting room of the sheriff's office. The day ground slowly on. Eva was passed from one to another, the only relief from the tension. Every few hours a deputy would return from the courthouse to report, "still no word."

The women left for the noon meal while Tom and Ben were served in the jail. In late afternoon, word finally came for them to assemble in the courtroom. When all were in place they were told to rise and Judge Blackburn came into the room, his face grim.

After he told them to be seated, he gaveled the court into session. Then he spoke. "I regret to inform you that the jury is hopelessly deadlocked and is unable to reach a verdict. Both counsels, see me in chambers."

When they were standing in front of him in the small room, he said, "Here's the deal. If I declare a mistrial, this thing could be hanging out there forever, Mister Shelby, until or if you choose to try again. Makes me regret I didn't dismiss. Never thought we'd come to this. What are your intentions?"

"I reckon I'll plan to have a new trial."

"Enlighten me, if you please, how the hell you think it would be different. What do you have you didn't present?"

Shelby looked flustered, "Well...we'd talk to more witnesses and just do a better job—"

"In other words, you don't have squat!" thundered Blackburn. "Here's what will happen: You bring this case again, and I'll walk into that courtroom and I'll dismiss the case with prejudice! And you'll look the fool! That jury in there has somebody on it with a motive. I don't see it any other way they deadlocked."

Shelby flushed red. "Your Honor, you have no right to influence—"

"Out there I don't, but in here I'm off the record! Do the right thing. We'll go out there and I'll declare a mistrial and you'll state that this case will not be considered for retrial due to lack of evidence."

When they were settled in the courtroom, Blackburn spoke, "As I announced earlier, the jury was unable to reach a verdict. Therefore, I declare a mistrial. Does either counsel have anything to say?" He looked toward the prosecutor.

Shelby slowly rose to his feet. "Thank you, Your Honor. Seeing as how we failed to provide sufficient evidence for a conviction, I believe it is in the best interest of society to state that we will not be seeking another trial…that is unless something unexpected comes up to warrant it."

He looked toward the jury. "I hereby release you from further duty. I thank you for your service." Then he faced the courtroom and continued, "Court is adjourned. Defendants are released from any further action on this case."

The spectators burst into conversation with no answering gavel as the judge left the courtroom. The Harveys and the Moses Shelby sat with heads bowed.

Anna didn't understand completely, but heard the word "released" and led the way around the rail, followed by Rebecca and they embraced their husbands. "Let's go home!" said Tom.

Charles Kilgore explained to all of them what it meant. "There was probably one holdout who wanted to punish you. I don't know why; maybe bribed, maybe not. It was an easy case; obvious what happened. Never should have been brought and now you'll probably never hear from it again. The sheriff and I talked yesterday and he was afraid this might happen. There's been some jury tampering going on in the county despite what he can do. I wish it could have been cleaner, but it's definitely better than guilty."

Tom and Ben shook hands with him with their thanks and he said, "Godspeed to both of you and your families."

They made their way through all the well-wishers, shaking hands, and finally they were outside. There were still reporters to contend with. As they finished answering all the questions as best they could, Margaret drove up in the surrey.

The man Ben had been observing in the courtroom approached Ben and introduced himself. "I'm Conrad Coleman. May I have a private word with you and your wife?"

"Of course," Ben said. He was about the age of Pa. A little shorter, but broad and strong of build. He looked at Ben with clear blue eyes.

Tom said, "I'll go get our stuff from the jail. You go right ahead."

When they were standing alone, Coleman said, "I've been following your case, and I congratulate you on your freedom. I was in the area buying yearlings to drive north. I'm in the cattle business and have a good bit of land up west of Springfield. Many years ago, when I was much younger, some men tried to rustle some of my cattle. Just like you, I had to stand trial for killing two of them in a gunfight. I was acquitted; you should have been. So you see why I was interested."

"That's really something," Ben said. "It's scary to be accused, no matter what."

"It is. Now, I don't mean to pry, but have you decided what comes next?"

Ben looked at Anna, "We haven't had time to talk much, but we do wonder if we can keep on next to those people."

"That's what I thought. I hope you don't mind my sayin' so, but you remind me of me when I was your age. And you, Miz Anna, I guess this has been hard on you."

"It has been." Anna said. "I'm glad this part is over."

"Well, here's something to think about. I just bought another farm on Honey Creek, north of a little town called Aurora. An older couple had it. What would you think of running it for me? You could help me drive these yearlings up there and have a look, then decide. I try to place a good couple on each farm of any size, and we go shares. Works out best for everybody."

Ben smiled at Anna. "I'll help with the yearlings anyway, and we'll think on it."

Coleman reached to shake hands. "Good! How about three days from now, in the evening, you meet me at the Hobart place on Swan Creek? I'm gathering them up there. We'll leave early the next morning."

"I'll check with Pa, to see if he can cover for me."

Tom arrived and Ben introduced the two men and explained the proposition. They shook hands and agreed.

The journey to Bull Creek that night was wearisome but happy. Tom and Ben spelled Margaret with the driving. Eva slept soundly with the motion of the surrey as she was passed from the loving arms of one to another. Margaret told them all of the pending changes in her life.

"The government has convicted my father, in absentia, of embezzlement during the war."

All voiced their condolences.

"I thought that's what it must be. Now that I've grown up, I look back and used to wonder where the money came from. Now I know. The upshot is they are confiscating the farm as a fine. There'll be prison if they catch him—or worse, depending on that marshal's death."

"Oh, Margaret, what will you do?" said Anna. "What will happen to Etta and Ike?"

"My plans are to buy a small place and build another cabin on it for Etta and her brother. They can raise enough for the three of us, and I have my school teaching. The government isn't taking our bank account or our cattle."

"That sounds good," said Tom. "You know we'll do anything to help."

Josie heard them arrive in the middle of the night and roused Jimmy. They had a joyful family reunion after all the separation and the trial. Margaret chose to keep going until she got home. Jimmy was thrilled and no longer sleepy when Tom asked him to saddle a horse and accompany Miss Margaret home. She said she'd have him nap and feed him breakfast before she sent him home. Rebecca found places for everyone to sleep. Peace, at last.

CHAPTER 55

In the morning, Ben and Anna were at last in their own wagon headed home. Anna sat as close to Ben as possible without interfering with control of the horses. Eva slept soundly, cuddled to her breast.

"Ben, I feel that the future is opening up for me and for us. My life has been up and down, some really lows and highs. The best times were when you took me in and we learned to love each other. Then this precious baby came along and it was even better."

"I feel the same way. I was just this overgrown boy, now that I think back on it, until you came along. Before then, I thought about fishin', huntin', things like that. What a change! Now I think about you all the time; what's Anna doin'? What would Anna think about that? I can't wait to see Anna again...stuff like that."

He smiled down at her.

She squeezed his arm and smiled back, "That's the way it's supposed to be. I want to be in your mind all the time, just as you are in mine. This thing with the Harveys was awful, but it made my feelings for you even stronger. While we're on that subject, I'm all back to normal after Eva being born." She looked down and said in a soft voice, "What I'm trying to say, when we are finally alone, I'm ready to be a real wife to you." She looked back into his eyes. "Do you think we can do that?"

Ben blushed, "Why, yes, I think we can work together and figger it out."

On the appointed day, Ben joined Conrad Coleman for the drive north to Coleman's farms in Lawrence County. Anna and Eva stayed with Ben's family while he was away and they hired Matthew Johnson to take care of their place and their livestock during those few days.

Ben and Anna made the decision to make the move after Ben's glowing description of the country and the place they'd be living. Tom contributed the newer wagon and Rebecca told him to keep the team of grays from her original farm. Tom told Ben privately that he planned to sell the Friedrich place. They had heard nothing out of the Harvey family since the trial, but he thought it best to put it behind them completely. "When I do sell it," he said, "whatever we get above the loan is coming to you for your inheritance."

"That's great, Pa! But you don't have to do that."

"You've earned it. Later on I'll help the others get a start."

On the day of the move, the whole family came to say their farewells. The distance was not so great that they couldn't get together every year or so in the future, but still it was a big change. The wagon was piled high and covered with canvas. Margaret Madison and George Zinn arrived, bringing Etta with them. Matthew Johnson came to help herd the livestock.

Finally, the moment came for hugs and tears and goodbyes.

Ben helped Anna into the wagon and Josie handed Eva to her. She gave her big brother one last hug before he climbed up also. Ben put his arm around Anna for a brief moment, then slapped the reins and they began their journey into the future.

AFTERWORD

About the time fictional characters Ben and Anna were leaving Taney County, Missouri, a real Ozarks settler named Reuben Branson opened a general store and post office in 1882 at a riverboat stop on the White River. Soon other settlers were drawn to the area and it began to develop as a community named Branson. However, lawlessness and disorder worsened in Taney County, with thievery and unsolved murders increasing. Outlaws and renegade holdovers from guerilla bands during the Civil War began to thrive and exercise control over law enforcement and jury selection. Even if law-breakers were arrested, they were often released.

Community leaders, frustrated at the lawlessness after still another murder, gathered in secret in early 1885 to decide what to do. They elected a newcomer, Nathaniel Kinney, to head up the group. He was an imposing figure, six-feet-six, and had been a captain in the Union Army during the war. He had also been an agent in the west for the Postal Service and had been a detective for the Santa Fe Railroad. They decided to form a vigilante group, which had been done in other parts of the country. Word got around and the organization grew rapidly. When they met on April 5, 1885, over two hundred men showed up on a hilltop south of Forsyth. After Kinney stated the goals of the organization, all of the members were sworn to secrecy. The hill where they met was named Snapp's Bald. The group was thereafter named the "Bald Knobbers."

A few days later, they began to take action. About a hundred Bald Knobbers broke open the Taney County jail and hauled out two brothers known for their vicious attacks on citizens. The Bald Knobbers took them out south of Forsyth and hanged them. The organization grew quickly to several hundred members. Before long, Bald Knobbers made night raids not only on lawbreakers, but on their detractors and anyone they felt "unworthy" of their standards. They wore knitted hoods with knitted horns to conceal their identities. Eventually they killed numerous men and women who disagreed with their tactics. The expected cure for lawlessness became worse than the problems they were trying to solve, so some of the founding members dropped out of the organization.

National press began to write about the actions of this vigilante group. When a judge called for a state audit against corruption of the county's officeholders, the courthouse was burned down. An Anti-Bald Knobbers group sprung up. In 1887, Bald Knobbers killed two more of their critics and injured several of their family members.

In August of 1888, a man named Billy Miles killed Nat Kinney in a Forsyth store where Kinney was working, claiming self-defense, although it was said to be a planned assassination. As there were no witnesses, Miles was tried and acquitted. Three Bald-Knobbers were tried and convicted of murder in Christian County, and hanged May, 1899, effectively bringing the era of the Bald Knobbers to a close.

R oger Meadows is the author of *DEVIL'S LANE* and two prior novels, *HANGMAN, A Deadly Game* and *A CHANCE ENCOUNTER*. After college and a tour as an Army aviator, he began a career in industry, completing graduate school along the way. He conducted business throughout the world, dealing with many cultures.

He has written dozens of essays and short stories, and edited the works of other writers. He has participated in writers' groups in Spartanburg, Greenville, and Hilton Head, South Carolina; and Knoxville, Tennessee. He and his wife, Wanda, are members of the local chapter of Sisters in Crime.

Mr. Meadows enjoys reading, sailing, kayaking, travel, and wooden boat building. He and his wife live in the Upstate of South Carolina.

They have three adult children and two grandchildren. He welcomes your comments to him at RDM730@aol.com. See his web page at https://www.amazon.com/author/rogermeadows

A CHANCE ENCOUNTER, a mystery novel by Roger Meadows, ISBN 9 781502 388537

Gideon Grant is a computer lawyer involved in the explosion of technology in the late 1990s. Dedicated to his clients, he grew his firm at an astonishing rate and his life was no longer his own, with frequent twenty-four-hour days. He decided to sell his firm, build a boat, and sail to the South Seas. Far off the coast of California, a wind shift causes him to encounter a sinking yacht, apparently abandoned. He boards it and pumps it out, and because of what he discovers, he is compelled to return it to its home port of San Francisco. There he becomes embroiled in the society he left behind and must defend himself against suspicion from authorities. He sets out to solve the mystery of who was aboard and what happened to them. In the process, he discovers what life and love are about.

"Not wanting to telegraph my intentions, I stayed in the second lane until the last minute, before cutting off another driver in a van to dart into the 4th Street exit ramp. The rear-view mirror was suddenly filled with a dark shape coming behind me from behind the van at a high rate of speed. As I entered the curve, he slammed into my right rear bumper with a crash that sent me into a hard left, into the wall with a loud clang. The airbags blew and my faithful Land Cruiser rolled over with shattering glass and screeching metal against concrete. It bounced over the wall to the street below."

HANGMAN, A Deadly Game, a suspense novel by Roger Meadows, ISBN 1 4196 2876 3

Hiking alone in the mountains of North Carolina, Matthew Cross faces a temptation so great that it overpowers his lifelong sense of right and wrong. Rather than turn away as he has in the past, he renews international contacts and explores unfamiliar subjects: deceit of friends, money laundering, and ways to change identity. His odyssey takes him from his home in the mountains to Europe, the Bahamas, and to the coastal plains of Florida and Georgia. Too late, he yearns for a return to the safety and security of the life he once had, loving someone who loved him. Control slips away and life-threatening dangers encircle him. A final betrayal springs a trap. Escape and redemption will require qualities he is not aware he possesses, help from an unexpected source, and a complex plan.

"I crept to the cable, rose, and sprinted for the Explorer. As I slid to a stop, I dived to the ground and felt for my key ring. I heard my pursuer running across the moonlit parking lot behind me, but at the same time saw another pair of feet in front of the car. I had miscalculated. There were three of them. I sprang to my feet to flee, but the dark figure of the third man came around the Explorer with a gun in his hand. He leveled it and fired at point-blank range."

Made in the USA
Charleston, SC
30 June 2016